The Dress in the Window

The Dress in the Window

Sofia Grant

wm

WILLIAM MORROW

An Imprint of HarperCollinsPublishers

HarperCollins
PUBLISHERS
Since 1817

P.S.™ is a trademark of HarperCollins Publishers.

HarperCollins books may be purchased for educational, business, or sales pro-
motional use. For information, please email the Special Markets Department at
SPsales@harpercollins.com.

FIRST EDITION

Designed by Diahann Sturge
Title page image by TanjaJovicic/Shutterstock, Inc.

Library of Congress Cataloging-in-Publication Data has been applied for.

ISBN 978-0-06-249972-1

17 18 19 20 21   LSC   10 9 8 7 6 5 4 3 2 1

For my dad

The Dress in the Window

Prologue

There is nothing lovely about Minisink Avenue. If it ever could have been said to enjoy a period of prosperity, when steam engines came along toward the end of the last century to boost the production of the tweeds and plaids, the blankets and shawls, the zephyrs and most of all the rough, heavy cottonade called "Negro cloth" everywhere but in the Center City salesroom—that period came at the expense of the stooped and mute workers, some of them as young as seven, working thirteen hours a day and never earning enough to rise out of the cheap cramped housing in the floodplain of the Schuylkill.

In the twenties, the English and Scottish and Germans gave way to the Italians and eastern Europeans moving their families into the cramped row houses. Across the river, Philadelphia may have been dubbed the "Workshop of the World," but in the mills, the spinners and carders and mules toiled as miserably as ever—making carpets, upholstery fabric, and woolen plush—and still only the bosses seemed to thrive, moving their families up the river to Roxborough. The mill complexes expanded, reinforced concrete and brick grafted onto the old stone, ingesting the workers hungrily before dawn and belching out smoke as though they had swallowed whole the modest dreams and hopes, the bodies bent by the work and crippled by swollen joints and spinner's phthisis.

The Depression delivered its merciless judgment and sent the last of the cotton south. Their eyes finally open, perhaps, the bosses strived and pleaded, but the workers—long accustomed to calamity and so inured to tragedy as to be nearly indifferent to their fate—took a gamble and demanded six more dollars a week. The last of the textile mills were shuttered, and the only smoke in the sky was from pulp and paper production. All those buildings, empty save for squatters and thieves, their forges and furnaces cold. When they occasionally caught fire and burned, the few souls who remained in the tenements on the hill watched from their filthy windows and cursed in half a dozen languages.

There is no reason for you to find yourself here. The odors wafting from the river are foul; the grit in the air, drifting from the rail tracks, will find its way into your eyes and nostrils and lips, until you taste ash that makes you think of the terrible stories coming back from Europe—the burnt skeletons they found in the pits, all those babies killed before they could ever find their mothers' breasts.

Or maybe it is this news that compelled you to walk here, leaving behind the golden-glow windows in the nicer streets away from the river and the mills, where widows and grief-dumb mothers and luckier women alike are washing dishes after the meals that still take us all aback, so accustomed are we to the penury of the ration books. Who knows what to do with a chop fried in butter, after all these months of watery stews bobbing with offal? It's as though our bodies recoil from plenty.

Of course you've lost someone, everyone has; but maybe you've lost more than most, or maybe you lost the one to whom you could tell your secrets, so now they echo in your hollow breast with nowhere to go. These secrets might propel you down these steep streets where the ghosts of the wretched seem to linger.

In front of the old woolen mill, you pause to light a cigarette and stamp your feet against the chill, your boots making prints in the thin snow that settled on the town like a feather tick since the weak sun surrendered. Inhaling with no great pleasure, you notice a faint glow from within the largest of the buildings, the original stone one that housed the mill's offices, where visitors were received; but it is not so different from all the others now: windows boarded and broken, anything of value carted off long ago. The cornerstone is carved with the numerals 1881; over the door the legend MURPHREE & SON stands stately and proud. There is no way for you to know that the younger Murphree perished from influenza before the doors of the mill ever opened for business. The last man to own the building was named Brink, and he had no sons at all.

Brink was a modest man, and a silent one, so the workers who loomed the fine wovens in his factory had no access to his inner thoughts and dreams, except on the few occasions—half a dozen, at most—in which he drank at lunch and came back maudlin and raging.

Brink died in 1939, without ceremony. The mill closed, the new war came, boys enlisted and were drafted, and soon there were no young men to plunder what was left for sport. The buildings and everything in them were as dead and decaying as the mill's last owner.

But that light you see emanating from inside—if you are curious, if you put your gloved hand to the knob you will find it unlocked; if you stay to the edges of the floor where the boards do not squeak, if you avoid stumbling over the stacks of pallets and broken chairs lining the hall leading to the open workroom, you will find yourself privy to a scene of such shocking depravity that it will take your breath. Surely, you have seen men and women naked; the mysteries of intercourse have long been revealed to you. Perhaps you have experienced a love affair or two, or even a great passion of your own. But it is unlikely that you have ever seen anything like these two.

The moldering bolts of soiled and ruined cloth have been pulled from the benches; yards and yards lie carelessly mounded to make a crude pallet. The light that caught your eye comes from sputtering, rough-made candles, the cheapest to be had at the mercantile, fixed to the workbench with no regard to the pooling wax or even the risk of the flame catching. And this building would burn—how quickly it would burn, its timbers and rafters exposed! But the lovers don't care; the lovers, anyone can see, care nothing for the future, the past, for anything but this moment, this single crack in the wretched crushing yoke of their lives. Look at how he seizes her hair in his fists; look at how he bucks like an animal. See her twist and groan below him; she pounds his chest with her fists until he catches her wrists in his strong, scarred hands. She shows her teeth; he calls her by another woman's name, by her own, by no name at all. There are long scratches that each will have to hide tomorrow. A sheet metal screw has dug into her hip as she fought and writhed, but later she will have no idea how the blood came to stain her skirts, how her skin was punctured and bruised. The sting of the iodine with which she will dress the wound tomorrow will not seem like nearly penance enough.

As for him, he'll find her blond hairs on his horsehair coat and curse himself. For his weakness; for his lack of courage, now and before. He has no doubt his debt will be settled at death's reckoning. Hell waits for him, but he figures he may as well get a head start on learning to live with eternal damnation. And so tonight he takes what he can, drinks deep of her intoxicating poison.

They carry on into the night, and even if you make a sound—even if you take a trumpet from your coat and blast its strident notes—they'll have no use for you, with your patched cloth coat and your darned socks and your thin pressed hand-kerchiefs. You are nothing to them. They are, for these few stolen hours, the only creatures left on this damned earth.

One

Taffeta

Taffeta is a cruel fabric, as fickle and delicate as it is alluring. Handle it carelessly, and you'll wreck a garment in any of a dozen different ways. Set down a glass of water while you're cutting out a panel for a gored skirt and you'll never get the ring out; use a dull needle and the hole will pop and run. A lazily finished seam will unravel at breathless speed. Even a bitten fingernail can leave a snag you can't smooth away.

November 1948

Jeanne

Nancy Cosgrove had seen the gown made up in taffeta in *Vogue*, and taffeta was what she had to have. Jeanne made a muslin first, at Nancy's insistence, even though muslin could never stand in for the stiff, slippery hand of the real thing. The muslin's skirt hung around Nancy's lumpy hips like wet rags and Jeanne thought she'd finally come to her senses—but Nancy just went home to get her crinoline. It made only a slight improvement: the muslin spread out over the stiff underskirt like leaves floating on a pond. But Nancy took herself across the river to the city, where she found a bolt of emerald green moiré taffeta in a shop at the corner of Fourth and Fulton.

When she brought it back, the bolt of fabric sitting in the passenger seat of her garish two-tone Packard Clipper like a visiting dignitary, it occurred to Jeanne that Nancy might still be trying to one-up her, even after everything that had happened. Never mind that Jeanne slept in the unfinished attic of the narrow row house that she shared with her sister and her niece and Thelma Holliman. She suspected that there was a part of Nancy that was stuck back at Mother of Mercy High School, where Jeanne had sailed like a swan through adolescence, winning top marks and courted by a steady stream of

St. Xavier boys. By contrast, poor Nancy had been as awkward as a stump, beloved by no teacher, no suitors, and none of the other girls.

Jeanne tried not to hold this belated vengefulness against Nancy: they badly needed her money. Still, Nancy had no head for sums, and there was not enough fabric on the bolt for the New Look dress she had hired Jeanne to sew for her. Unlike the wide bolt of unbleached muslin that Jeanne kept on a length of baling wire on Thelma's back porch, the taffeta that Nancy brought back was only forty-eight inches wide—a scant forty-eight inches at that, the selvages taking up the better part of an inch on either side. Jeanne could barely cut a skirt panel from it—even with Nancy's oddly short, bowed calves—and only by forgoing the deep hem she'd planned in favor of an understitched facing.

Jeanne had been up the night before until nearly three in the morning, hand-tacking that facing with a single strand of superfine Zimmerman and a straw needle. When she finally went to bed, she had an unsettling dream. It had been months since she'd dreamed of Charles, but suddenly there he was, wearing a hat that had hung on a nail in the carriage house of his parents' estate in Connecticut, a western style of hat that his father had brought back from a trip to Montana.

But in the dream Charles frowned at her from beneath its broad brim, while he pressed his hands to his stomach, trying to stanch the blood pouring from the hole in his side, while all around him in the trenches of Cisterna, his fellow Rangers were felled by the German panzers. Only six of them came home, out of more than seven hundred—but Jeanne didn't care about any of them. She would have traded them all to have Charles back.

War had made a monster of her, and there was nothing she could do about it—except to sew. A stitch, another, another. In this way the minutes and hours passed.

IT WAS THE second week of Advent and their little parlor was decked out in paper snowflakes and a wreath of fresh greens, but that was all for Tommie. The rest of the household was sick of pretending to be cheerful. Thelma had come down with shingles in the fall and spent long afternoons in her room, and Tommie had a cough that persisted through one week and then another, terrible racking coughs that seemed much too harsh to come out of a six-year-old.

"Stop pacing," Jeanne snapped, as Peggy swished by again to peer out the window, with Tommie clinging to her like a barnacle. Tommie was a stocky child, and too old to be carried like an infant. Jeanne didn't know how her sister managed—a few turns around the park could put Jeanne's back out for a week. But today it seemed to be the only way to get Tommie to stop fussing.

"You're the one who told me to keep watch," Peggy retorted.

"Girls! Stop bickering!" came Thelma's muffled call from the kitchen, where she was making stock, simmering last night's chicken carcass in hopes of getting another meal out of it. It galled Jeanne that Thelma still called them "girls" when she was twenty-eight and Peggy was twenty-seven, but she was not in a position to complain. She was the interloper here, the recipient of charity, a fact that she loathed but could not change.

Before Jeanne could respond, there was a knock at the door. She peeked out the parlor window, and there was Nancy's car, parked out front. Jeanne fixed a smile on her face and opened the door. Nancy wore a houndstooth coat too dowdy for a woman twice her age, and it was all Jeanne could do not to tilt her head in subtle disdain the way she'd once done, in the halls of Mother of Mercy a decade earlier. She had forgotten, during the long hours of sewing since fitting Nancy with the muslin, the way she leaned slightly forward on the balls of her feet, like an old dog ready to collapse; had forgotten Nancy's stomping gait as she came into their front room. The gown Jeanne had just finished was a thing of delicate beauty, and it was hard to bear the thought of Nancy's lumpish figure stuffed into it.

Still, it would flatter her as much as any gown could, and Jeanne was counting on the other guests at the ball to notice, to lavish Nancy with compliments. Jeanne knew Nancy wouldn't be able to resist telling people who had sewn the gown for her: girls like Nancy never forgot the cruel hierarchy of high school, and having Jeanne in her employ would be a card she would play for all it was worth.

Nancy was far from the only woman in Brunskill who was wealthier than most but still unable to afford to shop in Paris or New York, or even the finer shops in Philadelphia. Jeanne was her best-kept secret, but hoped not to be a secret for long. If she could get a commission like this one every week, it would pay for groceries for the household, even a chicken every Sunday night. And that would do until Jeanne figured out the next chapter in her life.

"Well?" Nancy said, barely nodding at Peggy, who stood swaying with Tommie in her arms. "Where is it?"

Jeanne went to Thelma's bedroom, where she'd hung the gown from the door of the closet, and said a quick prayer before lifting the dress from the hook and carrying it out in front of her. Thelma emerged from the kitchen, wiping her hands on a dishtowel, a faintly imperious expression on her face. Thelma, Jeanne knew, did not care for Nancy either. She considered Nancy common, a peculiar vanity for a widow of a drayage driver. But like the rest of them, Thelma had once been someone else too.

Nancy's sharp intake of breath belied her studied indifference. She touched the bodice reverently with nails filed into sharp points and painted crimson. "It's lovely," she said, "but don't you think . . . I mean, I wanted the waist nipped close. Like the picture, you know?"

Jeanne knew exactly what Nancy wanted. Every woman in America had seen those photographs in the paper, the fashion firestorm sweeping the nation ever since Christian Dior's scandalous collection launched last year in Paris. An outrageous reaction to the leanness and rationing of wartime, Dior's New Look was nothing if not controversial. It featured wasp waists, padded hips, and close-fitting sleeves—and flowing, voluminous skirts, falling to the ankle even in day length, all of it hinging on an hourglass of a figure that few women came by naturally.

All that fabric, all that weight—excessive, screamed the American press. MR. DIOR, WE ABHOR DRESSES TO THE FLOOR, read a placard carried by a housewife protesting in Chicago, in a photo that was picked up by all the major newspapers. Husbands in several cities called for a boycott.

But the tides of fashion would not be turned back. Women had emerged from the war in the worn, threadbare, much-mended clothes in which they entered it, their few wartime outfits lean and spare according to the penurious regulations of fabric rationing. No cuffs, no pleats or gathers, no trim or pockets. No dolman sleeves, no skirts past thirty inches. They welcomed the feminine silhouette and hungered for the ballerina skirts and soft shoulders, no matter how impractical or expensive to produce.

Jeanne had fitted the silk bodice as tight as she could without asphyxiating Nancy, whose waist had disappeared after the birth of her second child. She would see this for herself once she put on the dress.

But tact—even a bit of prevarication—was called for now. "Oh, don't you worry," Jeanne said, folding the dress over her arm at the waist. "A good corset will take care of that. I'll tell you what—why don't you put it on and I'll pin the adjustments."

Nancy shrugged in what she probably imagined was a queenly fashion. Peggy appeared at her elbow, Tommie suddenly nowhere to be seen. She had applied a slash of vivid scarlet lipstick, and that one simple addition made her appear radiant again. If Jeanne had once been the famous beauty of the family, Peggy had surprised everyone by blossoming late. It was as though tragedy had smoothed the sharp edges of her impetuous youth and given her a sense of languid melancholy, like Veronica Lake in *The Blue Duhliu*.

"Come into the changing room," Peggy said in the bored, throaty voice she sometimes assumed for company. Nancy glanced at Jeanne suspiciously before following Peggy into the larder, and Jeanne opened her mouth to speak—but was startled to silence by a rare, conspiratorial wink from Thelma. Only yesterday Jeanne had been on her hands and knees in the tiny, dank room, scrubbing a bit of onion skin that had adhered itself to the old wooden floor by a smudge of damp black mold, but now a flash of bright light emerged from the doorway.

"She wanted to surprise you," Thelma murmured, pinching Jeanne's forearm lightly. Jeanne could smell her rosewater perfume mixed with the yeasty scents of baking. Thelma pinched her a second time. "Don't tell me you've forgotten? You've got that head of yours in the clouds, birthday girl!"

Jeanne realized with a sickening sensation that it was indeed her birthday—her twenty-ninth. She stood helplessly, her mouth hanging open like a fish laid out on ice, as the pieces fell into place. Thelma in the kitchen all morning, the scents of allspice and cinnamon wafting from the oven, pretending to be cross and shooing Jeanne from the room. Peggy insisting that Jeanne take Tommie to Florence Park, at the bottom of two steep sets of steps half a mile away, because the playground at the public school down the street where they usually played was too marshy with melting snow. They'd been plotting a celebration!

Jeanne, only last night, had been feeling sorry for herself as she put the finishing touches on the dress. She felt her face warm with embarrassment. "Thelma, I . . ."

"Hush now." One last pinch, this one hard. "Go see to Queen Elizabeth in there."

Jeanne hid a smile behind her hand. Thelma could occasionally make a joke, a sly one. They'd read about the luxury ocean liner named for the queen, marveling at the glittering excess, the parties and formal dinners—and most of all the trunks and trunks of beautiful clothes the passengers brought along. But it wasn't the gowns Thelma was comparing Nancy to; it was the enormous ship herself.

There wasn't room for Jeanne to join the others in the brand-new "dressing room"—but what a transformation Peggy had effected! The walls were covered in pale shirred fabric, and a closer examination revealed it was Jeanne's very own muslin, gathered under hem tape and stapled top and bottom. Thelma's oval mirror had been plucked from her dresser and hung from the wall by a satin ribbon Jeanne recognized from the band of one of Peggy's hats, and the floor was covered by the rug from Thelma's bedside. The hooks that held bags of onions and potatoes were now adorned by glass knobs that looked suspiciously like the ones from Thelma's bureau. Nancy had slipped off her day dress and hung it on the wall, and now she was turning this way and that in the green silk gown, examining herself in the mirror and frowning.

The waist was stretched taut, as Jeanne had known it would be, and Nancy was tugging at the sleeves. They were done in the New Look style she'd requested, small tapered caps that hugged her doughy shoulders. Jeanne had made the armholes more generous than the tight cut featured in the Parisian gowns, but even so, the fabric cut into Nancy's flesh. She looked a bit like a washerwoman, her underarms jiggling as she moved.

"You've made these too tight," she complained, jamming a stubby finger under one of the curved caps.

"I've got an idea," Peggy said, before Jeanne could respond. There wasn't a seamstress in the world who could make a cap sleeve that would flatter Thelma's arms. Peggy and Jeanne, used to the labor of keeping house and carrying Tommie around, had the opposite problem—their biceps bulged with muscles.

Thelma crowded behind Jeanne, the four women squeezing into the little room like fraternity boys into a phone booth. Ignoring Nancy's ire, Jeanne was touched by her sister's ingenuity. There hadn't been money for a new pair of gloves or stockings, but the gift she'd given Jeanne was better than anything money could buy.

"What a gorgeous shade," Thelma said diplomatically. "Almost like jade, wouldn't you say?"

"What was your idea?" Nancy huffed to Peggy.

"Just give me a minute . . ."

While Peggy raced upstairs to the bedroom she shared with Tommie, there was a small commotion from the coat closet, and Jeanne suddenly realized where her sister had stashed Tommie. She exchanged an exasperated look with Thelma.

There was often an unspoken cooperation between Jeanne and her sister's mother-in-law. For her part, Jeanne's efforts were born of the desperate wish to make herself valuable in the household that had taken her in. She was well aware that her presence was a burden, that Thelma had offered her shelter more out of deference to social conventions than any genuine enthusiasm for Jeanne's company. As for Thelma . . . Jeanne liked to think that they had found they were kindred spirits: both practical women, clever in the way of women whose resources were few and needs were great. And without many options for passing their leisure time, both loved to read, and Jeanne suspected both of them might have been labeled bookish if their more obvious assets hadn't drawn greater attention. Yes, Thelma had been a beauty once, and her face—even now unlined and smooth—still commanded notice.

Thelma gave Jeanne a slight nod and went off to fetch Tommie, who'd probably been stowed among the galoshes and mops with nothing but a few saltine crackers to keep her busy, and Jeanne racked her brain for ways to hold up her end of the bargain—to distract Nancy.

"So tell me more about the ball," she said.

Nancy gave Jeanne a suspicious look. The Holly Ball was a fairly minor event in the Philadelphia social season, but to attend any ball in the city was a heady accomplishment for a

Roxborough matron. Jeanne herself had attended, once, with Charles. With his sterling manners and good looks, he'd been invited several times already, a handy date for girls making their debut. And he danced well—his mother had seen to that.

Nancy, on the other hand, had had to work her way up—laboriously, Jeanne suspected—to an invitation, serving on the committees no one wanted and looking for opportunities to gain a footing in Philadelphia society. "Well, it's still held at the National Guard Armory, of course," she began. "The Mo Bishop Band will be playing, and—"

Jeanne was saved from having to hear more of what she would be missing by her sister, who'd come back with one of her old sketchbooks in hand. She held up the book to reveal a quick drawing of Nancy's dress rendered in a few bold, assured strokes—but with a new sleeve, a rather straightforward elbow-length style with a little notch at the bottom, eased into a more generous armhole. The new sleeves were just shy of matronly, but they would hide the flabby extra flesh that had given Nancy pause.

"It's very chic," Peggy gushed. "I saw this style in *Women's Wear Daily*. It's barely made it to New York from Paris, but it will be everywhere this spring, I imagine."

Peggy didn't look at Jeanne—she knew better. She was a gifted liar, and had been since childhood, and Jeanne had learned to be constantly vigilant. Often Peggy would give up in a gale of laughter when Jeanne gave her a pointed glare—and they couldn't chance that now.

"Hmmm," Nancy hedged. "I didn't know you were an artist,

Peggy." She said it in the same tone that she might have said *I didn't know you were a laundress*, but Peggy's sketch really was quite good. Once, she'd hoped to go to art school, but after their father died during her last year of high school, she settled for working at an art supply shop. She'd draw anything, but she especially loved to copy illustrations from the department store advertisements in the papers and the magazines they read at the library, modifying the stylish outfits to suit her own taste; and she could suggest the turn of an ankle or the drape of a coat with just a few strokes of a pencil. It was a hobby that had taken a backseat since Tommie's arrival, but now Jeanne saw that it might come in quite handy.

"Oh, yes," Jeanne improvised. "Peggy's done tons of original designs. In fact, I'm wearing one."

She turned this way and that, hands on hips, to show off the dress she was wearing. In truth Jeanne had copied it from one she'd seen at Fyfe's on a trip to see the holiday decorations earlier in the month. The wool had exhausted her savings, but Jeanne was making Peggy and Thelma each a new dress for their Christmas presents, and she'd wanted something new to wear to church too. She'd even made Tommie a little matching dress, just for fun, but Tommie'd been sick on it and Jeanne couldn't get the smell out of the wool.

The dress was ice blue and it had a clever faux twist at the neckline, made by stitching down a band of wool with a thin rayon interfacing that allowed the wool to be ruched without adding much bulk. It hadn't been Jeanne's idea, but it had been simple enough to copy.

Nancy considered Jeanne's dress only for a moment before she returned her attention to the one she was wearing. Her fingertips idly caressed her bare shoulder. "Well, can you do it?"

Jeanne thought of the scraps, carefully folded in her basket. She'd coveted a bit of the green silk to use on a project of her own—but there wasn't enough to make much more than a dickey or perhaps to line the pockets of her old car coat. Making new sleeves for Nancy would be a stretch, but if she cut them on the bias, and pieced a gusset in the underside . . .

"I suppose," Jeanne said coolly.

"But she'll have to charge you twice her usual rate," Thelma cut in, "as it will mean putting off another client. And there won't be time for a fitting, of course, since the ball is tomorrow night."

Nancy glanced between Thelma and Jeanne, nonplussed by the older woman's intervention. "Well, then, I'll come first thing in the morning."

Jeanne could see that it had been the right move, from the rising color in Nancy's cheeks. It was just as it had been when they were at school together: girls like Nancy valued things by how much others wanted them, and creating a false sense of scarcity had excited that impulse in her.

A devilish idea occurred to Jeanne, born of the years she and Nancy had spent in their overlapping social spheres.

"Oh, I'm afraid that won't work," she said sorrowfully. "I'm to visit Sister Anthony this evening, you see, and the poor dear looks forward to my visits so much. She doesn't receive many visitors."

Behind Nancy, Jeanne could see Peggy trying to keep a straight face. She bent down and pretended to be busy wiping something from Tommie's chin.

Sister Anthony O'Connell had been simply the most dreadful teacher at Mother of Mercy. She'd always seemed to have eyes in the back of her head, and had a near-obsessive distrust of humor. A giggle in Sister Anthony's English class could lead to an inquisition, with her looming over a student demanding to know what exactly was amusing about the day's lesson. Also, she couldn't speak without spittle flying from her thin, cracked lips, and rare was the girl who'd avoided being spattered during a reproof.

Sister Anthony had seemed ancient even then, and shortly after Jeanne and Peggy graduated she'd moved on to the order's retirement home. Jeanne had heard she had dementia now; there was a rumor that she yelled like a longshoreman at her nurses. Jeanne had certainly never been to visit her, not once.

"Well," Nancy said, drawing a breath. "I suppose . . . I mean, I could go, to visit her . . . that would be the kind thing to do, wouldn't it? And you could—you could—" She gestured at the sketch she was holding.

Thelma coughed and took the sketch from her hands.

"And yes, the . . . extra charges will be fine," Nancy added.

Moments later, she was gone. The three women peeked out at her behind the drapes, giggling at her wide derriere when she bent to get in the car. Even Tommie joined in the laughter, delighted by a rare moment when none of the women in her life were in the clutches of despair.

THAT EVENING, AFTER she got Tommie to bed, Peggy came up to the attic, carrying her sketchbook. She reclined on Jeanne's pillow, her back against the iron headboard of the bed Jeanne had brought from their mother's house, her sketchbook propped up on her knees.

"I bet Nancy's bazooms hang down to her belly button," Peggy said. "You should sew a couple of saucers into the bodice to hold them up."

"You're terrible." Jeanne sighed, carefully lifting the presser foot as she eased in the new sleeve. In truth, she liked it when her sister came upstairs; it reminded her of their childhood, when they'd shared a room until they were teenagers. Even when Jeanne started high school and was given the guest room for her own, Peggy snuck in many nights and crawled in with her, keeping her awake with her whispering and giggling.

For several moments the only noises in the drafty room were the scratch of Peggy's charcoal pencil on paper and the hum of the sewing machine's motor as Jeanne made her slow and careful way around the armhole. The machine was her most precious possession, a Singer Featherweight with a special red and gold embossed badge on its narrow throat. It had been her mother's, a gift from her father when the pair made an anniversary trip to Chicago for the World's Fair in 1934.

Emma Brink was a daughter of the Philadelphia Burnhams. She'd grown up with money, beautiful clothes, servants, an elegant home in Merion—and given it all up to marry Leo

Brink, a poor son of Irish immigrants who promised her the moon.

Leo had done well for himself, working tirelessly in the mills until he was able to start his own company. Brink Mills had been a modest success; Leo had been able to move his family from the tenements above the river up to Roxborough and send his daughters to Mother of Mercy with the other mill owners' children.

Ever mindful of the promise he'd made his wife, Leo Brink spoiled the three females in his house. It was as though he never stopped trying to make up for the loss of her family, who never reconciled with their only daughter and refused to acknowledge their granddaughters, because they were being raised Catholic. There were closets full of beautiful clothes, fine linens for the table, Irish crystal Leo had shipped all the way from Dungannon. The one indulgence he put off year after year was to take Emma on a long-delayed wedding trip, because he never wanted to leave the mill. Finally, he hired his brother to be his right-hand man, and he was able to fulfill his promise.

At the fair, Leo wrote letters to his teenage daughters about the brand-new Museum of Science and Industry and the artillery that was rumored to have cost over one million dollars. But Emma was captivated by the Singer sewing machine being debuted in the Electrical Building. Perhaps remembering the early years of their marriage, when she'd sewn her husband's shirts and her daughters' layettes on a secondhand treadle, she declared it a miracle that would transform the American household.

They returned home, and the machine remained in its case. Leo went back to work, harder than ever, because the textile industry had started to shift and he saw the writing on the wall; hard times were coming. Emma, who had pneumonia as a child and had always struggled from her scarred lungs, grew weaker and spent more and more of her time sitting up in her bed, waiting for her girls to come home and tell her about their days.

Jeanne missed a pin and drove the needle down on top of it, snapping the needle in two. "Oh, rats," she exclaimed, giving the full skirt an exasperated tug. "I'll never finish this in time."

"Leave the pins in," Peggy suggested. "When she goes to the toilet in the middle of the ball, maybe she'll sit on one."

"You're awful," Jeanne murmured, gently removing the bunched fabric so she could access the throat plate and dig out the snapped needle.

"Maybe," Peggy agreed. "She has it coming, though. The way she swans around! She's probably spent the last ten years dreaming about putting you in your place."

Jeanne leaned back in the chair, rolling her shoulders, taking a break from the painstaking work. She looked around the room, at the exposed rafters, the coarse floorboards covered with a flea-market rug, the length of pipe along the wall that served as a wardrobe. Besides the bed, she'd taken her childhood dresser from her mother's home, as well as a few treasures that now sat on top of an embroidered Irish linen runner on the dresser top: her parents' wedding picture, her mother's comb and brush, a vase that Charles had given her for her twentieth birthday. The only other ornamentation in the room was the dressmaker's mannequin and her sewing cabinet.

How Nancy Cosgrove would smirk if she could see this room. But Jeanne would never forget looking out over the audience in the high school auditorium her senior year and seeing Nancy, stolid and unremarkable even then, in the front row. Jeanne, who'd been salutatorian and also voted both loveliest and most graceful, had given Nancy a smug nod before receiving her awards, then forgotten all about her in the ensuing standing ovation.

Jeanne had been beloved by all, and Nancy hadn't, and no reversal of fortunes would ever take that away.

Jeanne worked her fingers into her neck, trying to massage away the numbness from sitting too long bent over her work. "I suppose she can put me in my place all she wants, as long as she pays. What are you working on?"

Peggy held up the sketchbook: she'd drawn a fanciful hat, dripping with feathers and roses, on a faceless mannequin. The drawing was quite good, the detail of the veil rendered in a few lines, the roses lush and shaded. Peggy had loved to draw clothes and fashion since she'd received her first set of paper dolls and promptly made them a whole new construction paper wardrobe, but now that she had a child of her own, she limited herself to the sketchbooks she kept under her bed.

"And where are you going to get ostrich feathers?" Jeanne teased. "From a visiting sultan?"

"It's just for fun," Peggy mumbled, and closed the cover of

the sketchbook. Too late, Jeanne realized that she'd hurt her sister's feelings.

Even though Peggy was the one who'd married and had a child, who'd buried a husband and made a life with her mother-in-law, providing Jeanne a home by Thelma's good graces, Jeanne sometimes forgot that her younger sister had grown up.

"Your drawing is really good," Jeanne amended quietly.

"I'm off to bed," Peggy said, getting up and smoothing the covers where she'd lain. "I'll be up early with Tommie. Go back to burning the midnight oil."

❀ ❀ ❀

PEGGY HAD BEEN right: the modified sleeves balanced out the dress, drawing the eye up from Nancy's thick midsection and showing off her collarbones. "Her best feature," Thelma had observed wryly, making the others laugh.

The project had brought the three of them together in a way that had been rare in their little house. At the outset of the war, no one would have imagined the life they now had: three women and a baby, living on a service pension and Jeanne's earnings from her part-time jobs. Nothing had gone as it was supposed to. Before the Japanese bombed Pearl Harbor, Jeanne and her beau planned to marry, Peggy was caught up in a whirlwind romance, and Thelma looked forward to grand-children and time to spend in her garden.

But it was unfair to view that time through the wistful lens of the present. Even then, darkness had touched their lives. Four years earlier, in 1937, Thelma's husband had died in an accident, leaving her and her son, Thomas, with the house and an insurance policy that left little room for luxuries. Only two years later, Leo Brink was dead as well.

In those days the two families had been acquainted only through business: Thelma's husband, Henry, owned a small drayage company, and provided cartage for Brink Mills' yard goods, driving them from the mill to shipping ports and New York City's garment district. The sisters remembered Thomas Holliman from company picnics a decade earlier, when he was a ruthless plague upon the girls.

But at twenty-one, handsome and tall with patriotic fervor in his eyes, Thomas proved irresistible. He and Peggy started dating in the late summer of 1941 and were married on Valentine's Day 1942, weeks before he shipped out with the navy.

All these years later Peggy was prone to dark moods, as though she were the only widow in the house. But between them they had buried two husbands and a sweetheart. Still, that wasn't enough to elevate their misfortune above others'. Two doors down, Myra Lyall had lost both her sons and her husband had left her; when someone said hello to her in the street, half the time she didn't respond at all.

But the night after Jeanne finished Nancy's dress they had a little party of their own. There was Thelma's spice cake with buttermilk icing, and Frankie Laine on the radio. Jeanne and Peggy danced around the dining room, pretending they were at the ball, Jeanne leading because she was taller. Thelma acted annoyed and swatted at them, but Jeanne caught her humming in the kitchen. Peggy disappeared into her room for a few moments and emerged as Nancy, with couch cushions stuffed under her clothes and socks in her brassiere. She clomped through a waltz, while Jeanne made Tommie laugh by playing the rogue, pinching Peggy's bottom and sloshing imaginary champagne.

Hours later, after everyone had gone to bed, Jeanne lay under the mound of covers in her little bed, unable to sleep. Ice formed on the inside of the glass of the tiny attic window on nights as cold as this one, but Jeanne was warm under the quilts. She thought about the dress, about the compliments Nancy would receive and the business that might now come their way. In the end, she had charged Nancy nineteen dollars plus the cost of notions, a figure Thelma had come up with after studying the Fyfe's ad from the week before. Nineteen dollars was only half the cost of the featured gown—"and Nancy got an original," as Thelma pointed out.

On Sunday, Jeanne got ready for church with a flutter of anticipation. She wouldn't have to wait long. At St. Elizabeth's, she followed Thelma into their customary pew with her head held high. It was impossible to focus on the Mass, on the interminable sermon, and during Communion she watched the processional while pretending to pray, judging each woman's outfit as she walked by. Finally, the Mass was over, and she hurried to station herself strategically a few paces from the door, where Father Nowak was in the habit of greeting his parishioners.

The line grew long. Thelma and Peggy were delayed by

Tommie, who had undone the laces in her too-tight shoes. Jeanne chatted with Blanche Southwick, whose husband had been promoted to vice president at the bank where he worked, and who had most certainly been at the ball. Jeanne made idle conversation while she tried to figure out a way to bring up the dance, knowing that Blanche was far too polite to mention an event to which Jeanne had not been invited.

Peggy caught up just as Marjorie Reid joined their little group, adjusting the cherries on her hat. She had been several years ahead of Jeanne at Mother of Mercy, a toothy girl who had been president of the student council—never one to mince words.

"I saw Nancy Cosgrove last night," she announced. "She said you'd hemmed her gown for her at the last minute, Jeanne. That was awfully nice of you."

Jeanne stammered a response as Peggy dug her gloved fingers into her arm. Thelma was out of earshot, whispering in Tommie's ear, reminding her to curtsy for Father Nowak.

"She said you were a godsend," Marjorie continued. "What was it like, working on a Fath?"

"A . . . Fath?"

"Come now, Jeanne, you can tell us, now that the cat's out of the bag," Blanche interjected. "She told *everyone* that Lester bought her that dress in London."

"The skirt must have taken enough yardage to pitch a tent," Marjorie said. "Nancy's not exactly petite."

Suddenly Jeanne understood what was going on. Marjorie had always been a gossip in school, speculating on which girls might have allowed their boyfriends to go to second base, or tattling on the ones who smoked behind the band room. She would have been the perfect person to spread a rumor . . . particularly a rumor that one wanted spread.

And what asset would good old Nancy Cosgrove, as insecure and socially clumsy as ever, most want the attendees of the Holly Ball to believe she possessed—especially because she had neither beauty, wit, nor social standing to fall back on?

Money. Nancy would want everyone to think that she and Lester were rich—rich enough that he could bring back from his business trips a dress from one of the top couturiers in London. Of course everyone had heard of Jacques Fath, the French designer who had designed Rita Hayworth's wedding dress. A gown from Fath was a prize that could be won, or even purchased, only after gaining entrance into the salons, an honor that itself typically required an introduction. Charles's mother had owned a few gowns bought on her own European tour with her mother before her marriage, and Jeanne had been allowed a glimpse of them—the mothballed silk rustling gently under layers of tissue paper—in Mrs. Pearson's closet during a visit to their home in Connecticut.

Jeanne made all of these connections in the space of a few seconds—heartsick seconds during which she realized that Nancy had thrown her over, had won this round through sheer duplicity. But Peggy realized it even more quickly.

"Oh, but it wasn't just the hem," she said smoothly, producing a serene smile. Only Jeanne—and perhaps Thelma—noticed the twin spots of color on her cheeks that signaled her fury.

"Whatever do you mean?" Blanche said, her eyes narrowing as she leaned in closer, ever vigilant for a morsel of gossip.

"Oh, I—I shouldn't say," Peggy said demurely, placing her fingertips delicately over her lips.

Marjorie rounded on Jeanne. "Did you alter more than just the hem?"

That was all it took, the match that sparked the tinder of Jeanne's ire. She had once been a formidable presence, at least in the halls of Mother of Mercy, back in the days before any of them had known any real hardship. It had been years since Jeanne had summoned the poison from those hidden depths, a resource that all beautiful girls and women have, hoarded deep inside her like the bitter pit inside a peach, and she did Nancy one better.

"Well . . ." she said hesitantly, as though she couldn't decide whether to divulge the truth. Blanche leaned in too, and they all drew close, a coven of four, just a few yards away from the matrons offering their gloved hands to the pastor while they peered up piously from under their hats. "You see, she took it to be altered at Fyfe's in Plainsfield."

This was credible, because though the flagship Fyfe's department store was located just across the river in Philadelphia, it was actually easier to drive to the new store in Plainsfield, twenty miles away in the new Community Square mall. Center City society matrons would never make the trek, of course, but for a new generation of suburban housewives, flush with postwar success, the shopping mall beckoned with its wide avenues of parking and its imposing granite façade. The flagship's couture salon may have served ambassadors, first ladies, movie stars—but the new branch boasted the splendid Crystal Salon, which featured tall mirrors in gilded frames and sumptuous carpets and chandeliers rumored to have cost tens of thousands of dollars, as well as clothes from the most celebrated houses in Europe. Jeanne had pored over pictures of the salon in the pages of the *Inquirer*, the beautiful mannequins wearing gowns fresh from Dior and Balenciaga and Perrodin and Balmain, the women who could afford them seated on tufted brocade chairs, sipping coffee from bone china.

Blanche twitched her nose like a rabbit with a scent. "But why couldn't *they* do the hem?"

"*Well*." Jeanne had warmed to the lie, and now it had taken possession of her. "You see, Lester purchased the size that Nancy managed to convince him she wears. When she tried it on at the salon, she couldn't get the skirt up past her thighs. As for the bodice . . ." Jeanne shook her head sorrowfully. "There just wasn't any way. She tried to force it, and the zipper tore clean away from the faille lining."

"Whatever did you do?" Marjorie gasped. Jeanne knew that the story she was spinning, embellished for maximum impact, would soon make its way through the gossip chain of Brunskill society.

She shrugged. "The dress was ballerina length, thank heavens. I convinced Nancy that if we shortened it to slightly below the knee, I could use a bit of the hem"—here she paused to show that by *a bit* she meant a good eight inches—"to modify the bodice."

"But—I couldn't even tell. It looked perfect."

Jeanne nodded conspiratorially. "It took me two days just to piece in the gussets. I had to remove the boning and reattach it by hand, since the faille is so delicate." She accompanied these damning words with a covert gesture to indicate her rib cage and the bust darts of her suit, showing where the imaginary panels went and suggesting they'd been enormous. "Poor thing, I believe after the birth of her last, she's really had the hardest time getting her figure back. And with Lester spending so much time on the road . . ."

Jeanne gave the slightest emphasis to those last few words, just enough to communicate a bit of doubt, an unspoken suggestion that Lester's travels might not all be strictly necessary to his business, after all. Never mind that Lester was perhaps even more unattractive than Nancy—he'd have to have been to allow himself to be snagged by someone so unremarkable, despite his family's modest fortune—all it would take was a hint of a suggestion that his attentions were being lavished elsewhere.

That the Fath might have been—*just maybe*—a guilt present.

But Jeanne's work wasn't quite done. Revenge, no matter how sweet, wasn't going to put food on the table.

"Please don't let on that I've told you anything," Jeanne beseeched. "Nancy's quite a private person. I only agreed to tailor her gown because we've been friends for so long. It's not really . . ."

She let the words hang in the air, as though battling with herself on how much to say.

It worked, of course. "Not really what, Jeanne?" Blanche pressed close.

Jeanne fluttered her eyelashes modestly. "It's just that I prefer to work on my own designs. Mine and Peggy's." She nodded at the coat Peggy was wearing, one she'd begun several months ago when the first frost killed off the impatiens in Thelma's flowerbeds. The coat was flared in the back so that it hung in generous folds below its straight yoke, and when Peggy moved it swirled graciously around her hips. No one needed to know that the coat had started out as a man's balmacaan—quite a portly man, from the size of it—that Thelma had found in the St. Vincent de Paul shop. There'd been enough wool in the back alone to cut the sweeping gored panels.

"What do you mean, *your* designs?" Marjorie asked.

"Well, not mine exactly, of course. Peggy does the sketches. That one is based on a coat from the spring Balenciaga collection."

"They don't show those," Marjorie said, which was absolutely true. To gain entry into the salons, one had to have had an introduction from a long-standing client—and none of the women in the group qualified. Which was, of course, a fact that Nancy had gambled on when telling her outrageous lie: it was credible—just barely—that Lester might have made the connections to buy such a gift.

"Oh no, of course not," Jeanne said airily. "But Peggy is friends with the vendeuse at Fyfe's in the city. They met at Camp Nyakway."

And with that final, brilliant stroke, Jeanne sealed their

fate, the path that would wind through the years to come, leading them all down its treacherous, glittering twists and turns.

Many years earlier, Peggy had been sent to summer camp in a last-ditch effort to civilize her after her junior year of high school, when the nuns at Mother of Mercy had warned Emma Brink that her younger daughter was becoming unmanageable.

When Peggy returned at the end of the summer, tanned and sporting a new pin-curled hairstyle that she'd learned from the other girls, Jeanne had been hit with an unexpected wave of jealousy. She'd never had to share the spotlight, after all; she was accustomed to receiving the lion's share of the praise and attention of her parents and teachers and other girls. Peggy's transformation was surprisingly difficult to stomach, at first. But Jeanne had met Charles that summer on a fix-up date, and she buried her resentment by writing him long letters addressed to his family's home in Connecticut, where he was living while studying for his medical board exams, and looking forward to his visits.

Camp Nyakway was strictly for the daughters of affluent families, but Emma Brink was an alumna and somehow found the money to send her rebellious daughter. In her months at camp, Peggy had met girls from all over New Jersey and Pennsylvania and even New York—but none from Mother of Mercy. So she could say anything she wanted about the experience and there would be no one to contradict her.

Jeanne knew she'd struck a direct hit when Blanche's eyes lit up with excitement. "Wait a minute—you're saying you *copied* a Fath for Nancy? And she told you not to tell anyone?"

"Oh," Jeanne said, feigning confusion. "It wasn't like that—I don't mean to make it sound like Nancy—I mean, I'm sure she was just—"

"It's all right," Blanche said quickly. "I understand. You were trying to do something nice. But listen, Jeanne—I wonder if you might have time to stop by for coffee next week?"

January 1949

Peggy

It was well past time to turn out the light and get some sleep, but Peggy didn't set the square black Conté crayon down. She took a dainty sip of the bitter, cold coffee left over from the morning—yesterday morning, to be accurate, since it was nearly one-thirty—and made a bold, broad stroke down a fresh piece of newsprint. The piece of wood she'd rigged as an easel—taken from a cabinet face from a building being torn down around the corner—shifted on the bolster on which Peggy had propped it. Too bad they didn't know any carpenters who might make her a real easel, Peggy thought grimly. Too bad they didn't know any useful men at all.

On her little mattress not three feet away, Tommie shifted and rolled, her rosette lips pursed. She was a restless sleeper, as she had been a restless baby—she'd come into the world uneasy, as though she knew already that she'd be denied a father, denied the perfect charmed life that Peggy had promised her many months earlier, when she'd first made her presence known on a prodigious wave of nausea, harbinger of the difficult pregnancy to come.

No, nothing about Tommie was easy, and sharing a room with her—and yes, Peggy knew she was lucky to have a room at all, with her sister making up a bed each night in the freezing attic—was a daily torment.

Another curving black stroke of the crayon, to meet the first. In those two lines were the suggestion of the back, the shoulders, the curve of the hip. Peggy glanced at the latest issue of *Vogue*, open to a spread titled "The New Blouse-and-Skirt Formula," featuring full-circle skirts nipped in tight over balloon-sleeved blouses. The first wave of outrage over Dior's new look seemed to have abated, silenced, perhaps, by the unstoppable tide of women hungry for a bit of glamour. Peggy could sympathize. The wartime fashions, made severe and scant by textile regulations dictated by the War Production Board—had looked all right on angular, thin women like her sister. But on curvy Peggy, they looked downright ridiculous.

She sketched soft, feathery strokes to suggest a full skirt like the one in the *Vogue* layout. Underneath the skirt, there would be structured layers of tulle to give it shape, but her drawing would only show the fanciful outline, like a bell, with satin pumps peeping from the bottom. Peggy could wear such a skirt—if she had anywhere to go. She had retained her small waist even after Tommie's birth, and her bosom remained high and generous. She was still making do with her corset from two years ago, but if she could afford one of the new French-waisted ones, with the tabs that could be cinched tightly . . .

After Thomas's death, and Tommie's birth, Peggy had drifted through time for a while. She remembered the sleepless nights, the endless bottles, the sour smell of spit-up and soiled diapers as though they were one long fevered dream. Boys she'd known seemed to die every day, or be taken prisoner, and she couldn't seem to make herself care. The only time the war being fought on other continents felt real was when she saw some poor veteran soldier being pushed in a wheelchair, a blanket covering his missing limbs, and in his eyes saw something familiar—a blank resignation that resembled emptiness more than grief.

But now! Now, for reasons she didn't understand, Peggy was ready to live again. It was an amorphous urge, an undefined hunger for something she couldn't name. She longed for something of her own, something beyond caring for Tommie and carrying on the homely tasks of life with her sister and mother-in-law. Sometimes, she saw a man in public—his worn brown shoe as he stepped up on the trolley; his callused hand holding a folded newspaper—and she felt a physical longing so strong she nearly doubled over with the force of it.

Peggy, if she'd been allowed, if circumstances were different, would have greeted the New Look by wearing her skirt any damn length she pleased. She could have turned heads, could have been a provocateur herself, a trendsetter—if only.

She squeezed the narrow chalk tightly between her fingers and concentrated, adding short light strokes to define the head, the arm, the wrist turned just so. The feminine form came naturally to her, the shadowy suggestion of the anatomy that would disappear under the rest of the drawing, yet without which it would never come alive.

Once—Thomas had been away at war for nearly two months at the time, and Peggy was still in the first trimester of her pregnancy—she had snuck off to the library, a place she knew no one would expect to find her. She'd found a book titled *Anatomical Drawings of Albrecht Dürer* and spent a long afternoon studying how the great artist had prepared a sketch. Hands divided with crossed lines to indicate proper proportion, limbs moving along a curved axis—even drawings of skeletons and skulls to illustrate the structure under the skin. Peggy had been fascinated to discover that there were tricks and secrets to what she'd always assumed was the domain of pure genius.

She got that day's *Philadelphia Inquirer* off the heavy wooden roller and spread it out on the long table next to the book, ignoring the scowl of the librarian. Here—in the Wanamaker's advertisement featuring "smart hostess frocks"—she saw how the artist had fancifully altered the mannequin's proportions. Peggy held up her pencil with her thumb marking the hip bone, checked it against the Dürer illustration. Off by a factor of nearly one and a half. Languid fingers too narrow to hold a telephone—ankles so delicate they'd snap during a brisk walk. Waists and necks impossibly narrow and sharp, planed cheekbones you could practically cut a tomato with.

It was no secret that the sketches in the ads didn't reflect reality. But as Peggy traced the drawing with the eraser end of the pencil, beginning to learn the proportions in her muscles' own memory, she reflected that maybe they represented something better: possibility, which was in such short supply now that the grim reports were coming back from the front—

Peggy sneezed, drawing a sharp glance from the matronly librarian. But did the librarian have a husband who was serving in the South Pacific? A husband whose letter, received only yesterday, compared Peggy's breasts to "cantilopes" (okay, so Thomas wasn't a speller)—who promised that when he returned he was going to take her to Atlantic City, where they wouldn't leave their motel room for three entire days? A husband who was not yet aware of the incredible fact that he would soon be a father?

No, Peggy thought angrily, she undoubtedly did not. The librarian was too old and pruney and mean to have a husband or beau.

Peggy redoubled her efforts.

Now, nearly seven years later, she'd improved considerably. She'd done little drawing during the early sleepless nights with Tommie, the bouts of colic and croup and fever. But later, as Tommie grew into a willful toddler and exhausted herself with temper tantrums until she collapsed, Peggy learned to steal every peaceful moment for herself. She asked only for chalk and paper for her birthdays, and when her daughter finally slept through the night, Peggy waited until Thelma and Jeanne went to bed and drew to her heart's content.

A tap, a swish, and the door swung silently open. The figure who slipped inside, past Tommie's little bed, was her sister.

"What are you working on?" Jeanne whispered, pulling her robe tightly around her knees. Peggy's room was warmer than the attic, but not by much, especially at night when they turned the furnace way down to save oil.

Peggy tilted the sketch up. She'd finished detailing the skirt, and outlined a scalloped capelet over the shoulders. Jeanne picked up the paper and examined the Wanamaker's ad from which Peggy had been working. "That collar looks like it could stand up by itself," she said doubtfully. "I don't know if Brunskill is ready for that."

"You said you wanted to give Blanche something new," Peggy said. "Europe is doing everything crisp. You could do broadcloth . . ." The defensiveness that rose up in her was inexhaustible. If only Jeanne would spare a kind word now and then—Peggy often imagined that she could go for days on a bit of praise. But their mother had been gone for years, and with her, the indulgence Peggy never knew she would miss so much.

"Maybe . . ." Jeanne set the page down and sat on the edge of Peggy's bed, the same one that Thomas had slept in during his childhood. This had been Thomas's room, a fact that had given Peggy comfort in her early months here, before his spirit seemed to fade almost entirely away. "I just think that Blanche . . . she's going to her husband's sales dinner. Not a cotillion in Versailles."

Peggy heard the petulance in her own voice but couldn't

stop it. "Her husband is getting an *award*. She *said* so. She needs to look special."

Those had been Blanche's exact words, in fact. Peggy had busied herself with Tommie, on the floor with the wooden blocks that had also once belonged to Thomas, while Jeanne sat primly on the sofa and took notes. "I need something special," Blanche had said, "something that says 'regional manager material.'"

As if a dress alone could turn Blanche, a sow's ear of a girl with enormous thighs and a sloping chin, into a silk purse. But Peggy felt a duty to try. She felt strangely moved by the naïve hopes of Jeanne's clients, their bright-eyed longing for *la mode*. Peggy knew that no woman shaped like a proper mannequin was likely to walk through their door and ask for a dress, but she didn't mind. Their work—because even though Jeanne did all the cutting and sewing and fitting, Peggy considered it her work as well, as she did the sketches and maintained the "dressing room" and swept up the snippets and threads each evening—was to give the women of Brunskill and Roxborough an escape from their babies and children and husbands and household budgets. They were ordinary women with ordinary problems, trying to buy a little glamour at a cut rate, and Peggy was proud to provide it.

She knew it was different for Jeanne, who had gone to school with most of these girls. Peggy, two classes beneath them, had envied and worshipped them but never really known them. She'd been a willful, solitary girl given to spending most of her time alone or in the mother superior's office awaiting the latest in a never-ending stream of rebukes. Having never attained Jeanne's level of status, Peggy had never suffered the ignominy of a fall from grace.

"Bring the skirt in," Jeanne said, rubbing her eyes. "We'll do it in crêpe. Put some stiffening in at the hip if you must, but remember that Blanche probably doesn't want to draw the eye there. Her hips are not her best feature."

Peggy didn't want to bring the skirt in. She wanted it just the way she'd drawn it, outlandishly full and coquettishly flounced. But she bit back a retort; her sister looked exhausted. She'd been losing weight again; the robe's sash circled twice around her shrunken waist.

"Why are you still up?" Peggy asked instead, afraid to voice her fear. Their mother had grown very thin before her final illness. Peggy couldn't imagine losing Jeanne too: she needed her sister to be steady, to be her rock.

Jeanne smoothed the robe over her knees, ducked her chin, sighed. Finally she looked up and met Peggy's gaze with her own. "It's just . . . I can't sew fast enough, honey. I've got girls waiting. Aggie Hart called just this afternoon, wanting a coat, she was so happy with the dress I made for her. But it takes as long as it takes. And . . . and they won't pay. It's Brunskill and they will only pay Brunskill prices."

So it was money, again. Peggy stayed out of the household finances, but she'd seen Thelma and Jeanne with their heads together, going through the accounts. Thelma's medicine and Tommie's shoes, heating oil and groceries and detergent— Peggy knew they were struggling to get by. But there was her widow's pension and the money from Jeanne's part-time office job in addition to the sewing; how could it still not be enough?

"I can help," she said quickly, shamefully. Her main task, they all agreed, was to raise Tommie; but she knew that Thelma and Jeanne would also agree she wasn't well suited for the job. Tommie was in kindergarten now for several hours a day, but the peace of the school day passed so quickly, sandwiched between the chaotic mornings and evenings. Tommie was a demanding child, and Peggy secretly wondered which of her many failures caused her daughter's poor behavior. Surely there were other mothers who would welcome Tommie's boundless energy, her scabbed elbows and knees, the tangles in her flax-fine hair and the faintly spoiled smell about her. Mothers with experience, matter-of-fact women who'd take Tommie in hand and have her sorted out in no time, who'd braid her hair tightly and teach her to say "yes, ma'am" and take a hairbrush to her bottom when she talked back.

Peggy herself would have done well with a quiet, shy girl, one whose energies were restrained, who still napped and said please without being prompted. Or a boy. She would have known what to do with a boy—raise him to be athletic and strong and decisive. But what to do with a headstrong *girl?*

"I *can* help, you know," Peggy repeated, rubbing the black grime off her fingertips with a worn handkerchief she'd saved for the purpose. She would take up hems, cut out patterns, sew on buttons—simple tasks that she couldn't mess up. "I could chalk and pin and cut—I can baste and hem."

Jeanne barely acknowledged the offer. Those were the least difficult tasks and they both knew that Peggy couldn't set in a sleeve or fit a bodice or sew an invisible zipper. And Thelma—with her painful joints—was no help either.

"I'm going to have to take a job in the city," Jeanne said quietly.

Peggy stared at her sister. "City?"

"In Philly. I talked to Benny Frazier. There are openings in the typing pool at Harris Carton. I can start next week. I *will* start next week."

"But—" Benny Frazier had been in love with Jeanne since they were Little Saints together at St. Augustus. He'd married a Main Line girl after college and took a job at the same company where his father-in-law worked. What must have it cost Jeanne to ask such a favor?

"Who will finish Blanche's dress?" Peggy asked instead.

"I will," Jeanne said. "I'll work extra this week. I need to tailor my brown suit too, and maybe I can do something with Mother's old tweed. I'll need clothes for work."

Peggy picked up the crayon again, squeezed it hard enough to break. The little sticks were brittle, and she only had one spare. She set it down again. Who would she sketch for now? And who would help her with Tommie? And the little dressing room . . . would it go back to storing potatoes and onions, the rag bag hung from a nail, Thelma's coffee can rattling with coins?

For the last few months, as Jeanne's fingers flew over yards of wool and silk and cotton and the sewing machine whirred late into the evening, as Thelma stepped around the kitchen table covered with fabric and patterns, carrying the mail and the laundry and the hard round loaves from the bakery, and Peggy made a game of hunting for snipped threads and dropped pins with Tommie, she had allowed herself to hope. That the future might hold something for them—something finer than the life that had settled on them during the war.

But Jeanne was leaving. Jeanne—not technically a widow, still young, or at least young enough, and prettier than girls a decade younger—would find her chance, in the crowded streets and skyscrapers of the city. For Jeanne, now, there would be cocktails at smart clubs, lunches with other career girls. Banter with sophisticated men and women in the office, glances exchanged with strangers as she rushed for her train.

She would go on dates. There would be a wedding, perhaps, eventually—a proper one, with a gown and a veil and a mountain of gifts, not the rushed ceremony at City Hall that Peggy and Thomas had. What would be left for Peggy but raising Tommie under her mother-in-law's observant eye, watching her waistline thicken every year, discovering her first gray hair alone, with no one to comfort her?

"What a wonderful idea," she said, crumpling the half-finished drawing in her trembling fist.

Jeanne rose and slipped out of the room before either of them could cry.

Jeanne

Their poverty was a constant thread, though each of them suffered it differently. Peggy resented the meager meals most of all. She'd always had a sweet tooth, and when her government check came, she always bought a pint of ice cream on the way back from the bank before handing the cash over to Thelma. The rest of the time there was cabbage and meatloaf, stews and gristly chops, Malt-O-Meal and spaghetti and canned fruit. As for Thelma, she hunched over the black ledgers left over from when she'd done her husband's books, entering every penny of their household expenses, adding the sums over and over as though if she only tried hard enough, she might get a different result.

For Jeanne, the worst privation was having to make do with mended and redone clothes. All three women loved fashion, but for the others it was like a spectator sport: they read and re-read the remaindered fashion magazines Thelma got from her friend who worked in the drugstore until they were dog-eared and crumbling. They admired the beautiful clothes they saw in the department store windows, and devoured the newspaper photographs of movie stars in sumptuous gowns. For Jeanne, on the other hand, going out in public in a patched or worn garment engendered an almost physical pain. She had always taken pride in her appearance, and she could hardly bear to wear the things she'd owned for years, some of which she'd mended and tailored so often that they were virtually disintegrating.

Now she was faced with the prospect of walking into the midtown headquarters of Harris Carton in two days' time, under the gaze of all of those smart city girls and her new supervisor—she was to report to the assistant to Theodore Harris, the boss's own son and heir to the family business and hence a thorn in the side of her old friend Benny—and she could not bear to do it in one of her old dresses. There was humiliation enough in her age and bare ring finger.

Jeanne had finished Blanche's dress last night, and this morning had sent her home happy. Blanche had asked for another and Jeanne had put her off. So far, no one but Thelma and Peggy knew about the job, and that was how Jeanne meant things to stay until she was sure she could measure up. She'd learned typing and dictation before the war, when she thought she would work until her wedding to Charles—but then her mother had begun her steep decline and everything else was put aside. Since Emma Brink's death, Jeanne had done only a few hours of filing and simple correspondence each week for small local businesses. She wasn't certain, despite her assurances to Benny, that she'd be able to pull off the dictation and typing, and she wanted to spare herself any further humiliation.

She turned her mother's old tweed skirt over in her hands. It was at least a decade out of date, an A-line style that would never do, but tweed was back in style and Butterick had just published a pattern that had given her an idea.

Jeanne no longer worked from patterns. After discovering a passion for sewing the first time her mother opened the case of the Singer Featherweight, she had sewn perhaps a hundred garments, hungrily tackling each new technique with the passion of a master. She started with a Simplicity pattern for a blouse that was only slightly more advanced than the simple white middy she'd sewn, along with all of her classmates, for home ec, then moved through A-line and gored skirts, a tab-waisted pair of trousers, a shawl-collared jacket.

Her first designer pattern was a Joseph Sussman for Advance, and Jeanne discovered halfway through cutting it out that shortcuts had been taken—gathers rather than a proper bust dart, for instance, and a faced neckline that would never lie flat and really should have been lined. Jeanne had begged her mother to buy the four yards of raspberry crêpe for the dress, and planned to wear it to deliver her salutatory address—and she felt personally affronted by the pattern's shortcomings.

Jeanne studied the pattern envelope and saw how she'd been taken in. The illustrator's fanciful brushstrokes hid the underlying flaws; she should have noted that the back of the envelope bore the legend SEW EASY. She went back to the catalog counter at the fabric store and spent an hour poring over the catalogs. Simplicity, McCall's, and Advance all had designs advertised as "easy" or "quick" or both, for lazy, novice, or time-pressed seamstresses. But even Vogue's elegant catalog included designs that lacked fine tailoring, while others featured clever feats of fabric manipulation that it would almost take an engineer to plan and execute. A twisted keyhole top, for instance, was constructed of pattern pieces shaped like hour-glasses; the end result could not be divined from its parts.

She was studying a draped and bustled gown from the Vogue Couturier line when the woman next to her glanced over. "All those tucks," she tutted reprovingly. "And then what if you want to ease in a little extra?"

"I haven't done tucks yet," Jeanne admitted.

"Well, then you have no business with that one. You'll cause yourself no end of grief." She peered over her spectacles at Jeanne. "Such a lovely girl. Have you done a fitting pattern yet?"

"No—but I have my mother's dressmaker's dummy," Jeanne said, embarrassed. Her mother barely knew how to use it herself; sewing had not been part of her privileged upbringing. "I've adjusted it to my measurements."

"Oh, no no no," the woman said. "You're not ready for that yet. Here, let me help you."

Jeanne never did learn her name—but her benefactor spent nearly an hour patiently explaining how the fitting pattern would teach Jeanne to adjust her flat pattern cutting, to lengthen and shorten, ease for fullness or take in excess. "You won't be ready to drape on the dummy until you've mastered all of this," she said, using her thumb and index finger to mark off two-thirds of the Vogue catalog.

Years later, when Jeanne worked in the silent attic, allowing her mind to wander wherever it liked, she sometimes wondered about the woman. Had she no daughters of her own? Or were they too impatient with their mother's instruction? Jeanne had listened eagerly, soaking in the details that her basic home economics course hadn't covered, her fingers practically twitching with their eagerness to get started. She showed the woman the dress pattern she'd been working on, and together they found another—a McCall's evening gown with a pieced bodice and full-length side zipper—which she said would fit far better.

Jeanne went home with the pattern and recut the pieces she'd already pinned. The raspberry dress flattered her perfectly, and that summer Jeanne worked through the fitting patterns for blouses, skirts, trousers, and coats. She was wearing the raspberry dress the night she met Charles; she made a second version in teal acetate when he asked her to a dance.

That fall, when her father's heart attack took them all by shock, sewing became Jeanne's refuge and her solace. She made a mourning wardrobe for her mother, dark dresses that grew looser as her mother grew thinner. With their finances in a shambles—Uncle Frank was helping sort through the details, since her father had never given her mother access to the accounts—Jeanne learned to sew for economy. She made Peggy's prom dress and the dress she wore under her graduation gown. She began to page secretly through the bridal section of the pattern catalogs, dreaming of her wedding even as the war stole headlines and her mother's illness became impossible to ignore.

With each new garment she learned a new technique, a shortcut, a tailoring trick. She could cut a skirt panel from memory, or gauge a sleeve adjustment by holding the fabric up to her arm. She matched the neckline from one pattern with the sleeve from another; she made adjustments on the fly, using up a bit of extra silk for a piped collar or narrowing a hem to save fabric. By that spring, when Uncle Frank shuttered the mill for good and Jeanne was finishing her secretarial courses and Peggy had gone to work at the art store, she could copy a dress from a magazine with just a measuring tape and chalk and scissors.

All these years later, Jeanne rarely bought a pattern, but she still browsed the catalogs to see what was new. She lacked Peggy's imagination—she couldn't come up with a design on her own—and she drew her inspiration from the illustrations. She preferred Vogue for their designers and their intricate details, but always gave the Butterick and Simplicity books a cursory look. And there she'd found an ingenious pattern for yokes, fitted to the hip, that could be attached to an existing skirt to give the length and illusion of the abundant skirt that had become so popular.

Jeanne had taken a chance and cut the sleeves from the jacket, leaving only fitted short ones. She opened out the seams and picked the hand-stitched lining and was left with enough yardage to cut a trim front and back from the more voluminous ones of the old style. Had she not lost weight last fall, it wouldn't have been enough, but Jeanne had grown quite thin. She couldn't help thinking how disappointed Charles would be; he'd always liked a bit of meat under his hands, and he'd loved to squeeze the soft flesh of her hips, her waist.

Charles had been gone for five years. He'd died in Cisterna, watching helplessly at first light as seventeen German panzers bore down on his ranger division after a night of hard-won advances toward town. Some had suggested he'd been among the lucky ones, since hundreds of men were captured by the Germans that day and spent the rest of the war languishing in the camps.

Thoughts like this could seize Jeanne's mind and twist it into impossible knots of doubt and anguish. And there was no one she could turn to, because Peggy and Thelma had lost Thomas eighteen months earlier at Guadalcanal. At least Charles's family had been able to bury their son in the family plot in Woodbury. Thomas's remains lay on the other side of the world, in one of the makeshift cemeteries where they buried the endless tide of boys who were mown down by bullets or torn apart in blasts or felled by disease, starvation, or freezing.

Jeanne forced her attention back to the skirt, using her seam ripper to pick the waistband from the plain gathered waist, then separating the panels. She would reconstruct them as a bias-cut flounce, attached at the thigh of the new yoke so that the hem—which she remembered hitting her mother below her knees—now swirled about the ankles. She would have to piece in triangular pieces of black wool from another old dress to achieve volume, but the gussets would disappear in the folds of the skirt. As for the jacket, she would narrow the waist and cut down the lapels to a demure inch.

Hours later, as a final touch, Jeanne took a bit of the silk from which she'd sewn that traitor Nancy Cosgrove's ball gown and stitched a gathered rosette, which she tacked to the breast pocket.

Sunday morning, she skipped church without an excuse, and Thelma, eyeing the still-uncut old clothes on the sewing table, didn't ask for one. Peggy trailed Thelma out of the house, tugging Tommie behind her. Jeanne knew that they were trying to give her the time and space she needed to prepare for her new job. She was to earn thirty-eight dollars a week, money that would close the gap in their budget, but this had introduced a hierarchy into their home that was not there before. In the beginning she'd been the interloper, the odd one out, but in the years since then they'd become three women toiling equally, shoulder to shoulder like so many during the war.

Jeanne sewed all day, barely looking up when the others returned from church dragging a now tear-stained and snif-fling Tommie and a ham hock wrapped in butcher paper. She sewed while the soup simmered and took only a few minutes to eat with them, barely tasting the salty broth and Peggy's biscuits. By midnight she had finished a second outfit, which she planned to wear on her second day of work, after which she would alternate the two until she could afford a third. The dress that Thelma had worn the day they went to the train sta-tion to see Thomas off to war now featured a four-panel skirt that reached almost to the ankle, its pieced-in yoke concealed by a flounced peplum and bodice made from an old dress that had never fit Peggy properly.

Jeanne was in bed by eleven o'clock, exhausted. She knew that she would drop off quickly, that the strident tones of the alarm clock at six would interrupt a dead sleep. But she was not at peace. Since accepting the job, a nagging, anxious voice had taunted her: *What makes you think*, it demanded, *that you can do this? You had your chance, and it's over.*

It was this voice that had stolen Jeanne's appetite and plagued her moments of solitude. But unlike the terrible long-ago spring after her mother died and Jeanne had to come like a pauper begging for a crust to live in Thelma's attic, she had had enough. Some small spirit inside her refused to be snuffed out.

She turned over in her bed, pulling her pillow over her head so that her breath warmed her face and neck under the covers. She could give in to her fate and spend the rest of her days languishing here, until she died a penniless spinster. Or she could get up tomorrow and get on the train that would take her into Center City, where her future was waiting.

Jeanne had once been the envy of Mother of Mercy. She'd been pretty and popular and admired, but most of all she had been sure of herself and her place. If the pain of the intervening years had somehow loosed her from the gravity that moored her to earth and sent her floating aimlessly through her own misery, she was now ready to reclaim what she'd lost. She'd make them take notice once again. She'd show them all.

Two

Tweed

They've been making tweed forever, you know—don't be fooled by what they'll ask for a yard of it at Holland & Sherry. A hundred years ago, Scottish women hunched over the spinning wheels, the carding combs, the looms, everything done by hand, and most of it stayed right there in the islands. And what do you suppose they were paid for their toil? But you see, that's the way it's always been: a man sees no value in a woman's work until he can charge someone else double for it.

It's a pleasure to hand sew, though . . . the way the needle slips between the threads, like a hot knife through butter. And it's got lot loads of ease. If you can't match a Harris plaid seam, why, I suppose there's no hope for you at all.

February 1949

Thelma

The girl was up early, but Thelma was up earlier. She lay in the bed she'd once shared with her husband, and listened to Jeanne moving through her preparations for work. Two weeks into her new job in the city, she had perfected her routine, as brisk and tight as the girl herself. The slight creaking sound above the ceiling of Thelma's room—that was the drawer in the old dresser in which she stored her underclothes and hosiery. The scrape of metal was the hanger suspended from the length of pipe she'd hung from the wall in lieu of a closet. Muffled twin thumps were her shoes—shined and polished the night before, the narrow heels hitting the rug.

Then, the sound of her feet descending the steep stairs, the squeak of the floorboards. For many years, Thelma only went up into the attic to add some piece of junk to the pile stored there since she and Henry moved in all those years ago. All of that had been discarded, of course, when Jeanne moved in. Good riddance.

Jeanne performed her ablutions in the bathroom that separated the two bedrooms. She tried to be quiet—God knows she was a considerate one—but there are sounds that humans make that cannot be stifled. Thelma should know. She, at the advanced age of forty-seven, was a veritable catalog of the things that befell a body in maturity, or so she often thought in these early morning sleepless hours, when the sleep that had once come so easily eluded her and her gut churned and roiled. Her husband—she'd once known every detail of him: the creases in his neck, the snores that ended in abrupt gasping for breath (she has always believed he must have made a sound like this when the pallet fell from his truck and struck his head, killing him before he hit the street), the smell of him when he shifted in his sleep.

Thelma thought about getting up and fixing Jeanne some coffee, some toast. Lord knew the girl could use some meat on her bones. But Thelma had sensed from the start that Jeanne had no desire to replace her dead mother with a stand-in, that she would find her way best if she was left alone. Some girls were like that. Thelma herself had been, in fact. She'd shunned close girlfriends during her own school days, focusing instead on helping in her father's store. Thomas arrived quickly after her marriage (Henry's brief courtship seemed, in retrospect, almost insignificant when Thelma reviewed her life's history) and occupied her completely. By the time Thomas went off to school, Thelma was consumed with trying to make ends meet.

She helped in the classroom, volunteered at the convalescent home, scrubbed their little row house top to bottom, and grew vegetables to supplement Henry's meager earnings. It bemused her that Peggy and Jeanne thought their current circum-stances were dire: true, it was a struggle to pay the bills, but Jeanne often left food on her plate and Peggy thought Thelma didn't know she held back some of her government checks for herself. It wasn't their fault—they'd grown up coddled, wealthy enough for private school and pleasure trips. Perhaps because of this, Thelma had still not shared her secret, the one that might have saved Jeanne from this new career: How else was the girl to occupy her time? Hunched over the table for another seven years while her back grew humped and her fingers as arthritic as Thelma's?

Thelma had never sought out the attention of other women, but here she was living with two and raising a third, and none of them really knew her at all. Before Henry died, she had enjoyed doing his books. She was good with numbers and she found something like joy in preparing the invoices and depositing the checks and balancing the ledgers. Down in the basement, care-fully packed in excelsior, were her adding machine, her stamps and inks, her leather-bound books and stationery and desk cal-endars and blotters. She hadn't been able to part with any of it. The tools of a trade no one, not Henry or even Thomas, had ever acknowledged.

The soft sound of Jeanne's footsteps stopped outside her door. She lingered there for a moment, and Thelma wondered what she was doing. In between the bedrooms, was she listen-ing at her sister's door—or at Thelma's?

A secret-keeper by nature, Thelma couldn't imagine what

secrets the others might keep from her. Spoiled, tempestuous Peggy—unfit to be a wife, barely fit to be a mother, and made useless by being cast in the role of both. Jeanne, practically a spinster already, squandering a little more of her rare beauty with each passing day.

And what did they see when they looked at Thelma? A widow, mother of a dead son, in mourning for over a decade now? A walking ghost, with only the gray road between the present and her own death, persevering only to help provide for her son's wife and child?

Thelma rolled her face to her shoulder and bit down the frustration that stemmed from too much introspection, leaving teeth marks in her own freckled skin. A moment later Jeanne's soft footsteps shuffled away, down to the first floor, and then—there, the front door, opened and shut quickly because Jeanne was a meticulous and thoughtful girl and would be mindful of the house's heat seeping out into the chilly dawn.

The house was silent. The neighbors—a widow to one side, a childless couple to the other—would not be up for another hour at least. In the other bedroom, Tommie would soon wake, shift, demand attention. Thelma would go downstairs to warm her milk, then return and lead her from her bed. Her mother's job, but there was no use prodding Peggy. Thelma would take care of them all. Thelma, wrapped in her secrets and her plans, would move among them undetected.

March 1949

Jeanne

Jeanne's morning walk to the trolley stop took around eleven minutes in fair weather or foul. She liked to arrive at precisely 7:01 for the 7:04 trolley, keeping her eye on her watch (her mother's, which she had begun wearing the day after Emma Brink died).

She liked to sit in the fourth seat, next to the window. Arriving in Center City at the Ninth and Walnut stop, it was another four blocks to the Harris Carton offices on Sansom. At her desk at last, she took pleasure in finding the plastic typewriter cover precisely as she'd left it the night before, her coffee cup rinsed and dried, pencils and pen lined up on the blotter.

The work was not difficult. The memos and letters that came her way to type were simple. Jeanne typed as she sewed, with precision and determination, and she was rarely called on an error. By the end of the first week, the girls at nearby desks had taken to asking her how to spell words or to check their punctuation. This, however, was the limit of their contact. Jeanne was not invited to lunches; no one gossiped with her in the ladies' room over the stall doors.

Standoffishness had been one of her stock tools, back at Mother of Mercy, so Jeanne understood it keenly. She was almost glad of it. The well of her social graces had gone dry during the years of her exile, and she had no desire to curry the favor of the office queen bees or mock the ungainly ones. There was a hunger blooming inside her, but it was not for girlish confidences and petty feminine victories.

After the first day, Jeanne realized she had worried about her clothes for nothing: no one guessed the shabby provenance of her wardrobe. Other girls wore dated and unflattering and clearly homemade things; Jeanne's skill with the needle ensured that her suits fit and flattered her perfectly, and she let the others believe that she shopped for her fabric in the showrooms on Fourth Street. That lone insecurity vanquished, it was from an indifferent remove that Jeanne received her coworkers' envious glances.

At the end of the day Jeanne prepared to leave in reverse order, brushing off the typewriter's keys with the bristles of her correcting wheel and dusting her desk with a rag she kept in the drawer. Then she hurried out with barely a nod to her coworkers. Maybe they thought she had a fiancé. Maybe they saw right through her. It was hard to say.

But on a damp Tuesday several weeks into her new job, as she settled into her chair, she heard her name.

"Jeanne?"

There was Gladys, hurrying toward her between the desks, tugging anxiously on her faux pearls. Gladys was a transplant, a newlywed from the Midwest who'd married a soldier with whom she'd begun a wartime correspondence, a shy girl whose broad pale cheeks were forever bursting with pink. Her soldier was Theodore Harris himself, Benny's rival and son of the company's owner, and her employment here was sure to end just as soon as she managed to get pregnant. This sort of gossip was impossible not to know, even for someone like Jeanne.

"Oh, hi, Gladys . . ."

"You always look so elegant," the girl blurted. "And I need—I need some advice." She tugged at the hem of her skirt self-consciously. "I'm having lunch at my mother-in-law's club next Friday and I just don't—and I heard the girls saying that you can sew? That you make all your clothes and they're just so, and I don't have, I mean I can't buy anything *new*, and I'm a disaster with a needle and I just wondered. If you had time . . . I could. Well." She grinned a wobbly grin. "I could pay you back with a pie. That I can handle."

Jeanne hesitated, her mind already on the ride home, the bliss of sliding, at last, into her seat. The smell of damp wool and pipe tobacco and the leather of the seat, mixed with aftershave and perfume and exhaust from the traffic.

But there was something about this girl, with her hapless wholesomeness, her slightly protruding teeth, her guileless smile. Another girl would have made an advantage of her marriage to the boss's son, but in Gladys it backfired; she had an air of perpetual embarrassment, rendering her easy fodder for the sharp beaks. Jeanne sensed, perhaps, an opportunity to repent for her own long-ago cruelty.

"Well, sure," Jeanne said, smiling, casting back in her memory for something the girl had worn that had potential. "The blue crêpe—are you very fond of it the way it is?"

Gladys grimaced. "Ugh, no. Mama made that for Pearl—my older sister—but she had a baby last year and she hasn't got her figure back, which is why I got it, but it never has fit right."

Jeanne nodded; that explained the gappy neckline, the straining darts. "Well, I'll tell you what, why don't you bring it in tomorrow and let me take a look?"

A WEEK LATER Jeanne was standing at the door of an apartment just off Bainbridge along the northern edge of South Philly, a part of town she'd never visited before, where families of seemingly all nationalities crowded into tenements and apartment buildings together.

"I'm so sorry," Gladys mumbled at the sound of a wailing infant down the hall. "It's just—Teddy's parents have *gobs* of money, he grew up in a *mansion* on Rittenhouse Square, but they feel he should make his own way. And we do too, of *course!*"

Jeanne couldn't help smiling at the girl's earnestness. "I think it's swell. So cosmopolitan. Now let's see if you like what I've done."

She took the blue dress out of its garment bag. Gladys had given her an old ivory-colored skirt along with the suit, and Jeanne had shown the two garments to Peggy and asked her to come up with a design, describing Gladys's figure. Once she had a drawing to work with, she had cut wide bands from the skirt to set into the yoke so that they tied in a bow above a keyhole neckline, which solved the problem of the too-tight bust.

She'd also added a wide ivory band at the hem to lengthen the skirt and a single layer of tulle for a bit of fullness.

Gladys gasped as Jeanne laid the garment reverently on the young couple's worn davenport. "It's gorgeous, but—gosh, Jeanne, this wouldn't fit a flea! Look at me, I'm just as big as all get out!" She patted her hips, which swelled from a tiny waist like Peggy's.

"Don't judge yet," Jeanne said, hiding a smile. "Go try it on."

Moments later, a wolfish whistle could be heard from the back of the apartment. Gladys's husband emerged from the kitchen, a wrench in his hands, his old shirt hardly befitting his family name. "You must be the fashion wizard Gladys talks so much about. I must say, you have a new fan. Listen, I'd better not shake your hand—I've got grease up to my elbows."

"Hello, Mr. Harris," Jeanne said guardedly. She'd only glimpsed Theodore Harris once or twice in the office, since he worked in the executive suite upstairs—and always in starched shirts and ties. Today he looked more like the building's super.

"Call me Theodore. *Please.*"

Slipping past him, Gladys entered the living room, skirt swirling around her shapely calves. Jeanne couldn't resist clapping her hands in delight—the garment fit better than she could have hoped.

"Where on earth did you get this idea?" Gladys asked, fingering the bow at her neckline.

"Oh, I saw it in *Photoplay*. Rita Hayworth was wearing a dress just like it." For some reason, Jeanne was reluctant to expose her sister's secret talent. "I knew it would suit you."

"Say, Gladys speaks so well of you," Theodore said. "She says you're the smartest girl in the pool. You should meet my cousin Ralph—he lives nearby and he's always up for a good time. I bet he'd love to take you to dinner."

"Oh," Jeanne hedged. "I—I don't like to take the trolley at night."

She hadn't told anyone at work that she'd lost Charles in the war, since they were never officially engaged. When people asked if she had a fellow, she managed to shrug off the question, to suggest she was too busy to date or that the question was too intimate for her office relationships. This, she knew, had given her a reputation as a cold fish, which made Gladys's friendliness all the more touching.

Somehow, she'd let Gladys in. She had become fond of the girl, and that had turned out to be a risk. Jeanne hadn't stopped to think that by granting Gladys this favor, which had cost her only three evenings at home, for which she had no other plans anyway, she would open the door to further intimacy. But of course, Gladys would want to return the favor.

"Well, that's easy," Theodore said. "Ralph can drive you. He's got a car."

"Oh, you'll love him," Gladys said. "He's a real card!"

"I—well—maybe," Jeanne finally said.

Fifteen minutes later, the young couple had walked her back to the trolley stop, the echoes of their goodbyes ringing in her head as she headed up the stairs. A date—had she truly just accepted a date? And would Ralph be like his cousin, broad and cheerful and booming and ebullient?

Oh, Charles, Jeanne thought. In the early days following his death she had mourned the life they would have had together—the house in Woodbury near his parents, Charlie building his medical practice in the same office as his father. Evening strolls along Main Street and anniversary dinners at Dooley's. Filling her days with the Women's Club and long afternoons spent at the library, until the children came.

All these years later, that life seemed like a childhood fantasy, as unreal as her long-ago wish to be like Mary Lennox in *The Secret Garden* with her robin redbreast friend. Now, when she thought about Charles, it was with a twist of hopeless anger. Each year that he'd been gone had taken her further down a road she never intended to travel. *How could you leave me to this?* she implored his memory in her private hours, the lonely nights after she'd put the cover over her sewing machine and slipped under the freezing cold sheets. How could he have consigned her to a future whose best hope was a pension from her secretarial job, whose only connection to the future her niece?

It hadn't occurred to her to start again, as some girls did. Courtship, even with sweet, serious Charles, had been exhausting. To start again with a stranger—almost unthinkable.

But now she was being offered a chance. This job, these rain-slicked streets and tall glittering buildings, the stone fountain and park benches in the square where on pleasant days she sat to eat her lunch. And now a date. Could this be a gift from Charles? Had her one great love, who could not come back to save her himself, sent her all of this instead?

She could try, she supposed. She could dress up and make

conversation and let a man buy her dinner. She could cast off the invisible cloak of spinsterhood, and demand something more for herself. Not the fever-dream of romantic delusion: she'd put Charles on a pedestal that he could never sustain; she'd inadvertently distanced him with her talk of marriage and home and children when they both should have been enjoying the youth that would end prematurely for their entire generation.

She could kiss a man, if only to have something to talk about with the girls in the office pool. She could, perhaps, allow more to happen. She was nearly thirty years old, with a future as solid as a dandelion puff. The war's enduring lesson was that everything can be taken from a person in the blink of an eye. What was she saving herself for? Where was she to find any pleasure in this life, if she didn't seek it out for herself?

The trolley came and she climbed aboard, nestling into the corner of her seat, avoiding the gazes of the other passengers. Thoughts and emotions battered about in her mind, invoking murky longings that refused to come into focus. It wasn't infatuation she sought—one cloying taste, with Charles, had been enough—and it wasn't the social ascent that lay ahead for Gladys, who would someday assume the powers and obligations of the Harris matriarch. But something—there was *something* that called to her in the throbbing pulse of the city, in the confounding clash of wealth and poverty, crime and civic duty, old world and new.

When the trolley pulled to her stop in Brunskill, Jeanne got off and walked in the wrong direction, away from home, to the drugstore. She browsed the aisles as though she were searching for a box of clothespins, a cake of soap, when in fact she wasn't sure what she was looking for. Passing the cosmetics counter, she paused in front of a cardboard display for pressed powder. It featured a laughing beauty, her blond hair gleaming, her lips retouched cherry red. "You're a MODERN girl!" the ad copy read.

Was Jeanne, in fact, a modern girl? Since the day the telegram arrived—from Mrs. Pearson, Charles's mother, a full three days after his family was notified of his death—Jeanne had lived as an old maid. It had not occurred to her to demand or even desire more.

"Miss?" The clerk, an acne-plagued young man in a poorly knotted tie, stepped uncertainly from behind his register. "Can I help you?"

"Oh, no," Jeanne said, turning away. "But thank you anyway." She felt him watch her as she made her exit. Maybe he was admiring her, as teenage boys often admire women in the heady age between their sweethearts' and mothers'—but more likely, Jeanne thought, he'd noticed the change that had taken hold of her, as abrupt and consuming as if her heart had become a hungry furnace.

THE NEXT FRIDAY, Ralph picked Jeanne up from work, because she couldn't bear the mortification of him coming to Brunskill. He took her to Kelly's, and his manners were as fine as his cousin's. Though he shared Theodore's sun-flecked brown hair and square chin, he was a stockier and all-around ungainlier man; but he made up for it with a self-effacing sense of humor that Jeanne took to immediately.

It was Ralph who asked if she might like a second cocktail when their entrees came—veal cutlet for him, duck for her—but it was Jeanne who finished hers while unblinkingly holding his gaze.

It was Ralph who ordered the cheesecake with strawberry crème, but it was Jeanne who offered him the last bit on the spoon she'd licked clean.

It was Ralph who suggested a post-dinner walk in the square . . . but it was Jeanne who paused in front of the lion statue with her face upturned in the gilded lamplight. Ralph kissed her, tenderly at first, then less so half an hour later in the elevator of his building, to which they had taken a heady cab ride with her hand under his shirt.

Peggy

Tommie was the sort of child who could amuse herself for hours, given the right combination of books and pencils and scraps of paper. It did not look as though she was going to be a very good student, but Peggy had expected that; she had done poorly at school herself.

More puzzling was Tommie's indifference to her appearance, to the dresses her aunt sewed for her and the bows and ribbons Peggy tried to put in her hair. Tommie's socks were generally bunched at her ankles; she preferred pants and wondered why she couldn't wear them to school when the boys were allowed to; she wanted to play baseball, not softball.

In one way she resembled Jeanne more than Peggy: she loved to read. Every week one of them took her to the library, where she checked out all the books she was allowed—six— and conversed with the librarian about what she should choose next. She liked nonfiction, even the books she was too young to understand: children's biographies about U.S. presidents and famous explorers, foreign cities and scientific discoveries, astronomy and the discovery of gold in California. Anything, really, as long as the illustrations were nice.

That was the one way Tommie undeniably took after Peggy: her greatest passion was art. Not fashion illustration and figure drawing, the things Peggy most enjoyed, but puzzling little tableaus of everyday items and ordinary scenes. One day Tommie might draw a dead beetle she found on its back on the sidewalk; another day she would try to capture the water standing in a glass. She drew the carcass of a chicken after dinner; the basket full of laundry. And she was good, even exceptional, for her age—or would be, anyway, if she drew things anyone wanted to look at.

Today, an unexpectedly balmy spring day, Tommie trailed Peggy on a trip to the Community Square mall in Plainsfield. Touted as one of the first and finest suburban shopping centers in the nation when it had been built nearly a decade ago, it was anchored by the magnificent three-story limestone Fyfe's department store. From the start, Peggy preferred this Fyfe's to the stuffy granite columns and arches of the flagship store in downtown Philadelphia, its echoing, fussy marble atrium. She loved the modernity of the new branch's art-deco flourishes, the stately, imposing entrance. They were not here to buy anything, and Peggy had only enough money in her pocket for a shared milkshake on the Silver Terrace. But spending a few hours window shopping was better than idling the day away at home, waiting for Jeanne to return from work while Thelma grew irritated at having Tommie underfoot.

On the bus ride, Tommie kept her nose in a book about trains. She was wearing overalls that barely fit, hand-me-downs from a family several doors down, and Peggy had let her get away with them because she didn't feel like fighting today. It was warm out and Tommie's neck was sweaty, her hair matted, her dense, chubby torso straining against the canvas. Peggy wondered if her daughter would develop curves like her own someday, the genetic gift from their father's side, glimpsed in photographs of aunts long since dead and buried. It seemed unlikely that she would thin out like her willowy aunt.

Once they disembarked from the bus, Peggy tugged impatiently at the overalls' strap, willing Tommie to walk faster. They approached the enormous windows along the side of the department store, whose displays were changed every two weeks to feature the newest merchandise. Peggy loved to browse, even if she couldn't afford so much as a pair of stockings.

Today the windows had been done up in a bridal theme to showcase the new gowns. The floor was draped in yards of satin and strewn with silk rose petals, and mannequins peeped shyly under their veils while faceless plastic flower girls held their skirts. Wedding dresses had been among the few garments excluded from the War Production Board's General Limitation Order restricting fabric usage, along with burial clothes and baby layettes, but these gowns were still a far cry from the more austere wartime fashions. Each skirt featured dozens of yards of tulle or organza, with nipped waists and highly ornamented bodices. Peggy's favorite was rendered in Alençon lace, with dainty scalloped sleeves and dozens of tiny silk-covered buttons. The veil was attached to a crown of silk flowers . . . Peggy touched her hair, imagining her platinum curls mounded under such a veil, and nearly jumped when Tommie poked her in the side.

"Can I have my drawing pad, Mama?"

"Oh." Peggy shook her head, embarrassed that she'd allowed herself to get caught up in such a silly fantasy. "Well, all right. Here, let me put your book away."

She took the sketchpad and pencil box from her purse—she was in the habit of carrying both—and on impulse tore out a page before handing them to Tommie. She sat down on the bench facing the window and patted the warm wooden boards next to her for Tommie. Propping the book on her lap to lay the sheet of paper on, she took one of Tommie's pencils, and the two of them sketched side by side.

She drew the gown she'd admired, making small changes

as she went. Her drawings were getting quite good now; she'd learned to define the spine with a single stroke, to suggest a background with a few shaded blocks for buildings, or feathery curves for clouds and trees.

Occasionally, when she was drawing in public, someone would stop to admire her sketch, and ask if she was a professional artist. Once or twice when she was alone, Peggy had said yes, just to see what would happen. It was both thrilling and disappointing that the answer was . . . nothing. Some lies, it seemed, went unpunished.

Unless . . .

Unless they weren't lies at all.

Peggy stared at the plate glass windows thoughtfully, her finished sketch flapping lazily in the breeze. She was wasting the afternoon, and if she waited too long to buy their milkshake, Tommie would get restless and cranky. But the tantalizing notion that had flickered into her mind refused to go away.

Well, she'd never gotten anything in this life for nothing, had she? Senior class secretary (despite her poor marks), a good part in the spring musical that year, even handsome, gregarious Thomas—she'd had to seize upon each of these goals herself, had to make an opportunity that ordinarily would have gone to someone else—someone richer, more important, more experienced, better educated.

Peggy had always played her best advantage back then—the fact that she had nothing to lose. And what did she have to lose now?

She made a show of admiring Tommie's drawing—three

dogs frolicked next to a lake, though there was neither dog nor lake anywhere in sight—and suggested they move along. "Mama has to make one stop, and then we'll get a treat," she promised, relieved when Tommie showed no interest in what that stop might be.

They walked into the department store, past the cosmetics counters and displays of gloves, to the elevator. Up to the top floor, where they passed the bridal and couture salons and the entrance to the grand Ruby Room, where lunch was being served, all the way to the customer service counter. She whispered to Tommie to take a seat in the waiting area and read her book quietly, and approached the desk, where a woman in tortoiseshell glasses resting on a pocked red nose was filling out a long form. She looked up and smiled. "May I help you?"

Peggy felt her resolve slipping, and tilted her chin up higher, as though to stanch the leaking of her confidence. "I have a portfolio of illustrations. I'd like to show them to someone in the advertising department."

The woman's eyebrows lifted fractionally. "Oh, I don't think . . . they don't do the ads here," she said. "That would be in New York, wouldn't it?"

"Well, of course," Peggy said, feeling a blush creep across her face. Had she been so stupid to think they had a team of illustrators somewhere in the back, drinking cold coffee and sketching at long tables? Most likely they worked in ateliers and studios, like the great artists of Europe—as inaccessible to Peggy as easels and live models for figure drawing and redolent tubes of oil paints, all the trappings of true art.

But she was here, wasn't she? And if all it cost her was some embarrassment—well, who was this pinch-faced girl, with no wedding band of her own and some unfortunate skin condition, to judge her?

"The employment office, then," she said coolly.

"Well, you're in luck there," the woman said. "Mr. Friedman's one o'clock interview canceled. Would you like me to see if you can take her place?"

"What sort of interview was it?"

"For runner in the Crystal Salon. The position reports to Miss Perkins."

The woman recited this information deferentially, and Peggy didn't feel like asking who Miss Perkins was or what a "runner" did. Of course she knew what the Crystal Salon was, though she'd only ever been as far as the entrance to the couture collection, close enough to glimpse the brocaded chairs and tall mirrors and chandeliers. It took far more money than she'd ever had to get any closer than that.

It was a moment of decision, and out of nowhere Peggy felt the electric thrill of daring that she'd experienced several times before when her life brought her to the brink of adventure. She could take the safe road, the proper one . . . or plunge down the unknown path, give in to the lure of the dare.

Most girls would always choose the former. A good mother, good sister, good daughter-in-law, would do the right thing, the proper thing.

But Peggy could never resist the allure of the unknown. And if her impetuousness hadn't always worked out well—if it had sometimes doomed her to regrettable and even tragic outcomes—still she could not turn back.

"I'd love to," she said.

The woman pushed a button on her sleek black intercom box. "Mr. Friedman, will you see another candidate who just arrived with no appointment?"

After a moment she set down the phone, smiling. "You're in."

"Oh, thank you. There's just one thing . . . I'm babysitting my sister's daughter today," Peggy said, lowering her voice conspiratorially. "Would you mind terribly if she sits out here with you?"

"I was wondering how you were going to pull that off, " the woman said, winking. "But don't worry. You just leave her right here with me, and we'll be fine, won't we, sweetheart?"

Tommie, chewing on a fingernail, didn't even look up. Peggy thanked the woman, took a deep breath, and walked down the hall. If only, she thought, every burden could be so easily handed off, even for a moment.

Thelma

May God forgive her, on the day that Thomas's child was born, Thelma had walked out of the church and planned to never return. She had made it clear to God, had fallen on her knees so many times over the weeks and months leading up to the birth to beg: she who had lost everything had asked God only one thing and he had refused her.

Tommie was to have been a boy.

A boy with Thomas's pale cowlick, his blue eyes so thick-lashed they could break your heart, his dimples at the corners of his mouth, and yes, his long and awkward toes and gap between his front teeth and slightly hunched shoulders, these too, for they had been Thomas's and thus they were precious. Thomas lay now in the cursed soil of Guadalcanal, but his grave should have been next to his father's, a lovely spot where a sycamore had grown to shade it in summer and shield it from the snow and ice in the winter, not too far from Thelma's own mother and father and her sisters, who'd been taken early. There, Thelma had planned to walk with the boy—Thomas Junior—to tell him stories about his father, stories his mother could not be counted on to remember or care about.

On the day of the birth, the nurse had come into the room where Thelma waited with Jeanne and given them a too-bright smile that should have been a clue. "A lovely, *healthy* girl—and quite a big child at that! Eight pounds, four ounces!" she'd said, as though such a large number could be consolation.

Thelma had gotten her fury under control by the time Peggy came home from the hospital, though the truth was that had she known the child was to be a girl, she might not have offered the spare room to her daughter-in-law. It wasn't that Thelma disliked Peggy, exactly, it was just that she found her unexceptional, and was rather disappointed in Thomas for falling so easily for her insubstantial charms. Thelma of all people could have explained to him that good looks are no bulwark against difficult times, and since his own father as well as Peggy's were dead, there was no family business to welcome him.

A few days later Thelma had realized the error in her thinking, because of course a baby will worm her way into one's heart; one truly is helpless against her tiny fingers, her soft neck, the downy fluff on her soft head. So: the baby would stay, and so would her mother. Thelma would find a way—because finding a way was her lot in life.

Now, six years later, by some miracle—and yes, Thelma had returned to the church to pray for the baby's continued good health, but she chose her own words now and cast dark glances at the statues of St. Katherine and Mary of Magdalene whenever she passed—both girls had jobs, though Peggy wasn't making enough for the government to stop sending her widow's pension. There would be money for the dentist and Tommie's school uniforms, and even new spectacles now that Thelma wasn't able to make out the fine print in the newspaper without squinting.

The girls agreed to hand over what was left of their paychecks after their lunches and necessaries, and Thelma would take care of the household expenses, as she had been doing since the day she married. The girls did not need to know that even with their combined earnings, they were barely breaking even. Peggy's job at Fyfe's turned out to be serving as a glorified gofer, fetching dresses chosen by the mythical Miss Perkins and her salesgirls to show to their fancy customers, then standing at attention like some lavatory attendant while the gowns were modeled by the mannequins and the rich ladies made their selections. And there was no future in Jeanne's typing pool, where the girls were paid a fraction of what their bosses earned, even if they had equivalent educations.

Oh, to be young again—young-*ish*, anyway, since the girls were both closing in on thirty—when one's sleep was untroubled by thoughts of disintegrating plumbing and expensive dentistry and one's own looming decline. Jeanne and Peggy didn't lie awake at night worrying about the bank coming for the house, but of course, that was Thelma's fault—she'd led them to believe it was paid for. Well, those decisions had been made and could not be unmade. At least now, finally, Thelma had a few moments to herself during the day. The girls were at work, and it would be several hours before Thelma needed to walk down to the elementary school for Tommie.

Thelma had already bathed and her hair and makeup were done. Now she reached to the back of her closet, where a zippered garment bag contained her wedding dress (such a waste of silk and lace) and her good suit and, in a satin fabric envelope at the bottom where no one would see, a chemise constructed of a scant yard or two of China silk, a gift purchased for her in a city she would never visit by a man who had been instructed to park a block away and walk to the back door.

Thelma stood in the doorway of the second bedroom and took one last look at Peggy's dresser, where, among the clutter of her combs and brushes and mirrors, there were framed photos of Thomas on their wedding day and in his uniform.

Then she quietly closed the door.

May 1949

Jeanne

"Please!" Gladys begged, her eyes shining with excitement. "You must. It's the least you can do, after breaking poor Ralph's heart!"

Jeanne pushed a safety clip around on her desk, stalling. She hadn't exactly broken anyone's heart—and she was still surprised that Ralph Harris had called her after the date that had ended with a silent two A.M. drive home, in which the faint, embarrassing odor of sex hung between them in the car. But surely he had found someone more suitable by now, someone who would laugh at his puns and share his self-declared goal of visiting every one of the forty-eight contiguous states by automobile.

But this was something else entirely. "I'm sure you misunderstood her," Jeanne hedged.

"I did not. She's been talking about it ever since she saw what you did with my old dress." Gladys burped delicately into the back of her hand. She was in the third month of her pregnancy and nothing sat well with her at lunch. She was planning to quit in another few weeks, as soon as she could be sure, she said, that "this one would stick."

"And besides," Jeanne countered, "according to you, she can buy anything she wants."

"Not for this," Gladys said. "It's a charity fashion show—she has to wear the outfit they give her, but she can have it tailored any way she pleases. Look, it's just lunch. Oh, but wear something smart!"

ON THE SATURDAY of the luncheon, Jeanne met Gladys at the Nineteenth Street trolley station and they walked together to her in-laws' house, a four-story Pompeian brick mansion facing the square.

"Let's hope the cook doesn't have the day off," Gladys giggled. "Mrs. Harris is a terrible cook. Practically all she can make is chipped beef on toast."

"I don't think I could eat a thing," Jeanne said. She'd barely been able to get down half a grapefruit that morning. It had been well over a decade since she'd been in a home half as swanky as this one.

Wealth had hovered over her childhood like a family portrait over a mantel. It was impossible to miss its long shadow on her mother's life. Besides the excellent bearing and elocution, products of her days in finishing school, Emma Brink was unintentionally imperious to merchants, demanding of her children's teachers, and exacting in her home. The Brink family may not have been able to outfit their home like a Main Line mansion, but it was well appointed with books and music and art, even if phonograph records stood in for tickets to the symphony, and the framed prints in the dining room were mere copies.

When Jeanne moved in with Thelma, she'd deliberately stifled the remnants of her mother's influence. Thelma was certainly not coarse, but she was sensitive about what she perceived to be her own inadequacies. She cared little for politics and less for the arts; she had received only a primary school education and, later, taught herself accounting and bookkeeping. She was mistrustful of Peggy's new clientele and contemptuous of high society.

For all of these reasons, Jeanne had no intention of telling her about Mrs. Harris's fashion show. Even knowing that Jeanne had gone to lunch at her home might well feel, to Thelma, like a slight; Jeanne had told her she was going to the movies with friends, and waited until Thelma went to the market before dressing for the day.

She'd worn her most recent creation, a smart suit modeled on one from the British couturier Hardy Amies, in a tweed that was a reasonable copy of an Irish handwoven but could be had at a fraction of the cost. The suit was her most conservative, its only nod to trends a slight flare in the skirt, and when Mrs. Harris opened the door Jeanne realized she had made a mistake.

Gladys's mother-in-law was wearing green twill pedal pushers and a simple white blouse, a colorful scarf knotted at her waist—hardly the conservative outfit of the dowager Jeanne had been expecting. She was perhaps ten years older than Thelma, but her skin was remarkably unlined and her silver hair arranged in the new "swirled" cap style. She made no attempt to hide the fact that she was sizing Jeanne up while she kissed the air next to Gladys's cheek.

"Welcome, welcome, dear. I've heard such wonderful things."

"I've—me too—I mean, Gladys has told me—"

"Come into the conservatory," Mrs. Harris interrupted, turning on her heel and saving Jeanne from her painfully tongue-tied attempt at conversation.

The two younger women followed her into a glass-roofed addition off the dining room. There was a magnificent view into the courtyard behind the house, but Jeanne's attention was drawn to the table, also made of glass on iron filigree legs. It was elegantly set with white dishes and yellow woven mats, matching napkins tucked into bamboo rings. A platter in the center of the table held scoops of chicken salad nestled into lettuce cups, sliced pickles, and hard-boiled eggs. At each of the three place settings was a dish of canned fruit cocktail, and a silver platter held melba toast arranged in a semicircle and what Jeanne was fairly certain were sterling ice tongs.

Mrs. Harris followed her gaze. "I'm sure Gladys has told you I don't cook," she said, a bit acidly. "I can't be bothered, I'm afraid."

A clatter of heavy footsteps made them all look down the hall. A man in stained, worn canvas coveralls entered the dining room, his face obscured by an enormous stone urn he was carrying. "You sure you don't want it in the courtyard, Mrs. H?" he was saying with a pronounced Italian accent as he walked through the door. "Because I could . . ."

His voice trailed off as he realized that she wasn't alone.

"Anthony!" Mrs. Harris exclaimed. "Set that thing down before you drop it."

He immediately set the planter down, his broad shoulders straining against the fabric of his shirt. He dug a hankie from his pocket and wiped off his face. Heavy, wavy dark hair fell over his eyes, and his face, flushed with exertion, was the most beautiful that Jeanne had ever seen. It looked as though it had been carved by a master sculptor, like the statues she'd admired on visits to the Museum of Art with her mother.

"Please meet Anthony Salvatici," Mrs. Harris said, "who is undoubtedly the worst gardener in the state of Pennsylvania. Possibly on the entire East Coast. And Anthony, you know my daughter-in-law, Gladys, and this is her friend from work, Miss Jeanne Brink."

"Pleased to meet you," Anthony said, flashing white teeth and a roguish grin.

"It's very nice to meet you as well," Jeanne said. Her face and neck felt hot.

"I'd better, uh . . ."

"There's lunch in the kitchen, but it's just rabbit food for us girls," Mrs. Harris said. "Maybe when you finish outside you can run down to the restaurant for the lamb."

"Lamb?" Gladys echoed, perking up. "For tomorrow?"

"Yes, and please tell my son to be prompt, as you know it's not nearly as good cold."

"We wouldn't miss it!"

While they talked, Anthony rolled his shoulders, took

a breath, and picked up the urn again, staggering under its weight. Turning to leave, he glanced at Jeanne once more. His eyes bored into hers for a fraction of a second, as though he was making a critical calculation, and then he was gone.

"Well," Mrs. Harris said. "Let's eat, shall we? I do apologize, Jeanne, but with Cook gone for the day, we all have to do what we can."

❈ ❈ ❈

AFTER THEY'D NIBBLED their way through the unremarkable lunch, Mrs. Harris sent Gladys to the kitchen to make coffee.

"So, did Gladys tell you I've got a little project I wanted to talk to you about?"

"She . . . mentioned that you're interested in fashion," Jeanne said carefully.

"I *love* fashion," Mrs. Harris exclaimed. "If my husband wasn't such a tightwad, I'd spend all our money on clothes and drive us both to the poorhouse."

Jeanne studied the crumbs of melba toast on the platter, trying to think how to respond. Her own mother had worked tirelessly to drill the lessons of polite discourse into her girls; she'd hoped to pass along, from her own privileged childhood, the tools that Jeanne and Peggy would not learn from their own friends and neighbors. Now that she had a chance to put them into use, however, she had discovered that Mrs. Harris was nothing like the stodgy society matron she'd expected.

"I've got entire closets full of things," Mrs. Harris said with a dismissive wave of her hand. "I've got a girl at Fyfe's who helps me and I hide the bills from Noel. But I have the hardest time finding anything really . . . *unique*, do you know what I mean?"

"I think so," Jeanne said.

"Do you?" Mrs. Harris gazed doubtfully at the suit Jeanne was wearing. "You certainly have exquisite taste, dear. Oh, I know I should just behave and let the girls dress me up like some—some nice old matron, I suppose. But where's the fun in that?"

"You've got a great eye," Jeanne said. "That green . . . it's really striking. And the scarf is a wonderful accent."

"I thought so! I do love a touch of the bohemian, don't you? Oh, Jeanne, if I can confide in you . . . I *adore* Gladys, I truly do, but I was rather hoping Theodore might bring home an artist. A café singer, or a poet, or a gypsy girl—or perhaps a socialist." She grinned wickedly. "Do you know, when Noel and I met, I had been expelled from Wellesley? His parents were utterly shocked."

"I—my goodness . . ."

"Oh, you don't want to hear about all that. My avant-garde days are long over." She chuckled fondly. "My more immediate problem is this wretched Junior League fashion show I've got to model in."

Gladys came back in pushing a tea cart with the coffee and a plate of cookies.

"Oh, did Anthony bring those? What a dear!" She plucked one of the sugar-dusted cookies. "They're called *biscotti a ric-*

cio, Jeanne, and you truly must try one. I was just telling her about the fashion show, Gladys. I'm afraid I'm in a heated battle with the old hag who's chairing it this year."

Gladys laughed. "She's not really a hag, Jeanne. I've seen her picture."

Mrs. Harris rolled her eyes. "Well, her heart is as black and evil as Sinbad's. Anyway, just wait until you see what she's making me wear."

As she went to get the outfit, Gladys poured the coffee and Jeanne tasted a cookie. "These *are* delicious. The . . . gardener brought them?" Jeanne asked, as casually as she could, remembering his smoldering eyes, his insouciant smile.

"Oh yes, but he's really not a gardener. I mean, his father was, before he opened a restaurant. Teddy says that he and Anthony practically grew up together because Anthony's dad worked for the family since he was a baby, and his mom died so his dad had to bring him to work until he was old enough for school. Mr. and Mrs. Harris were always good to him, and now that Anthony's in college he works here for extra money."

"He's in college? He looks older."

"Oh, I think he's twenty-seven or twenty-eight. He only gets to take a class or two at a time because he works so much."

Mrs. Harris returned with a garment bag emblazoned with the Gimbels logo.

"Letty gave me 'Picnic,'" Mrs. Harris sniped. "Can you believe it? She gave all the best categories to her horrid friends—'Venetian Nights' and 'Monte Carlo' and 'Seven Seas' and so on. So, I need something that'll blow their socks off."

"All the stores sent clothes," Gladys added. "Fyfe's, and Strawbridge and Clothier, and Gimbels."

"Letty had the nerve to act like she was doing me a favor, choosing for me," Mrs. Harris said. She unzipped the bag with a flourish, revealing a flared blue poplin A-line skirt and a puff-sleeved blouse with a Peter Pan collar.

"If I were a fishmonger's wife on wash day, this might be fine," Mrs. Harris fumed. "But I am not getting up in front of two hundred women in this. Tell me, dear . . . can you do something to make this any less dreadful?"

Jeanne examined the coarse, inexpensive fabric, the thin elastic, the topstitched appliquéd pockets, and decided that Mrs. Harris wasn't exaggerating: Letty must truly despise her.

"I think I can help," she said.

Mrs. Harris lifted her coffee cup to her lips with a wink. "Wonderful. And I insist that you and Gladys attend as my guests."

An improbable bargain had been struck.

BEFORE THEY PARTED ways at the trolley stop, Jeanne made one more attempt to steer the conversation back to the Harris's handyman. "Those cookies were so tasty," she said. "Does . . . the restaurant prepare the lamb too?"

"Oh, yes, you'll have to come to Sunday supper sometime! Mr. Salvatici makes everything so Cook can just heat it up when she gets back on Sunday night. The lamb is so scrumptious, and there's always noodles and sometimes fancy desserts. It's why I've gotten so fat! But Jeanne, do you honestly think you can do something with that awful outfit?"

Jeanne looked down at the garment bag slung over her arm. "I'll do my best," she promised.

She'd once made a collar for a coat from the fabric that covered a chair that was partially burned in a fire. She'd sewn Tommie's rompers from the sacks that rice and grain came in. She'd been making do from the time she first picked up the needle—and she wasn't about to back down from this challenge.

It would make an excellent distraction from the other matter, the one that lurked at the edges of her mind like a cloud growing more ominous with every passing day.

June 1949

Thelma

"She had knees like a *goat*," Peggy said, while she attempted to pry something from Tommie's clenched hand. "Miss Perkins tried everything to get her to agree to a longer skirt, but she wouldn't listen to reason. What on earth have you got?"

"I gave her a cinnamon stick," Thelma said, stirring the

spaghetti sauce that she'd started when Peggy came home. It would be ready when Jeanne walked through the door. "Let her keep it."

"Cinnamon? That's not a toy," Peggy rebuked, but she released Tommie's wrist.

"I didn't *say* it was a toy," Tommie sulked, holding the gummed and moist end she'd been chewing out to her mother. Peggy batted her hand away.

"Anyway, we were all trying to pretend that the dress flattered her. It was a Molyneux, from the spring collection. The most beautiful pale yellow silk moiré—and it cost one hundred and sixty-nine dollars. The sale would have made our week. She said she wanted to talk to her husband about it."

We this, *we* that, Thelma thought darkly; you'd think the girl had been invited to view the collections in Paris. "Mmm," she said, sprinkling in half a teaspoon of tiny celery seeds.

"And Miss Perkins told me to fetch a Lanvin fox-trimmed stole to go with it. It didn't suit the dress at *all* but Mrs. Booth kept complaining about the bodice gapping at the shoulder. It wasn't the dress's fault, it was her shoulders—seriously, Thelma, they stick out like giant lumps—but Miss Perkins was trying to distract her. But when I was back in the storeroom I saw this citron Jean Dessès that had come in. Really, it's too European for our market, Americans aren't ready for it. But I had an inspiration. The bateau neckline was much better for her figure and there's no easy way to hem the Lyons lace, so she couldn't possibly insist we shorten it. So, I brought it out."

Thelma glanced at Peggy, who'd plopped herself in a kitchen chair and crossed her legs, grinning smugly. Like she'd signed the constitution itself.

"Well, I thought Miss Perkins would just about die, staring at me with her eyes bugging out—her eyes really are unnaturally large, you simply have to see for yourself—but before she could say anything I said, quick as you please, 'Mrs. Booth, I do believe this dress was destined for you,' and for a moment it could have gone either way—she looked at me like I'd brought her a bug on a platter—but then she saw the clever little rhinestone trim at the waist, and she just had to have a look. Like a magpie, that woman, anything that sparkles . . . anyway, it turned out I was *right*. The lace overlay bells out, you know how lace can have a stiff hand to it, and it just covered up all the protruding parts, and made her look—well, I was about to say it made her look a dozen years younger, but that would still make her at least fifty."

Thelma, stirring the pot, felt her face warm in the steam. Her own fiftieth birthday was less than three years away. Under her dress, an old brown shirtwaist she'd owned forever, the marks she'd received that afternoon were still fresh. Jack had held her down with his fist in her hair, and when he entered her with a single savage thrust, her cry of pleasure was muffled by his hand over her mouth. The memory dulled her irritation with Peggy.

"She bought it, of course, plus a pair of net gloves that Miss Perkins convinced her she needed. Another twenty-two dollars, on top of the dress! And as I was getting ready to leave tonight, Miss Perkins said, 'Well done, Peggy.' Which, from anyone else, would be heaps of praise."

"Well, that's good," Thelma said. "Now would you mind setting the table?"

Peggy got up and shooed Tommie from the room, sighing heavily to communicate how disappointed she was in her audience as she got the dishes from the cupboards.

Thelma turned down the flame and set the lid back on the pot. Another half hour of simmering would tenderize the ground beef and mellow the flavor of the herbs. When Jeanne got home, Thelma would slice the bread she'd picked up from the bakery.

She went to her room and took off her apron. In front of the mirror Henry had bought her when their marriage was only weeks old and he still came to life when she walked into the room, she tugged open her collar and examined the skin above her breast. There . . . the faint outline of teeth marks. A shiver went through Thelma at the memory. Jack could still surprise her, even after their many stolen afternoons, the long stretches apart punctuated with their fevered reunions.

She opened the narrow drawer at the top of the dresser. Once, it had held her husband's cuff links and handkerchiefs. Now, banded by a ribbon, there was a stack of bills, mostly singles with an occasional five, insurance against a reversal of their fortunes. With both girls working, Thelma tried to set a little aside whenever she could.

The money was not the only thing in the drawer. She took

the other two objects out and unwrapped their tissue carefully before laying them on the lace runner on top of the dresser.

Two price tags, bearing the Gimbels logo, from their Better Sportswear shop. She'd found them on the floor of the attic when she'd gone up with a stack of folded laundry.

One was for $5.84, the other for $4.98. Both were marked size 8. There was no way on earth Jeanne was more than a 4. Peggy might be a 6 . . . and Thelma herself hovered between an 8 and a 10.

Thelma had stood in the drafty attic with the tags in her hand, trying to figure out the mystery for quite some time before she resorted to snooping. It hadn't taken long to find the garments, hanging behind all the other clothes on her makeshift rack: a homely, prim little blouse and a stiff, plain skirt in a dull marine blue.

This puzzling find did little to answer Thelma's questions. She was the only person in the house who could possibly wear the outfit—but Jeanne had made every one of her birthday and Christmas gifts since moving into the home. There were dresses, a burnt-orange swing coat of which Thelma was particularly fond; there were cloches and fur-trimmed gloves and a quilted robe. There was a tea cozy with a matching set of pot holders. A clever cloth bag to hold her spectacles and magazines, that could be hung over the arm of her reading chair. A braided rug made from scraps and selvages for the back door.

They'd never given each other anything store-bought—and if for some unfathomable reason Jeanne were to do so now,

Thelma was quite sure it would never be as frankly ugly as the outfit hidden in her room.

She smoothed the clothes on the rack, making sure to hide the outfit as she'd found it before she went back downstairs. She would bide her time. Eventually, all mysteries were revealed . . . especially to one as well-versed in secrets as Thelma.

THURSDAY EVENING, THE sun broke through the clouds just in time to sink below the horizon after a few days of drizzling rain. Peggy seemed distracted at dinner, and soon it became clear why. She had been invited by Miss Perkins to have coffee the next morning before her workday officially started. To get there in time, she needed to leave an hour earlier, which meant that someone else would have to help Tommie dress and make sure she ate her breakfast.

"Please, please," she'd begged. "I promise I won't ask again. But this could be important!"

Jeanne stirred her lentil soup across the dinner table and stayed silent.

"Is that so." Thelma sighed. "Tell us exactly why your boss wants to have coffee with you."

"Well—I don't know," Peggy admitted. "But I do know that she hasn't asked any of the *other* runners."

In the two and a half months that Peggy had been employed, she'd earned an hourly wage even lower than Jeanne's, and since she was not paid for her lunch, it was only fifteen hours a week, barely worth the effort she put into getting dressed and made up each day, or the two-hour round-trip on the bus. But the hours she spent at Fyfe's had brought her sparkle back in a way motherhood had never done.

To be fair, Thelma herself had gone through a period of profound melancholy when Thomas was small. It had passed, of course—but there had been one endless winter when each morning seemed to bring an echo of the dreary day before, spooning cereal into the child's mouth only to have him smear most of it on his high chair, ironing her husband's shirts and preparing his lunch. Putting the folded paper sack into Henry's hands at the door, tilting her face for a perfunctory kiss as the vicious winds stirred a burst of icy snow crystals up into the folds of her skirt, then closing that door and turning to face the long, empty hours until he returned again.

Made guilty by the memory, Thelma tried again. "Of course, I would be glad to take care of Tommie tomorrow morning, but you'll have to pick her up yourself after school, because I've got an errand I need to run. You go ahead—enjoy yourself."

"This isn't about *enjoyment*, Thelma, it's work," Peggy scolded, already rising from the table, probably to spend an hour pinning up her hair in paper strips and putting cream on her face and neck while Tommie helped dry the supper dishes and put them away.

But Thelma didn't much mind, as caring for Tommie would distract her from worry over the errand she had planned.

In the morning, she made a special effort for Tommie. She gave her an extra slice of bacon and trimmed the crusts off her toast before spreading it with butter and jam, and then poured herself a second cup of coffee and sat down to keep Tommie company while she ate.

"Why don't Mom and Auntie Jeanne ever eat breakfast?" Tommie asked, making short work of the bacon.

"That's a good question," Thelma said. What was she supposed to say—that Peggy was worried about her figure? Tommie's baby fat still hadn't melted away, and Thelma supposed she was going to have to do something about the matter of her weight one of these days, but she didn't want the child to turn vain or, worse, crippled with insecurity.

Thelma had taken extra care with Tommie's hair this morning, plaiting it into two braids that met at her nape and became one. She'd attached a wide navy grosgrain ribbon that went with her dress. She'd had only seven years to prepare for her audacious plan: to send Tommie up the road to Miss Kittering's, where Thelma meant for her granddaughter to receive an education that would prepare her for anything. In Thelma's childhood, no Catholics were allowed at Miss Kittering's, and even now there was rumored to be a quota. So that was the third problem with Thelma's plan, along with the challenges of getting Tommie accepted and paying the tuition. And, of course, convincing Peggy to allow it, but Thelma didn't anticipate that would be a problem.

Still, no need to stir up a commotion in advance. For now, she would simply do what she could to help Tommie be a little less . . . odd; there simply wasn't another word for it. "All right, let's wash hands," she said, taking Tommie's plate, "and then you can go and play with your friends in the playground until school starts."

Tommie's face fell, but she did as she was told. Thelma knew that friendships were scarce for Tommie. There were few young children in the neighborhood anymore, and Peggy hadn't exactly sought out the company of other mothers, so Tommie had grown up without the constant stream of playmates that had filled the house when her father was a little boy.

These thoughts were still in Thelma's mind as they walked the quarter mile to school. "How would you like to take a dance class?" she asked, thinking Tommie might make a friend there.

Tommie shrugged. "I could take a painting class," she suggested.

Thelma winced inwardly. The last thing Tommie needed was to have her artistic temperament encouraged, even if that was what had attracted Thomas to her mother. He'd loved Peggy's outrageous zeal, her colorful ensembles, her unabashed way of speaking her mind. "Isn't she something?" Thomas had asked the first time he brought her home.

"You know," Thelma said carefully, "I knew your mother when she was a little girl."

"I *know*," Tommie said patiently. "Grandpa Henry and Grandpa Leo and Uncle Frank were friends. Mama and Daddy used to play together at company picnics. And you used to be friends with Grandma Emma."

Thelma winced at her recitation, but she herself was responsible for this narrative, which she'd been fine-tuning practically since Tommie was born. Never mind that all of the child's grandparents but her were dead—if Thelma was to keep Thomas's memory alive, Tommie must be made to learn his history.

Even if she'd taken a few liberties. Henry and the Brink brothers had never exactly been *friends*. Henry would grumble, when he was drinking, that they were going to put him out of business by refusing to give him an exclusive contract. But Henry could never have kept up with the work alone during the mill's busiest years. As for Emma Brink—she had been all right, Thelma supposed, though her memories of the picnics under the great waterfall were of the mothers dividing their attention between serving the food and trying to keep the little ones out of the water. Little Peggy Brink could always be counted on to have a tantrum at some point, while pretty Jeanne had been uppity, pretending not to notice the younger girls following her around like ducklings.

Oh, if only all those people could look down from the afterlife—a concept in which Thelma put very little stock—and see what had become of them. Emma Brink was already ill when Thomas and Peggy began their whirlwind courtship, and if she'd disapproved, she'd never let on during the one lunch to which she invited Thelma. Henry would have probably been pleased that his son had married the boss's daughter. Leo—Leo had been an inscrutable man, but by all accounts a good one.

And then there was Frank, of course. Frank was still alive, though Tommie had never met him.

They arrived at the school, joining a stream of children with their mothers. Tommie's hand tightened around Thelma's. "You could stay with me," she said fiercely. "Until the bell rings."

Her reluctance to part broke Thelma's heart. She knelt down so she could look Tommie in the eyes. "You don't need to be afraid of them, Thomasina," she said. "You're every bit as pretty and smart as any girl at Saint Katherine's."

Tommie blinked, frowning at the lie, but she was too polite to correct her grandmother. "They don't like me, though."

"Only because you haven't given them a chance. Tell you what. I want you to talk to two girls today, and tell me all about it tonight."

"Talk to them about what?" Tommie asked despairingly, as though Thelma had suggested she turn straw into gold. "I don't know what they like."

"Tell them you like their dresses," Thelma suggested. "Or ask them—I don't know, if they have any pets." It was terrible advice, but Thelma had nothing else to offer. *Just try to be a little less unusual*, she pleaded silently.

Tommie accepted a kiss and trudged off as though she was headed for the gallows. Thelma watched her go, thinking that her love for this child was the most painful thing she'd ever endured.

THELMA HAD RIDDEN the trolley into Philadelphia many times as a child, then less often when Thomas was growing up, and hardly ever since then. She didn't care for the city, with its noise and smells and traffic, the way strangers would step right in front of you if they didn't think you were walking fast enough. Waiting for the trolley, she looked around the platform and thought about how change had finally gotten the best of her, how the years that remained for her would be eclipsed by the advances of the second half of the century. The government had developed a machine that could solve problems faster than the world's leading mathematicians, and there was talk of sending rockets into outer space. During the war, women were allowed to do all kinds of jobs that would have been unthinkable even ten years earlier. Young women in Brunskill had worked in converted factories to support the war effort.

Should Thelma have joined them? It hadn't occurred to her then, so mired in grief was she after Thomas's death. Still, she'd had other skills. She'd run every bit of Henry's company except to drive the truck herself. Maybe she should have tried harder to provide for herself, for Peggy and Jeanne and Tommie.

But that's what she was doing now, in a way. The trolley arrived, and Thelma found a seat next to the window so she could watch the scenery go by. The trolleys were closing down now; in another year or two, they would nearly all be replaced by autobuses. The end of another era.

When Thelma got off on South Broad, it took her a moment to orient herself. The buildings seemed taller than ever, the crowds denser, the smells and sounds sharper. Or maybe that was all in her mind. Thelma let the sidewalk traffic carry her the few blocks to an address she hadn't visited in years—almost a decade, in fact, and yet there it was, looking almost exactly as it had back then. The letters on the windows spelling POLKS to the left, BAR to the right, heavy black curtains behind the glass. The heavy wooden door that allowed no light through.

That onslaught to the senses when she pulled the door open: the uprush of cool, dank air on her face, the slightly sickening smell of rotting hops and ash and cigar smoke, the stolid clunk of glasses being set down deliberately on rift-sawn oak . . . the yellowish glow of the old brass fixtures that gave everything it illuminated a febrile energy.

She'd come here only twice, ill-considered outings both. But there had been some domestic urge, then, to be seen together, to be acknowledged even in the most casual way—even in a place such as this. What did she know of coupling, then, besides Henry? Such romantic notions had evaporated quickly, of course . . . but there lingered in Polks the shadow of that once-dear illusion.

He was sitting on the same stool, almost at the end of the bar, the one he'd always gravitated to. There were glints of silver in his thick brown hair, and in profile he looked more like his brother than ever. Leo Brink had been a smaller man, thinner, stooped later in life—but the nose was the same, the squared-off chin, the workingman's raw and blockish hands.

The stools on either side of Frank were occupied, and he appeared to be in the middle of a story, the men nearby paying attention. A recent round, the glasses still brimming, was probably the reason why.

Thelma waited for a lull, ignoring the curious stares. When all the men laughed at something Frank said, the man on the left slipped off his stool and lumbered to the men's room. Thelma walked toward Frank on legs that did not feel like her own, and sat on the still-warm stool with her purse clutched primly on her lap.

Voices fell silent, and Frank—alert to the shifts in his audience, as always, turned her way. The transformation in his face was almost comical. "Thelma?" Then, "My God!"

He recovered himself quickly, of course—it was one of his best tricks. A papery kiss, a smooth smile, a compliment— "You're looking exactly the same"—none of them could erase his momentary unmooring, and Thelma plunged in, to take advantage of it.

"How are Mary and the children?"

Frank blinked, and a tremor seemed to pass through him. Thelma smiled to herself. She'd learned a few things since she sat in this same spot, mooning like a schoolgirl. There was a time when nothing could have made her say their names . . . but that was before she lost Thomas, before she lost everything. Before she started over with the ones God, in His dubious wisdom, saw fit to send her. The ones she had to care for now.

"They're—they're fine." He recovered himself a bit, hitching himself taller on the stool. "Elizabeth just had another boy, and Gil—"

"I need a job, Frank," Thelma interrupted. She wasn't here to make small talk. "I need money."

Frank goggled at her, as though wondering if it was really her, or some other woman masquerading as Thelma. "I'm not sure what you came here hoping to find," he finally said. "If you are having . . . financial difficulties, if you need a small loan, perhaps I could—out of respect for our friendship—"

"Oh, we were never friends," Thelma said mildly. "But perhaps things can be different now. I don't need a small loan—what I need is a job. An *income*."

"Well, surely you know that I am no longer in the textiles business. I am employed by Gleaner Manufacturing, in fact."

"Though you do still have a *mill* complex." Thelma focused her gaze on the bridge of his nose. "A total of thirty thousand square feet on Minisink Avenue, an area that has enjoyed a considerable escalation in land value. And there's also equipment valued at several thousand dollars. It's all in the public record, you see."

"You—now, Thelma, what you're talking about—"

"Your brother's property, his company, that he purchased himself, before he ever brought you on. The one which you told everyone he deeded to you before he died. Remember? You actually managed to convince Emma not to consult a lawyer, that you would handle all of his affairs." Thelma let that settle in. "But you used to confide in me, Frank. I was your secret-keeper—you said so yourself. You used to say you could tell me things you could never tell another soul."

"That's—I don't know what you're talking about," Frank said, glancing around. "See here, I'm not sure what you're getting at. I mean, even coming here, to a place like this—"

"Let me show you something." Thelma reached into her

purse for the envelope and drew out the thin, folded sheet of paper. "This isn't the deed, of course," she said. "I've taken the precaution of engaging an attorney to hold my papers." That was not true—she had no idea how to find an attorney, or, more to the point, how to pay one. The box of papers that she had brought home from the mill, all those years ago, was stowed in the basement.

Frank stared down at the folded paper but didn't take it, so Thelma was forced to open it and hold it up in front of his face. It was a mimeograph duplicate of the original deed of sale, the faint outline of the Recorder of Deeds seal. The owner was clearly listed as "Leo Wallace Brink and Wife."

Frank gazed at it for a long time. Thelma slid the paper into its envelope, the envelope into her purse, and folded her hands on top. "It's time for the mill to reopen," she said.

"You know that's not possible," Frank said.

"It is if I say it is."

He pressed his lips together and for a moment he looked almost as though he might cry. "And what—you'll tell them . . . you'll tell them . . ."

Thelma watched him squirm, but she was remembering another Frank—the man who'd first taken her with her face pressed into the blotter on his desk while all around them the stacks belched smoke and the spinners whirred and the looms clacked and sighed. The man who could catch her wrist and twist it, gazing into her eyes in the stolen twilight, just to the brink of cruelty, to the place where reason gave way to the roaring furnace of need.

She *had* loved him, though she'd never admit it to another soul.

"I'll tell them only what's necessary," she said. "That you decided the market seemed right, that you're getting back in. That you asked me to do the books. I'll pay myself, by the way," she added calmly. "A fair wage."

"Why don't you just hand it over to them?" Frank demanded. "Just—just take that paper you've got there and ruin me?"

"Don't be dramatic," Thelma snapped. "You landed on your feet. That mill hasn't earned you a cent since 1940."

"I couldn't go back into production," Frank protested.

"Not without cutting Jeanne and Peggy in, you couldn't. Not without telling them the truth."

"They were supposed to be *married*," he said bitterly. "They were supposed to be taken care of. I had a family to look after, you know, I had—"

Thelma found that she didn't have the appetite to hear any more. She stopped him with a look and got up from the stool. "We all had our burdens," she said. "You just made the mistake of thinking that yours mattered more than everyone else's. I'll plan on starting on Monday. I'll meet you at the office."

"Wait—why this way? Why not just tell the girls?"

Thelma was silent for a moment. Because she wanted, finally, something for herself. Because she'd tended that stove and cleaned those rooms for too many people, for too long. Because keeping secrets had become as natural to her as breathing. Because . . . because she couldn't quite bear, despite everything, to hurt him.

But she couldn't afford to be sentimental now. She squared her shoulders and turned to go, then remembered something.

"Don't worry about opening the place up for me . . . I still have a key."

Peggy

"Have you enjoyed your time here, dear?"

Miss Perkins gazed placidly at Peggy through the slightly distorting, thick lenses of her glasses. Set with a sparkling rhinestone at each uptilted corner, they gave her the air of a predatory bird—the sort that eviscerates its prey with its claws for sport before plunging its beak deep into the still-beating heart. That, at least, was the image that had come to Peggy on the occasions when one of the girls had erred, bringing the wrong dress, taking too long, or—worst of all—addressing the customer directly instead of fading into the plush surroundings of the Crystal Salon.

Miss Perkins had explained the rules on Peggy's first day on the job. "You're a good-looking girl," she'd said. "That could work against you." *Consider yourself a part of the wallpaper,* she'd gone on to counsel. Ornamental, pristine, yet unobtrusive, just like the chinoiserie paper decorating Fyfe's rarified inner sanctum.

We may not be Paris, the furnishings seemed to announce, the deep velvet upholstery of the chairs and the scrolled occasional tables. *But Plainsfield, for the few, can also be exceptional.* In the Crystal Salon, an effort was always made. Class distinctions were acknowledged and maintained. The wives of the wealthy, the distinguished, the influential could feel welcome here; the inherent promise of the Crystal Salon was to do its part to secure and maintain the social prominence of its clientele.

And by dressing in the fashions carefully selected by the legendary Annabel Ingram, couture buyer for the Fyfe's chain and direct boss of Miss Perkins, the Crystal Salon's clientele could rest assured that the gowns they would wear to occasions in suburban Philadelphia—or the city itself, or even Manhattan—would be appropriate, exquisite, and singular. That, most important, they would not see themselves coming and going. Miss Ingram attended the shows in New York and Paris and London, and in recent months had added Ireland and Italy to her trips. She purchased pieces from the collections presented by Balenciaga, Jean Dessès, Balmain, and Schiaparelli, and ordered slight modifications to make them more appropriate to the Fyfe's customer, generally forgoing the most outlandish flourishes and details for more understated versions.

All of this Peggy had picked up by listening, taking any opportunity to observe Miss Perkins at her desk and listen to her telephone conversations and review her correspondence. "I've been really happy here, Miss Perkins," Peggy said, smoothing her skirt. "I've learned a lot, and I enjoy helping our customers."

This wasn't exactly true. Peggy did not enjoy helping the wealthy wives, some of them only a few years older than she, who pretended not to see her. She did not enjoy bringing armloads of dresses that she would never get to wear, that she, in fact, was allowed to touch only while wearing white cotton gloves. She did not enjoy standing at attention with her head bowed and her hands clasped in front of her like a novitiate, and she most especially did not enjoy the way the salesgirls treated her with disdain, never letting her forget where she was in the pecking order.

"I'm so glad to hear that." Miss Perkins's smile turned calculating. "You've caught my eye, you know. Tell me, what do you think of the way we conduct business here in the Crystal Salon?"

Here it was, the critical moment, the one Peggy had been preparing for since her first day. The autumn collections would be arriving in the next few weeks; the best customers would be invited to informal showings. Scheduled several times a day at the start of the season, ladies came two or three at a time, and the store's mannequins tirelessly modeled the pieces selected for them by Miss Perkins. Diplomacy was critical, and it was here that Miss Perkins showed her true talent, because she had to anticipate which pieces would suit which clients. A gown promised to one woman could not be shown to another; the promise of a much-anticipated gown could be used to reward her loyalty or pique her hunger for it. Customers could try on the samples, but of course they never fit; the real work would come later when the clothes arrived and individual fittings— typically at least three per garment—were scheduled.

The collections served another purpose: illustrations of couture gowns went into the newspaper advertisements that brought the ready-made customer to shop. She had no illusions that she would be going home with a two-hundred-dollar Balenciaga, but she might be more than happy to pay eighteen dollars for a dress from the misses department that borrowed details from the designers' latest styles.

Peggy had done a little discreet inquiring and knew that Lester Creighton, the illustrator who'd created Fyfe's advertisements for many years, was approaching seventy. It seemed reasonable that he might want to retire—or that a mild stroke or heart attack might force the issue. At the very least, wouldn't a man of his age welcome a reduction in his workload?

Peggy drew a breath and prepared to take a gamble. She was counting on Miss Perkins, herself known for ruthless ambition, to appreciate her audacity.

"I believe there are specific reasons why Wanamaker's continues to out-perform Fyfe's not just in ready-to-wear but in couture," Peggy said, a slight quaver to her voice. She had practiced in front of the bathroom mirror late at night, whispering in the silence of the tiny house. "Our customer service is exceptional and of course, Miss Ingram's taste is widely admired. But I can't help but wonder . . ."

She paused on the cusp of the words she would not be able to take back.

"Yes, Peggy?" Faint bemusement glittered behind those obscuring lenses. Miss Perkins clicked her vermillion-lacquered nails on the desk.

"Well, it's the newspaper advertisements. As I'm sure you know, the circulation of the *Inquirer* alone is nearly three hundred fifty thousand households, and Fyfe's purchases a full-page spread in at least three regional papers most Sundays. We have the exposure, but—well, I just wonder if the presentation couldn't be a bit fresher."

Glitter, glitter. Miss Perkins's perfectly plucked eyebrow lifted. "Fresher?"

Peggy reached for her handbag and pulled out the small sketchbook she'd carefully crafted into a miniature portfolio.

"This is last Sunday's ad," she said, flipping the book open to a page on which she had pasted the illustration. She'd trimmed the ad to focus on Lester's rendering of a boy's romper. It was unfair to the old man, because it was the weakest of his drawings that week, the tot's legs out of proportion, his face obviously erased and reworked. "And this is the text style that we've been using for at least two years."

"I am quite familiar with our advertising," Miss Perkins said drily.

Peggy swallowed and flipped the page. "And here is a *New York Times* ad for Neiman Marcus. You see they are using the new typeface, and their logo is larger. But what really sets these apart, I think, are the drawings. Mr. Creighton has a beautiful command of his medium, of course. But you see in these other ads, there is a move away from technical precision. The figure is sketched with a minimum of detail and here—where you see this ink wash—the fabric's folds are merely suggested. I've made a few sketches of my own in this style, from the new collections."

One more flip of the page: there, on the creamy paper, worked late last night in the light of the bedside lamp while Tommie slept a few feet away, was Peggy's best effort.

Miss Perkins took the sketchbook from her hands, pushing her glasses up her nose. She studied the long, languid leg, the fall of crêpe de chine, the figure's face in profile. Finally she set the notebook on the desk.

Then she burst into laughter. "My, my, Peggy, I had no idea we'd hired an *artiste*."

The way she pronounced it—Miss Perkins was in the habit of peppering her conversation with French words—did not sound like a compliment.

"But, Peggy, dear, I'm afraid I haven't been clear with you. I invited you here because I'd like to offer you a new position."

Peggy kept the smile fixed in place, willing herself not to show any emotion. The girls who proved themselves as runners occasionally worked their way up to mannequin, but these were usually girls with figures like Jeanne's, tall, thin girls with long necks and endless legs and graceful arms. Peggy knew some of the other runners hoped for the position, but these were the same girls who had few other aspirations other than to marry a wealthy man. Peggy, whose figure had been curvy to begin with and had weathered Tommie's arrival with only a slight lowering of the bosom and rounding of the stomach, knew she possessed the most common sort of good looks, the kind that would play well only in places where they didn't know better. The head of the famous Powers modeling agency was famous for saying that "an interesting face is more effective than a flawless one," and Peggy had nothing like Jean Patchett's beauty mark or Elizabeth Gibbons's heavy eyelids, some minor imperfection that might make her stand out.

Peggy's looks, she knew, were as interesting as a box of baking soda. She'd languish as a mannequin, and soon she'd be too old, anyway. But put a pencil in her hand and she felt transformed.

"Miss Perkins," she blurted, "it's just that I've worked really hard on my illustrations. I've got stacks and stacks I could show you, and I can do different styles too, I—"

"Dear, I don't have the first thing to do with advertising." Miss Perkins cut her off impatiently. "I see the sheets about ten minutes before the rest of you girls do. It's really not our concern—the marketing department is responsible for getting the customer in the store. It's our job to sell to them once they're here. Do you understand the distinction?"

Miss Perkins's gaze was unflinching, assessing. It was, Peggy understood, her do-or-die moment. She was being given a choice. Only there wasn't really a choice—she couldn't be a runner forever. The mannequin's job could at least be parlayed into a future. The mannequins went out with men with good jobs and cars and bank accounts; they were taken to the theater, restaurants, clubs. It would be tricky for Peggy, burdened with a child, but she could pass for twenty-five, and she could have more children—

Miss Perkins interrupted her reverie. "Dear, I understand that you have artistic leanings. But anyone can be an illustrator. Take a few classes at Pratt and I guarantee you could do every bit as well as Lester. He's a drunk, you know; he turns in work with gin rings on the paper."

She pinched her lips and reached across the desk to pat Peggy's hand with cold, waxen fingers. Was there a living heart beating inside her bony chest? "Besides, what you're doing isn't drawing, it's designing. I know this ad—I see what you've done to the hem, the neckline. And listen to me, sweetheart, no one wants to buy a dress designed in America. Europe—even Canada—maybe. But 'Peggy Brink of Plainsfield'? It's simply never going to happen."

Peggy nodded, biting her lower lip hard enough to taste the hot, salty blood. She would not cry. She'd known disappointment before. She could be a mannequin. She could make it work.

"I see," she said quietly. "Of course, you're right."

Miss Perkins sat back in her chair. "But, Peggy. I've seen you with the customers. You don't realize it now, but you have a gift. It's a rare thing, a subtle thing, but absolutely critical to the sale. The Crystal Salon customer wants to deal with women on her own level, you see. She doesn't wish to be pandered to, nor does she wish to be patronized. She enters the salon with an expectation of being among those who understand her needs. Women who speak her language, so to speak—who can address an unflattering hemline but also know where it might be appropriate to wear the gown. Who know that the hour between tea and cocktails makes all the difference in the world. Who know what to do with a berry spoon, for heaven's sake, or a fish fork."

Peggy nodded, confused.

"There is a reason why our runners and mannequins are directed not to speak to the customers."

"Yes, ma'am."

Miss Perkin's shook her head in frustration. "Do you know why I got this job, Margaret?"

"No, ma'am."

"Not many people do. I was engaged once, you know."

She paused, waiting for Peggy's response. She had to know what the girls said about her—that she'd been born under the famous clock at Fyfe's flagship store, and raised in its tenth-floor salon. That she had no sense of humor, that she was still a virgin in her late forties, that her own family didn't speak to her. She was as feared as she was respected. It was impossible to imagine her caught up in a love affair.

"To whom?" Peggy asked timidly.

"To Richard Meade. Of the Woodbridge Meades."

Peggy willed her face to remain impassive. Everyone knew of the Meades' fortune—half a dozen buildings in Plainsfield bore their name. Decades ago—before Peggy was born, before her parents had met and married—her mother had gone to parties given at the Meade mansion. Peggy had once seen the dance cards her mother had saved, hidden under the silk in her jewelry box.

"He lives in the South now," Miss Perkins continued. "Hasn't, I'm afraid, lived up to the family name. He is what is politely known as *convivial*, which is what one calls a man with an undue thirst for alcohol. It was probably a mercy that he broke off our engagement. But you see, his mother had become fond of me. I used to study her carefully—her every word, gesture, her social calendar, the calls she returned and the ones she didn't. I had thought I would need this knowledge when I married her son. When that didn't happen . . ."

For a moment Miss Perkins stared moodily out the window of her office, which gave a tall, narrow view onto the other shops of Community Square, where merchants were unlocking doors and beginning their days. "She gave me this ring, which had belonged to her grandmother." She held up her hand, but Peggy knew the ring by heart: a cabochon emerald set high in a gold setting. "And she spoke to Morton Fyfe, whose couture department she had shopped for years. A week later I had a job."

"That's very . . ." Peggy searched for the proper response, the meaning she was meant to take from the story.

"Let me be clear. Dorothea Meade had noticed my interest. She noticed my drive. She guessed, correctly, that that drive would see me through the challenges that would come my way. And, I suppose, she felt that the family owed me." A wistful smile flashed across Miss Perkins's face, a smile that briefly transformed her into someone else entirely. "Well. I did not let her down, as you see. I studied fashion with the same dedication I had once studied her. I learned my clients' needs and tastes better than they knew them themselves. I've done well for this company; very well, in fact. And now I've been rewarded. I'm being moved to the flagship store in Philadelphia, Peggy—I'm taking Annabel Ingram's place. A significant promotion, I'm sure you'll agree. And it's my job to fill the position I'm vacating."

Peggy's mind swam. "You're—you're giving *me* your job?"

Miss Perkins's laugh was as brittle as shattered glass. "Don't be stupid, Peggy; of course not. Lavinia Cole will assume my position. But you're to be her assistant. Every client, every dress, every sale, you'll be right there. You'll earn twenty-seven dollars a week, which I believe is significantly more than you're earning now, though of course you'll be working longer hours. You'll attend the shows with her in New York—maybe even in Europe this fall, if she can build it into the budget. It's a start."

"I—I don't know what to say."

"Say thank you. And don't make me regret this."

Thelma

Thelma listened to Peggy while she stirred the apples in their simmering bath. They were the worst of the lot, cheap because they were bruised and wormy, old and spotted with rot, but after the bad bits were cut away they were suitable for applesauce.

With any luck, Thelma wouldn't be shopping the bruised produce for much longer. But the more Peggy talked, the more irritable she felt.

"And what about Tommie?" she finally said, once Peggy had shared her news. "When you're off in Paris for weeks at a time, who's supposed to be taking care of the poor little thing?"

She glanced over at her daughter-in-law and experienced a strange pleasure at her discomfort. She felt her own news inside of her like a coiled spring. She had wanted to tell the girls together—that was the excuse she'd given herself, anyway. Jeanne was upstairs, sequestered in the attic, where she'd been spending every spare moment, probably working on a new outfit for work. Maybe Thelma should call her down right now and have it out. No time like the present, and all that— except that every time Thelma thought about what she'd done, she was overwhelmed by the inevitable questions that would follow.

How, for instance, was she to tell the girls that she'd known they were being cheated of their inheritance all these years? That their financial troubles could have been dispatched—or at least greatly lessened—by the sale of the mill complex that rightfully belonged to them? How was she to explain the way she'd come to know the truth?

From the start, Thelma had known she had no future with Frank, who had a wife and three children. And yet for five years, she'd returned again and again to the mad distraction of his arms. Sometimes he slipped extra bills into her pay envelopes, but the money was never discussed and—to Thelma, at least—had nothing to do with their trysts. Sometimes months would go by, and she'd thought she was shut of him at last, but then some setback or disappointment or inexplicable mood would send her back to him, as dumb and helpless as a dog scratching at fleas. Only Thomas's death had had the power to end their affair, as it ended everything else that mattered.

Maybe it wouldn't occur to either girl to question why Frank was beginning production again. Maybe they would never have to know the truth. No matter what, Thelma had to tell them soon, because she would start work the next week, after the workmen Frank had hired finished repairing the equipment. Raw goods had already been ordered. Frank had come around, once he finally accepted that he was to be part of the enterprise, and had quit his sales job and thrown himself into the new venture.

Thelma was counting on Peggy understanding, once she showed them the calculations she had done, that her job made no sense at all, that she needed to stay home with Tommie. But it would not be an easy sell. Since Tommie had turned six, Peggy was constantly complaining about how difficult she'd become. She quickly grew bored with the lessons Tommie brought home from school, and made it only a few pages into the books Tommie begged her to read before turning out the light.

"I—I'll hire someone," Peggy said now. "I'll be earning more money, Thelma. And it's for us. For all of us."

"Mmm," Thelma muttered darkly. Even with a raise, Peggy would be hard pressed to pay a sitter. "And what about your drawing? Where are you going to find time for that, now that you're going to be a saleswoman?"

"Assistant to the director," Peggy corrected her. "And I wasn't drawing so much as I was designing, which is going to come in quite handy. When a customer wants to modify a gown, I'll be able to offer them a quick sketch of what they can expect."

"Is that right," Thelma said. She had to admit that it was clever of the girl to find a way to make money from her hobby. Her drawings were very good, at least to Thelma's untrained eye, but she was certainly no Norman Rockwell.

"Plus now I'll be expected to wear our clothes! I'm to be a reflection of the Crystal Salon at all times." Peggy grinned, looking for a moment like the young, enthusiastic girl that Thomas had first brought home, all those years ago. "And I'll get clothes for you and Jeanne too."

"How would you manage that? Those clothes cost a fortune."

"Well, I get a discount, and then there's the pieces that are refused by a customer after they are already tailored—we can't resell those, but Jeanne can make something of them."

"I see." *Tell her,* Thelma's conscience urged. *Tell her the truth now.* Before it became even harder, even more complicated.

But Tommie came running into the room, wailing, having cut her hand on something, and the moment was lost.

Thelma returned to her applesauce, stirring down the sugar that crystallized on the sides of the pot. First Jeanne, then Peggy, and now her—all of them had ventured out of the house that had been their sanctuary for so long. Thelma could scarcely believe it—but maybe the time had come to stop living in the past and start creating some sort of future for them all.

Jeanne

Gladys was giddy with excitement, her nausea having finally abated enough for her to enjoy the outing. They found their places near the front of the hall, at the second-best table, no doubt thanks to Mrs. Harris's intervention.

"Teddy said I should buy something nice after the show," she confided as she eased her thickening body into her seat. "He's so happy that his mother finally seems to be warming up to me!"

During the lunch service Gladys chatted happily and ate everything on her plate and three dinner rolls too, while Jeanne brooded. The outfit had turned out well, she thought, though she'd resorted to sneaking a page from one of Peggy's notebooks to copy the design, because she was too angry at her sister to ask her instead.

Peggy had taken a promotion at work and was now earning a bit more—and she'd had the audacity to ask Jeanne if she'd quit her own job and stay home with Tommie. Jeanne loved her niece to distraction—but Peggy's request had unleashed a bitterness that she hadn't realized she was still hanging on to.

In the frigid first months of 1942, as the war began stealing headlines every night and boys she'd known her whole life were shipping out to fight, Jeanne had counted her blessings that Charles, a newly minted M.D., would be beginning his medical practice with his father. He'd passed his boards in the fall, and his father was having a second examining room outfitted at the building downtown where he practiced general medicine. Charles had inquired about her preferences in rings, and they'd discussed the advantages of living in town, near his parents, versus building a home in one of the new neighborhoods. All that was left was the formal engagement—and then there would be an announcement, the date would be selected, the church booked, the registry composed, the stationery ordered, and Jeanne's life would finally begin.

Thoughts of her future with Charles had sustained Jeanne through the fall, when her mother grew sicker and sicker, until she barely got out of her bed. The doctor told Jeanne, in hushed tones, that these holidays would be her last, and Jeanne exhausted herself trying to make them festive while Peggy was out every night with Thomas. It was as though Peggy was trying to outrun their mother's illness, while Jeanne dutifully saw to her needs and cared for the house and fretted over the bills, all the while still numb from losing her father.

Charles visited when he could, usually twice a month, staying in the city with the college friend who'd introduced the pair. Their courtship had mellowed over time, their engagement delayed until he finished school, and Peggy's fevered romance seemed indulgent and silly, by comparison. Where once she and Peggy had talked endlessly about her wedding, the gowns and flowers and gifts and seating arrangements, now all Peggy wanted to talk about was Thomas. Christmas was a strained affair, a visit from Charles spoiled when Jeanne, exhausted from caring for her mother, came home early from a Christmas Eve party they all were to have attended, and Peggy stumbled into the house during the wee hours and then stayed in bed, hung over, on Christmas Day, while Charles went back to Connecticut early.

And then, one crackling cold February day, Peggy had burst into the little house and announced that she had gotten married. *Married!* She proudly held up her hand, with its narrow gold band on her ring finger, and their mother moved her parched, pale lips and managed hoarse, lung-rattling congratulations while Jeanne stood by, shocked to silence. *How dare you*, she wanted to shout—she hadn't even brought Thomas along to ask for her hand. Thomas was to ship out in less than a month, and as the days passed, a steady stream of cards and gifts arrived at the house and their mother asked Jeanne to give a dinner, one she would not be able to attend. Jeanne did so—she did it all, wordlessly spooning broth into her mother's sunken mouth while the party went on downstairs, cleaning up the mess when the last guest left.

"What about us?" she'd begged the next day, when Charles stopped by the house to say goodbye, before he drove back to Woodbury. Surely *now* they could announce their engagement? Better to wait, Charles said, for the Allies to defeat the Axis, for his practice to take off, for a thousand reasons that Jeanne had stopped believing. She'd known then, somehow, that her dream was over. There would be no glittering wedding, no beautiful children, no comfortable home in Connecticut. And she couldn't help believing that Peggy had stolen it all.

And now, when Jeanne had finally found something for herself again, all these years later, Peggy was trying to take it all away, expecting Jeanne to babysit so she could rub elbows with the wealthy women at Fyfe's. Two days ago she'd waited until Peggy was taking a bath to sneak into her room and take her sketchbook, flipping through the pages before she found what she was looking for and tore out the page with a sketch of a romper with a ruched and piped bodice and a flirty attached culotte.

It had seemed utterly justifiable in the moment, but as the show began and the members of the Junior League took to the runway amid cheers and applause, guilt took hold. Jeanne hadn't even told Peggy about the luncheon, and without her unwitting help she'd have had no idea what to make for Mrs. Harris.

"And now . . . it's picnic time!" the emcee announced, a battleship of a woman with diamonds the size of pecans on both hands. She squinted at her cards and added, "Modeled by Mrs. Noel Harris. Mrs. Harris is wearing an original design by Miss Jeanne Brink."

Jeanne was startled—she hadn't expected to hear her name. But her surprise was quickly drowned out by gasps and murmurs all around her, as Mrs. Harris strutted out in the beguiling, playful jumpsuit that Jeanne had made sure fit her as though she'd been born in it.

It *had* turned out well, she thought, as spontaneous applause turned to cheering. She'd completely reconstructed the skirt to create the sassy, knee-length pantaloon, and cut the blouse into bias strips, which she used to pipe the pockets, yoke, and armholes of the bodice she sewed from a yard of sheer snow-white batiste. Peggy had sketched the design based on a young Italian designer's debut collection; no American manufacturer would cut a leisure outfit so fitted and spare or embellish it with such lavish details. The knee-length pant was daring, to say the least, for a woman of Mrs. Harris's age, but as she rounded the end of the runway she was the picture of confidence, and applause thundered through the room.

Jeanne stole a glance at Mrs. Harris's nemesis, the event's chairwoman, whose face was red as a beet. The show concluded moments later, and as the ladies began to gather their coats and purses, Mrs. Harris—still wearing the outfit Jeanne had made—threaded her way to their table.

"We're a hit, darlings!" she said, kissing Jeanne and Gladys. Her eyes glittered as she touched up her lipstick in a silver compact. "I've been asked to chair next year. Letty just about fainted. Let me tell you, my dear, I've got plans for you."

Thelma

Thelma liked to get Tommie ready for church herself. She didn't trust Peggy to tame her wild hair or remember her white gloves or make sure she wore her good socks, with the lace trim. Tommie loved going to the Little Saints because she was allowed to help with the younger children, making up elaborate games of make-believe for them during free time, and she allowed herself to be fussed over for fear of being forced to sit through Mass with the adults.

It had rained again last night, and as the women walked to the church they passed flowerbeds and bright green grass heavy with raindrops. The scent of lilacs and dirt warming in the sun teased Thelma's nostrils and stirred a familiar feeling inside her. Fecund—everything around her seemed ready to burst with new life, everything but her, who would never give life again, but who had somehow not thrown off the cloak of need as other women her age did. Thelma had not asked for this appetite; sometimes she thought it was God's rebuke. But what did He expect her to do? Why give her such a thirst only to deny her relief?

It was in this mood that she arrived at church. After dropping Tommie off in the church basement, they walked down the aisle in order of age, as always, and sat in the pew that Thelma had occupied since her marriage, fourth from the front on the left. Some Sundays she imagined Henry sitting next to her, but most of the time it was Thomas she thought about: on her lap as a new infant; squeezed between her and Henry when he was a boy of ten or eleven, and—finally—her favorite memory, when he was all grown up and she'd sat between her two men, beaming with pride at Thomas's good looks and manners.

Today, she was so distracted that she barely paid attention to the Mass. Afterward, as they were filing out with the congregation, she didn't see Father Nowak greeting parishioners until she was practically upon him. She preferred Father Zabek, but the older priest seemed to be slowly withdrawing from the daily life of the church, letting Father Nowak take on more and more of his duties. Father Nowak, in Thelma's opinion, was not ready for the job. In fact, he looked barely old enough to shave.

"Ah, good morning, Mrs. Holliman, Mrs. Holliman, Miss Brink," he said unctuously. Thelma resisted rolling her eyes— she sometimes thought he stayed up late at night with the parish directory, memorizing names. "Jeanne, I trust you enjoyed the fashion show yesterday. Mrs. Carson mentioned that she saw you there. A very good cause, indeed."

"I—I'm sure you're mistaken," Jeanne stammered. "I was visiting a friend. In Roxborough."

"Oh dear—" Father Nowak playfully tapped his forehead and laughed. "I must be confused. So many parishioners to keep track of."

But Thelma realized that he wasn't confused at all. That he was poking into Jeanne's business, probing to see what he could unearth.

Thelma could not stand prying, particularly from a man—it seemed unnatural—and most especially from a man who wore the collar. She suspected Nowak was not, as others had suggested, merely a sycophant, aspiring to greater power in the parish. He was something worse and more dangerous: a compiler of clues, a hoarder of details, a merchant of secrets. Men like that were drawn to the priesthood, Thelma suspected, because of the inherent power linked in the position: literally God's incarnation on earth, if one was a believer.

Jeanne had gone to see some friend from high school—or so she'd said. If she had reason to lie, well, it was certainly not the business of the contemptible Father Nowak.

"And Thelma," he said, as if reading her thoughts. "You're looking well. We would still love to see you at the women's club."

Thelma held his gaze. "What a kind invitation," she said coldly.

That, at least, seemed to set him back—there was no retort as they passed, and he didn't react even to Peggy's hip-swishing, perfumed presence. Perhaps he was one of those, the funny ones, if even her daughter-in-law could not capture his attention.

Peggy went around to the basement entrance to collect Tommie, and Jeanne and Thelma waited under the branches of a cherry tree, away from the rest of the parishioners chatting in the parking lot. "About what Father Nowak said," Jeanne said anxiously. "About yesterday."

"It's your business," Thelma said, suddenly weary of her own secrets. "You don't owe me an explanation. And actually . . ."

It was on the tip of her tongue; *There's something I've been wanting to tell you,* she could say, as though it had just occurred to her, as though the news she'd been carrying around hadn't felt like a stone inside her.

But not here. Not yet.

A strange feeling stole over Thelma. Jeanne had taken a little time for herself, for an innocent outing to a fashion show—and Father Nowak couldn't let even that go, a small recompense for a life mostly bereft of pleasure. Thelma had not wanted to make room in her heart for this thin, quiet, beautiful girl who carried the yoke of misfortune with her like a birthmark. She had been a burden that Thelma could not think of a way to refuse. But as Jeanne trudged on ahead, Thelma felt the walls inside her begin to crack.

Three

Tulle

You may have heard it called "illusion," because tulle is used to trick the eye, to perform feats of deception no less impressive than Jasper Maskelyne's sleight-of-hand. Clouds of it veil a bride in mystery; gathered lengths of it make a limp skirt seem full. There is a rumor that no less than sixty yards of it went into a Balenciaga evening gown worn by a Manhattan socialite who was likened by the press to a "gossamer faerie."

But here is something you might never guess: tulle is strong. The weft thread is wrapped around the warp thread, practically knotting it in place. If you ever find that you are to be suspended from the top of the Empire State Building, tulle would make a better choice than cotton rope.

July 1949

Jeanne

An unexpected distraction arrived that afternoon, when they'd returned home after church. Peggy's new boss, a sharp-nosed woman in her forties, arrived in a screech of tires and a cloud of Je Reviens, holding a stack of order books.

"I'm so very *very* sorry to disrupt your afternoon," she said when Jeanne opened the door. "My manners are perfectly awful, I'm afraid, but now that I've been given an assistant I plan to work her to the bone!"

Peggy, who'd been in the kitchen trying to fix a tear in the suede covering the heel of a brown shoe with a homemade concoction of glue mixed with coffee grounds, came rushing to the door when she heard her boss's voice. She practically pushed Jeanne out of the way, stepping in front of her. "Please come in," she said, and Jeanne detected the frantic note in her voice.

Tommie, who'd been reading on her stomach behind the couch, rolled onto her knees and peered at Miss Cole. She loved adult visitors—brush salesman or neighbor, it made no difference; she seemed endlessly fascinated by people who were neither her teachers nor related to her.

"Oh, what an adorable little girl you are!" Miss Cole exclaimed, taking a step back, her expression implying the opposite.

"My niece," Peggy said hastily, avoiding Jeanne's gaze.

Jeanne quickly covered her surprise. Was it really any surprise that Peggy hadn't told her boss that she had a child? She probably was afraid it would keep her from getting the job. But who knew what Tommie would make of the lie.

"Come on, Tommie, let's go feed the ducks," Jeanne said before Tommie could react.

"I've got some stale bread," Thelma said, rushing to get the heels from the bread box and put them in a paper bag. She exchanged an opaque look with Jeanne as she handed them over. "I think I'll join you."

In moments, the three of them were out the door. Peggy and her boss, their heads together over the paperwork and the last of the coffee, barely looked up.

"Don't be angry with her," Thelma said once they reached the park and Tommie was busy tearing off bits of bread and throwing them in the pond, where half a dozen ducks circled and quacked.

"I'm not." Jeanne tried to decide if that was true. The lie, that Tommie was her child, wasn't so outlandish. It might as well be true, given the amount of time the two of them had spent out alone together. Jeanne had no wedding ring, but not every widow wore one.

Once or twice, when Tommie was younger, Jeanne had even allowed herself to pretend. "You'll ruin your appetite," she'd say loudly when Tommie paused to peer into a bakery window, or "She gets them from her father," when a stranger complimented her long, thick eyelashes. These moments felt, strangely, more like thefts than lies. Jeanne would never understand fate's handiwork, why some were given so little and others so much, but she still felt guilty when she allowed herself to imagine having what Peggy did.

Since she was a little girl, she'd dreamed of having children of her own. It wasn't until Charles's death that she accepted that it truly might not happen for her—and it took several more years for her to mourn the loss of that dream.

Lately, though, something had happened to change things. Or rather . . . something had *not* happened. Jeanne hadn't given her missed cycle much thought at first—since she'd lost weight, she missed months as often as not—but as each day ticked by, she had started to wonder. It had only been the one time—and Ralph had pulled out, as he had promised, only it had seemed to happen faster than he'd expected and she wasn't quite sure if he'd been all the way out when . . . it happened. It had all been so awkward, Ralph apologizing and unable to look at her as he pulled up his pants, Jeanne dressing hastily in an agony of embarrassment.

The thought nagging at the back of her mind was simply unthinkable, but with each passing day it encroached further. It all seemed to circle back: there was one child in their household, and three grown women to watch her—and still Tommie was passed among them, her presence one more obligation, one more endless source of chores.

For years now, Peggy had put herself first—her needs, her

whims—while the rest of the household worked overtime trying to accommodate her and her child. The unfairness of it weighed more and more heavily on Jeanne the longer she thought about it.

"If I tell you something, do you promise not to tell Peggy?" she blurted.

A strange look passed over Thelma's face, but she quickly recovered herself. "Of course."

"I wasn't with a friend yesterday. I mean, I was—but we were at the Junior League fashion show in the city. Remember Gladys? The girl from work, the one I made that blue dress for? Well, her mother-in-law asked me to make an outfit for the show, and it was a huge hit, and now she wants me to do more. And not in secret, either, like I did for Nancy and Blanche and the rest of them. And if I started sewing for her, I'd have to quit Harris—"

"But I thought you liked your job," Thelma said.

"Well, yes, I do, but—"

"And you wouldn't make as much sewing as you do there, right?"

The flame inside Jeanne flickered and she felt her face flush. "I—not at first, anyway. I mean, we didn't talk about what she would pay me, and maybe it would be more than I charged the others. *Definitely* it would be more," she amended, with more certainty than she felt. How to explain this wasn't about the money—when *everything* was about the money?

How had she thought she could make this work—without Peggy's help, with the mountain of bills under which they were all suffocating?

"It's just that it would be for *me*," she said. "I mean—working for myself, not—not—"

Not for the subtly cruel and competitive Miss Bream, whose reaction to a perfect draft, one in which she could not find a single typo or misspelling, was to grunt and roll her eyes and load Jeanne up with more work. And not for *her* boss, a man who took three-hour lunches and was famous in the office for his flatulence and for his habit of waiting until a girl went into the supply room to follow her, pretending to drop his pen on the floor so he could look up her skirt.

"I just want to be something other than one more girl in the typing pool," she finally said. "They're all the same—they just work for a couple of years and then they get married. And I . . . and that's not going to happen to me."

Thelma was watching her carefully. "What is it you want?" she asked, finally. "For you, for your life. I don't flatter myself that you want to live with me forever and take care of me in my old age."

What did she *want*? The old rage filled Jeanne, and then immediately drained away. It was so long ago now. She had wanted Charles not to be dead. She had wanted to be married, with three perfect children, in a perfect home. She had wanted her parents to live long enough to meet their grandchildren.

She would never have any of those things. For a while, the path left to her had seemed to be to merely wait to die, whether it took a year or a decade or half a century. But there was something . . . when she picked up her paycheck at the accounting department every other week. When she handed the stack of bills over to Thelma. When Mrs. Harris had looked at her appraisingly, as though she had something of value to offer. There was a seed of something inside Jeanne that had somehow sprouted into a hunger, perhaps even a need.

"I want to *matter*," she said. "To do something important. I thought, back when we first started, with Nancy, I thought maybe Peggy and I could do something together. With her designing and me sewing—maybe even open a little shop. But now she's got this new promotion, and—and I did something."

Jeanne's urge to confess was suddenly strong—but how to explain? "I took one of Peggy's designs, for the jumpsuit I made for Mrs. Harris. I took it out of her sketchbook without asking. I didn't ask her first and she doesn't know. I . . . I pretended I designed it myself."

I lied, she wanted to say, *I cheated, because Peggy gets everything and she doesn't ever appreciate it.* But even in her thoughts, the explanation sounded pitiful, even contemptible.

"Ah," Thelma said. "Well, your sister knows how to land on her feet. I wouldn't worry too much about any of that. But maybe there are other things you can do. Other jobs, where you could have more responsibility than you have now."

"Like what?"

Thelma dug the last of the bread from the paper bag and handed it to Tommie, who went back to tearing off tiny bits and casting them onto the water, while the ducks swam nearby.

"Before I tell you . . . there's something you should know. Something that affects all of us."

"All right."

"It's just that—you see, our financial situation has been worse than I told you. We're in danger of losing the house."

"What—I don't understand. It's *yours*. Mr. Holliman *left* it to you."

"It was never really mine," Thelma said wearily. "That house has belonged to the bank for years."

"But I thought—Peggy said—"

"Never mind what Peggy thinks," Thelma interrupted. "When Thomas died, I did what he would have wanted me to do. I told her what she needed to hear, that the house was mine. I didn't want her to worry, you see. And, of course, I wanted the baby under my roof."

"But what about your savings, the money your husband left you? Was that—something you told Peggy too?"

"Oh, there was a little money," Thelma said. "From my father. I never told Henry about it. There wasn't much, but my father gave it to me before he died. He never liked Henry."

Jeanne tried to process what Thelma was telling her. The house, modest as it was, was the only place she'd had to land. The attic ceiling, its contours now as familiar to her as her childhood home. The small table on which her sewing machine sat, the yellow paint showing through where the green had worn away. The pantry that Peggy had worked so hard to transform.

"But how have you been paying for things? Groceries and—and heating oil and Tommie's things?" And the collection on Sunday, the man who came to fix the stairs, the cake of soap on the bathtub ledge and the Borax under the sink? All the little expenses added up to an enormous sum, as Jeanne knew from the months she spent managing the house as her mother slipped away. She'd squeaked by on what was in the bank, and then after her mother died, the sale of the house had barely covered the doctors' bills and the funeral.

"There's been enough for that," Thelma said briskly. "I made do. I stretched what Father gave me. But now, that's not possible anymore."

"I'll keep the job," Jeanne stammered with a growing sense of panic. "And there's Peggy—her new position—"

"That stuck-up stick she works for barely gave her a raise," Thelma said. "Just a new title, though your sister acts like they gave her a scepter and a crown along with it. And even if you kept your job   and don't get me wrong, I appreciate every cent you give me. But Tommie is going to need things. She deserves more than Saint Katherine's. I want her to go to Miss Kittering's. I won't have her ending up . . ." Her voice trailed off, but Jeanne knew she meant: *like us.* Thelma didn't want Tommie to end up like them, poor and desperate.

"I don't understand what else we can do," Jeanne said. Something occurred to her. "Unless . . . should I go? So you can get a paying boarder?"

"Oh, Jeanne, where would the boarder sleep? In that tiny attic, like you do? No, that's not the answer. God put us all together and that's not going to change. But you're going to have to do some things. Some . . . things to secure our fortunes."

"I can type and file and—"

"Wait, Jeanne. Let me tell you my idea. It's a way that we

could make enough for all of us, for Tommie to wear a new dress to school every day of the week, for me to pay off this house once and for all. For you to go to Atlantic City with a girlfriend, for heaven's sake." She took a breath and said the rest in a rush. "Your uncle Frank is reopening the business. He's asked me to come work for him doing the books, and I've agreed. And—and I think you should work there too."

"The mill?" Jeanne asked in surprise. "Brink Mills?"

"Yes, he saw an opening in the market, and he thinks he can get it operational within a few months. We could use the money, obviously," Thelma said. "He's going to pay well."

"I haven't talked to Uncle Frank in years," Jeanne said. She wondered how much Thelma knew—or suspected—about the rift between them. Or perhaps *rift* was too strong a word . . . but the last time Frank had come to see any of them had been their mother's funeral, when he barely stayed for the Mass and skipped the reception entirely.

"You're not close."

"Maybe I should have tried harder to stay in touch," Jeanne said, but she *had* tried; she had sent birthday cards to her younger cousins for several years, had written notes to her aunt Mary. They lived in Chestnut Hill, but Jeanne heard things now and then—that their eldest, Arnold, did nothing but stare out the window all day; that Frank was earning enough money selling combine harvesters to buy a new car. Her resentment stemmed, in part, from that success—her father had always complained that his younger brother wasn't helping enough at the mill.

"Oh heavens, don't blame yourself," Thelma said briskly. "People drift apart. And besides, this is business. He needs help, and I know that operation inside and out."

Memories of the mill flooded Jeanne—of the dust motes dancing in the sun streaming through the narrow windows, the sound of the looms humming, her father's office with its pipe tobacco smell and books full of silky sample squares. The workers tipping their caps respectfully when their mother brought her and Peggy to visit.

Jeanne especially had loved those visits, had loved dressing up and holding her mother's gloved hand, had loved how one elderly worker in particular used to bow and call her "Miss Jeannie" and let her move the handle that lifted the warp threads. Jeanne had felt so safe there, so sure of her place in the world. To recapture even a little of that feeling . . . but it seemed impossible.

"What about Tommie?" she asked.

"I'll need to talk to Peggy," Thelma said. "She's just going to have to face facts and realize she needs to stay home. It's not even another year until Tommie's in school all day, and maybe she can work something out with Fyfe's then."

"But, Thelma, all I know how to do is type and file."

"Don't sell yourself short," Thelma snapped. "You're a smart girl. I'll teach you. You can take over invoicing and sales processing."

Could she really do it? The possibility was tantalizing. "But why wouldn't Frank just hire someone with experience?"

"I *am* the person with experience," Thelma said. "Frank

knows that. He was good with sales, but your father always took care of follow-up with the accounts. And they were both hopeless with the books."

Jeanne had never seen Thelma this animated, her eyes bright and hopeful. Possibility fluttered within her. More money, more responsibility—and Peggy would have to do her part too, for a change.

Jeanne shrugged off the ugly combination of resentment and guilt that accompanied every thought of Peggy these days. If what Thelma was saying was true, and Jeanne could earn more working for Frank than in her current job, then Peggy couldn't possibly expect her to pass up the opportunity.

"Yes," she said breathlessly. "Yes, I'd like to come work with you."

"Well, that settles it," Thelma said. "Come, let's get that child before she falls in and ruins her dress."

August 1949

Peggy

The first week on the job was an education, a view of the couture salon through a new lens. Before her promotion, Peggy had come to the store in her old leather shoes with her suede pumps in her purse, and stored her lunch and bag away in the employee locker room along with everyone else employed at the store: the sales staff from every department, the accountants and cleaners and shipping clerks. Now, she changed her shoes on the trolley, arriving half an hour before the store opened. She used her very own key to go in the side entrance, and took the elevator to the third floor, where she walked through the ready-to-wear dress department to the gilded entrance to the Crystal Salon.

This was her favorite moment of the day. Without the buzz of activity, the customers and the ringing cash registers, it sometimes seemed as though the entire store was waiting for her arrival. Long ago, before the war, before Tommie, before she'd even met Thomas, Peggy had loved to walk into a party, loved the moment when everyone noticed her and there seemed to be a break in the humming pulse, just because she was there. Now, it was as though the mannequins were lined up for her approval, their long elegant hands upturned, their smooth chins raised regally, luscious handbags dangling from their wrists, shoes slipping from their narrow heels.

Each day she examined the store with a critical eye, trying to apply whatever she had learned the day before. This cotton skirt might have suited Mrs. Pendegast from church, who'd finally shed what she called her "winter weight." That one really shouldn't have been made in seersucker—a better-draping fabric would have kept the waist from puffing out awkwardly. A notched collar was a poor choice for this slim jacket, as it would make all but the leanest women look too wide in the bust.

And this was all while she was still on the floor in ready-to-wear! Once she entered the salon, it was another matter entirely. The gowns presented to the salon's clientele were selected carefully for each woman's shape and size, and would undergo a series of fittings before they were ever worn in public. Flaws would be concealed and assets emphasized. Moreover, the entire staff worked hard to shield their clients from unsuitable dresses, as there was nothing worse than having a customer fall in love with a gown that could never be made to flatter her—or, worse yet, a gown one was saving for another client, who very well might see her at luncheons and balls and dinners.

On the other hand, the women who shopped in ready-to-wear did not have that luxury. The racks might hold four of a dress in blue, but only one in yellow in the wrong size; clever girls might be able to take in a bust dart or shorten a hem, but most of these garments would be worn just as they were. Peggy sometimes heard laughter and conversation when she passed the communal dressing room, women shopping together, praising or evaluating each other's choices. Other women left armfuls of clothing in the dressing rooms and gave up in frustration, unable to find anything flattering to wear.

It was these women Peggy found herself most interested in, despite the fact that she now held a job coveted by all of her former peers. The runners and mannequins looked at her differently now. Their easy camaraderie had turned hollow, their envy laced with resentment. How had she, no more remarkable to look at than most of them, curried Miss Perkins's favor?

How had the more senior girls, the more obsequious employees, been passed over for her?

Until her promotion, Miss Perkins had worked alone. That Lavinia Cole was granted an assistant was a result of not only the money that the Crystal Salon brought to the chain's balance sheet, but also—even more important—the status conferred on the Fyfe's name by the salon's rarefied clientele. This complicated social calculus seemed beyond some of the other girls.

Adding to their consternation was Miss Perkins's selection of Lavinia Cole to succeed her. Peggy too had been briefly surprised that it was Lavinia, not especially remarkable among the sales staff, who had been plucked out of the pool and placed in charge. But over her first few days in the new position, Peggy gradually realized why Lavinia was perfect for the job.

She didn't come from money.

She hadn't gone to a prestigious college.

And she wasn't especially ingratiating with her staff.

But what Lavinia had, the quality that was easy for others to miss, was a flawless rapport with the Crystal Salon customers. She moved easily among them, neither cowed by their wealth nor contemptuous of their flaws. She mirrored their mannerisms when she was with them and dropped them the moment they left, reverting to her impatient, demanding ways with the staff. Moreover, she cultivated a quiet air of authority, whether by accident or design, that made women listen when she advised them on trends or style.

"That shade invokes royalty," Peggy had overheard Lavinia

say one day while she was helping a customer to choose between two gowns, and whether it was true or not, her words had struck Peggy as much less important than the fact that the customer believed them. The customer purchased the mauve dress recommended by Lavinia, along with the gloves and shoes and bag that she suggested.

Peggy watched. She learned.

Morning coffee became a ritual. Peggy arrived before Lavinia and laid out the service, making sure the silver shone, the linens were neatly pressed, and the coffee was blistering hot. When Lavinia arrived, she dotted her face with a handkerchief if the morning was warm, and took a seat behind her desk. Not until she'd had her first sip—eyes closed, followed by a luxuriant sigh—did she greet Peggy, who would be waiting with the date book open on her lap.

Peggy would then lay the book on the desk blotter for Lavinia's review. If the salesgirl who made the appointment had been sloppy, if there were misspellings or careless abbreviations, Peggy erased and rewrote them. She also copied relevant notes from the file that they kept in a lacquered box. Each card held details about a customer's measurements, coloring, and personal tastes; there were notations for husbands and children, board and club memberships and associations. There were also notes about what each client had spent each year that she had ordered clothing from the Crystal Salon, which was one of the reasons the box was locked up whenever Lavinia or Peggy was not in the office.

Some of the cards, those belonging to their longest-term

clients, had entries going back twenty years, copied from the records kept in the flagship store. Some of the cards bore the handwriting of women who were no longer working—and some who were no longer alive. Some of the oldest clients had daughters and even granddaughters with their own cards. Some things were too delicate to be written directly, even in this closely guarded resource: a weight gain was signaled with a mere "+" and the new measurements; a scandal such as a husband's affair or a financial reversal was indicated by a star and the notation "see Miss Perkins." An unpaid bill earned a delicate red border made with a pen that Lavinia, like Miss Perkins before her, kept in the top drawer of her desk.

Together, Peggy and Lavinia reviewed the day's appointments, discussing the dresses that were to be shown, the sales strategies to be employed. Peggy had learned quickly: the best outcome was a dress that flattered the wearer, and thus indirectly the store, so care had to be taken that a client not fall in love with an unsuitable garment. A large invoice was good news; a repeat customer was even better news. Referrals had to be handled with tact. In Europe, a couturier might refuse admission to anyone not known to the staff, but at Fyfe's, subtler strategies had to be employed. A prospective client with insufficient means might be told there simply wasn't anything in the current collections that would flatter her, and referred to another department. One who had offended an existing client, or been late to pay her balance, might receive the message in starker terms.

Peggy and Lavinia also reviewed the sales from the day

before, the tailor assigned to each client, the schedule of fittings and any updates concerning the garment's purpose. If the dress was to be debuted at an important occasion, a note was made of that as well: the customer counted on Fyfe's to ensure that no other woman would show up wearing a similar dress.

A week into her new role, Peggy stepped into the back room one morning, where the girls assembled before the store opened. Abruptly, their conversations stopped; their laughter died. Peggy scanned the room as she hung her jacket, and her gaze fell upon a crumpled puddle of hosiery in the corner.

"Oh dear," she said mildly. "What happened here?"

"Tildy got a run," one of the runners explained, earning a dark look from the unlucky owner of the stockings.

Peggy checked her watch. "Well, luckily there's still ten minutes before the store opens. Why don't you go get a new pair from downstairs, and tell them to bill me. You can pay me back later."

The girls glanced at one another. Peggy saw their uncertainty, their pooled resentment, and felt it flow through her like her own hot blood. She suppressed a smile.

"You can't tell her what to do," the haughtiest of the mannequins said. "You don't write our checks."

"You're right," Peggy said amenably. "But I'll do my best to get you my discount, all right? And I'll tell you what, if Lavinia gets angry, I'll say they were for me. I won't even mention your name."

The tone shifted. The owner of the stockings exhaled. There were reluctant nods of acquiescence.

Peggy took her seat in the chair next to Lavinia's desk, the one that everyone now knew to leave vacant for her. She took a small notebook from her purse, the gold-plated pencil that had long ago been a gift upon her graduation from high school. She flipped the notebook open and wrote something. No one needed to know that she had merely sketched a star next to a drawing of a shoe she'd seen in *Harper's Bazaar*. It didn't matter what she wrote; the girls' imaginations would fill in the rest.

She would tell Lavinia, of course. She'd tell her that the girl came to her, unsure what to do about her stockings, and was it all right that Peggy had taken care of it? She'd let Lavinia decide. For now, she'd let Lavinia believe she was in charge.

LAVINIA TURNED OUT to be a surprisingly adept mentor.

The next day, Peggy came to work in the same woolen skirt and charmeuse blouse she'd worn on her first day on the job. When Lavinia arrived, she took an assessing look at Peggy before closing the door behind her, something that happened so rarely that Peggy had forgotten the back room had a door.

She unlocked a cabinet in the corner of the back room, the one in which the declines were stored—the items ordered and tailored for clients who refused them for whatever reason: issues with tailoring, the properties of the materials, or simply (and most commonly) because they had changed their minds. Only the most valuable customers could get away with this last excuse, but as Lavinia had once said to Peggy, "If Elizabeth

Craig keeps buying two-hundred-dollar suits, then I'm not going to quibble about a sixty-dollar blouse."

"This one, I think," she said, taking out a navy jersey Balmain that the intended owner had judged too form-fitting. "Now you'll need to check the appointment book before you wear it. It wouldn't do for you to have it on when Mrs. Reinhold comes in, not after she called the dress 'ghastly,' and we agreed."

"She didn't think it was *ghastly* when she ordered it," Peggy said. She had still been a runner the day the imperious woman had sent her to fetch gown after gown. "She had to have it the moment she saw it."

"Our clients' memories can be short," Lavinia chided. "But they pay for that privilege."

"But what do they think we do with the returns?"

Lavinia shrugged. "Who knows? Perhaps they think we donate them to the urchins on the street. More likely they don't give it a second thought. Still, we must preserve the illusion that their taste is above reproach, which means they really shouldn't see their discarded garment anywhere. Now listen, you're going to need a tailor who knows what he's doing. Not our staff—they talk, and that won't do; you'll need someone outside the store, especially since Mrs. Reinhold has a waist like a longshoreman. I can recommend someone—"

"I've—I've got a girl," Peggy stammered.

"Good. Now, since you're going to be helping me with the books, let's go ahead and put this one through." Lavinia got the large linen-bound order book down from the shelf behind her desk.

"Lavinia," Peggy said haltingly, "I'm not sure that—I mean, even after the discount, I don't know if I can—"

"Ah, Peggy," Lavinia said, sliding on her glasses and motioning her to sit at the chair across her desk. "No, no, no. You see, this is altered merchandise, which means we can't possibly sell it to a customer. Now you're going to have to start thinking like a businesswoman. Let me introduce you to the beauty of the internal write-off."

Later, when she showed the dress to Jeanne and Thelma that night, Jeanne asked Peggy to explain the practice twice. "But that doesn't make any sense," she said. "The balance sheet still has to balance. If you take a loss on that dress—a hundred and forty-five dollars, you said?—it has to come from somewhere."

"Well, yes, of course," Peggy said, feigning confidence. "But that's for Central Accounting to deal with. All I have to do is turn in our books every Friday and they . . . do the rest."

"Reconcile them," Jeanne said, barely looking up from the dress, which she had turned inside out so she could examine the seams. Of course Jeanne would know the right term—she'd probably done it herself, in the city, before she quit. The old envy—Jeanne coming home from school with As on every paper from the same teachers who seemed to take such pleasure in giving Peggy Ds the following year—flared inside her and extinguished the pride she'd been feeling. "This would take a *lot* of work, Peggy—I'd have to take apart the entire thing and cut the panels down. I can't just take a few inches off the waist, you know."

"But I'll be ever so grateful," Peggy wheedled, barely keeping her impatience in check. Wasn't a genuine couture piece worth a little effort? And after she had been there a bit longer, maybe she could "buy" returns for Jeanne and Thelma too.

Still, you couldn't just *say* something like that to Jeanne. Jeanne was the more delicate sister and always had been. Jeanne's feelings had to be anticipated and nurtured and soothed; a careless word or the smallest act of thoughtlessness could send her into a funk that could last for days. It hadn't been so bad when their mother was alive; Emma Brink could cajole and tease Jeanne out of her dark moods, even at the end, when her hold on life was so tenuous that she was little more than a whisper in a darkened room.

Jeanne laid the jersey dress down on the kitchen table, and Peggy immediately snatched it up—the surface was still damp from Thelma wiping it off after dinner. Thelma and Jeanne exchanged a glance.

"Peggy," Thelma said. "Jeanne isn't going to have time to tailor your dress."

Tommie, drawing at the little table Thelma had set up in a corner of the kitchen, looked up in surprise at Thelma's curt tone.

Since the argument about Peggy accepting the new promotion, things had been fairly peaceful; she'd made a point of getting Tommie ready before school, and taking her off Thelma's hands when she arrived home after work. She'd completely given up any semblance of time to herself, and went to bed each night exhausted from Tommie's bath and nighttime routine. She'd done everything she could to show that she was doing her part—and yet it *still* wasn't enough for them?

"It's not just for me, you know," she said in exasperation. "After I'm there a while, I can get things for you two. Returns, like these, that we could never afford."

"*Peggy.*" Thelma folded her dishtowel and laid it on the counter. "Jeanne and I are going to work for your uncle Frank. He's opening the mill up again."

"Uncle Frank?" Tommie echoed.

Uncle Frank? The name rang in Peggy's mind. When had this all happened—and when exactly were they going to tell her? "The mill?" she echoed stupidly. "Dad's mill?"

"Thelma just found out," Jeanne said defensively.

"When?"

Thelma hesitated. "I talked to him last week. He asked me to come back and do the books. But it's more work than one person could do—there used to be a full-time accounts manager back when your father was in charge—and he—we, Jeanne and I, thought it made sense for her to work with me, rather than in the city."

"It's more money," Jeanne said. Neither of them would look her in the eye. "More than they pay at Harris, even the senior stenographers."

"With what he's paying Jeanne and me, you won't have to work anymore," Thelma said. "You can stay home with Tommie. In a year or two, when she's in school full-time, maybe you can do something during the day, at Fyfe's, or—"

"Wherever you want," Jeanne said. "Once Tommie starts first grade, you'll have six hours every day for yourself. You can help in the classroom, or down at the rectory, or get a little job."

"A *little* job?" Peggy said, rage choking her words as she rounded on her sister. "You want me to give this up—the best job I've ever had, something I'm really *good* at—somewhere they actually *appreciate* me, they *believe* in me—just so you don't have to go to the *city* every day?"

"That's not why—"

"That's enough, Peggy," Thelma snapped, raising her voice. "Up to your room, Thomasina."

Tommie began to cry, and Jeanne automatically bent to comfort her. Peggy pushed past her and grabbed Tommie, lifting her into her arms. Her face was hot and teary against her neck. She was heavy—so heavy. "I *love* my daughter," she said, her own face wet with tears. "My job—I want her to be proud of me. I want her to know I'm somebody."

"You *are* somebody, you don't have to—Peggy, please," Jeanne implored, as Peggy backed out of the kitchen.

"Let her go," Thelma said darkly, not bothering to lower her voice. "She's going to have to get used to taking care of that child sometime."

Peggy rushed up the stairs, Tommie jouncing in her arms. Safely in her room, she leaned against the door, letting Tommie slide from her arms to the floor, where she promptly threw her arms around Peggy's legs and hugged her tightly. "Don't be mad," she sobbed against Peggy's skirt. "I hate it when you and Aunt Jeanne fight."

But Peggy hadn't started the fight, and certainly not with Jeanne, who was just parroting Thelma. Maybe Thelma even pushed her into taking the job.

But if only they would listen to Peggy—she was finally doing something she was good at. She had a future at Fyfe's, she was sure of it. The rumor was that Miss Perkins earned nearly one hundred dollars a week in her new position, more than Thelma or Jeanne could ever hope to earn in the mill, and while it was true that Peggy had a long way to go to catch up with her, she had already advanced further than any of her peers.

And instead of recognizing that she'd done something impressive—that she'd earned a position the other girls would give their eye teeth for—Thelma and Jeanne had gone behind her back to come up with a scheme that completely turned her world upside down, that took away every hope of ever building a life of her own. She might as well simply cut the Balmain dress to ribbons and put on a washday dress and put her hair up in a rag.

"Mommy, are you all right?" Tommie asked, peering up at her with her tearstained face.

Peggy took a deep breath and patted her cheeks, angrily brushing the tears from her eyes. "Yes," she whispered. "Yes, Mommy's fine."

She *wasn't* fine, not just at the moment. But she would be. Resolve took shape inside Peggy: she wouldn't accept this without a fight. She wouldn't let them steal this chance from her.

Jeanne

Jeanne couldn't sleep: dread roiled inside her every night now, the knowledge of what she must do weighing heavily on her heart. It had to be done soon, before she started her new job, before it could grow into a problem that could not be solved. "It"—always it. To indulge what-ifs would be as dangerous as walking along the tracks by the river in the dark with a train bearing down on her.

In the wee hours, when there was nothing to do but wait for dawn, something surprising happened. She heard the squeak of the stairs that signaled someone trying to tread quietly, and a moment later someone slipped through her door and stood silhouetted in the dim glow of the streetlamps through her narrow window.

"Peggy?" she whispered.

"Can I come in?"

Jeanne moved over on the bed and pushed back the covers, and Peggy—still warm from her own bed, her nightgown bunched around her knees under Thomas's ancient river shirt that she wore in winter—slid in next to her. She wriggled her back up against the iron headboard and sighed. "I couldn't sleep."

"Me either," Jeanne said. Her anger at her sister was too big a burden to pick up now, in the silent hours.

For a while neither spoke, but Jeanne could sense her sister thinking next to her. She imagined the flutter of Peggy's long eyelashes against her cheek, the way her corn silk waves curled against her neck. She knew the contours of her arms— still plump, as they had been in adolescence—and the sweet, slightly curdled smell of her sleep.

What would it be like, to tell? To confide the thing that was so unthinkable that Jeanne had not allowed herself to name it, even in her own mind? She remembered a night like this, years ago, when Peggy had come into her bed on Placer Avenue, before she'd moved out, before their mother had died. Jeanne's bedroom in the old house was much larger, the walls papered in a beautiful soft green with a print of floppy pink camellias, the floors covered in a carpet that had been a gift from her godmother, her mother's sister. It had been the same bed, however, that Peggy had clambered into that night, after announcing her elopement.

"What was it like?" Jeanne had asked then, and Peggy had sighed happily and stretched her legs luxuriously under the quilts. *Fine*, she had said. *It didn't hurt at all. And he was so happy after.*

If Jeanne was to confess now, she would have to say that it did hurt, though not a lot; it was like getting your fingertip pinched in the wringer's rubber rollers. But that night Peggy had radiated happiness, an almost smug contentment. Jeanne, on the other hand . . . when Ralph rolled off of her, already apologizing, she'd felt little more than a detached sort of disappointment. That, and relief that it was done, like the feeling she had after a vaccination; that something unpleasant had been gotten over with, a necessary task checked off a list.

"Peggy," she said carefully, and then didn't know how to proceed. How to explain, for instance, that it truly hadn't occurred to her that this disaster could result. For something so momentous to happen, Jeanne felt as though she would have had to be more engaged, more deliberate. More . . . participatory. How could it be that while she lay there—attuned to Ralph's every breath and sigh and grunt, but as still as a stone in the nave of St. Katherine's—her body could have been silently betraying her, gleefully acquiescing?

"I need this job, Jeannie," Peggy whispered, turning her face against Jeanne's shoulder so that her words were muffled by her flannel sleeve. "I can't have it taken away. Can you understand? . . . Please?"

"I did something," Jeanne said. But instead of unburdening herself of what she had done the night of her peculiar date, she confessed to Peggy about Mrs. Harris and the fashion show.

"I tore your drawing out of the book," she said. "The romper with the piped trim."

"Doesn't matter," Peggy said, yawning. Jeanne was surprised—she'd expected her sister to be furious.

"But don't you get it? I pretended *I* designed it. Mrs. Harris loved it—she wants a gown now. When I gave my notice, she thought—I mean, I didn't tell her I'm going to work for Uncle Frank. I let her think I wanted to design and sew full-time. She wants to help me; she says she can get her friends to come to me."

"Like before?" Peggy rolled her eyes. "Like Nancy Cosgrove in the living room?"

"Peggy, you don't understand. I *stole* your drawing. And based on that one outfit, Mrs. Harris—who has more money and influence than everyone I've ever sewn for put together—is ready to make me her personal designer." She took a breath, praying that Peggy would understand just how significant this was. "If I tell her, if I can find a way to explain it was you—*you* could do that for her. You can get your designs *seen.*"

"I can't sew like you," Peggy said. "It'll never work."

"I can help you at night, after work," Jeanne said. She'd thought of this already—Peggy could do much of it on her own: the cutting and joining, pinning in zippers and darts, gathering the fabric for a waistband or a cuff. Jeanne could do the difficult parts, like attaching a collar or easing in trousers' crotch seams, and then Peggy could finish stitching down facings and hemming and sewing on buttons. She would teach Peggy to fit and tailor; she'd teach her everything, in time.

"Mmm." Peggy wriggled farther down under the quilts, pressing her face against Jeanne's side, burrowing under her arm like a cat. Jeanne realized she'd stopped listening.

It wasn't the best plan, maybe, but it was something. Peggy could sew for Mrs. Harris; she could draw to her heart's content, and still care for Tommie. It wasn't a fancy position in the Crystal Salon, perhaps, but Mrs. Harris was every bit as rich and important as any lady who shopped at Fyfe's. Maybe she would introduce Peggy to some people. Maybe she would invite her to parties.

It wasn't exactly what Peggy wanted, but then who got to choose anymore? Peggy would have to do as Jeanne had done, and seize the imperfect opportunities that offered themselves. They weren't children; it was time to let go of childish dreams.

Jeanne lay awake in the darkness, her eyes wide, while the rhythm of her sister's breathing evened and slowed and eventually turned to gentle snores. Jeanne ought to push her out, she knew that. They were much too old for Peggy to be getting away with her spoiled baby-of-the-family routine. Theirs were real problems, with real consequences, not like their childhood squabbles over a pretty ribbon or a piece of pie.

But there was something so comforting about having someone next to her in the night, about matching her breathing to Peggy's without even being aware of trying, about the way she mumbled in her sleep and pressed even closer against Jeanne's body. A hundred nights, a thousand, they had clung to each other like this, and as Peggy's fine hair fluttered against her neck, Jeanne drifted into deep, dreamless sleep.

But when she woke in the morning, there was no evidence that Peggy had been there at all.

Thelma

In the morning, Thelma was tired and cross from not getting enough sleep; she'd heard the footfalls on the stairs late in the night and lain awake wondering what the two were talking about. She'd never had a girl; she'd only had Thomas. And her own sisters had died before they were old enough for girlish confidences.

Thelma had stumbled upon the two before, crammed into Jeanne's narrow bed like sardines in a can to stay warm, as if they were seven and nine, rather than twenty-seven and twenty-nine. The volatility of the sisterly bond was, frankly, incomprehensible to Thelma. Only yesterday, they'd been at each other's throats. Now, it seemed, all was forgiven, as Jeanne poured coffee and Peggy nestled a sleepy Tommie in her lap.

"I have an appointment with the doctor," Thelma said stiffly. "I'll be gone much of the afternoon. So you'll need to pick Tommie up at school, Peggy."

"Fine," Peggy responded shortly.

The girls never questioned Thelma's visits to the doctor for her sciatica. Thank middle age for giving her the excuse, at least—she had suffered annoying pains in her hips for years, which no amount of stretching and resting seemed to help.

Peggy herself had no trouble inventing maladies of her own so she could leave early when she wanted to. "Mysterious female troubles," she had once confided with a knowing laugh. "Lavinia is too well bred to pry, and the other girls are barely speaking to me."

Thelma marveled that Peggy wore this exile like a badge of honor. She'd never coveted the attention of other girls—since moving in with Thelma she'd had only a handful of outings with friends. Even before she took the job at Fyfe's, Peggy didn't seek out other mothers, neighbor girls with broods of their own. She was aloof with them in the street; she showed more interest in the man who came door to door selling knives than she did the new family down the street who had twins a year younger than Tommie.

Once or twice Thelma had tried to talk to Peggy about building a new social life, comparing her situation to her own, the inevitable shrinking of a woman's circle as she aged, but of course Peggy couldn't see the parallels. It was like that with the young—Thelma herself remembered all too well what it was like to believe your life stretched endlessly ahead of you, to believe that you'd never find silver in your hair and pain in your joints in the morning.

Thelma hadn't been entirely dishonest when she said she was visiting the doctor, of course, but when on the way home she developed an ache in her heel, she accepted that it was her due. Ordinarily the hours after she left Jack were pleasant ones, the aches under her clothes a delicious souvenir. But today, even Jack couldn't distract her entirely from her preoccupation. Her mind was a mass of conflicting thoughts and fears. What if they couldn't convince Peggy to quit her job? Who was to care for Tommie then? The child's growing unhappiness at St. Katherine's made Thelma even keener to find the money for Miss Kittering's, a bigger expense than any of their others combined. And Jeanne deserved something for herself, didn't she?

Thelma was limping by the time she reached the house. She let herself in the front door, hoping for one more hour of solitude before they all came home. But there, on the kitchen table, was Jeanne's purse.

It wasn't surprising that Jeanne had come home early; she had already given notice at Harris, and this was her last week. But her presence meant a possible witness to the outfit that Thelma had worn to her "doctor's appointment": a dress that hadn't been out of her closet in years, a slim, fitted style that was now out of fashion but that accentuated her still-lush curves. A dress whose shade of blue, in better days, had been compared to a turbulent sea by a man who was desperate to get it off her.

It was hardly an appropriate dress for day, and Thelma would have to get to her room, slip off the shawl she'd worn as camouflage, and change into something more appropriate before Jeanne saw her. Luckily, the bathroom door was closed, so she had a few minutes.

She hurried to her bedroom, but in the short hall, she paused at the bathroom door. A strange sound issued from behind it, a low moan followed by the sound of something thumping dully on the tile.

"Jeanne?" Thelma asked. "Are you all right?"

When the moaning continued, she pushed open the door, all thoughts of her dress forgotten. The door had no lock—hadn't since it broke years ago—but the door opened only a few inches before hitting an obstruction. Frightened now, Thelma pushed harder, and the obstacle yielded enough for her to be able to squeeze inside.

Jeanne lay on the floor, her skirt pushed up her painfully thin legs, a seeping pool of deep red beneath her. Her skin was frighteningly pale, her lips colorless, her eyelids fluttering.

"Jeanne? Jeanne!" Thelma knelt, the hem of the blue dress

in the blood, and reached for her wrist. Jeanne didn't resist; her arm flopped uselessly, like a sawdust-stuffed cloth doll.

Thelma found a pulse, a faint and irregular one. "What have you done," she whispered, as blood continued to trickle from her.

"I didn't . . . I don't . . ." Jeanne mumbled as her head lolled on her neck like a tulip past its prime.

Oh, these stupid, stupid girls. Didn't they know that it didn't have to be like this, that there were precautions one could take, precautions Thelma *still* took, even now? And in the same instant Thelma wondered, *When—who—how?* Had she really been so mistaken in her judgment of Jeanne; had she known the girl at all? For years they'd shared a house, a table, this very bathroom; had they both shielded their real lives from each other? Had they merely gone through the motions of living, like actors in two separate plays taking place on a single stage?

If Thelma didn't move fast, Jeanne could bleed out on this cold tile floor. She'd heard the stories; she knew about the places one could go, the alleys and windowless rooms. As Thelma felt the helpless ebb of Jeanne's veins beneath her skin, she knew she alone could save her; and instantly it was as if Thomas himself were in the room. It wasn't a hallucination; his ghostly form didn't appear and there was no voice whispering in her ear. But Thelma was suddenly certain that he would expect better from his mother. If Thomas were here he would insist that she act. There would be time for reflection later.

"Up we go, then," Thelma said briskly. Jeanne could not be allowed to think she had a choice, that she could be allowed to exit this world, or even this house. She could not be allowed to leave *Tommie*, who, God knew, was going to need every one of them to have a chance in this life.

Thank God Jeanne was so thin; Thelma couldn't have managed this with Peggy. Though Peggy would never get herself into such a fix.

Peggy was a survivor. Just like her.

That was a thought for later, and not a welcome one. Thelma pushed it from her mind. She knew how to handle crisis. She'd been handling crisis for years. One didn't view one's husband's crushed body at the morgue, didn't receive the telegram from the army, didn't decide between paying the mortgage and paying for medicine, without developing a certain strength.

Thelma wrapped both towels around Jeanne's waist and led her, stumbling, to the couch, where she helped her lie down with her head on a bolster.

"Jeanne, listen to me."

The girl lay unmoving, her lips slightly parted, her eyes all but closed, the feathery lashes quivering. Thelma patted her lightly on both cheeks. Not quite a slap. "Jeanne, I'm going next door to use the telephone. I'll be back in a moment and we're going to get you some help. Jeanne. *Jeanne.*"

There was no indication that the girl had heard her. "Do not die on me, do you hear me?" Thelma muttered as she backed toward the front door, but there was so little she could do but pray.

She would play the part she had been dealt, and God help all of them.

Peggy

Peggy hurried down the street, the rain whipping around her legs, cold and wet beneath her coat. She wasn't wearing the proper shoes for this, and her heels twisted on a crack in the pavement, threatening to cause her to fall. She should have taken a moment to change into her flats, but when she'd come home from the movies with Tommie, Mrs. Slater came bursting out of her door.

"Your sister's taken ill," Mrs. Slater said breathlessly. "Thelma's with her. She says meet them if you can. I'll watch the little one."

Then she rattled off an address in Northeast Philadelphia, a place none of them ever went, where eastern Europeans had immigrated to the apartment blocks and crowded houses above Pennypack Park.

"But—what are they doing *there*?" Peggy asked, Tommie squeezing her hand in alarm. Tommie didn't care for Mrs. Slater, who had a mean little dog she kept in her kitchen.

"I'm sure I don't know," Mrs. Slater said, distaste flashing across her flat, doughy face. Peggy had never liked the old widow, who spied on people all day long from her front window and wore men's trousers to wash her windows. But she absolutely hated her now. "She just said to come, if you can. Here, give me the child."

Mrs. Slater had grandchildren of her own, three or four of them, sturdy little things with trunk-like legs and unruly brown curls, but their visits were rare. Mrs. Slater wasn't the sort of woman any child wants for a grandmother, with her oniony breath and thousands of dusty knickknacks and the carpets stained with dog urine. Peggy hesitated: "I'll just take her with me."

But of course, that was an impractical thought, especially as she had no idea what was wrong with Jeanne or why she was in the Ukrainian part of town. All of it was frighteningly strange, especially as Jeanne had been fine enough this morning, despite the headache she claimed was keeping her from joining their movie outing. Jeanne had headaches all the time. But what if this one was different? The uncle of one of the girls at work had come home on a recent weekday, poured himself a glass of lemonade, turned to his wife and uttered four words before dropping dead—and the words weren't anything one would hope to choose as one's exit from this world, like "I love you, darling" or "Keep our children safe" or even "Oh God help me"—they were "Crack it all soon," as well as the girl's aunt could make out. Or perhaps "That's a monsoon." Nonsense, at any rate.

Had something similar befallen Jeanne? Could she—and this was the thought that spurred Peggy to thrust Tommie at Mrs. Slater and turn and run back toward the trolley stop—be dead? *Oh, please please please God no, no no don't take her—*

Peggy ran, her suede heels chafing as she went, giving her blisters that would rub painfully for a week before the skin finally tore away, the one on the left becoming infected and eventually forming a crescent-shaped scar that would never fade. Peggy ran, Tommie forgotten for the moment, and she begged God for everything to be all right, if necessary to take her own life for Jeanne's. *Please just don't let her die.*

Now she limped past one little house after another, her heels in agony in her shoes, peering up onto each sagging porch, looking for number thirty. In this part of town, entire families squeezed into flats carved from the humble buildings. She could hear squalling infants and husbands yelling at wives, smell smoke and rot. There—that one, a single story with a peaked roof, automobile parts strewn on the lawn, the brass numerals crooked on the siding. Peggy clattered up the wooden steps, and by the time she reached the top the door had already been thrown open.

Thelma stood in the doorway, clutching her collar against the wind and rain. "Where's your umbrella?"

"Is she all right? Oh God, is she all right?"

"She's fine," Thelma snapped impatiently. "Practically good as new."

Relief flooded through Peggy like water in a sponge. "But . . . what are we doing *here*?"

Behind Thelma a chorus of voices erupted at once, speaking quickly over one another in an incomprehensible cacophony. Thelma stepped aside for Peggy to enter. "We are the guests of the Petrenkos, of whom there are quite a few. Mind your manners."

This last, Peggy soon realized, had been a bit of sarcasm,

because the conduct of the people inside the front apartment wasn't the least bit mannerly. No one greeted Peggy as she entered, though a woman of about twenty-five yanked her coat from her hands and threw it on top of a hassock on which Thelma's coat was already wadded. An old woman in the kitchen didn't even bother to turn around, but continued muttering in her Slavic tongue while she scrubbed a pot in the sink. Two men in undershirts stared unabashedly at Peggy, until a thin, tired-looking woman with a baby in her arms entered the room, who Peggy assumed must be one of their wives. She handed the baby to one of the men and disappeared into the recesses of the house. Children—four, six, it was impossible to say—ran around the room in various states of undress while yet another woman yelled at them in a mixture of English and Ukrainian.

In the center of all of this, Jeanne lay on a sofa, her legs folded under herself to make room for the man sitting next to her. She was wearing a dress that Peggy didn't recognize, a faded flower-print housedress that was too large on her thin frame. The man on the couch clearly was not part of the large extended family who lived here. He was perhaps fifty, his silver hair slick with pomade, his cuffs folded neatly, even meticulously, over hairless forearms. He wore a wedding band and a gold watch, and above the crust of mud on his shoes, the leather was shiny and new.

"Oh, Peggy," Jeanne said from the couch, struggling to sit up, only to be stilled by the man's hand on her arm. She lay back obediently.

"Hello, Peggy," the man said formally, rising from the sofa.

His gaze darted to Thelma and back. "It's . . . a pleasure to meet you."

"You're a doctor?"

"Your sister is going to be fine."

"But what's wrong with her?" Peggy seized one of Jeanne's cold hands. "What happened?"

The man cleared his throat and looked at Thelma. "I should go."

Thelma crossed her arms over her chest. "You're *leaving*?"

The older woman in the kitchen set down her rag and hobbled into the living room. Now, nearly all the adults were crammed into the small front room, clustered around the couch. The old woman tugged on the sleeve of the blond woman who had let them into the house, and let loose a burst of rapid-fire speech. She jabbed a bent finger in Thelma's direction before turning her back on everyone and returning to the kitchen.

Peggy turned to the younger woman. "Do you speak English?"

The woman, who Peggy belatedly noticed was rather pretty, rolled her eyes in disgust.

"Well, can you tell me what's going on?"

"Ask the whore," the woman snapped.

"That's enough, Katrya," the doctor said angrily. "Thelma, I've done what you asked. I've given you my professional opinion. If you refuse to take her to the hospital, you may as well take her home."

"And you'll bring the medicine."

The man closed his eyes and exhaled before opening them. "Fine. We can discuss that later. Now please, we all need to go."

"We need a ride."

Peggy had never seen her mother-in-law speak so disdainfully to anyone, much less a man of position. And even more astonishingly, the man shrugged and nodded. "Very well."

"Well?" Thelma gestured at Jeanne. "It doesn't look like she is going to get up and walk out of here on her own."

The man bent and gathered Jeanne up into his arms. She whimpered and pressed her face to his shoulder. The man carried her to the door, while all the adults looked on. Even the children stopped running around and stared.

"I'll call," the doctor said. The blond woman ran from the room, down the dark hallway, slamming a door behind her.

"Thank you," Thelma said stiffly to the remaining adults, before following the man outside.

Only Peggy remained in this room full of strangers. She took one more look around, at the rosary hung from the crucifix over the couch, at the plastic flowers arranged in a painted vase, at the half of a waxy green cabbage resting on the counter next to a heavy cleaver. She imagined the children crammed around the table, the amount of food it would take to feed them all.

"Thank you," she echoed. But no one answered.

THE DOCTOR DROVE a new black Buick that smelled of pipe smoke and women's perfume. Thelma sat in the front, her posture painfully rigid, her hands clutching the handles of her bag.

In the backseat, Peggy stroked her sister's stringy hair and tried not to notice the odd smell that clung to her and murmured to her that everything would be all right, when she didn't even know what was wrong.

Going by car took a fraction of the time it took to go by bus and foot. In moments they were home. It occurred to Peggy that the doctor hadn't had to ask for directions.

"Well," Peggy said as the car pulled to a stop, "thank you. Again."

"I'll help you into the house," he offered, his hand on his door handle. But Thelma stopped him.

"I think we'll manage on our own."

Between Peggy and Thelma, they were able to get Jeanne out of the car, her arms around their shoulders. She was starting to seem more lucid, and as they started up the path to the door, she tried to walk, taking stumbling little steps.

While Peggy fished for her keys in her purse, Thelma stepped back.

"You go ahead in," she said. "I'll just be a minute."

But it wasn't just a minute. Long after Peggy got the door unlocked and helped Jeanne inside; after she'd helped her undress and seen the heavy, bloodied rags under her clothes and survived the shock of understanding; after she'd practically carried her up to bed—she'd turned all the lights off in the house but one small lamp in the room she shared with Tommie, and sat on her bed staring out the window onto the street. Next door at Mrs. Slater's house, Tommie was sleeping in a strange bed; tomorrow morning Peggy would have to go and get her back. Tonight would be the first time she'd slept alone since Tommie was born.

She peered out into the night. The car was still there. It was too dark to see much of anything, but when the clouds obscuring the moon parted for a few seconds, it looked as though there was no one in the front seat at all.

September 1949

Thelma

After the first night, Thelma installed Jeanne in her own bedroom. She boiled a chicken carcass and brought the broth to Jeanne in steaming bowls, along with thick slabs of rye bread bought from the Jewish bakery and smeared with butter, then sat beside her until she ate it. She made a pie that none of them besides Tommie touched, the sugar-dusted crust glinting in the sun on the center of the table.

Peggy came home from work carrying asters wrapped in white paper, sugared almonds, a paperback novel from the drugstore. Tommie got into the act; Peggy found a white cloche in a trunk and told her it was a nurse's hat, and pinned on a red paper cross cut from a magazine. Thelma gave Tommie cups with an inch of water to carry to their "patient," and Tommie curled next to Jeanne in the afternoons, exultant to be in the bed from which she was usually excluded, reading her library books.

These sessions slowly seemed to lift Jeanne from her funk. Thelma watched, hidden around the corner, as Tommie turned the pages of her books, sometimes reading aloud to her aunt. After the first day it was Jeanne who read out loud all afternoon long, and Tommie who listened with a rapt expression.

Back in her kitchen with her apron stained with chicken grease, a wooden spoon in her hand, Thelma felt a long-dormant stirring in her breast. But it wasn't a longing for the days when Thomas had perched on her knee with a book of his own, sounding out the words on the page. It wasn't fear for Jeanne's health, because Jack had assured her that all her body needed to heal was rest and nutrition and the pills he had delivered to calm her nerves.

No, what Thelma felt was not sentimental longing. It was impatience.

As Thelma listened to the sound of her granddaughter's chatter, as she inhaled the traces of her daughter-in-law's perfume that lingered long after she'd gone to work, something occurred to her that she'd never really considered before. She deserved more. She had married at nineteen and within a year known the bitter disappointment to which her own mother had alluded vaguely on the eve of her wedding. At twenty, she'd held her newborn infant alone, her mother in a fresh grave and her husband at the corner pub, not one to pass up the free rounds being purchased for the new father.

She'd helped her husband in his business and kept their home; she'd stretched the money he brought home to keep Thomas dressed and fed and educated. When Henry came home with other women's lipstick on his collars, she said nothing. When he sold her mother's signet ring to pay a gambling debt, she'd locked the bathroom door before allowing herself to cry.

When he'd died, she'd done what she had to do. She'd been fueled by desperation, but she never let that show. She held her head high through the funeral Mass before vowing never to return to the Church, but when her son begged her to change her mind, she swallowed down her bile and returned. When Thomas and Peggy eloped she kept her mouth shut.

When the telegram came, she'd wished herself dead. She wasn't even to be allowed to bury her son. **ON ACCOUNT OF EXISTING CONDITIONS THE BODY IF RECOVERED CANNOT BE RETURNED AT PRESENT**, the telegram read. **IF FURTHER DETAILS ARE RECEIVED YOU WILL BE INFORMED.**

But there was nothing else to do but to pick herself up and open the door to the foolish girl Thomas had left behind, the girl who now bore their name. When Peggy announced that she was pregnant, Thelma had vowed to raise her grandson in the house his father had grown up in, and that was the only miscalculation she ever made.

When Peggy's mother died and her sister had to sell their house, Thelma welcomed Jeanne too. What else could she do?

Two young women and a child, and only Thelma and a bit of government money—slim payment, for her son's life—to support them. And yet she'd found a way. She'd stretched her savings as far as she knew how. And yes, she'd stolen moments for herself here and there and she would not apologize; she would fight God himself if He dared to judge her for them; she'd march proudly down to Hell before she'd give up even a single stolen night or clandestine afternoon. Because it was those moments that had sustained her, that kept her going through the darkest days, that reminded her that her obligations were here and not yet on the other side, where someday she would find repose in death.

She had done everything for everyone, borne humiliation and hardship. Now, just when she had a chance to put that all in the past, God had nearly taken Jeanne. Was it punishment for treating her as merely the extra one, the refuse that had washed up on her shore? "It will be better," she whispered fiercely that day as she listened to Jeanne reading to Tommie. "It will be different now."

She called Frank. "One more week," she said in a tone that didn't invite argument. For the moment, he was still cowed by her threats; that was an advantage she didn't expect to keep. Men, especially men like Frank—soft men who balanced a tendency toward shiftlessness with keen awareness of their own interests—did not stay cowed forever. Look at how things had ended with Frank and Leo—had Leo not died first, Frank's laziness and underhanded dealings would have ruined the business.

But Thelma was not Leo. And she had no intention of giving Frank the free rein that Leo had—something he would learn in time.

BEFORE SHE COULD put her foot down and insist that Jeanne get out of bed, something else happened that made it unnecessary: Jeanne received a visitor.

On a Saturday afternoon, when Peggy had taken Tommie to the library, Thelma was dusting in the front room when she looked out and saw a gleaming Packard touring sedan cruising to a stop in front of the house. A plump girl in suede heels nearly tripped stepping up to the curb—and a dark-haired young man jumped out of the driver's door and raced around the car to help her.

"Jeanne!" Thelma called. "Are you expecting anyone?"

A moment later she heard a muffled crash upstairs. "Thelma, tell them I'll be down in five minutes," Jeanne called frantically. "Tell them—oh, tell them I just got out of the bath. Something, anything!"

There followed the opening and closing of dresser drawers, the sound of hangers being pushed on the makeshift closet rod.

Interesting.

Thelma dashed into the pantry—her mirror still hung on the wall, even though no one had used it as a dressing room in many months—and smoothed her hair away from her face and pinched her cheeks. Luckily, she'd worn one of her better dresses today, for no other reason than her workaday house-dresses were drying on the clothesline. When she opened the door, she felt as composed as possible under the circumstances.

"Hello," she said stiffly.

The young woman on her stoop was smiling broadly. "Hello, I'm Gladys!" she chirped. "And you must be Thelma!"

Thelma cocked her head to the side in confusion, but recovered enough to usher the girl in. Over her shoulder she watched the young man leaning against the car, staring out over the river as he lit a cigarette. In profile, Thelma could see that he was magnificent: strong jaw, defined brow, olive skin, a prominent but narrow nose—and the brooding musculature of a working man. A chauffeur, then?

"I'm so sorry to pop in unannounced," Gladys said, standing primly in the front room with her hands folded. "But I've just missed Jeanne so much since the accident."

Ah. The girl from work. Jeanne may have even mentioned her name, though Thelma couldn't remember, other than it had been commonplace. Jeanne hadn't said a thing about her being wealthy, however—and if the girl was rich enough for a chauffeur, what in heaven's name was she doing working as a secretary?

"She's mending well," Thelma said. The day after Jeanne's near-fatal procedure, Thelma had called the Harris Carton switchboard and asked for Jeanne's supervisor, explaining that Jeanne had twisted her ankle and was on strict bed rest for at least a week. *Dr. Blaylock says to keep it elevated at all times.*

"I'm sure she'll be down in a moment—she just got out of the bath. Would you like coffee?"

By the time Jeanne came down the stairs—she'd wrapped cotton around her ankle and changed into her coral worsted, and even put on powder and lipstick—Thelma and Gladys were chatting like old friends. Gladys popped up off the couch and rushed to Jeanne, offering her arm.

"Where are your crutches?"

"Today's the first day I'm managing without them," Jeanne said smoothly, ignoring Thelma. "I'm much better."

"Well, good, because it's just awfully dull at work without you."

"How . . . how did you get here?" Jeanne asked. "Don't tell me you took the trolley?"

Gladys laughed. "No, silly, Anthony drove me. He had to take Mrs. Harris to her luncheon, so he said he could bring me here after, and then we'll go pick her up. Anthony is my mother-in-law's handyman," she added, for Thelma's benefit. "Jeanne, I think he may have been there one day when you were visiting."

Then she changed the subject to Jeanne's accident, peppering her with questions that Jeanne answered with surprising ease, making up a story of carrying garbage to the alley and tripping over a broken flowerpot.

Thelma faded into the kitchen, where she started preparations for supper while the girls chatted. By eavesdropping, she learned that Gladys was married to the son of the company's founder, that she was expecting her first child, and that Jeanne was apparently her best friend.

And she learned something else too. Jeanne couldn't keep her gaze from drifting to the tall front window, through which she could catch a glimpse of the young man named Anthony, who smoked and brooded . . . and cast his own covert glances at the house.

As though they were joined by an invisible length of thread.

Four

Broadcloth

What can you fashion from broadcloth? It might be better to ask what you cannot. The goal of every step of the manufacture process of this hardworking fabric is durability. Loomed fifty percent wider than its finished width, broadcloth is treated to a scalding bath and beaten with hammers, worked and fulled until it has drawn up as clean and tight as can be. It will not ravel, fray, or pill. It is not so different from certain women, who only become stronger the more hardship they are forced to endure.

September 1949

Jeanne

Jeanne scrubbed her skin so hard in the bath that it had turned red. She was done resting—she was as healed as she would ever be. The thing she had unwisely done had been undone, and if she'd had to suffer for it, at least she had been lucky enough to be pulled back from the brink of death.

All that fuss, all that blood, for a few minutes of grunting and sweating and discomfort. Now she couldn't remember why it had seemed so important to experience the act. She certainly hadn't *cared* for Ralph, beyond a vague affection. She had been curious, and she had ceased believing the church's insistence that lying with a man outside of marriage was a sin . . . and that was really all there was to it.

Except: seeing Anthony outside the house—when she'd walked Gladys to the door, limping for effect, there had been a moment when he'd looked up and their eyes met. And there had been a sensation of heat that rocketed through her, a yearning that was indifferent to her ruined womb, to her shame. She wanted him in a way that she'd never wanted another man— and she didn't even know him.

She scrubbed harder.

When she emerged from the bath, her skin was raw and

pink and smelled of Peggy's French-milled lavender soap. Peggy would be miffed later, but in this peculiar moment, Jeanne didn't care. She pulled her slip up over her hips, noticing how it stayed up on its own, rather than sliding down to her hipbones. She'd gained a little weight lying in Thelma's bed, eating the rich meals she made. She rummaged through the clothes hanging from the pipe in the attic, past the suits and dresses she had sewn and altered, and chose an old shirtwaist that fit loosely.

Downstairs, Thelma had put away the coffee things and laid the table for lunch, setting out cold sliced chicken, canned peaches, and the thickly sliced rye bread she had been buying every day.

"Your friend seems nice," Thelma said.

"She is." Jeanne tried to find something to add, and came up short.

"You'll have to tell them you're quitting, you know."

"I know." Jeanne had said nothing to disabuse Gladys of the belief that Jeanne would be back at her desk on Monday. "I'm trying to figure out . . . how to say it."

"Sit," Thelma ordered her. "Eat something, and I'll tell you what I think."

Dutifully, Jeanne served each of them. The food tasted good, better than she could remember chicken tasting, the bread dense and flavorful. After she'd eaten everything on her plate, she dabbed at her lips with her napkin. "You were going to tell me what you think?"

"Well." Thelma sighed and pushed her own plate away.

"What I think is that working at the mill is going to do you good, more good than wasting your talents at that company. You can always stay friends with the girls you met there outside of work. But at the mill, you'll learn things—everything I can teach you, and more."

"You don't have to convince me, Thelma. I've agreed—and I'm feeling much better." They had never discussed what Jeanne had done—the closest they'd come was when Jeanne overheard Thelma talking in low tones with Dr. Blaylock as she drifted in and out of consciousness that first night—and Jeanne was grateful for the tacit agreement between Thelma and Peggy never to bring up what had happened. It was as if she were recovering from a particularly virulent case of the flu. Maybe, in time, her memories would soften and shift, the way they sometimes did, and she'd be able to forget the worst of it herself. "I'm ready to begin. I'll call my boss this afternoon and quit."

Thelma shifted uncomfortably in her chair. "Good. Yes. But before you do . . . it's just that there are a few things I left out, before. When I told you about Frank opening the mill again."

"What kind of things?"

"Well. You see, the mill doesn't belong to Frank."

"It doesn't?"

She looked Jeanne in the eye, and in her expression Jeanne saw shame and fear reflected back. "It belongs to you and Peggy."

IN SEPTEMBER OF 1937, *Thelma was returning from a trip to the thrift shop, where she'd sold all of Henry's clothes for a few dollars, when she saw a familiar car in front of the house.*

It was lunchtime and Thelma was hungry. Thomas wouldn't be home from school for a few hours, and she had planned to fix a sandwich and then go through Henry's tools in the garage. Maybe there was more that she could sell.

The car in front of the house belonged to Frank Brink, the younger of the Brink brothers, one of Henry's largest accounts. She girded herself for the visit, suspecting it wasn't just a social call. Twice in the past weeks, acquaintances of Henry's had come by to tell Thelma that he owed them money. One, a man who knew Henry from the tavern, had graciously forgiven the debt when he saw Thelma's humble circumstances: the threadbare furniture, the worn rugs, the front steps that needed fixing. But the other, a man Thelma had never seen before, had done the opposite, making veiled threats until Thelma agreed to go with him to withdraw the money from the bank.

Henry had been friendly with the Brink brothers—the younger, Frank, more so than Leo Brink, who was a taciturn man, serious and shy. Thelma knew them only from the bi-annual company picnics, when Frank made the rounds among the customers, shaking hands and telling jokes, while Leo stayed on the sidelines, looking pained.

The door of Frank's car opened as Thelma drew near, and Frank stepped out, holding a potted lily. So apprehensive was Thelma about the purpose of his visit that she didn't realize that he meant the gift for her.

"Hello, Mr. Brink," she said, standing uncertainly between him and her walk.

"Thelma. I'm so very sorry for your loss."

Belatedly she realized he was holding out the lily to her. She blushed as she accepted it and before she could thank him, he spoke again.

"I'm sorry that I didn't attend the funeral. The truth is that we didn't hear until . . . afterwards."

It was true that Thelma had insisted on holding Henry's funeral two days after his death, but that was for Thomas's benefit. The sooner his father was buried, she reasoned, the sooner her son would come to terms with his loss. As they had little family and few friends, the arrangements were simple. The notice appeared in the paper the day of the service. But this was the first time anyone had implied that they might have attended, if they had known.

Thelma was unexpectedly moved, to the point of not knowing how to respond. And then she felt she needed to make up for the uncomfortable silence and blurted out an invitation for coffee. To her surprise, Frank Brink accepted.

As she let him in the house, she wished she'd known she would have a visitor. The house was tidy, but she'd neglected the dusting in the days since the funeral, and a faint odor of oil used once too often for frying hung in the air.

Thelma hadn't invited a man into her house in many years, and she felt suddenly tongue-tied. She busied herself making a fresh pot of coffee while Frank made awkward conversation, sitting in Henry's chair at the head of the table. The demand for silk *was plummeting, he said; some of their competitors had abandoned it entirely to go into rayon, the new and popular fabric woven from viscose that could be had for a fraction of the cost.*

"I'm not sure how much longer we'll be able to keep the doors open," Frank admitted with more cheer than the comment seemed to warrant.

"I'm sorry to hear that," Thelma said, setting a cup down in front of him. "Would you care for milk or sugar?"

But she never got an answer to her question, not that day. Because Frank ignored the steaming coffee in front of him, and looked up at Thelma with something close to reverence.

"Won't you sit with me?" was what he said.

"IF HE HAD told me I was beautiful then, I would have thrown him out," Thelma said.

Jeanne was aghast. "You can't be saying that Uncle Frank . . ."

"He says he never planned on what happened," Thelma shrugged. "But most men are like that. If they aren't proud of something they've done, they'll come up with a new version of events and convince themselves that's how it was."

"But he was *married*." Jeanne hadn't seen her aunt and uncle in years, not since her mother's funeral. There had been some sort of falling out between her father and Frank before her father's death, an episode her mother refused to discuss. Aunt Mary had cried as they lowered Emma Brink's casket into the ground.

Thelma laughed. "Jeanne, dear. Lots of men are married. But that doesn't stop them from having urges."

She went on to explain how, during that visit, they'd simply talked. Frank had been kind, asking after Thomas, if she had everything she needed. Of course, Thelma lied and said everything was fine—her pride prevented her from even hinting at the hardship in which Henry had left them.

But Frank seemed to guess at it. Later, of course, she understood that Frank knew a lot more about Henry's character than he admitted. But on that day, his simple kindness had been enough to unleash the flood of emotions she'd been keeping locked up. She found herself confiding in Frank Brink, about how hard it was to fall asleep alone for the first time in over two decades. About how she sat down to answer letters and found herself staring out the window for hours instead. About how the hours seemed to stretch out endlessly while Thomas was at school.

"Is that when he, you know . . ." Jeanne asked, fascinated despite her shock.

"Oh, no. That came later. The first day, he only fixed my steps. And offered me a job."

FRANK BRINK MADE *it sound like she would be doing them a great favor. He knew about her bookkeeping skills, he said, because Henry had bragged about how helpful she was to him. Thelma*

suspected that was a lie, but she also saw the offer for what it was: an opportunity to bring in much-needed money. Frank said she could come in when it was convenient, that a few hours a week would be fine to start.

The first time she went to his office, a Tuesday, he was wearing a fine tailored pinpoint shirt and his hair was combed flat. That was when she knew that her instincts had been correct.

Thelma did not tell Jeanne everything that happened that day. That as they sat close together behind the desk, reviewing Brink Mills' accounts, she had grown warm under her dress, merely from the scent of him. That it was she, not he, who first allowed a hand to graze his knee as she turned a page.

That, two weeks later when they first stole a few hours together late at night in the company offices, each of them having snuck out of their sleeping households, he had cried afterward.

It was not the last time a man would tell Thelma that she was an incredible listener.

❋ ❋ ❋

"BUT HOW LONG did it go on?" Jeanne said. Then she had a thought that made her light-headed. "—or are you still . . . ?"

"Oh, no," Thelma said. "After Thomas died . . . I just couldn't anymore. And their boy Arnold came back from the war, the way he was . . . we just couldn't be together after that. Frank wasn't himself anymore. He said he needed me to help him get through it, but what he needed was to be home with Mary and the other children. I saw it, even if he couldn't." Thelma shrugged. "I don't know what you think of me now, Jeanne, but I did have some standards for myself."

"I don't think anything." Jeanne realized how ridiculous her lie sounded, and tried again. "I can't understand what it was like for you."

"Did you love Charles?"

"Did I . . ." Jeanne had heard the question, but couldn't begin to think how to answer it. Of course she had loved him. From the moment they met, she'd found him easy to talk to; they never had a single argument. They were interested in so many of the same things.

"What I'm asking is, and I don't mean to pry into things that aren't my business. But did you *need* him?" Thelma pressed a fist to her stomach, and her expression was almost pained. "Did you feel like you'd die if you couldn't have him?"

"Thelma," Jeanne protested. She had allowed Charles to put his hands under her skirt, and there had been a moment—something about his warm, strong fingers splayed on the bare skin near the edge of her panties' elastic—when she'd felt something—a warmth, a sort of moving along an unfamiliar continuum.

But what Thelma was describing . . . Jeanne had felt a confusing rush of need only a few days ago, when she looked out the front window at Anthony Salvatici leaning against a car. She'd felt it for the first time when he set down the heavy urn and looked at her with an intensity she was certain no one had looked at her with before; she had felt seen—every part of her, the ones she kept secret as well as the ones she tried to hide even from herself. Watching him walk away, watching him drive out of view, was like gasping for breath. Thinking of Anthony—which she'd done every night—was like catching an intoxicating scent, only to have the breeze spirit it away.

Thelma's eyes bored into hers, and Jeanne understood that she was asking about the man who'd made love to her. The dalliance whose end had been the cold porcelain floor of the bathroom, slicked with blood. Jeanne dropped her gaze, her face aflame. With Ralph, it had never risen above affability, and the instinctive pleasure of warm skin on hers. That, and the taut anxiety when she placed her hand on his belt. It had been a kind of excitement—but not what Thelma had described.

"Well, all right, I guess I don't need to know. But for my part, all it took was that first time with Frank and I couldn't get enough. Don't look at me like that, Jeanne, because you weren't in my shoes. I had so little that was mine, you see. But when I was with him, for a few minutes I could forget everything else. And he felt it too, I know he did."

"I'm . . . sure he did."

"I didn't feel what we did was right," Thelma said, misunderstanding her hesitation for judgment. "I wouldn't let him talk to me about Mary, about what was wrong between them. But I know that he never felt like he escaped your father's shadow. It was hard for him. When we were together, I think he could forget all that for a while."

"Dad adored him," Jeanne said. "I don't know what Uncle Frank told you, but Dad would have given his right arm for him."

"I'm sure that's true. But sometimes I think it's possible to love someone too much. It makes you do things for them they'd be better off doing for themselves. And then they end up weak."

"Is that what you think happened to Uncle Frank? That *Dad* made him weak?"

"No, Jeanne, and there's no sense getting cross with me. I'm just trying to explain to you how things ended up the way they did. Your father was a good man. But Frank might have been a good man too, if things had been different. If he'd had a chance."

For a moment Jeanne didn't say anything, trying to picture Frank, with his pockets full of butterscotch candies and his mustache that curved up when he smiled.

The immense implications of Thelma's revelations ricocheted around Jeanne's mind, jumbling anew all the facets of the past. The things she thought she'd known were now distorted, like reflections in the mirror at the carnival.

Her father and Frank hadn't been as close as she'd believed. Frank had lied to them—even as her mother lay dying in the house her father bought for her. And Thelma . . . Thelma had known the truth all along. Was she, in her own way, just as culpable as Frank?

Jeanne rarely walked past the old mill because the memories of her father were still too painful, but she could envision every window, every brick in the arched entrance, every peeling letter in the painted sign.

The money from the sale of that building could have changed their lives. They wouldn't have lost their house. Jeanne could have hired help to care for her mother, could have gotten her all the best doctors.

She would have been free to marry Charles, back when he brought up the possibility in that first feverish year, before he heeded the call of the war.

That was the thing that galled the most. Jeanne had had to learn to force her bitterness into a manageable pill that she swallowed over and over. And still she could never forget that *she* had been meant to marry first, not Peggy. She'd had her entire wedding planned, had envisioned the gown she would sew down to the last detail, her mother's dress and her brides-maids'. Peggy would have been her maid of honor, holding her skirt while she walked down the aisle.

She would have had children, four or five of them.

"You knew all along," she said, her voice little more than a husk.

Thelma sighed heavily. She looked, for once, every one of her years. "I don't expect you to understand," she said. "Frank made it seem . . . Frank was confused himself, I think. Oh, Jeanne, I don't mean to make excuses for him. Or for me. Early on, when we first . . ."

Her voice drifted off and she stared out the window for a moment before continuing.

"I don't expect you to forgive me, Jeanne. When we were together, Frank made the kind of promises that men do. I was naïve then, and I wanted so badly to believe. And I think he believed what he was saying, at least some of the time. He talked about the future we could have together, one day. The mill would give us a chance to start over. We just had to wait until . . ."

Jeanne felt like she might be sick. "Until my mother died," she guessed.

Thelma's reluctant nod confirmed it. "Your mother never understood your father's will. Frank was to receive the mill only after her death and in the event that you girls married, and at the time your father had the will made, she was perfectly healthy. I'm sure your father thought it would see her through her old age."

"But she never got to be old."

"No. I know. But you have to understand," Thelma added quickly, "Frank and I . . . we never imagined how it would end up. You had Charles. Peggy and Thomas had only just begun dating and we thought—Frank said—"

Her face flamed with shame and she stared at her lap.

"What? Tell me, Thelma," Jeanne demanded.

"Frank said Thomas could come on board with him someday. When he had the new business up and running. You had Charles, Jeanne, you had a *doctor*. We thought you were going to be fine. Better than fine. All I wanted was for Thomas to be able to support a wife. A family."

Jeanne put her hands over her face and saw it clearly. Charles, coming home at night to their brood, while she served his dinner and did the dishes and bathed the children. There would be housekeepers eventually, of course; school recitals and charity drives, clubs and tennis. Charles would have flowers sent on their anniversary and her birthday. They would join the same club his parents belonged to.

All of that, everything she'd dreamed of, and the thought of it now made her feel like she was suffocating. She wasn't sure exactly what she wanted—not an attic room, and not a typing job, but something. Some existence that pushed so hard against the confines of what she knew that it broke clean through, into a future that was hers alone.

"Jeanne, please," Thelma said, as the silence stretched. Jeanne knew that Thelma thought she was angry, and she wanted to correct her, but had no words to describe the emotions inside her. "I was wrong. I know I was wrong."

"It's all right."

"I've . . . look, ever since Peggy came to live here, and then you, I've tried to make it up to you. If I could go back and do things differently—but I can't. If you want me out—if you don't want me to work at the mill, I'll understand."

"Tell me something," Jeanne said thoughtfully. "The doctor who took care of me. That place—that place where you took me. Is he . . . do you . . ."

"He's my lover, yes," Thelma said wearily. "If that's what you're asking."

"But he—but why did he take me there? To that house?"

"Oh, Jeanne," Thelma said, shaking her head. "Do you really need to know all this? Do you want to?"

"I want to know *everything*. If you're making me talk about these things, then I want to know all of it."

"All right, fine. I met Jack—Dr. Blaylock—last year when Dr. Swenson couldn't see me. It was when I had the shingles, just a follow-up."

"And you started—"

"It was an affair, Jeanne," Thelma said. "Neither of us wanted more. He's married. It was four times, five, I don't remember, it doesn't matter. Then he met that Ukrainian girl—she's a nurse's assistant—and that was the end of things between us. Only when I found you that day, I needed someone who would come right away, who wouldn't ask a lot of questions, do you get it? He took you to that house because he knew they wouldn't say anything. I imagine he gave the girl some money."

Jeanne followed the story with dizzy fascination. Was this the way things worked, outside the doors of her sheltered world? People meeting and doing things with each other, without a care for what other people would think . . . because they simply wanted to? Needed to? Was that what love really was—not a ring and a gown and letters kept in a ribbon-tied box, but what a person *felt* when she looked at her lover?

The doctor had been kind. His hands had been gentle.

And Thelma . . . if it hadn't been for her, Jeanne might have died. Thelma had saved her.

How could they be evil? Jeanne had cared so much about what people thought of her, had believed they could see all the way inside her, all her fears and failures and humiliations. Thelma had been the opposite—fearless, taking whatever she wanted, indifferent to what anyone thought.

But neither of them had been rewarded. It wasn't clear which of them fate favored, or if fate played any part at all. Thelma had offered her a chance, a new direction, without being honest about what it meant. Jeanne had accepted, without asking the questions she should have.

"Does Frank know that you were going to tell me all of this? The part about—about you and him?"

Thelma surprised her by laughing. "Of course not. He can't imagine I'd tell you because he thinks it would shame me."

And does it? Jeanne wanted to ask, but she chose a different question. "So he gets to keep the company? It stays in his name, and we're his employees?"

"Well . . ."

"Wait, I have a few more questions. Are we planning to keep producing woolens?"

"We have the looms," Thelma said. "The carding and spinning equipment. It would be a waste not to."

"I think we should do synthetics." Jeanne's mind was racing ahead. "Dacron's all over *Women's Wear Daily*, Thelma. There's huge demand, the existing supplies can't keep up, even with Dupont building factories all over the East Coast."

"Dacron? But that's just polyester. And you don't need an entire mill to make polyester. You could do it in a garage."

Jeanne knew it was true; she had seen the mom-and-pop operations herself, former gas stations in which pure petroleum was processed into fibers.

"I'm not talking about cheap polyester slips, Thelma. I'm

talking about high-end blends. We could do polyester and wool. Polyester and cotton."

"But who'd buy that?" Thelma asked. "You've seen what your sister wears. They're not doing anything polyester at the Crystal Salon."

"No, that's true. The European designers will be the last to try it, I imagine. But we're *Americans*, Thelma. Americans are innovators. Look at Sears! There's pages and pages of synthetic fabrics in the new catalog."

"But that's just housecoats and lingerie."

"Not for long, it's not. Once women see what a little polyester can do for a fabric—the drape, the wearability, the stain resistance—there will be no stopping it."

"Jeanne," Thelma said. "How on earth do you know all of this?"

Jeanne blew out a breath in frustration. "For the last five months I've been taking dictation from a man who can barely spell his own name. He's gone for hours at lunch, and nobody looks for me until he comes back. So I walk, Thelma. I go to the newsstands and I read the papers. I window shop. I look at things I can't afford to buy."

Thelma shook her head in admiration. "You're a smart girl, Jeanne. But what you're talking about . . . it's all new equipment. New processes. Hiring workers with new skills . . ."

"That's not all." Jeanne thought of the care Thelma had taken to save her, the home she had given her. "We're going to be partners."

"What do you mean?"

"We'll hire a lawyer. I want—I want half, for me and Peggy. A quarter for you and a quarter for Frank."

Thelma looked at her in astonishment. "Half of what, Jeanne? It's some dusty old buildings and equipment that we're not even going to use, if we do this your way. Where are we going to get the money to get started? How are we going to pay ourselves until we start making a profit?"

"Loans," Jeanne said, with more confidence than she felt. "We'll go to the bank."

Thelma was already shaking her head. "You're an unmarried woman," she said. "I'm a widow. No bank is going to give us the time of day."

Jeanne allowed herself a smile. "That's why Uncle Frank gets a quarter."

Peggy

On a tart autumn morning cool enough for a wrap, after exchanging their customary greeting, Lavinia surprised her. "You won't need the calendar this morning. We're going upstairs for a meeting."

"A meeting? With who?"

Lavinia gave her an unreadable smile. "You'll see. Come on, you don't need to bring anything."

As they walked through the store, up the elevators to the general manager's office, Peggy's curiosity turned to alarm. "What are we—"

"Mind your p's and q's," Lavinia said, with an uncharacteristic grin. "You're about to meet Archie Fyfe."

Archie Fyfe was the grandson of Prescott Fyfe, as every employee knew. Before Peggy could ask why she was being invited to meet the man in charge of the entire Fyfe's empire, Lavinia had whisked her inside the office overlooking the mall's courtyard. Seated at a polished conference table were two men and an elegantly dressed woman in her fifties.

"Peggy, you know Garrett McAuley, our general manager," Lavinia said, as the men rose from their seats.

Peggy recognized the shorter man with a shiny bald spot, but she was quite certain he had never noticed her.

"Mr. Fyfe," Lavinia continued. Archie Fyfe did not much resemble the photo that hung in the employee lounge. He was grinning, for one thing; and he'd gained weight since the photo was taken. He was wearing a three-button suit in a flecked beige tweed that would have flattered a younger and leaner man.

"And Mrs. Virginia Harris," Lavinia said. The elegant woman nodded coolly, but Peggy was too shocked to respond. Mrs. Harris . . . Jeanne's boss. She'd found out about the drawing—she knew that Jeanne had lied. Had she come here demanding that Peggy be fired?

"Peggy, please take a seat," Lavinia prompted, taking her own place next to Mr. McAuley.

"Ginny here has made a most unusual request," Mr. Fyfe said. "She came to see me with a drawing of a dress that she said you'd made, and asked us to produce it for her."

He opened a folder that was lying on the table. There was a drawing Peggy had made only a few weeks ago, of a fanciful ball gown loosely inspired by a pair of dresses she'd seen in the *Women's Wear Daily* coverage of the Paris shows. Ever since the Chambre Syndicale de la Haute Couture had begun requiring the Paris houses to present their collections to the press several years earlier, Peggy eagerly awaited the first photographs to appear in the American papers, because the trends that began in Paris inevitably ended up being adopted all over the world.

Peggy's drawing had been a caprice, a juxtaposition of a sleek velvet Givenchy column gown with Jacques Griffe's signature voluminous, poufy silhouette. Peggy had been pleased enough with the result to shade it with her colored pencils, and her version featured an obsidian velvet bodice and lean, pleated gold silk skirt—overlaid with a cloud-like bustle of vivid scarlet sashing over the hips.

"There's your signature," Lavinia said, tapping the corner of the page, where Peggy had dashed off her stylized "P. Holliman."

"That dress is a stunner, all right," Archie Fyfe said admiringly, lighting a cigarette with a gold lighter. "I'm no expert, but I think it's safe to say that Fyfe's has never sold a dress like that before."

No one had been meant to see that drawing. Peggy had

signed it almost as a joke, a plaintive reminder to herself that she drew for an audience of one. Her face burned with embarrassment and anger—Jeanne had not only pilfered another drawing, she'd evidently confessed the truth to Mrs. Harris.

But no one was mocking the dress. In fact, Ginny Harris had liked it.

"When your sister admitted to lying about the outfit she made me, I will admit that I was angry at first," Mrs. Harris said. "But then she explained about your mother."

Her mother?

"I didn't know, Peggy," Lavinia said, in a gentler tone than Peggy had ever heard her use before. "I do wish you had been comfortable confiding in me, dear. In the days ahead, should you need . . . extra time, we'll work it out."

"A hell of a thing, pancreatic cancer," Mr. Fyfe said, shaking his head. "Lost an uncle to it. Real sorry for your mother."

"She must be so proud of you," Mrs. Harris said. Turning to Mr. McAuley, she explained, "Mrs. Brink's lifelong dream was to see Peggy's talent recognized. That was why Jeanne made the outfit for the fashion show—she was just trying to help."

"She—she was so happy," Peggy said, scrambling to keep up as the pieces fell into place. She should have guessed that Jeanne would come up with a whopper to explain what she'd done—Jeanne always talked her way out of the jams she got into when they were younger, usually leaving Peggy to take the blame.

"Naturally, we understand that Jeanne had to quit working to care for your dear mother," Mrs. Harris said. "And Jeanne assumed that you would have to quit too. But she is *so* proud of your work here at Fyfe's—and that gave me an idea."

Of course she acted proud of me, Peggy thought, faintly queasy at the magnitude of the lie Jeanne had told—which gave her a convenient excuse to quit her job at Harris Carton, so she could go to work for Uncle Frank. She'd stolen the drawings to bolster the lie, thinking she was paving the way for both of them to make a graceful exit from their jobs.

"Mrs. Harris is convinced that what you've come up with is something entirely new," Lavinia said.

"You've got a unique talent, young lady," Mrs. Harris said.

"Ginny here knows her stuff," Mr. Fyfe said. "Don't suppose you happen to know what her maiden name was?"

"No, sir."

"Elliott. Her father is Gordon Elliott. Does that ring a bell?"

Peggy's head spun. The Elliott family held a minority interest in the store, though their main fortune was tied up in steel. Gordon Elliott's grandfather had served as New Jersey's lieutenant governor several decades earlier, and his descendants were still socially prominent.

"I'm so sorry, I had no idea. If I've overstepped—"

Mrs. Harris laughed, waving the comment away with her elegant, ringed hands. "Hardly."

"I've known Ginny for years," Mr. Fyfe said. "Our families summered together when we were kids. She and my wife are good friends. Anyway, she has made something of a campaign of convincing Fyfe's management to give you a new role."

Peggy was still recovering from Jeanne's lie, trying to understand what it meant for her. To have one of her designs produced for an actual department store—even a design such as this, which Peggy had never intended as a serious piece—was more than she had ever dared to imagine. "Are you saying you would create the dress for the salon?"

"Eh, no," Archie said, puffing on his cigarette before crushing it out on the heavy crystal ashtray on the table. "The economics don't make sense. Our margins on imported couture aren't something that can be replicated domestically. But what we do well, what we'd like to do more of—we want to offer something really distinctive to the Fyfe's ready-to-wear customer."

"A branded collection," Lavinia explained. "All American. Not only are we not trying to duplicate anything being done in the European houses, but we want to make a statement—that American fashion suits American women."

"That's pretty good, Lavinia," Mr. Fyfe said. "'American fashion suits American women'—do me a favor and write that down for me."

"Imagine this," Mrs. Harris said, holding up a finger and drawing an imaginary scroll in the air. "*Peggy Parker Originals.* I think it works a bit better than 'Holliman,' don't you?"

"Your own line, Peggy," Fyfe explained. "Under the Fyfe's label, of course. I'd take credit, but Helen Perkins put the bug in my ear after Ginny called her too. You would design for the store—perhaps half a dozen pieces for the inaugural collection and then we'd see how it goes."

"You mean . . ." Peggy felt faint at the suggestion, and at the fact that Miss Perkins had put in a good word for her. "I would have the freedom to design whatever I wanted? And it would be sold in the stores?"

"Yes, in limited release. The collection would be debuted in Philadelphia, though Ginny insists that she would have her pick of it here in Plainsfield."

"I'd—I'd be in charge of the whole line?"

"Well, yes and no. You're still green, I think you'll agree. We'd arrange for you to meet with our manufacturer's reps. And the marketing department would review everything before any decisions were made. Honestly, for the first season, we probably won't deviate much from what we've got on the drawing board. Our existing suppliers won't have any trouble with a limited release, but we'll need to focus on growth right from the start. Because if this is successful, then we'd need to be prepared to produce the collection in far greater numbers, for distribution to all the stores. It would be exclusive to Fyfe's, of course." He drummed on the table with his fingers. "How is this sounding to you so far?"

"I'm—I have no idea what to say," Peggy said. "I mean, yes. *Yes.* I don't even know how to begin to thank you."

Jeanne had only been trying to cover her tracks; Ginny Harris, never imagining the implications of the gesture, had put something much bigger in motion. Peggy had lied when she led Lavinia to believe that Tommie was her niece—not her own child. Jeanne had lied when she made Mrs. Harris's outfit for the fashion show, pretending the design was her own; and again when she offered Mrs. Harris the drawing of the gown. All of the lies that led to this moment had one thing in common—they left no room for Tommie. And yet Peggy had just said yes to the tantalizing offer, as eagerly as Judas had accepted the silver coins. And just as Judas must have felt the weight of all of that silver in his hands, Peggy tasted the implications of her words that still echoed in the room.

"It's Ginny you should thank," Fyfe was saying. "Her and my wife, and Miss Perkins and Miss Cole here. Hell, we all agree this place could use a little fresh blood. As long as you don't start coming after my job."

"I never, I wouldn't—" Peggy said, as Fyfe chuckled.

"It's all right. I like you, young lady. You've got a heck of a future. Free of the distraction of marriage and children . . . frankly, we could use more gals like you." Fyfe slid a business card across the table. "I think that about does it for now. Until we see if this takes off, of course, you'll stay here in Plainsfield, and continue reporting to Lavinia. But if the response to the first collection is good, we'll talk about moving you over to the flagship store."

"I haven't told your sister any of this," Mrs. Harris said, looking extremely pleased with herself. "I thought you might want to do that yourself."

Lavinia stood. The meeting was over. Somehow, Peggy managed to get through the goodbyes and follow her back to their own office, where she collapsed in her chair.

"Naturally, you'll need to keep this all to yourself for now," Lavinia said, opening the date book as though she hadn't just turned Peggy's life completely upside down. "We've got plenty to do here until I can figure out who can take over some of your duties."

"Lavinia, I think I'm dreaming."

"No, dear, you're not. You've got talent. Mrs. Harris knows you were made for better things than kneeling on the floor with pins in your mouth. And, of course, once she found out about your mother she wanted to help. But just imagine—down the road, you could get a darling little flat in Center City."

Down the road, after her long-dead mother expired. "I just . . . I've never lived anywhere but Roxborough and Brunskill."

"I know it's a lot to think about, but there would be a raise involved."

Peggy tried to focus her many emotions. If this really did happen, there were many steps to be taken before the first collection debuted. It would be a full eight months before the pieces could be made available in the store, another few months until they could assess the sales data. By then, Tommie would be a first-grader, in school from eight-thirty in the morning until three o'clock in the afternoon.

There had to be a way to make it work.

"I'm honored," she said. "I never dreamed that I would have an opportunity like this."

"Well, keep it under your hat for now," Lavinia said. "Mr. Fyfe is a bit of a loose cannon. I'm not saying he didn't mean the offer, but as you could probably tell from what he was wearing, the finer points of fashion tend to escape him. And we still have the entire fall season to sell. Not to mention the fact that you know how gossip travels among the girls. They already resent you for your success. If they get wind of this, there's likely to be an all-out revolt."

PEGGY FOUND TOMMIE in the backyard, riding her tricycle around the tiny patch of lawn while Jeanne sat in one of the metal chairs with a stack of papers in her lap. All Peggy could think of, staring at her sister, was the lie that Jeanne had told, thinking that Peggy would never know.

"Mommy, look!" Tommie said, as she pedaled as fast as she could, only to lift her feet from the pedals and coast into the shrubs separating their yard from the neighbors'.

"Hurray!" Peggy cried, clapping her hands. Tommie clambered off the tricycle and ran over for a hug.

"It's nearly four," Jeanne said, annoyed. "You said you'd be back early today. I've got all these bids to go through. Thelma and I need to make a decision about the tuck-pointing."

"I'm sorry," Peggy said. She couldn't tell Jeanne what had happened yet—not when she'd promised to quit her job at Fyfe's by the end of the month, when the mill was slated to reopen. Three weeks—she had three more weeks to figure out how she was going to handle Tommie and the job, all on her own. "Thank you so much for watching her."

Jeanne said nothing as she went back to the paperwork.

Peggy desperately wanted to confront her about the lie. *How could you say those things about Mother*, she wanted to know. How could Jeanne have used those terrible months, when the house they grew up in echoed with their mother's stifled moans of pain, to concoct her ruse?

There was a coldness to her sister that she hadn't seen before, a willingness to say and do things Peggy would have once thought beyond her capacity for calculation. As a child, Jeanne had thought nothing of lying about a spilled glass of milk or a broken dish, blaming Peggy with stunning indifference. But Peggy had always assumed that was simply the way of sisters, especially sisters as close as they had been.

Now, she watched Jeanne for signs of change. When had she hardened, when had she become so calculating? Had any of it been true—had Jeanne thought of her when she showed the drawing to Mrs. Harris, had she felt any pride in Peggy's talent?

All of their lives, Jeanne had effortlessly earned the admiration and envy of others. Peggy chafed at the knowledge that despite her popularity and her accomplishments, Jeanne could be as petty and selfish as any other girl. Jeanne's specialness had been accepted for so long, by their parents, their classmates, their teachers, that Peggy had begun to believe it herself— and its inverse, that she was lesser, standing next to her sister's bright light.

I've been offered my own line of clothing, she longed to say. *I matter too.*

But Tommie wandered away from the tricycle, wiping her hands on the dress she'd worn to school, the dress Jeanne should have made her change out of when she got home, except that Jeanne was busy with her own plans, her own schemes.

"Mommy, I'm *starving*," Tommie said mournfully.

"All right, darling, we'll have a little something to tide you over." She really ought to insist that Tommie wait—she barely fit into any of her clothes, and as they all got busier they had taken to pacifying her with sweets and crackers. But Peggy didn't have the energy for an argument. Not today.

"Three weeks," Jeanne called after them as they reached the back door, and Peggy stopped with her hand on the handle, biting back her retort. The lie Jeanne told had given her this chance. Did that make it wrong? Or could she, for once in her life, seize the chance she'd been given?

PEGGY WAS EATING lunch at her desk as she usually did, paging through the latest *Harper's Bazaar* and nibbling at the cottage cheese plate she'd had sent down from the lunchroom, when one of the runners poked her head shyly into the office.

"Excuse me, Peggy, I'm sorry to disturb you."

Peggy gazed at her coolly, dabbing at the corners of her mouth with her napkin. This awkward, strawberry-blond girl was the most deferential of the staff, but she was also hopeless at her job: impossibly shy, she could barely look at the clients when she brought out their garments.

"It's all right, Mavis," Peggy said generously. "What can I do for you?"

"There's a woman in the waiting room who doesn't have an appointment."

"You know we can't accommodate her this week. Tell her that we are simply unable to find room in the schedule and send her downstairs. Nicely, please."

"I know that, Peggy, and I did try to tell her, but she was very . . . insistent. She says she is a personal friend of yours."

Peggy's fingers stilled. Slowly, she lowered the napkin to her lap. "Did you get her name?"

"Yes. She said you'd know her by her maiden name, Rose Scopes. She says you were in the AWVS together."

"I see." As calmly as she was able, Peggy pretended to look at her watch. "I vaguely remember a girl with that name. Well, I suppose I could take the rest of my lunch with her. Please let Lavinia know that I might be a bit late."

"Of course, Peggy . . . thank you."

Peggy sat for a moment in the quiet office, her appetite completely gone. Of course she remembered Rose Scopes, Rose with the narrow face and uneven teeth, the beautiful wavy red hair.

Those days in the American Women's Voluntary Services, when she and Jeanne and dozens of other Roxborough girls had hemmed sheets for hospitals and collected scrap metal and paper for the war, were a blur all these years later. She remembered smoking together out on the steps of the side entrance to the USO building, and Rose's red ponytail bobbing when she laughed, which was often. Rose had been sharp as a whip, if catty toward most of the other girls, but she and Peggy had gotten on fine. After their scrap-sorting shifts, she and Rose would sometimes stay late and help clean up, and Rose brought a little silver flask in her purse, and when everyone else had gone home and the USO hall was shut tight and locked for the night, they would sit on the steps and look up at the stars and marvel that thousands of miles away, the same stars shone down on the soldiers on the other side of the world.

They'd talked about other things too, when the whiskey was gone and the night grew cold but they couldn't bear to go back to the lives that were theirs now, lives of waiting and not knowing, lives that were more absence than presence.

Peggy stood and dumped the remains of her lunch into the wastebasket, and set the plate on her desk, where one of the girls would retrieve it and take it back to the cafeteria.

Outside in the waiting area, one hunched figure seemed to fade into the shiny gold brocade cushions of her chair. It took Peggy a moment to confirm that it really was her. Rose had lost at least twenty pounds and with them the pleasant roundness that had made up for her small, sharp features: a narrow, pointed nose, eyes set too close, a thin, compressed mouth. Her hair was no longer the gay red, but a dull brown, sagging from a careless set. Rose's blue cotton dress had been tailored by someone not nearly as adept with a needle as Jeanne, the waistband tacked in lumpy folds, the neckline gapping over bony shoulders.

"Peggy," Rose rasped. Even her voice seemed worn down by the intervening years. Her smile revealed a broken tooth, which she tried unsuccessfully to cover with her hand. "Look at you."

Peggy did just that. She looked down at herself, at the voluminous sleeves and gathered hip panels of an ivory day dress that had been made for a client who discovered she was expecting for the second time and canceled her entire order. She knew she looked chic and pretty.

She looked back up at Rose. "Let's take a walk."

PEGGY LED THEM down St. Georges Street, away from the Community Square and into the long tree-shaded avenues with their sprawling old homes.

Neither spoke until they reached the bus stop at the corner. The noon bus had come and gone, and there wouldn't be another for several hours. This was as good a place as any. "Why don't we sit for a moment?" she asked politely, as if Rose were a guest in her living room, and they settled onto the bench.

"So, Rose," Peggy said, "what's new with you these days?"

Rose shrugged. "Nothing you probably want to know about. I married Dickie, I guess you can tell." She held up her left hand, where a thin gold band spun loose on her ring finger. The little diamond solitaire, of which she'd been so proud back then, was gone. "I've got two boys now. Ricky's three and Sid is two."

"How wonderful," Peggy said. "Congratulations."

She wondered if they'd inherited their father's coarse, dark hair and stubby limbs. She'd never met Dickie, but during those AWVS shifts all the girls passed around pictures of boyfriends and fiancés and husbands. These photographs were the currency of their lives as the ones who were left behind; they were the threads that united the girls.

"*Congratulations,*" Rose echoed in a mocking tone. "Well, thanks a lot."

Silence stretched between them.

"How's Jeanne?" Rose said after a while, taking a pack of cigarettes from her purse. She offered it to Peggy, who shook her head. She hadn't smoked since Tommie was born.

"Jeanne is fine," Peggy said. "How kind of you to remember her."

"And she never married?"

"No . . . not yet."

"Of course not. She was so very devoted to Charles."

The hairs along Peggy's forearms tingled. Fear clogged her throat. "She was."

"And do you miss Thomas, Peggy? Do you still think about him?"

The fear thinned and spun, curdling with anger. "What do you want?"

"Me?" This time when Rose smiled, she didn't bother to conceal the broken tooth. Now that they were outside, Peggy could make out other evidence of damage in Rose's face. Tiny broken capillaries traced red lines that she had been unable to cover up with makeup. A faint yellow patch on her neck looked as though it might have been a bruise. "Why, I've got everything I could ask for. A husband and kids. Isn't that what we always said we wanted, Pegs? Only, it's not quite what we thought it would be. I hate to tell you that. To take away the dream. And you a widow and all. But having your husband come back from the war . . . it's not what I thought it would be."

Peggy didn't know what to say to that. She watched Rose exhale twin wisps of smoke through her narrow nostrils and wished she'd said yes to a cigarette.

"He has dreams. Bad ones. Sometimes he doesn't sleep at all. He says drinking is the only way to make it stop, but some days he's drinking before he goes to work. When he can keep a job, that is. Do you know how many jobs he's had since the war?"

"I thought he went back to Sears," Peggy said stupidly. Before the war, he'd been an assistant manager at the Wayne branch.

"Oh, *that*," Rose laughed. "No, Peggy, he's not at Sears. He worked at the Ford dealership for a while. Now he's working as a mechanic. But he's already had a reprimand. And . . . anyway, you don't want to hear our troubles. I came here to ask you if you remembered those talks we used to have. Dickie loves to hear about them. Sometimes, on a good night, he wants to know all about what happened to the girls I knew. I like to keep him talking, you know. It's better that way."

She kept her gaze fixed intently on Peggy. Peggy refused to squirm or blink, even though she could feel perspiration popping out along her hairline, under her arms.

"We need money, Peggy," Rose said abruptly, crushing her cigarette on the bench. "Dickie sent me to ask you. He says he thinks you won't mind. What with your fancy job, and having help with your baby. It must be so nice to have help. Your mother-in-law and your sister. You got on well with Thomas's mother, as I recall."

"Yes," Peggy whispered, because Rose's purpose was suddenly, horribly clear.

"You must be a great comfort to her. After losing her son, at least she has you and the baby. Her granddaughter."

"I don't have a lot of money."

Rose laughed, throwing her head back so that the dress gapped even more and Peggy could see that the bruise purpled farther down. She wanted to leap up off the bench and run and keep running until she'd left Rose far, far behind—where she should have stayed in the first place. Those days were over. They had been nothing but a dream, anyway—a cotton-fluff intermission between the lives that came before and after.

"Well, Dickie and I don't need a lot. Only what we deserve, for helping you keep this pretty little life you've made for yourself."

❀ ❀ ❀

PEGGY LEFT WORK early that afternoon, claiming cramps. She could see the relief in the eyes of some of the girls. Unease had replaced envy among them as Peggy learned from studying Lavinia how to distance herself from them, how to assign each the right responsibilities to keep her compliant, to know when to join in their gossip and when to keep herself apart.

"Have a nice evening, Peggy," one of the salesgirls called after her, but Peggy barely heard.

This numbness stayed with her all the way home. On the walk from the bus, she looked into the windows of the homes she passed, seeing families gathering at the dinner table, men and women going about their lives together. Had she ever really wanted what they had? Rose had reminded her of a time when they'd looked ahead and envisioned domestic happiness. But all it had ever been was a girlish game, a version of the rope-skipping rhyme they played in childhood: *A my name is Alice, my husband's name is Al, we live in Arizona and we bring back apples.*

She walked into the house and set down her purse before she noticed that Thelma and Jeanne had set the table with the good linens, the china plates that had belonged to Thelma's mother. A roast chicken sat cooling on the counter.

"Surprise!" Tommie said, barreling out from the bedroom. She was wearing a little paper crown that Thelma had cut from paper and allowed Tommie to decorate with her crayons. "Uncle Frank is coming to dinner!"

"Tommie," Thelma scolded. "Please don't run in the house. I've asked you a dozen times."

"Frank is coming here?" Peggy echoed. "Tonight?"

So far, Frank's return to their lives seemed strangely formal and cloaked in the details of the venture from which she had been excluded. She had not laid eyes on her uncle since their mother's funeral seven years ago. He had sent a silver-plated serving tray after she married Thomas, but the card had been written in Aunt Mary's hand.

She'd never really missed him during those years—during

the war, no one had the appetite for social gatherings, and then afterward, their grief created a gulf that seemed impossible to cross—but now, looking back, Peggy felt petulant and resentful. The fact that her uncle had decided to reopen the mill seemed in poor taste to Peggy, an insult to her father's memory. Frank was just one minor feature of a tableau that Peggy had assumed would be forever frozen in time—and his return had also occasioned the crisis she was currently trying to navigate.

"Someone could have told me in advance," she snapped. "I had no idea we were having company."

Thelma and Jeanne exchanged a glance. "Go to your room, honey," Thelma told Tommie. "This is grown-up conversation."

Tommie looked to Peggy, deflated, before trudging off, the crown sliding off her head.

"It's . . . a bit more complicated than just dinner," Jeanne said when Tommie had closed the door. "Frank is coming to sign some papers."

"What kind of papers?"

"Articles of incorporation," Thelma said, pointing to the little desk she had set up in the corner of the dining room, where she'd put the boxes she'd brought up from the basement. "For the mill."

Peggy looked from Thelma to Jeanne. They were behaving strangely, but then again Peggy had made a point of staying as far out of their undertaking as possible. It may have been childish to pretend that if she just ignored it, the reality would go away; but with the completion of the renovations, the delivery of the equipment, and the hiring of the workers under way, it was getting increasingly difficult to pretend that change wasn't headed her way like a steamroller.

"What does that mean?" she asked. "And what does that have to do with you?"

"It means," Thelma said firmly, taking the cooling pan of chicken from the stove, "that we are formally creating a partnership. You and Jeanne and I will own a majority of the new company."

"And Frank too, of course," Jeanne said. "This is about all of us."

"*What* is?" Peggy demanded. "How can we be *owners* of the mill? Dad left it all to Frank."

"It turns out that he actually left it to us," Jeanne said. "You and me. It all got mixed up after Mother died and—and anyway, what matters now is that we own the mill together, and we're going to get it running again."

"Wait a minute," Peggy said, the familiar rushing in her head making it hard to think. Yet again, Jeanne had lied to her—or held back the truth. "When did you find that out? That we own it?"

Jeanne was already shaking her head. "Only very recently. It wasn't something that—"

"So let me understand. Dad left it to us—to me and you—but now Thelma and Frank are going to own part of it too? Who decided all of this? And what about Tommie?"

"But that's just it," Jeanne said. Her face had drained of color, the way it always did when she was nervous, and she was talking faster. "All of this is for Tommie, and you, and our future. Once we get it going again, and we start to make money, we can set some aside for Tommie's education. We won't need your income, and there'll be enough to fix the roof and buy a new furnace and—"

"But I still don't understand," Peggy said coldly, because she was beginning to understand all too well. "How could Frank, and Thelma, how could they make decisions about something that you say belongs to *me*? How could you do all of this without ever telling me? Without asking me what I think?"

There was a silence, as Jeanne wouldn't meet her eyes, and Thelma stood with her hands on her hips, looking like she was spoiling for a fight.

"You've been so busy," Jeanne finally said. "And this—it all kind of just happened. No one ever wanted to deceive you, Peggy."

"And yet, you have."

She listened as Jeanne described how there had been a mix-up in the deed, how Frank had been thinking of opening up again for a while but when he began looking into bringing the production line up to date, he discovered his error.

"That seems like an awfully big mistake to overlook," Peggy said. None of this sounded right—Uncle Frank had sworn when he closed the business that he was done with textiles for good.

"We need Frank," Jeanne said. "The banks won't talk to us without him. And we need his connections to hire the production workers, and to get into Dad's old accounts."

"Well, it seems like you have this all figured out," Peggy

snapped. She had been working up to telling the others about the offer she'd received from Archie Fyfe—but they'd been withholding an even bigger secret from her.

"I know you aren't happy about having to quit your job," Jeanne said. "But don't you see that this is the solution for all of us? That job at Fyfe's barely pays you anyway."

"And everything you're doing for Fyfe's, you can do for us," Thelma said. "You can even design the sample sheets. You could make up a little catalog. And when Tommie gets older, maybe you could work on sales with Jeanne. Or I could teach you bookkeeping."

There was something pitying in her tone, and Peggy realized that they must have had many conversations to figure all of this out—and all without her. The old familiar hurt returned: in high school, Jeanne excluded her from her friendships, her interests, saying she was too young and too irresponsible to be included. Even their parents had never consulted her on the kinds of decisions they discussed with Jeanne.

Peggy knew she'd brought at least part of that on herself, with her impulsivity, her recklessness. But it had never felt like she had a choice: she could never be smart or successful or popular like Jeanne, so she'd settled for being the life of the party, the outrageous one. She gained her parents' attention by acting up when she couldn't get it by impressing them.

And now they were offering her scraps, trying not to hurt her feelings. A few hours filing or sketching dresses could never make up for the feeling of *mattering*, of doing something important, of making her own way in the world.

Peggy thought of all the ways the job had changed her life—the time to herself on the trolley, the coffee waiting for her in the porcelain pot, the way the other girls deferred to her, the closet full of beautiful clothes—and felt despair. She couldn't go back to being a pale ghost who haunted this pathetic little house, an inadequate mother, a petulant sister. For the first time in her life she had something she was proud of, and it was all about to be snatched away.

"Well, I have some news of my own. I've been offered a new position," she blurted. "In the Philadelphia store. They want me to design a line of ready-to-wear. A signature collection."

Now it was Thelma and Jeanne's turn to gape at her.

"You? But why?" Jeanne demanded.

She could have told them about the meeting, about Mrs. Harris and Mr. Fyfe. She could have confronted Jeanne with the fact that she knew about the lies. But suddenly none of that mattered. Nothing mattered, except that she had been given a chance—a glorious chance—to have something that was all her own. "They want someone new, someone fresh," she said. "They want to project youth, an all-American feel for modern women who can't afford couture."

Thelma regarded her skeptically. "You're one rung above shopgirl. And there are girls pouring out of the Fashion Institute all the time, girls with degrees. Why not one of them?"

Because I'm good, Peggy wanted to say—but deep down she wondered if it was true. Shame prickled at her, reminding her that it was luck—pure chance, and Jeanne's unintended interference. "It's only an experiment," she settled for saying. "If the first season fails, they won't have lost anything—I can go back to working at the Crystal Salon."

"And what are you going to tell your daughter?" Thelma asked. "How do you plan to explain to her that this job is more important than she is?"

Peggy looked from her mother-in-law to her sister and understood that there was no way to answer that question. They would never understand—she barely understood it herself. Something was wrong with her. She loved her daughter—loved her more than she cared for her own life—she just couldn't stand to be around her all day long, day in and day out.

If Peggy took the job, they would never forgive her.

There would be no line of her own. No office in the flagship store, no stationery printed with her name. She'd never know the thrill of seeing her designs produced and sold to real customers. Desperately, Peggy shuffled her prospects in her mind, trying to salvage something. She couldn't give up her job. Couldn't return to being nothing more than a wife with no husband, a mother with no future.

"I—I'll talk to Lavinia and see if I can do the job part-time," she said. "I'll use my own money to hire someone to watch Tommie when I need to."

"Your own money?" Thelma echoed. "While Jeanne and I work to pay for everything in this house? If I didn't know better, I'd say you didn't want to be with your own daughter. You'll have your time, Peggy. Tommie won't be a child forever."

"I know that," Peggy snapped. Tears threatened, and she couldn't bear to cry in front of them. Crying would show them the broken place inside her. Crying would only support what they already suspected: that she didn't love Tommie enough. She cast her gaze frantically around the little house, but there was nowhere to retreat. "I—I'll be back."

She raced for the door. Tommie ran out of the bedroom after her, and Peggy realized she'd been eavesdropping the whole time.

"Mommy, don't go!" Tommie cried. "Take me with you!"

But Peggy went out into the night and shut the door behind her, silencing her child, the constant reminder that she could never be enough.

Thelma

Tommie could not be consoled. Thelma knew it was because she was overtired, riled up, and didn't eat what she was given for dinner—but none of that helped. It was impossible not to remember the look on Peggy's face when she realized that she was going to have to give up her job and stay home. Even a child would have some understanding of what was going on.

Thelma held Tommie's twisting, fevered little body, wishing they'd been more careful not to let her overhear. She spoke soothingly even when Tommie's elbow connected painfully with her jaw, when she screamed right next to her ear.

"I want to go with *Mommy*!" she wailed over and over again. "I don't *want* you! I hate you!"

"Do you want me to take her, Thelma?" Jeanne asked.

"No, I'm fine."

Jeanne had never been a mother. She made a fine aunt, but she didn't have the experience to understand the child's words for what they really were: uncertainty and need, her growing independence in conflict with her attachment to a mother who was gone more than she was home.

It wasn't the same thing, of course, but Thelma remembered how it was with Thomas. Henry worked long hours and then frequently went to the tavern at night. There were stretches—weeks at a time, sometimes—when he barely saw his son.

Thomas became inconsolable, in the interminable late afternoons when it was too early for dinner and Thelma's patience was worn thin. He screamed for his father, threw his toys, refused to eat. Thelma had tried to be matter-of-fact, swatting Thomas's behind with a wooden spoon or locking him in his bedroom, where he kicked his door until he collapsed, exhausted, sometimes falling asleep on the floor just inside the door. But when Henry came home she tamped down her resentment and weariness, pleading with him to spend time with his son.

"What does it matter?" he'd scoffed when Thelma confronted him. "Kid won't remember a thing when he's older."

And that had certainly been true. Once, a few weeks after Henry's death, Thelma had asked Thomas what he remembered most about his father. The details Thomas recounted—a balsa wood airplane model they'd made in the garage, the annual tradition of penciling Thomas's height on the kitchen doorframe—were not untrue. His fierce love for his father, Thelma knew, was genuine.

"But didn't it bother you?" she couldn't resist asking. "That Dad was gone so much?"

Thomas had stared at her blankly. "Everyone's fathers are gone a lot."

It was a hard truth about her son that she would never share with anyone else. A dead son was eternally heroic and no mother could allow his memory to be otherwise, but if Thomas had come home from the war, if he'd married Peggy and they'd had more children, he would have been just like his own father: an indifferent presence when his children were infants, a distant figure in their adolescence; interested, finally, only when they were teens. And he only would ever have been comfortable with boys. Tommie would have been perplexing to her father until the day he married her off.

A rogue wave of sympathy for Peggy hit Thelma. As unhelpful as Henry had been, at least Thomas had had two parents. Peggy had no man to share her burden with, and though Thelma knew that she and Jeanne did far more for Tommie than any man ever would, she also understood that Peggy was pinned to her life like a moth to a board.

"She'll be back soon," Jeanne tried, as Tommie wiped her nose on Thelma's blouse. "She didn't mean anything by—the things she said."

There Jeanne went, defending Peggy. Thelma had mixed

feelings about the sisters' relationship. After all, it was Thelma who'd accommodated Peggy's moods and forgiven her lapses. Jeanne didn't see inside people the way Thelma did, didn't understand their motivations and needs. Jeanne loved her sister dearly, but she didn't *know* Peggy, couldn't read the need on her that was as plain as paint to Thelma.

No, Jeanne didn't understand people. But she would thrive in their new venture, which would run on schedules and numbers and deadlines. She'd grow as the business grew. Perhaps, someday, there would be a suitor, a man who was plainspoken and firm, who would treat her like a lady. When that time came, Thelma would do her best to help.

For now, however, Jeanne could not give what Tommie needed. Which left Thelma at this familiar crossroads yet again, having to decide just how much of herself she could afford to give.

"I'll put her down in my bed," she said wearily. Tommie had finally worn herself out and was fast asleep, draped like a drowned kitten on Thelma's chest. "She can sleep with me tonight."

That night, when she finally got into bed next to her sleeping grandchild, Thelma thought about how if things had worked out differently, she might be lying in the guest room of a pretty house where her son came home every night to his devoted wife. There would be a corsage on Mother's Day; her help would be appreciated in the kitchen.

Instead she was here—in this same tired old house, with the worn floorboards and leaning porch and faded curtains, where she had spent nearly three decades of her life. Her husband and her son were dead. But Tommie lay curled up next to her, sighing in her sleep, and that felt like a second chance.

Peggy

Peggy walked for hours along the streets of Brunskill, memories her only companions.

She'd once strolled these same streets with her mother and sister, and strangers had stopped to compliment Emma Brink on her daughters' charm and beauty. Peggy hadn't known then how vast the world was, how difficult the challenges were beyond the boundaries of her sheltered life. Perhaps that was why some girls never left Roxborough: if they'd grown accustomed to being special, if they needed praise like they needed air and water, then staying here could give them that, after a fashion. In the city there were lots of successful men and beautiful women; but there was also opportunity, a chance at money and fame, if you were strong enough to take the gamble.

Peggy believed she was strong enough.

She'd done well so far, hadn't she? Who would ever have guessed that Peggy Brink would get as far as she already had? She'd worked hard and taken every opportunity that came her way.

Why, then, did the fates keep conspiring to knock her down?

It wasn't fair. Long after midnight, Peggy stood in the shadow cast by a streetlight, staring through the windows of Mortimer Jewelers. Thomas had bought her engagement ring here, on a layaway plan. The little platinum ring with its row of diamond chips was tucked safely in her jewelry box now. Someday, it would belong to Tommie.

In the jewelry counter at Fyfe's, there were no rings as modest as hers. There were diamond solitaires big enough to choke on, pins and bracelets encrusted with rubies and emeralds and jade. Peggy had felt only a twinge of disappointment all those years ago when Thomas slipped the ring on her finger. But now? Now she would have expected more.

It wasn't *fair.*

Why had she been delivered into the elegance of the Crystal Salon if it was all to be snatched away from her? Why would God encourage her gifts if He only meant to squash them, to force her back into domestic drudgery? Why had He given her a child at all, if she was to have to bear the responsibility alone?

Immediately Peggy felt chastened. She had Thelma and she had Jeanne. Far less was required of her than of many, many other mothers.

And still it was too much.

She walked on. At the butcher shop she paused again, staring inside at the sausages hanging from the ceiling, the cold cases wiped down and covered for the night. She inhaled the peppery, spicy aromas with their faintly rotten undertones. Rose Scopes, it occurred to her, was like a chop that had turned. Bad meat gave off a smell that Mother Nature intended as a warning; eat it anyway and She would not be responsible for the consequences.

Rose had been turned, had gone bad. It wasn't her fault. A husband who beat her, poverty she hadn't counted on, children who sucked the life from her—no wonder she was nothing but a decrepit husk. But she was dangerous too. She had the power and the will to lash out at Peggy, if she didn't get what she wanted.

Peggy could not allow her to win.

She walked on, along the river, past humble homes giving way to shacks. Across the river was the neighborhood where months earlier, Jeanne's life had been saved by a stranger. Peggy was cold, the damp air seeping into her shoes, her glove-less hands. But as she shivered, her resolve grew. She would not allow Rose to hurt her. She would take care of Rose, and then she would turn her attention to the problem of Tommie. If only she could convince the others to simply sell the factory—if only she hadn't noticed the stirring of excitement in Thelma's eyes. There were few things, Peggy knew well, as dangerous as an ambitious woman.

But that was supposed to have been *her* role in the family.

When she finally returned home, the house was quiet. Jeanne was asleep on the sofa, her face to the cushions, her knees pulled up to her chest so that she almost looked like a sleeping child. The door to Thelma's room was closed and Tommie's bed was empty.

Guilt nagged at Peggy as she prepared for bed. Another woman had cared for her child while she had been out, walking for hours.

But she slept well that night.

Five

Ninon

The French invented ninon, of course, because who else would have the patience for its delicacy, its tendency to catch on every little thing? If you must use it, consider a nylon blend, at least. Then you won't have spent a fortune only to rip it on your date's cuff link as he leads you off the dance floor.

In 1947, or maybe it was 1948, there was a beautiful rose-colored silk ninon in a fabric store on Eighth Avenue. It had a tone-on-tone embroidered edge that almost called to mind Lyons lace. It was a bolt end, so it languished—but eventually someone bought it, just to have it folded in a drawer, to take it out and look at it from time to time.

Be warned, however: printed rayon ninon will never look anything but cheap.

Though some girls seem to like that.

October *1949*

Peggy

Rose waited two weeks before contacting Peggy again.

An envelope arrived for her at work, a sheet of cheap stationery folded with a newspaper clipping.

It was the notice that had run in the Brunskill *Morning News*, announcing that the former Brink Mills would be operating as Charming Mills, producer of fine textiles for the garment industry. Jeanne was listed as the "Representative Director and President."

The accompanying note was short, written in a spidery, tremulous hand.

"Congratulations on your new Family business. Like we talked about, please send Twenty dollars to this address in a plain envelope. Cash. I think this is very fair. Every two weeks unless you hear from me again."

Peggy quickly refolded the papers and stuffed them into her purse. On the one hand, twenty dollars was not an enormous amount of money. If she cut out the little luxuries she'd enjoyed since her promotion—the new stockings and beauty salon hairstyles and restaurant lunches—she could cover it from her paycheck.

On the other hand, what did that money buy? It wasn't like

the installment plan with which their mother had once purchased a silver tea service: after paying Rose for months—or even years—she would own nothing. Rose couldn't unlearn her secret. No pledge of silence was worth a dime if she ever decided to tell what she knew.

Paying her was not the way.

An idea had begun to form, one that shamed Peggy as much as it appealed to her as a possible solution.

What if she and Tommie simply left? What if, come Sunday, she were to wait until the others had gone to church, claiming that Tommie had a fever, and pack her suitcase with a few dresses and notebooks? She had enough saved in her dresser drawer for a deposit on a little apartment. She'd promised Lavinia an answer by the end of the week. What if that answer was yes?

Fyfe had suggested that if her line ever became a hit, she might be moved to the flagship store in Philadelphia. But what if she were to move there now and commute to Plainsfield? If she found someone to take care of Tommie during the day—perhaps a woman with children of her own—then why should it matter where she lived? She could give Tommie things in Philadelphia that she would never have here in Brunskill. Culture—they'd visit the museums and the symphony. Travel, perhaps. A better education than she could get at St. Katherine's or even Miss Kittering's.

And she could laugh in Rose's face. "So tell them," she imagined saying. "Tell them everything."

But at the thought, a chasm opened inside her, and her

bravado evaporated. She could imagine a life for her and Tommie in Philadelphia; she could imagine Tommie with a whole new set of friends. But she could not imagine life without her sister. And Jeanne had come under the influence of Thelma in ways Peggy didn't understand. The household had realigned, with the two of them in league as they'd never been before. Peggy sensed a break in the line that connected her to Jeanne, a vulnerability where there had been none before.

"Is everything all right?" Lavinia asked, frowning. Lavinia had been unusually attentive as the deadline approached.

"Lovely," Peggy said, in the bland, disinterested voice she had cultivated for work. "Just a bit of a headache."

"It's because you don't eat enough," Lavinia said. "How I envy you."

Peggy felt a little better. This landscape—of deprivation and jealousy and competition among friends—was comfortingly familiar. There were ways to deal with Rose—there was always a way, when you were strong and fearless. When you were willing to do what must be done.

As she left the store, she tore Rose's letter into a dozen pieces and flung them down into the sewer. Then she stepped on a trolley headed away from home.

Fifteen minutes later she was standing in front of the dilapidated house on a run-down street. A flash of dizziness passed through her as she remembered the angry women who lived there, and Jeanne lying on their couch, barely alive.

But this time, she knew why she was here and she knew

who the enemy really was. Resolutely she walked up the steps and knocked. Inside she could hear children yelling and the radio being turned down.

The man who opened the door was the man she'd come to see. Actually, either of them would have done, these brothers or cousins of the young woman who'd looked at Thelma with such hatred. He regarded her curiously in his suspenders and stained undershirt as he wiped a heavy wrench with a greasy rag. The wrench seemed to confirm that Peggy had made the right decision by coming here.

She looked past him, into the small house with its smell of cabbage and cooking grease. Little had changed. On the couch where Jeanne had lain, the old woman sat darning a sock. The children were stacking fruit crates; they'd put a baby in one, where he sat roly-poly and dazed. They paid her no mind. There was no sign of the young woman who had been so hostile that night—but the wilted roses, arranged in a milk bottle on the table, suggested an entire narrative. If she was shrewd, she'd have worked the situation for all it was worth. And girls like her were often shrewd.

"Your family did mine a favor," Peggy said. Inside her pocketbook was every cent that she'd managed to save from her paychecks. She took out the envelope and for a moment allowed herself to feel its heft, its thickness. *She* had earned this. She alone. She held out the envelope, showing the man the edges of the bills. "Now I want to do one for you."

FOR A WEEK Peggy heard nothing. During this time she endured the nightly talk about the new business, from which her sister and Thelma excluded her as casually as if she were a child.

One evening, her uncle Frank stopped by. It was the first time she'd seen him since their mother's funeral, and yet he barely appeared to have aged. His hair was peppered with silver and he favored one leg slightly as he walked, and his smile seemed forced, but his hug still smelled like peppermint and aftershave.

Nothing was said about Peggy's absence the last time he visited. After dinner, he and Thelma and Jeanne pored over documents Frank had brought in a leather valise, Thelma tapping the table lightly with the point of a mechanical pencil.

Thelma seemed energized by the new business. She had unearthed her old adding machine from the basement, and her fingers flew over the keys like birds attacking spilled seed. It was as though she suddenly spoke a language none of the rest of them knew. Even Tommie had noticed; skirting the edge of the table, she looked forlorn, clutching the French curve that Thelma had given her to play with.

There was no place for Peggy in the discussion of the new equipment they would buy, the experienced tradesmen they would hire, the suppliers who would deliver polyester and cotton and wool from which they would create their new, blended fabrics. When talk turned to potential customers, she recognized some of the brands that were mentioned, the makers of clothes that would never see the inside of the Crystal Salon:

moderately priced dresses and skirts and blouses that every housewife in New Jersey had in her closet.

Peggy had other things on her mind. Every moment of the day was devoted to worrying about whether Olek Petrenko (a name she learned only after money was exchanged) had done as she asked yet. Sometimes it was like wondering about the ending of a book she'd misplaced; but at other times she imagined being arrested, jailed, tried in court. She focused her attention on Tommie, bathing her each evening with great care, setting her hair in pin curls, which, in the morning, she'd arrange just like Jeanne Crain's. She coaxed Tommie to tell her about school, the girls who had excluded her, the teachers who'd scolded her. She heaped praise on the drawings Tommie made and encouraged her to make more.

All the while, Thelma and Jeanne planned and schemed and seemed to forget she was there. But Peggy knew she wasn't entitled to resentment, not yet. Not until she'd fixed the problem she had created for herself all those years earlier, the one that had come back to haunt her in the form of Rose Scopes.

Monday morning of the next week, after an eternity of a weekend in which Tommie clung to Peggy like a milkweed pod on a branch, Peggy got her ready for school and they left together for the quarter-mile walk to St. Katherine's. Autumn was moving in fast now that it was October, and Peggy tugged her headscarf tighter against the inhospitable wind and tried to hurry Tommie along. But they'd made it only to the corner of their street when she saw him.

Olek Petrenko was leaning against a lamppost, smoking a

cigarette. He was wearing a wool cap pulled low on his brow, his heavy work boots crusted with mud.

"It's done," he said as they came abreast of him, then flicked his cigarette into the street and strode away.

"Who was that?" Tommie asked.

"I've no idea," Peggy said, watching him go, waiting for the heaviness to lift from her heart. Instead she experienced something else: a premonition that everything she'd worked for, all of her careful plans and sacrifices, had taken her to a place she'd never intended to go. It was as though a door was slowly opening, and through the opening could be glimpsed a kaleidoscope of colors, the whole not yet discernable. And Peggy felt excitement mixing with dread. The future was unstoppable, it was her fault, and she was about to tumble into it.

Thelma

Thelma spread the newspaper carefully over the table. This was her favorite time of day, with Tommie off to school and Peggy at work, the breakfast dishes done and put up, a second pot of coffee perking on the stove, and Jeanne taking her time getting dressed. She savored the solitude that had once been her bane and was now her singular pleasure.

She read the local news first, then the business section,

and finally the lifestyle and obituary pages, which she combed for news of people she'd known through the years. This last was a bitter pleasure, a balance of longing and pain, where she learned the news of Thomas's friends' marriages and their children's births, the deaths of people she'd grown up with. Garden club prizes awarded, vacations taken to Florida and Lake Placid, silver anniversaries and gold-watch retirements— all the pleasures that had slipped away from her but that now did not inspire yearning as they once did. Because after the newspaper and the coffee, when Jeanne joined her at the table, came the balance sheets and invoices and payrolls that she'd once thought she'd put behind her forever.

She skimmed the obituaries, recognizing the name of an elderly man who had once been an undertaker himself, clucking at the loss of a child who hadn't made it to his second birthday, and her eyes caught on a grainy photograph of a girl. She was pretty, smiling shyly, her hair pulled back in a severe style that showed off delicate earlobes and a long neck. Rose Coffey, the obituary read, age thirty. Survived by loving husband, Richard, and children, Richard Junior and Sidney, sisters . . . mother and father . . . Thelma read the announcement a second time, looking for clues. A girl so young, and it wasn't an accident and there was no mention of a "long illness," so it had been suicide, then—a sin that always seemed like the worst one of all, when men like her Thomas would have gladly lived out all the days she had thrown away.

The girl hailed from Wayne, but in the last lines of the

obituary Thelma saw that she had served in the WVAC in Roxborough. She would have to ask the girls if they'd known her.

Jeanne came into the room, humming and adjusting an earring. "Good morning, Thelma."

"Good morning. Did you know someone named Rose Coffey? Her maiden name was Scopes."

"A little bit. She was in the WVAC with us. Peggy knew her better than I did."

Charles hadn't joined the Rangers until late in 1942, when he decided he was needed as a medic on the front lines and left his newly formed partnership with his father. And Jeanne hadn't joined the WVAC until their mother died and Charles left, when she finally had nothing else to occupy her besides serving with the other women whose men were overseas.

"Well, she passed away. Left behind two children too."

Jeanne peered over Thelma's shoulder to read the obituary. "That's her," she confirmed. "I wonder why she did it?"

SEVERAL DAYS LATER, on a Monday, Thelma was alone at her table, paying invoices for the raw materials that had been coming in almost daily now that they were in production. Jeanne and Frank had left for the day to visit a manufacturer in Newark, to close an order for nearly eight hundred yards of polyester-cotton, one of their largest yet.

Frank had arrived early in the morning to pick Jeanne up,

and they left the house in a cloud of Jeanne's perfume and tangled nerves. Next week she was going to the city to meet with several large wholesalers in the garment district. Thelma would go along for that trip, but she'd thought it would be wise to let the other two go on these early calls without her; with her growing responsibility, Jeanne seemed to be blossoming, her confidence increasing every day.

Thelma wrote out checks and recorded them carefully in the new register, only yesterday delivered from the printer with their new company logo engraved at the top. Each time Thelma wrote a check, she paused to admire the stylized letters spelling out "Charming Mills." The "Char" in "Charming," of course, was for Charles, but secretly Thelma also thought it could be for Thomas, who'd been charming when he wanted to be.

The mail came through the slot in the door, and Thelma glanced up at the clock and was surprised to see that it was already half past noon. She stood and stretched and thought about making some toast for lunch, to go with last night's cold chicken, and then fetched the mail, her mind having moved on to wondering how Jeanne and Frank were doing. Having lunch in downtown Newark, perhaps, after concluding their morning appointment; if it had been a successful call, perhaps they were celebrating a bit.

On top of the stack of mail was a square blue envelope, Thelma's name and address written in a delicate, spidery hand. The postmark was Wayne. Curious, Thelma opened the letter with the long steel opener that she'd unearthed, along with the adding machine and her old office supplies, from the basement. She pulled out several thin sheets of inexpensive stationery and laid them flat on the table, pushing the check register out of the way, and began to read.

Dear Mrs. Holliman,

I hope you don't mind me writing to you but you see I feel as though I know you already. Us girls sure talked a lot when the war was on and the boys were gone and we had all that time just to wait for them to come back. Peggy told me all about you and I will give her this, she always said she got a good mother-in-law, unlike some we knew of.

They say I should feel lucky to have my Dickie back but there is no luck in having a grown man like a child crying in the middle of the night so you can't get any peace and angry all day long so you don't ever know when it is he's going to turn on you. Or on your children which is worse. It's for my kids I'm doing what I have to do, they will go to my sister and he won't see them any more and that is better then never knowing when he will treat them bad.

But before I am gone I thought you should know something about the Girl you have taken into your home who you have been so kind to, treating her like your own Daughter which I understand because, as a mother myself I can not imagine the pain of losing any of my Boys. But I did lose a brother in the war so I know a little bit, maybe, about it. Peggy and me used to talk about him, too. We used to joke that if Peggy and Thomas hadn't gotten hooked up, maybe she would have made a good match for Paul. I confess I used to think about that sometimes, please forgive me, if Thomas didn't come back and Paul did, but those are thoughts best forgotten.

I know I am beating around the bush because what I have to say to you is hard for me. But I feel you deserve to know and also Peggy has left me no choice. Peggy and me, sometimes we would stay late talking after the scrap sorting and you know how girls are. We talked about everything, sometimes the next day I wish I'd kept my mouth shut. But Peggy one day she couldn't stop crying. I said Peggy what's the matter, what could be so terrible, and she said she was pregnant and I said but that's a good thing, that's wonderful news (even though it was natural to have mixed feelings, all the girls who were expecting did, with their husbands gone) and she said no it isn't and then she told me something that shocked me as I know it will you. Thomas isn't the Father, she said, and she was in such a state, no matter what I said I couldn't calm her down. I tell you I was afraid she would do something terrible, which is kind of funny because if I am brave by the time you read this I will have done the same thing. She told me that it was Charles, Jeanne's fiancé, who got her Pregnant and she felt so awful about it but what was done was done and Thomas could never find out, and they all had to make the best and move on. But her biggest fear was, what if the baby favored Charles and she was so sure he would, Charles being so tall and Dark with those dark eyes. She showed me his picture, the picture I think it was taken at his Family's house in Connecticut. So I knew it was true and she was right to worry with Thomas as fair as he was. That Irish blood with the blue eyes and the blond hair, just like Peggy, and how are two people like that going to have a baby with dark hair and eyes.

Well I guess it all worked out because I never did hear anything bad. I heard about the baby from Sue Pierce because by the time she came, Peggy and I weren't speaking really much. Once she started showing she quit coming to the WVAC and the one time I came to see her, you weren't home that day, she was in your Front room with her feet up and it was Jeanne who fetched me a glass of tea and asked after my family, Peggy said she was so uncomfortable she could barely talk. Well I had two babies of my own so I know how it is when you get close. But mostly she just let me know in that way of hers that she didn't really consider us Friends any more. Which on the way home I thought to myself, well isn't that fine because I had a husband and a house of my own and she was living with her mother-in-law, no offense, and still Peggy could make anyone feel like she was looking down on them no matter if they were a Queen or a Movie star.

I got over that though and that is not why I am writing to you today, to get even with her for that. Only I thought you ought to know. From everything Peggy told me I know you loved your Son Thomas and you were a very Good mother to him and especially with him having no father and I just didn't think it is right for you not to know the Truth.

Sincerely yours,
Rose Martha (Scopes) Coffey

By the time Thelma came to the end of the letter, she was sitting rigidly straight in the chair, her hand pressed to her mouth as though suppressing the scream building there.

If what this girl said was true—

This dead girl, from whom no more secrets could ever be pried—

But Tommie. *Thomas.* Everything she had left of him, everything she cared about. His daughter . . . who wasn't his daughter at all.

Bile rose up inside Thelma and she could barely push herself away from the table fast enough, running to the bathroom and kneeling on the floor, her hands gripping the bowl of the commode while her breakfast splattered everywhere. She heaved and heaved until there was nothing, until her insides felt bruised and her throat raw. Then she pulled herself up-right, holding the sink, feeling a thousand years old. She stared at herself in the mirror, stepping carefully over the mess. Some of her hair had come free of its bobby pins and clung to her sweat-dampened forehead and cheeks. She looked like a wild savage. Her eyes were glittering coals tossed in ashes, her color-less lips those of an old hag.

There was nothing in the reflection to show she'd been a grandmother, a mother. Thomas might as well have died in her womb, all those years ago, and his history would be more scoured from the earth than it was now. He had no child. He had no wife—because any wife who could do what—what—

At the thought of Peggy—whom Thelma had taken in, whom she had treated as her own, no, *better* than she would have treated her own daughter, because she would have ex-pected more grit and spine from her own daughter—Thelma felt sick all over again. But she had nothing left to expel. She was empty, as empty as a worn and faded flour sack.

She reached for her toothbrush by rote and mechanically scrubbed the foul taste from her mouth. She splashed water on her face and used one of the rough cloths she kept folded in the bathroom for cleaning to scrub her face, until it was as raw as she felt. Then she went to fetch the bucket, and filled it with the hottest water the tap would give and enough bleach to scorch her hands. She cleaned her mess without gloves, her knees painful on the hard tile. Pain was all she deserved. Pain was all she had left.

Peggy

Peggy stopped by the bakery after work and picked up four tiny iced cakes. One for each of them, but mostly for Tommie; the thought of her sticky kisses eased the dread of what lay ahead.

But when she let herself into the house, it was cold and dark. The kitchen was empty; nothing simmered on the stove, no bread sat cooling on racks. A thin pool of light came from underneath Thelma's door. Bewildered, Peggy knocked.

"Come in," came Thelma's tired voice.

Peggy eased the door open.

Thelma was sitting at the little desk where she wrote letters, but the stationery box was closed and her hands were clasped on her lap. When she turned to face Peggy, her face was stony.

"Is . . . is everything all right? Where's Tommie?"

"Tommie's fine. Jeanne's taken her to get a hamburger."

Peggy tried to process this piece of information. They never went out for hamburgers during the week—the only time Thelma would agree to eat lunch at the diner was on the rare Sunday after Mass.

"Wasn't Jeanne with Frank today?"

"Yes. Earlier. They got back a couple of hours ago."

"Did the meetings . . ."

"*Peggy.*" Thelma barked her name, standing up abruptly from the desk. She crossed the room in two strides and Peggy had no idea what was happening until Thelma had slapped her hard across the face, sending her staggering into the door-frame. She put her hand to her stinging cheek in astonishment, tasted blood where she'd bitten her lip.

"For *years* I have given you a roof over your head," Thelma said in a voice as sharp and cold as ice. Her face was pale, the lipstick she'd applied a harsh slash on her mouth, her hair loosed from its pins.

"I know, and I'm grateful, and—"

"I got a letter from Rose Coffey today. She's dead, did you know that? I saw the notice in the paper the other morning. I showed it to Jeanne."

Rose Coffey.

A chill sliced through Peggy like lightning striking a stump in a field. She sagged against the doorframe. But if Rose was dead—but how could Rose be dead? She'd come to see Peggy only two weeks ago. She had *children.*

Had Olek . . . ? But that couldn't be. *Just frighten her,* she'd told him. *Push her around a little. Make her believe there'll be worse in store for her,* she'd said, even though the threat was an empty one, because Peggy would never be able to follow through.

Thelma was shaking with rage, her lips pressed together so hard that her jaw trembled too. She picked up a letter from the bed—Peggy hadn't seen it lying there, the stack of rumpled blue sheets—and shook it in Peggy's face.

"Rose wrote to *you?*" she asked, faint with confusion.

"Yes. What happened, Peggy, did you cut her off because

she knew, all those years ago? You thought that if you never spoke to her again, your secret would be safe?"

"She's dead?" Peggy echoed stupidly. "But—how?"

"'Died suddenly,' the paper said, but I know people. I made some calls. That fool girl jumped off the Dubuyk Bridge. Left behind a mess—two children and a good-for-nothing husband. But we've all got our troubles, don't we, Peggy? I mean, look at you." Spittle had collected in the corner of her mouth, and her hands hung useless at her sides. "Look at *you*."

It was the disgust in that single syllable that finally made Peggy understand: Thelma knew.

Peggy swallowed and backed toward the doorway. "I . . . have to get Tommie," she mumbled, her voice quavering. "We'll go somewhere. I'll—there are some girls from work."

"Is that what you think?" Thelma said, seeming to swell with fresh fury. "That you'll just take her and go? Without—without even *explaining* yourself?"

Somehow Thelma had managed to back Peggy away from the door and into the corner of the small room, where the wallpaper was peeling up from the baseboard. Peggy felt the walls against her shoulder blades and wished she could be swallowed up inside them, wished she could be anywhere but in the relentless beam of Thelma's fury.

"But there isn't anything to explain," she whispered.

Thelma threw back her head and made a sound of such anguish that Peggy winced. Thelma would hit her again, and Peggy wouldn't stop her; maybe Thelma would keep hitting her, over and over.

"He was my *son!*" Thelma screamed.

"I know that." She was crying now, crying hard. This was her greatest fear, come to life, worse even than the telegram saying that Thomas was dead. "I loved him too."

"Don't you dare say that. Don't you *dare.*"

Peggy was silent, but she wanted to say it again—she had, she had. She had done her best to love him with all her heart. Thomas knew that. It wasn't his fault, but somehow it wasn't not his fault either. Because she had tried to tell him, right before he went away, right before their quick secret wedding—she had tried to warn him that what they had was cooling too fast to last a lifetime, that when they kissed, already she felt a heaviness, a reluctance. But he'd said it was just jitters. He'd been so insistent, he'd begged, comically, singing her made-up words that he claimed were an aria of love . . . she could still see him as he was that day, kneeling before her in the park in front of the courthouse, a little crowd of their friends cheering him on. *Marry me*, he'd shouted, not caring that people passing by could hear. *Marry me, Peggy, and make me the luckiest guy alive*, and she couldn't resist, how could she be expected to resist? When every day another batch of them shipped off, another bevy of girls stood crying at the train station, how could she resist the tide that swept her in with the rest of them?

And by then it was done, and she felt the shame so thick it smothered her, strangled her. She would have done anything to take back that night. It was Christmas Eve—Christmas Day, by the end of it, the cotton-mouth early morning hours when Charles dropped her off in front of the house before driving back to the house of the friend who'd first introduced him to Jeanne.

It was too much champagne, dancing in that living room—it had been a sort of going-away party, three of them would be shipping out in the first week of the new year—and the boys had urged each other to drink more and more and coaxed the girls to kiss under the mistletoe. They had been drunk—of course they were drunk. Peggy was fearless that way, had a bit of a reputation, in fact. The truth was she liked the lightness it gave her, the way it loosened her words and made her seem carefree. Peggy was never carefree, but no one needed to know that.

Jeanne hadn't felt well and one of the girlfriends, Peggy couldn't even remember her name, had offered to drive her home, and a thousand times Peggy blamed herself for not going with them. But Thomas—Thomas had pouted comically and begged her, *Just stay until midnight, kiss me on the stroke of Christmas,* and then passed out half an hour before.

She'd gone to get her coat. She was sure of that. She was going to get her coat and then find the friend, Bart was his name, because Bart had a car and even though he shouldn't be driving, it wasn't so very far. Thomas would stay on the divan where he'd fallen asleep, and in the morning Charles would drive him home.

She remembered hearing laughter, a girl's teasing scolding, and she'd gone looking for the girl because the girl was with Bart and maybe she would come too, all three of them would drive back to her house, she could offer to make them coffee. Instead she opened a door and there was Charles. He had looked at her and she had looked at him, and there had been a moment when she could have simply turned around and walked back out again, but there was something so curious in his expression. Something sharp and wolf-eyed, but also sad and almost regretful. *What's the matter*, she was about to ask, when he took her wrist and pulled her to him while with the other hand he pushed the door shut.

"Oh, Peggy." He'd sighed against her mouth, before kissing her. At first it was a soft kiss, and Peggy was inert with shock but also . . . she had been strangely electrified. She had never wanted him, never longed for him, never thought of him when she was kissing Thomas. Charles was like a middle-aged man in a young man's body; Peggy made fun of him with her girlfriends. That striped tie—that signet ring.

But now he was kissing her and with a breathtaking rush of understanding Peggy knew that he had watched her from the start, that all those times he'd watched her, with what she told herself was brotherly concern, it had been something else.

He was Jeanne's—but it was Peggy he wanted. And because of the secret thrill of that knowledge, she hesitated a second too long.

She knew it was her fault, because why else would he have shoved her up against the wall, filling her mouth with his tongue so that she couldn't speak, crushing her hands against the plaster so she couldn't push him away? He'd felt her hesitation, he'd known her betrayal. She tried to cry out but he was breathing right into her face, hard, fumbling with his belt, his pants, her skirt. She was crying—*please, please, please,* chanting and sobbing—but she didn't dare raise her voice because what if Bart heard, what if he came running, what if he threw open the door and found them like that? The thought of Jeanne finding out silenced her as Charles grabbed her breast right through her dress and squeezed.

At some point he pushed her onto the bed and her ankle jammed against the bedpost. That pain, sharp and instant, was what she focused on as he pushed himself against her. Until this moment Peggy had allowed one boy to touch her that way—through her underpants—and that boy was Thomas and it was Thomas she had promised this to, what was happening now *please please* in this bed in this house. When he shoved her skirt up and pushed himself into her he growled against her ear, "You want this you know you want this you want this Peggy you made me do this," over and over again, as she squeezed her eyes shut and bit her lip so hard she tasted blood.

After, he didn't look at her. "It would kill your sister to know what you did," he said matter-of-factly as he pulled up his pants. "Don't make me tell her."

He left the room and he closed the door very softly behind him and Peggy knelt on the floor; the rug was a braided rag rug, she remembered that detail. Some mother or grandmother had made that rug with the rags from her basket, and in the rug were scraps from the clothes that the people in the family had worn. Peggy rested her forehead on the rug and pinched her wrists, hard, to make herself stop crying, because she still had to get home somehow and she couldn't let the others know.

But when she finally came out of the room, Charles was waiting with her coat over his arm. He helped her into it, and he was back to being the Charles that she knew, the one whose stuffy manners she had mocked. He walked her down the drive and held her elbow because the streets were icy. He said nothing on the drive home—it was a short drive, maybe five minutes, and they didn't pass another car—but when she got out of the car he told her "Good night" as though it were any other night.

So. That was how it happened.

She'd have walked the entire earth to be able to rewind that evening, except that there had also been a part of her that had known, the next morning, through the headache and the nausea—that had felt a tiny pinpoint of surprise deep inside her as Tommie was begun like a match to a sparkler.

"Thomas never knew," she pleaded, unable to look at Thelma. "I never told him and he never—I wanted him to believe that the baby was ours. I never would have told him. I would have been a good wife, I swear it."

"Get out," Thelma said. "Get out of my house and don't come back."

"But—Tommie—"

"Go!" Thelma grabbed Peggy's upper arm so hard it felt like she'd yank it from its socket, and pushed her out the bedroom door. She half dragged her through the house, Peggy stumbling and nearly losing a shoe.

Somehow Peggy was out the door and on the street, and it had begun to rain, huge splattering cold drops that hit her scalp and ran down her face. The door slammed and lights came on behind the drapes, and for a moment Peggy thought she would demand to come back in, that she'd pound and pound until Thelma at least told her where Tommie was.

She stood, chest heaving, her clothes sodden and hair plastered to her face, for what felt like a very long time. Behind her, a car slowed, stopped, then moved on when she didn't turn around.

Finally, she turned and walked away in the darkness.

September 1950

Jeanne

"Where's Tommie?"

Thelma came into the front room carrying a box, handing it off to the movers. "I sent her next door. Mrs. Slater said she'll keep her busy until we're ready to leave."

Jeanne nodded, pressing a hand to her forehead. It was pure chaos in Thelma's small house. It was almost impossible to imagine, but tomorrow, she and Tommie would be living somewhere else. Thelma would be alone here for the first time in years. Everything was happening so fast. Sometimes Jeanne just wanted to make everything stop so she could take it all in one last time before it all changed.

She went to the bedroom that she had been sharing with Tommie since Peggy left, where her suitcase was lying on the bed. Under her camisoles and stockings were two things that Thelma didn't know Jeanne had packed. The first was the framed photograph of her and Peggy, taken in Atlantic City when they were seven and eight, their mother's shadow falling across the sand while they squinted in the sun and laughed.

The second item was a white handkerchief. Embroidered in pink thread, not nearly as skillfully as Jeanne's handiwork, were the initials MAB, for Margaret Anne Brink.

Peggy had stitched the handkerchief when she was thirteen, in the home economics class she despised, before stowing it at the bottom of her dresser drawer, where it lay forgotten until the day she left. Jeanne had saved it from the box of Peggy's things that Thelma gave to St. Vincent de Paul.

Jeanne closed the suitcase and set it on the floor. There were only a few more boxes from the kitchen and then Frank would be coming to drive them across the bridge and into the city. In less than an hour they would arrive at the sunny two-bedroom apartment on Spruce, with a maid's room that would be Thelma's when she stayed over.

As Jeanne passed through the house, she paused at the door of the pantry that, for a while, had served as their dressing room. She put her fingertips to the nail hole where Peggy had hung the mirror for their customers to see themselves during their fittings. A lump caught in her throat.

She'd sent at least a dozen letters to Peggy in New York City, using the return address she'd copied from a letter Peggy had sent Tommie. "Miss Thomasina Holliman, c/o Jeanne Brink" was how Peggy had addressed the envelope. No mention of Thelma at all, but when Thelma saw the letter in the stack of mail she'd snatched it away and never shown it to Tommie.

And Peggy had never answered any of her letters. Thelma refused to discuss her departure, and the few times Jeanne had mentioned her name, Thelma had retreated tight-lipped and angry to the kitchen, banging pots and pans until she settled down. Jeanne knew that Thelma would never forgive Peggy for abandoning her grandchild without even a note. But she also believed in her heart that there was more to it, that Peggy must have suffered quietly for quite some time until she reached a breaking point that none of them had been able to predict.

Looking back on the days leading up to her leaving, she knew that Peggy had been trying to tell them all along how badly she wanted to take the job in Philadelphia. They'd underestimated the power of Peggy's hopes and wishes. If she had stayed in Brunskill, it must have seemed to Peggy that those dreams would have died forever . . . but couldn't they have found a solution together? It was only a few years until Tommie would be old enough to stay by herself. Couldn't Peggy have waited?

The front door opened and Frank stood there with his hat in his hands. "Big day," he observed with customary understatement, as Thelma came back into the room.

"Let's go," she said. "We should get there before rush hour."

Jeanne followed her outside. At the curb she turned and

took a long, last look at the house where she'd washed ashore for the past eight years.

THE FIRST NIGHT on Spruce Street was full of the sounds of night in the city. The traffic never stopped, not even as the small hours of the morning ticked by. At four o'clock the trucks began their deliveries. Workers called to each other. A woman sounded like she was crying somewhere in the building.

Jeanne lay alone in the wide bed that had come with the furnished apartment, staring at the bars of streetlight that snuck in between the draperies and splashed across the ceiling.

Tommie's room was at the other end of the apartment, a sweet little space with built-in bookcases and a dormer window, and Jeanne couldn't stop worrying about her waking in the middle of the night and not knowing where she was, walking through the darkened rooms where stacks of boxes cast ominous shadows. She'd offered to let Tommie sleep with her, but Tommie was so delighted at the prospect of having her very own room that she refused.

Jeanne tossed and turned, the old building creaking and cracking through the plumbing ducts. Tomorrow they would begin their new routine. She and Tommie would have breakfast together—Thelma had packed a cooler with bread and milk and eggs so they wouldn't have to go to the store right away—and then Jeanne would walk Tommie to the Academy of Mount St. Agnes, where she was enrolled in the first grade. They had deliberately timed the move so Tommie would start a new school year right away, so she would focus on new friends and teachers instead of missing her old home and routines.

From Mount St. Agnes it was a four-block walk to the trolley stop, then forty-five minutes to the mill—the reverse of the commute she'd made when she worked at Harris. The new showroom had just been completed, the floors buffed, the paint dry, the display racks installed and the furniture moved in. Later that week Jeanne and Frank would receive their first customers and take their first orders from the new location. The mill had been operational for a year now, and there were dozens of bolts of finished goods in the showroom and several thousand bolts at the warehouse, awaiting shipping.

The wheels had turned at astonishing speed. In the last month, Charming's first invoices had been sent out, and paychecks were beginning to trickle in. They'd already made the first payment on the loan they'd secured to start the business. And there would soon be more than enough money for the apartment, for Tommie's school, for everything in their new life.

Jeanne would take them all out to dinner at the Bellevue Stratford to celebrate, she decided. Tommie would love the crystal chandeliers, the white-gloved waiters. Thelma had promised to come and stay in the city apartment on weekends. She had a fondness for window shopping, and Jeanne would take her strolling along the shops.

As Jeanne had searched for an apartment that would allow

her to give Tommie all the advantages a life in the city offered, a hollowness had settled inside her. It was Peggy's absence, the thought of her living in her own apartment in Manhattan that Jeanne had never seen, separated by miles that might have been continents. Jeanne had started and abandoned a dozen more letters, all of them attempts at an apology for failing Peggy, though she didn't know what she had done that was too little or not enough or simply all wrong.

How had it come to this? By now, Jeanne nearly thirty-one and Peggy twenty-nine, they were supposed to be busy with their children, their husbands, their homes. The childhood promise they'd made each other to always live on the same street, to raise all their children together—three girls for Jeanne, twin boys and twin girls for Peggy.

Instead, they had one child between them, and Peggy had let her slip quicksilver through her fingers, a lost little soul living in a world without men, except for Uncle Frank. Now it had come to be Jeanne's turn to keep her, and she would do the best she could.

Six

Brocatelle

Italians have for centuries woven a fustian of cotton and silk, with linen threads in the weft making it extraordinarily strong. You might put brocatelle on a chair cushion—if you wanted that cushion to last for the rest of your life. It is not like a chiffon scarf or a satin glove that will last only a season before showing signs of wear: it is made to endure. Sewing with brocatelle requires skill and dedication; use a nap layout and only superfine pins, and be prepared to devote a great deal of time to matching seams.

Do not undertake brocatelle until you are certain you are ready for it.

Come ti vidi m'innamorai, e tu sorridi perche lo sai.
When I saw you I fell in love, and you smiled because you knew.
—Arrigo Boito

Jeanne

She had taken the day off for Tommie's first day of first grade, but when she arrived—fifteen minutes early, because she'd been so afraid of being late that she'd rushed Tommie through breakfast and the short walk to Mount St. Agnes—the nun waiting at the front door told her that parents were to say their goodbyes outside, and that any tears or reluctance on the part of the children should be ignored.

"Otherwise, they'll think they can get away with it every morning," the nun explained grimly.

Tommie was gripping Jeanne's hand so tightly she was cutting off circulation to her fingers. She looked up at Jeanne with terror in her eyes.

"It's just—she's new to the school," Jeanne said.

"Mrs. Holliman, *all* of the first-graders are new to the school."

Jeanne seethed. The nun could be forgiven for not knowing she was *Miss Brink*—that she was Tommie's aunt, not her mother—but couldn't she see how frightened Tommie was? But maybe she was right. Maybe this was how every child behaved, in every school in every city in the country. In this, as in a thousand other details of child rearing, Jeanne was ignorant.

She crouched down and straightened the ribbed waistband of Tommie's navy blue cardigan. Her braid was already
threatening to come out of its matching ribbon, and there was
a smudge—syrup, from their rushed breakfast—on the collar
of her blouse. Tommie wrapped her arms around Jeanne's neck
and squeezed tightly.

Suddenly Jeanne was certain she'd made a mistake. What
did she know of raising a child? How could she possibly care
for Tommie, when her heart was full with all the things that
could go wrong?

"Are you going to be here after school?" Tommie whispered.
"To pick me up?"

"Oh yes, darling, of course I am!" Gently, Jeanne pried her
arms away and forced a smile. "You'll have so many things to
tell me about your day."

"No, I won't," Tommie said gravely. "None of the girls will
like me."

"Oh, sweetheart." Jeanne knew that if she didn't leave now,
she would cry, which would be awful for the poor girl. "That's
nonsense. Now, up the stairs you go, we mustn't keep Sister
waiting."

Tommie gave a barely perceptible nod, then trudged away
without looking back.

"It's so sweet, isn't it?" a woman's voice said.

Jeanne turned to see a woman with a stroller and a toddler
in her arms.

"Your first?" the woman continued. When Jeanne nodded
dumbly, she smiled. "I could tell! But I promise it gets easier.

Five minutes from now she'll be playing with all the other children, and she won't want to come home later."

"Thank you," Jeanne said. The woman was already turning away, the toddler squirming in her arms.

Should Jeanne go after her? Should she introduce herself, find out her daughter's name, perhaps plant the seed for future get-togethers for Tommie and the other girl? By the time Jeanne made up her mind, the woman was halfway down the block, and the opportunity was lost.

The day stretched out with nothing to do. Thelma was overseeing the installation of new display racks for the sample books; Frank was interviewing candidates for second-shift manager in the office. Jeanne's presence was completely unnecessary. But she didn't relish the thought of going back to the apartment, with its bare walls and boxes waiting to be unpacked.

Jeanne decided to walk along South Street, with its many clothing stores, haberdasheries, and tailors. Frank was drawing up lists of potential customers, including accounts that Brink Mills had served as well as new ones, and in a matter of weeks Jeanne would be joining him on sales calls to some of these stores. Maybe she'd stop in somewhere to drink coffee and read the newspaper from front to back, an indulgence she'd had no time for lately.

The shops were opening up for the day, merchants sweeping the sidewalks out front, delivery boys wheeling garment racks and unloading trucks, seamstresses strolling in twos and threes. Jeanne heard conversations in Yiddish and Italian and

English; she passed pushcarts and produce trucks and fish-mongers transporting their wares on beds of ice. Jeanne felt her spirits lift in time to the pulse of the city.

When she reached Fourth Street, she decided to walk a little farther. She would never tire of looking in the fabric shops at the bolts lined up in the windows, especially knowing that soon, some of those bolts would come from her very own company. The sun was rising higher in the sky, and her legs felt pleasantly invigorated from the walk. Her stomach growled, but Jeanne wasn't quite ready for this simple pleasure to end. Perhaps she'd buy a yard of lace or a packet of buttons, or some ribbon for Tommie. Maybe, if she drummed up the nerve, she'd approach a merchant or two and tell them about the gabardine, serge, and doeskin that would comprise Charming Mills' new season.

She was standing in front of a trim shop, examining a sample board in the window, when she heard her name called.

"Jeanne? Jeanne Brink?"

She turned, searching for the source of the deep, amused voice, when a hand touched her shoulder. She turned and found herself face-to-face with Anthony Salvatici. He was wearing a stained white apron over a chambray shirt with the sleeves rolled up to his elbows. His hair had been cut shorter, but otherwise he looked very much as he had the last time she'd seen him, standing at the curb outside the house.

"What are you doing over in this part of town?" he asked.

"Oh, I—well, actually, I live here now. With my niece. We

have an apartment on Spruce." Immediately, Jeanne wanted to take back her words—did she sound snobbish? Would he be put off that her niece lived with her?

And then she was overcome with mortification for even having those thoughts. It was miraculous that he even remembered her.

"How's your sister's dress business coming?"

"My—oh—fine," she stammered. She had not seen or spoken to Peggy in eleven months and two days, a painful number she tallied alone, ever aware of trying to divert Tommie's attention from her mother's absence. "She moved to New York City."

"Yeah, Mrs. H says that's where you have to be, in that business. Although, I don't know, seems like we have plenty · of fabric stores right here."

"I'm, um. I'm working for a fabric mill, actually. It was my father's."

"No kidding?" He whistled. "I asked Mrs. H about you, but she said you quit the company. I was sorry to hear about your mother. Is she . . ."

"She's passed away," Jeanne said, and suddenly the lump in her throat was as real as if it truly had been recent. Why she should react like this now, she wasn't sure—but there was something about the kindness in his voice that dissolved every shred of her composure. "And—and you," she said desperately, "how is school?"

He raised an eyebrow. "I graduated. It only took me eleven years, but I'm the first Salvatici to get a college degree."

"Oh, that's wonderful. What did you study?"

Anthony laughed. "English literature. Nearly killed my pop. But I'm making it up to him now." He pointed at his apron.

"You're helping in the restaurant."

Anthony raised an eyebrow, studying her. "You could say that. Pop retired, and me and my brother are expanding into wholesale. Tell you what, how about I give you a personal tour?"

Peggy

The man with the clipboard and the Kelly green tie came into the little anteroom for the third time. "Still doing okay, doll?" he asked with a familiarity that set Peggy's teeth on edge.

His name was Mr. Crouse and he had been hired to orchestrate today's event, so Peggy could not evade him. "Mmm," she murmured, giving a slight smile, trying to appear more confident than she felt—under the table her hands were clenched tightly, and she'd taken one of the little pills her new doctor had given her to calm her nerves.

"We're just getting the girls settled down now," Mr. Crouse said. He consulted his watch. "You'll be on in five."

Peggy closed her eyes after he left the room. She could hear them out there, all the women who'd been invited for this exclusive preview of the Fall 1950 Peggy Parker collection, the ones whose purchases put them in the top ten percent of Fyfe's ready-to-wear clientele. The chain hadn't tracked these customers as carefully as the Crystal Salon tracked theirs, but that was going to change. Sales of the store's first exclusive line by an American designer would be examined with an eagle eye. Her future hung in the balance, and it wasn't an exaggeration to say that it could be decided in the next two hours.

Peggy couldn't fail now. She had no home to return to.

She drew a deep breath and stood, smoothing down her skirt and adjusting her collar. The dress she had selected for today was not the one that would be featured in the advertisements; that one was the star of the line, a dress and jacket ensemble with scallops on the collar, the peplum, and all the way down the placket. But Peggy had made the decision to wear one of the least expensive pieces, a sailor-collar day dress in navy and white sailcloth, trimmed with blue braid and a rope belt. At eleven dollars and ninety-eight cents, the dress could be had for less than a tenth of the price of dresses Peggy had sold only a year ago—a price that was in reach of every woman in the room.

Peggy had put on a crinoline, which she rarely wore due to the scratchiness of the netting, to make the skirt flare out dramatically. Her front-lacing French corset had been a special welcome gift by Miss Perkins herself, who was now the head women's fashion buyer for the whole chain. The corset lifted her bosom and whittled her waist and forced her shoulders back, which added up to a measure of discomfort that, as Miss Perkins liked to say, was a small price to pay for the envy of others.

Peggy took her compact from her bag and checked her lipstick. "Orange Absolu" was not Max Factor's best-selling shade—but Peggy knew that in a sea of women wearing red, she would stand out. Even her hair had been a daring choice: she'd had it dyed reddish-blond and cut her bangs nearly as short as Bettie Page's.

Mr. Crouse appeared in the doorway, flushed with excitement. "You're on, love!" He stepped out of the way with a flourish and Peggy swept past, sashayed to the stage they'd erected at the front of the room, and clasped her hands with feigned delight.

"Oh my gracious, just *look* at all of you!"

Every word she would say for the next few moments was scripted and well rehearsed; Peggy would have said her lines even if only half a dozen women had attended. But as she went through her prepared welcome, she counted the women in the seats, aisles, crowded in the back of the room. There had to be fifty, sixty, maybe seventy-five of them.

"I know you've all come for the lingerie bag," she said modestly, picking it up from the table where she'd placed it earlier. It was an inexpensive giveaway the store had had made for the collection's debut, the Peggy Parker logo stitched into the pink satin. One hundred was the manufacturer's minimum, which was a good thing, because they hadn't anticipated such a high turnout.

Laughter and a scattering of applause filled the room—and Peggy knew she'd succeeded. Earlier in the week, Archie Fyfe had expressed doubt in a marketing meeting: wouldn't the ladies be more impressed by elegance, by a show of glamour and wealth that transcended their ordinary lives? The "Peggy Parker story," manufactured for the fashion reporters, hinted that Peggy had come from a lofty background, that she'd come to designing by way of a fabulous debut and social seasons in New York and Europe.

But Peggy had taken a gamble motivated by a memory of Thomas. On a wintry November evening just months before he left for the war, she'd come downstairs to discover that Thomas had gotten off early from his hardware store job and come for a visit. She had no plans for that night other than laundry, and she was dressed in an old plaid shirt knotted at her waist, her hair in a ponytail.

She'd been mortified, but Thomas had hooted appreciatively and swung her around in his arms. "You're something special, Pegs," he'd said. "I'm a lucky man."

"But look at me!" she'd protested. "I'm a mess."

"Nope. You're home and heartland. You're the reason the boys are signing on in droves. Look at you, Peggy—you're every man's American dream."

Peggy had glowed with hopeful pride. She knew that Jeanne was the true beauty of the family, dark where Peggy was fair; elegant where she was ordinary, elusive where she had always been just the kid sister.

Only years later, long after he was dead, did she understand what had caught Thomas's eye that day. But now she meant to use that knowledge to show these women that in the right dress, even an ordinary girl could have extraordinary appeal.

"The American girl's life is busier than ever, isn't it?" she asked, letting her gaze flit from one woman to another, taking in their expectant smiles. There were young and old, thin and fat, mothers and daughters and neighbors and friends. They wore gingham, rayon, dotted Swiss—inexpensive, washable fabrics suitable for homemaking. "We take care of the children and the home, we have our husbands' favorite suppers ready when they come home. We do the wash on Tuesdays and the dusting on Thursdays and next week we start all over again."

More applause. This had been a bold claim, because all of them knew that she was an unmarried woman. There was no mention of husband or children in the biography that had been printed on the invitation, which featured a smiling photo of her with a pen poised over a sketchbook.

But Peggy was counting on them to believe that she understood their lives. Where she came from didn't matter. Where she went in the evening after work, where she lay her head at night, none of that mattered. *I see you*, she telegraphed with all her might. *I know you. I want the best for you.*

Lies, all of them, because they were a mystery to her. How could they smile like that, these women with their lumpy figures and unremarkable husbands and too many children at home, their scrimping and saving, their humble dreams of electric sweepers and Memorial Day picnics on a crowded beach?

"All of us girls could use a little glamour once in a while," she continued. "Even if it's just a trip to the market, a special blouse can make all the difference." She picked up a cotton plissé blouse from the rack that she'd positioned nearby on the stage. She glanced up and saw Miss Perkins standing at the back of the room, an unreadable expression on her face. "Look at this darling self-fabric loop trim at the collar. I call it 'spaghetti trim' because it looks like noodles, doesn't it?"

More laughter.

It was time to move into some of the pricier items in the collection. "Now let's see how a few clever details can transform a plain dress."

On cue, one of the models walked out into the crowd, threading her way among the tables, pausing to pose with a hand on her hip. Her name was Pammy—or Patty, something like that; all the girls looked alike, perky and wholesome and more pretty than beautiful.

"All of our cottons are Sanforized," Peggy said, "including this gorgeous cadet blue number." The women oohed and aahed, leaning in to examine the pinwale pique fabric, the topstitching along the pockets.

"And here's a lovely three-piece ensemble for an afternoon of bridge," Peggy went on, gaining momentum. A dark-haired girl walked out and took a spin at the front of the room, making the full skirt flare out. "Notice the bat-wing sleeves, the matching trim on the sweater. And, ladies, we guarantee shrinkage at less than one percent!"

This got hearty approval from the crowd. Unlike Peggy's former customers, these women would all be laundering their clothes, pinning them to clotheslines, expecting to get a lot of wear from them. Peggy had been unrelenting when insisting on snag-proof zippers and only preshrunk fabrics, knowing quality issues could sink her line before it had a chance.

Another model emerged, wearing one of the few evening outfits of the show. "Oh, here's a favorite of mine." Peggy was ad-libbing now, getting into the spirit of the presentation. "Just look at that embroidered linen. Only guess what—it's actually a printed *Dacron-cotton blend*! Would you ever guess? I don't think anyone else will. Oh, and it's machine wash and drip dry, and costs a mere ten dollars and ninety-eight cents!"

Actual gasps were heard in the crowd, followed by a hearty round of applause. Peggy beamed. In her final days in couture, there had been a spirit of contempt for the new synthetic blends. Lavinia had vowed never to let them through her doors; she had asked Peggy, genuinely perplexed, "Are we to expect women to toss their gowns into the laundry with the dishrags, then?"

But these women had no such hesitations. They were ready to embrace the future, with its promise of time-saving ease and miracle fabrics. And their enthusiasm was what she hoped would make Peggy Parker a success.

"I've got another special garment to show you," she said, sorting through the clothes hanging from the rack, searching for the one she wanted. Mr. Crouse raised his eyebrows questioningly from the wings, and Peggy nodded at him and hoped he'd get the hint that she was going off-script. She found what she was looking for and held the hanger aloft. "At eight ninety-eight it's a bit of a splurge for a simple skirt, isn't it? But I don't think you'll mind saving up a bit for this beauty when you see it for yourself. Come on out, honey"—because she didn't remember the girl's name, or even which mannequin had been chosen to model the skirt, which until this moment hadn't been a star of the line—"let's show them the fabric that's going to change their lives!"

There was a breathless hush as the model—too bad; she was one of the homelier girls with a profile that showed too much chin and a bit of a swayback—came tottering uncertainly out. Peggy tamped down her impatience; the girls were stupidly slow to improvise. She smiled and linked arms with the girl.

"This may look like ordinary chambray," Peggy said, and indeed, the skirt was among the plainest pieces in the line. She'd originally designed it to go with a piped dolman-sleeved blouse, but manufacturing issues had forced the blouse to be cut, too late to cancel the skirt. "It does have some lovely details, such as a hidden zipper and this faux button front. But the true genius of this skirt is . . . *acrylic*."

One of their vendors had offered Fyfe's a deal on a run of a new synthetic blend fabric. In anticipation of greater demand, he'd made too much and was willing to let it go at a discount. Peggy had discussed it with the buyer who was working with her on the line, and convinced her to take a chance on the fabric.

"There's a reason he can't sell it," the buyer had protested. "Europe won't touch anything like this."

"Europe is not America." This had become Peggy's mantra

ever since accepting the new position. "We're practical here. We have a chance to be innovators."

The buyer had finally given the go-ahead, lured by the savings. Now Peggy tried to remember what the vendor had said that warm day last August. He was sweaty from lugging his sample case to the offices on the top floor of the flagship store, and doing his best to sell her on his overstock.

"This fabric is made from a blend of sixty percent cotton and forty percent acrylic, and it's virtually wrinkleproof."

Peggy dared a glance at the back, where Miss Perkins watched with an inscrutable expression on her face. She could have been bemused . . . or furious.

Peggy plunged ahead—what choice did she have? *In for a penny, in for a pound*, her mother had been fond of saying, all those years ago.

"Yes, *wrinkleproof*!" Peggy repeated the word she'd just made up, her take on *waterproof*. "Tell you what, everyone, let's let you girls see for yourselves." She stepped down from the stage, dangling the skirt's hanger from her fingers, and offered it to the first table she came to. Two heavyset blond women, sisters perhaps, touched the hem reverently.

"Go ahead—try to wrinkle it," Peggy encouraged. One of the women gave the hem a cautious pinch, then crumpled it in her fist, looking up at Peggy with a tentative smile on her face. Then she released it, and gave a yelp of surprise that was better than Peggy had hoped for. "Tell the girls, honey—how does it look?"

"It's—it's perfect!" the woman said. That was an exaggeration, of course; there were faint impressions of folds in the fabric. But Peggy knew, because she'd tried it herself, that a quick pass with a cool iron would take them right out. So would a few minutes in the bath in the steam from a hot shower.

But she wouldn't share those ideas now. They were the homely details of real life, and she was here to peddle magic.

"What's your name?"

"Ida Cyrus," the woman answered, blushing.

"Everyone, we're going to have a skirt sent to Mrs. Ida Cyrus in gratitude for her help today." Cheers erupted as if every woman in the room had been the recipient of the gift. The feckless mannequin, who was loitering at the edge of the room, finally caught on and joined Peggy among the tables, women reaching out from all sides to touch the fabric of her skirt. Lively conversation swelled around the room, and Miss Perkins gave Peggy a little wave before disappearing through the doors.

❋ ❋ ❋

MISS PERKINS CAME to her office several hours later. She clutched a folder to her chest and smirked.

"Guess how many pieces were ordered today?"

Peggy, who hadn't been able to concentrate all afternoon, tried not to let her nerves show. "How many?"

"All of them."

Peggy opened her mouth but couldn't think of a thing to say. "You mean . . ."

"We've had to cut into Newark's shipment. We'll pull advertising from that market and see if we can order a second run, but from now on we're focusing on next season. If things go as well in the other markets as they did here today, there's no way we'll be able to meet the demand this fall. But that isn't necessarily a bad thing. Anticipation might be our greatest ally right now, my dear. Deprive the ladies of what they want and it only makes them want it more—we learned *that* back in the Crystal Salon, didn't we?"

"Wait," Peggy said weakly. She thought she might faint. "You're telling me . . ."

"Every skirt, every dress, every blouse. All right, we've still got a few things in sizes two and four. You were right about that, I'll admit it now." Peggy had tried to remind Miss Perkins that the ready-to-wear customer didn't have the time or means to starve herself, as many of their old customers did. "But other than that—poof!" She flapped her hands to mimic the clothes vanishing into thin air.

"It was the chambray skirt that did it," Peggy said. "They ate it up."

Miss Perkins gave an exaggerated shudder. "'*Wrinkleproof.*' God help them."

"We really should be using a net underlining," Peggy said, her mind already on to a new direction. "The gathered waistbands we're seeing aren't going to be stiff enough in the blends, and they'll end up emphasizing the stomach."

"Then maybe the ladies should be introduced to cottage

cheese," Miss Perkins sniffed. "Glamour isn't free. It takes work."

But Peggy barely heard her. The *entire* collection . . . gone. And to think she'd been worried about keeping her job. "So there's definitely to be a second collection?" she asked.

Miss Perkins laughed. "Oh my, yes. I shouldn't say this, but Archie is absolutely ecstatic right now. I wouldn't be surprised if he offers you your own office. He wants you to do your show in all the markets. They've already started making the arrangements—it has to be booked fast. We want to make it seem as though we planned it all along. I've got to call the papers—talk to marketing—oh, I've got a thousand things to do. Take the rest of the afternoon off, Peggy, you've earned it."

"But it's almost four-thirty."

"Is it? Imagine that!" Miss Perkins turned to go. "Well, enjoy an extra hour off, then. Go to the movies. Treat yourself to a martini."

And she was gone.

The delirious first blush of success stayed with Peggy only for another few seconds before it began slipping away like sugar between the planks in a wood floor.

Something amazing had happened today, and there was one person in the world Peggy wanted to share it with. But Jeanne was lost to her.

Seven

Crêpe

You can manufacture crêpe out of anything: wool, silk, acrylic, nylon, or a blend. Frequently it has a slightly crimped or puckered appearance, achieved with a twisted ply. The lighter and smoother the crêpe, the more pins you should use, because it can be slippery and shift during cutting. And use a walking foot so it doesn't bunch in the bobbin case!

You do know, don't you, that crêpe is not to be confused with crape? The latter is for mourning, and who among us has not pressed our tear-stained face to the stiff black bodice of a grandmother or great-aunt? That is crape—that matte black tight weave that seems to suck the very life from a garment. As, I suppose, it should.

April 1951

Jeanne

As the weeks ticked by, Tommie settled into her new routine without complaint, though her prediction seemed to have come true: there were no invitations from other girls, and when Jeanne picked her up in the afternoons, she was never part of any of the little groups of girls assembled in front of the school. And things weren't much better academically. After a promising early start, her teacher praising her quick wit and strong reading skills, she'd begun having behavioral issues. "Strong-willed," the teacher said, "uncooperative and reluctant to participate."

Just like her mother, Jeanne thought, but of course she couldn't share that, because the subject of Tommie's parentage was one she'd deliberately left vague. She'd hinted that her sister suffered from anxiety and had to be institutionalized, and the nuns accepted that information without comment; when Tommie insisted her mother was living in New York City, they gave each other knowing looks.

The nuns were a judgmental and sour lot; she imagined them gossiping behind closed doors, looking for signs of early madness in Tommie. And these years mattered. It wasn't fair, of course, but Tommie must rise above her circumstances, above the abyss of orphanhood into which Peggy had flung her, and make her way in the world.

There were girls in the classroom for whom the social graces came easily. Jeanne recognized them as her own. How she'd ruled the halls at St. Katherine's! She saw in Tommie's classmates the beginnings of a pecking order, the calculated rejections and snubs. At the ages of seven and eight, they were still experimenting, but soon there would be invitations to parties, mixers with the boy's school; then it would be on to college, and in the blink of an eye the girls would be caught up in dating, engagements, marriage.

Against this backdrop of anxiety and worry for Tommie, however, lovely things had happened. The mill was fully operational and production for their third season was under way. Orders were trickling in, with the promise of more as word spread.

And—best of all—she was dating Anthony Salvatici.

She'd gone with him to the restaurant that day seven months ago when she ran into him on Fourth Street. Anthony had introduced her to his brother, Marco, as "the girl I told you about," and served her a four-course lunch that left her barely able to move. Since then there had been many wonderful outings, when a sitter could be arranged or Thelma was visiting and could watch Tommie. There had been movies and a baseball game and long walks—and always dinner, in one little restaurant after another, all over the city. Anthony loved food, whether it was borscht in Northeast Philadelphia or pastrami in Oxford Circle or pierogi in Port Richmond, and Jeanne had already gained a few pounds.

One drizzly Wednesday morning, the plumbing in the showroom sprang a leak, nearly ruining a display of vibrantly colored cotton-polyester bengaline, and a plumber had to be called. Jeanne canceled her appointments for the rest of the day and stole out half an hour early for lunch, leaving Ned, the salesman they had hired when their volume exceeded what she and Frank could handle, in charge.

She had a date with Anthony that night, and she was glad for the extra time to get ready. He was taking her to the restaurant, where she would meet his father for the first time.

She headed back into the city, her mind on what to wear. As she walked past the newsstands at Broad Street Station, she browsed the racks of magazines, perusing the glossy covers and headlines of *Vogue, Charm, Madrigal, Harper's Bazaar,* and *Mademoiselle,* all of which she studied for trends. She glanced at *Good Housekeeping, Women's Own,* and *My Home.* And then an image on a cover stopped her in her tracks.

Around her, the tourists and con men bumped and jostled against panhandlers and preachers, the hustle and noise of noontime at its peak. A woman hissed, "Watch where you're going!" and pushed past. But Jeanne could not tear her eyes from the cover of *Women's Wear Daily.* Because there, in a small piece on the lower corner of the front page, wearing the smile she knew like the back of her own hand, was Peggy.

The headline read: *Peggy Parker, Fashion Designer, Builds Her Empire.*

The name was different but it was Peggy, so familiar and real it was as if she had just told a joke and was laughing at her own punch line. The newsprint blurred as Jeanne stared, her mouth going dry. Finally, she snatched it from the rack and carried it to the counter and asked the man to put it in a plain wrapper, as though passersby could guess what the image meant to her.

She read the article under the awning of a bakery, gusts of rain blowing in on her. "Look at Fyfe's own Designing Miss!" the caption read below another photo of Peggy. In this one, she was standing next to a plastic display mannequin in an empty dress department, her hand on its shoulder. The mannequin was wearing a dress with a wide, flaring skirt.

Even now, Jeanne could see Peggy's work in the design: the clever draping of the bust, the shirred waist panels. But it was her sister she was more interested in. She searched the photos for clues, but Peggy's expression was empty. She was wearing lipstick in a shade of orange that was jarring against her pale skin, but maybe that was just a result of the printing process.

"It's Peggy's year!" So says Helen Perkins, the director of women's fashion at Fyfe's, the beloved and venerable department store launched in Philadelphia in 1888.

Why all the excitement surrounding this young, attractive debut designer? For one thing, she's among the first to test the waters in America that Europeans have long dominated: the namesake label. Sure, the wealthiest customers have long been able to shop at Fyfe's ultra-exclusive couture salon for designer fare, where an evening gown can cost as much as a family automobile and women are served coffee and tea by chicly dressed attendants as they thrill to the latest haute fashions.

But Peggy Parker aims to change all that. "Fashion is for everyone," she gushes, meeting this reporter at Cedar Tavern, a fixture for the in-the-know in Greenwich Village. Miss Parker sipped at a champagne cocktail and barely touched her sole almondine as she explained her take on the glamorous business.

The article went on to tell the story of how Peggy had wanted to design fashions from an early age, sewing clothes for her dolls to match her own and begging for scraps from the ladies in the neighborhood. Jeanne felt her face grow hot as she read stories drawn from *her* childhood that Peggy had appropriated and made her own. Then came a quote that blurred her eyes with tears:

"My mother died when I was young, and my father traveled a great deal for work. I had no siblings, only a series of housekeepers to keep me company. So I lived in a world of my own creation, of paper dolls and make-believe."

In a single sentence, Peggy had written Jeanne out of existence.

And what of Miss Parker's personal life? Though a rising star on the Manhattan social scene, the never-married 28-year-old claims to be far too busy for romance. Rumors of suitors abound, which Peggy declined to address, with an infectious laugh. After all, the wise entrepreneur knows that many a legend has been built on a foundation of intrigue. But a source who wished not to be named confided that Miss Parker has been seen on the arm of a certain handsome widower, a surgeon who is well known for his generosity to many worthy causes.

Peggy had wiped them all away—Thomas, Tommie, Thelma, and even her. It was as though she'd willed her life to become a canvas as blank as the sketchbooks into which she had once poured her heart.

Thelma

Thelma too had seen the article—Mrs. Slater brought it over. She'd been visiting her daughter and had seen the magazine on the coffee table.

"It *is* Peggy, isn't it?" she'd asked. Thelma had been frozen in shock, but as Mrs. Slater rattled on about fresh starts and God's plan, she reclaimed her wits.

"We're really pleased for her, of course." The words were bitter in her mouth. But she needed time to absorb this development, to reconcile it with her sense of betrayal and her anger, which had dimmed only slightly in the days since Peggy left.

But Thelma hadn't gotten where she was without the ability to take the long view, and she had a fine-tuned talent for choosing her moment. She smiled pleasantly and added, "But we were honoring her wish to keep mum about the new line. Peggy insisted on doing it her way, out of the shadow of her elder sister. It's been hard for her, you know, with Jeanne having been such a beauty, so talented in school, and now such a success in business."

Mrs. Slater tutted. "No one deserves a fresh start more than that poor girl. And you too, of course, Thelma."

Mrs. Slater seemed sincere in her wishes. It was she upon whom Thelma had debuted the story that she and Jeanne had come up with to explain Peggy's departure—and the fact that Tommie remained behind: nerves, she'd said, made worse by recurrent dreams of Thomas, dead in the war. The physicians had recommended rest, a less demanding routine.

It was just that Thelma had never expected Peggy to succeed. She'd been certain that the job offer was merely Peggy's desperate attempt to escape—her, Jeanne, the house, but most of all Tommie. Once she'd learned the truth about Tommie, Thelma had come to see Peggy's mothering in a new and unflattering light. It was guilt, she was sure, that made her reject her only child. In Tommie's face she must have seen a daily reminder of her infidelity, of the fact that she'd sent her husband to war—to his death—after squandering her virtue on another man.

That night she stared at the magazine photograph of Peggy, memorizing every detail. The gossamer, spun-silk hair. The bright green dress. The rose gold earrings, which had once been hers, and which Thomas had given Peggy before leaving for the war.

Inside Thelma new seeds of bitterness sprouted and began to grow. It wasn't right that Peggy should thrive after what she'd done, and yet Manhattan seemed to have welcomed her with opened arms and celebrated her in its glittering center.

But Thelma knew something that Peggy didn't, not yet. No sin goes unpaid forever. The triumphs of youth eventually fade, and one is left to face the things one has done. The lucky have their children to comfort them, lovers to console them.

But for most, aging brings clarity that is a cold comfort indeed.

As the night grew late, Thelma tore the pages from the magazine and crumpled them, tossing them into the fireplace. Flames licked at their edges briefly before they went up in a blaze of orange, and Thelma bent close to feel the heat on her face.

As she straightened, she felt a pain deep in her lower back, somewhere near her kidney. It was a new pain, dull rather than urgent; but Thelma knew that it was the price of her bitterness. She had declared vengeance, and she would have it—and then she would be made to pay.

May 1951

Jeanne

"Tell me, please, precisely what Tommie has done to warrant this conversation," Jeanne said tightly.

She was seated in an uncomfortable hardback chair in Sister Eustace's office. There were echoes of St. Katherine's in the austere furnishings, the drafty tall ceilings; but Mount St. Agnes was also worlds away, just as Brunskill was worlds away from downtown Philadelphia, and not just because Tommie's fellow students often arrived in the company of nannies and servants. There were expectations of student and parent—or guardian, in her case—behavior here that Jeanne was still learning to navigate.

"She refuses to focus in Sister John's class."

"Her marks have fallen, then?"

Sister Eustace's mouth folded in on itself, a thin, disapproving line. "Her marks are superior. But if she applied herself, they could be exceptional. Instead, she does *this*."

Sister's hands had been folded on an exercise book. Now she spun it around and opened it. On one page was dutifully copied a list of times tables, in Tommie's familiar, lazy, slanting handwriting. On the other side was a drawing of a bird perched on a flowering branch. It was quite good, actually.

Jeanne started to speak, but then Sister flipped a few pages forward to a drawing of a nun with a comically angry expression on her face, her open mouth featuring long, pointed teeth dripping with blood.

Sister slapped down the open notebook and slid it across her desk.

Jeanne sighed. Tommie, increasingly sullen and uncommunicative at home, had refused to talk about what she'd done to get in trouble. In fact, she rarely wanted to talk about anything at all, spending her afternoons by herself in her room or sitting at the kitchen table with her sketchpad. Jeanne had wondered if she should take Tommie to a doctor—a specialist of some sort—but a few discreet inquiries produced only a shockingly expensive psychoanalyst. It had been only a matter of months since she and Thelma had been struggling to find a way to pay the heating bill; wealth was still an untested tool, as unreliable as the weather, and it seemed irresponsible to spend it on something of such dubious merit.

"I will speak to her about this. But you must admit, Tommie has talent, which if it were properly cultivated—" She pointed past Sister Eustace's office doorway to the reception area, where a small Renoir sketch hung. It had been a gift from a wealthy alumna and was featured on every tour for prospective students. "Perhaps her work could hang here someday."

Sister hacked out a mirthless cough, showing her long yellow teeth, no doubt the ones that had inspired Tommie's drawing. "I'm sure every parent wishes to find talent in her child, Miss Brink. But surely you recognize that suggestion is fantastical."

Jeanne bristled, but held her tongue. Was it her imagination, or did the old nun always put unnecessary emphasis on the word *Miss*, so as to underscore her unmarried status? And the unsubtle use of the word *parent*—which of course Jeanne was not? Still, Sister herself was the ultimate spinster, with her sham marriage to God. The church had lost its hold on Jeanne when she moved to the city, and Jeanne had stopped attending Mass, something else Sister probably held against her.

"This has escalated beyond a problem that can be addressed with conversation. If Thomasina's behavior does not improve, there will not be a place for her here at the Academy of Mount Saint Agnes."

Jeanne felt her fury rise, fury not just at Sister Eustace and her failure to understand what Tommie had been through, how much loss she had suffered—yes, perhaps she and Thelma and Peggy had not disciplined her adequately, perhaps they had allowed her to run free in a household of all women for too long, unfettered and unmolded—and how far she had traveled to come here. And her art! If only Jeanne could explain about Peggy, how at the same age she too had a head full of dreams and a pencil in her hand.

Peggy had been pretty and brash, though, and people naturally excused her temperament, because her eyes were wide and blue, her blond hair fell naturally in perfect ringlets, her creamy soft skin was pink and chubby. Sister Eustace had obviously never been a beauty herself; but of course Jeanne could not appeal to her in that way. *You ordinary girls,* Jeanne longed to say. *You had to work for everything, and now you want to hold it against those of us who didn't.*

"I understand," she said abruptly, standing and reaching for her handbag. "One more thing. I trust our donation to the Building Fund arrived?"

Now it was Sister Eustace's turn to look down uncomfortably at her desk. "Yes."

"It was for three hundred dollars, I believe."

"The check came from Charming Mills," Sister Eustace said pointedly. "Our gratitude to the company will be expressed in the parish bulletin."

"The check," Jeanne said tightly, leaning forward for emphasis, "was written by *me.* Charming Mills is *my* company. I am not married, as you know. Further donations will occur precisely the same way, at the pleasure of Charming Mills's president. That person, it is my duty to remind you, is me."

Sister Eustace looked up at her defiantly then, her scowl filled with such hatred it nearly unsettled Jeanne. *She hates me because of my power,* Jeanne realized. *She hates me because I dared to take it.*

Here in her drafty third-floor office in the brick building wedged into a not particularly fashionable block on Chestnut, Sister had risen as high as she could in the parish—and still she was despised by students, parents, and her fellow nuns; still her authority carried only as far as those she could bully. She'd made an error in thinking she could bully Jeanne. For a moment Jeanne almost felt sorry for her. Jeanne could manage the other parents' censure by making large donations, ensuring Tommie's gloves and veil were clean and pressed, and attending those events at which her presence—or absence—would be remarked upon. And she could, if necessary, manage Sister Eustace with a call to the diocese and the promise of a larger check, assuming Charming's revenues continued as they were.

Sister Eustace had no such choice. She'd already played all of her best cards, and they were a pitiful lot.

With a mixture of pity and scorn, Jeanne nodded goodbye. But at the door, she couldn't resist adding, "Who knows? Perhaps Tommie's art will pay for her own children's tuition one day, long after you're gone."

July 1951

Peggy

"Peggy, darling . . . you're a thousand miles away."

Peggy smiled reflexively and focused on the man seated next to her. He'd purchased a table at the ball, a fund-raiser for the new New York City Ballet—one of the best tables, right in front of the stage where the orchestra would play—and during the seemingly endless speeches, he'd been making little circles on her knee with his fingers. No one at the table knew; none of them would guess that Daniel Griffin, handsome surgeon tragically widowed when his wife suffered a terrible riding accident, would indulge in such illicit activities.

She gave him a smile and patted his hand on her knee, and was saved from having to reply when the event's chairman began his introduction and the spotlight followed Daniel up onto the stage. There he had to wait until the long list of accolades was over to make his own remarks, all while Peggy kept her face carefully composed.

She had to tell him. Not tonight—tonight was for him, the crest of a wave of success he deserved to ride, a triumph over the dark days following his wife's death. But soon. Before the next time Claudia, his daughter, visited from Vassar. Before the web Peggy found herself in drew itself so tightly around her that she could never escape.

Daniel spoke briefly about his involvement in the arts and thanked the organizers for putting on a splendid event, earning applause at every pause. Peggy could feel the envious glances directed her way.

"Fortune has smiled on me in recent months." Daniel's voice was one of his best features, Peggy decided as she listened, its rumbling timbre that she loved to feel against her skin when he held her after their lovemaking. It wasn't just the women in the room who were drawn to Daniel, but the men as well; he had the rare gift of making other men feel greater in stature in his presence. He was generous in that regard, as in most. "As some of you know, I have been fortunate enough to have won the heart of a beautiful woman. I cannot imagine what she sees in me, because she captures the affections of everyone who meets her. Peggy Parker . . ."

He held out his hand, inviting her to join him at the podium—and Peggy understood the gravity of her miscalculation. He wasn't waiting for Claudia's visit—wasn't even waiting for the six-month mark. Why hadn't she listened to Helen, who'd warned her that no man who's been married can return for long to the bachelor life?

An excited murmur filled the room. Next to her, the wife of the chief administrator at the hospital put her hand to her mouth in delight. "Oh, Peggy! Get up there!"

She had no choice. She laid her napkin on her chair and smiled, smiled, smiled for all she was worth, and then she was moving toward the stage, only vaguely aware of her painfully high satin heels. She was walking up the stairs, she was accepting his hand, his kiss on her cheek—careful not to muss her makeup, always so considerate that way—and she was turning, looking out into the sea of faces, the thunderous applause.

"As you know," Daniel began, then had to wait until the applause died down. "As you know, Peggy is a success in her own right. Her line of women's dresses is doing smashingly well here in New York."

Tri-state, Peggy mentally corrected him. Fyfe's had grown to eleven stores in three states, something she was quite sure she had told him. And it wasn't just dresses, of course.

"So I'm hoping she might be able to carve out room in her busy life for this hopeful suitor," Daniel said, reaching into his pocket for a small velvet box.

Don't kneel, Peggy frantically prayed. Please, for the love of God, don't kneel . . . because suddenly she remembered Thomas, that freezing February night outside the courthouse, the thin platinum band with the diamond chips that he'd spent every cent of his savings to buy. The way he'd knelt right there on the icy pavement, grinning up at her with nothing but guileless love in his eyes.

She needn't have worried. Daniel opened the box, and the lights reflected blindingly off the massive brilliant-cut diamond flanked by sapphires and set in platinum as he slipped it on her finger. There was something of the showman in Daniel: he held the microphone at just the right distance when he spoke his next words, so that the audience would have to strain to hear, and a hush fell throughout the room—

"Peggy, my darling, what do you say, will you have me?"

And what could she do? Under the heat of the spotlights, Italian silk fluttering against her legs, the only people she loved hundreds of miles away, she blinked away the memory of Thomas, of Charles, of all of them. The ice around her heart thickened as she held up her hand to catch the light, giving the audience her best profile. Already the ring felt impossibly heavy on her finger.

"Yes," she gasped, and the light shone directly in her eyes so she could not even see the man standing inches away. "Yes!"

❋ ❋ ❋

THAT NIGHT DANIEL made love to her twice, her dress in a puddle on the floor of the suite he had taken. He was even more tender the second time, if it was possible, holding himself up on his elbows while he took his pleasure so as not to let his weight rest on her. Afterward, she shut herself into the bathroom and used one of the fluffy white towels to wipe herself clean.

"Darling," he said when she'd come back to bed. "Let's drive to Vassar tomorrow and surprise Claudia. I'd like us to tell her together."

"Oh, I—I wish I could," Peggy said, casting about for an excuse. Claudia had been perfectly lovely when they'd met, but Peggy had seen it in her eyes—the affront of a girl whose mother had been replaced by someone, anyone, else. "But I'm going to the Pittsburgh store on Monday. I need to pack and organize the samples."

Daniel sighed and continued stroking her back, his hands making idle circles. After a moment he said, "You know that once we're married you can retire and never work again. I love you, Peggy. I don't expect you to be like the rest of those women—with their luncheons and their balls. You don't need to serve on committees or even give interviews if you don't want to. You can give yourself to art, like you've always wanted."

Peggy stared out into the room, the strip of streetlight seeping between the drapes. He pretended he was offering her freedom, but Daniel really just wanted her available to him, whenever he could find a break in his schedule. She could dabble, he was saying, as much as she liked—he'd build her a studio, convince a gallery to show her work, even. She might, if she was lucky, build a small following.

But in return he wanted something she didn't have left to give. Her love. Her devotion. Her commitment.

It wasn't Daniel's fault that he couldn't see how broken she was, or how she had brought it on herself. How God had punished her by taking not just her husband; had not been satisfied until Peggy had lost her daughter and sister and Thelma too. How she would never in her life be able to right the wrongs she had committed.

"Perhaps . . . perhaps we might even consider having a child, Peggy," Daniel said gently. "A child would occupy your time."

Peggy froze. There would be no child. She'd already made sure of that, but Daniel did not need to now about the doctor downtown, the one with no nameplate on his door.

She suspected that Daniel didn't really want a baby, anyway. It was just one more step in making her his, in lashing her tightly to his life.

And inside Peggy, who knew she deserved nothing, who'd already squandered every indulgence God could ever give, the quiet spark of rebellion refused to be extinguished. As she feigned sleep, the spark took flame and burned bright.

Jeanne

The first few weeks of second grade seemed to agree with Tommie. The miserable Sister John had given way to the considerably kinder Sister Aloysius, who smelled like spice cake and told Tommie she was clever. On a wave of optimism, Jeanne suggested a party for Tommie's birthday. But of the thirteen invited girls, only eight came.

The regrets of the others had trickled in late in the week. First was Hope's mother; Hope was the meanest—and prettiest—of the girls in the class, a bright little thing with tumbling auburn curls. The rest quickly followed, and Jeanne imagined the gossip among the mothers, about the homely little girl with no parents, the one whose aunt worked to send her to the academy.

Jeanne had done her best to make light of the other girls' absence, but Tommie had started the day solemn and quiet, barely touching the cinnamon babka for which Jeanne had made an early morning trip uptown to the bakery.

Thelma had arrived the night before and been up early to bake the birthday cake, and she was finishing it in the kitchen, piping on roses, when Jeanne came in half an hour before the first guests were due to arrive. Thelma didn't hear her come in, and Jeanne paused at the door, alarmed. Thelma was hunched at the sink, holding her stomach and whimpering softly in pain.

"Thelma?" she asked in alarm. "Is everything all right?"

"Oh, I'm fine," she said, instantly straightening. But her face was pale and the lines around her eyes seemed deeper.

"You'd tell me," Jeanne said, "if something was wrong—wouldn't you?"

Thelma's expression softened. "It's nothing for you to worry about."

"Thelma—please." There was more that Jeanne suddenly wished she could say. That she loved Thelma . . . that she was all she had left, besides Tommie.

Thelma turned away. "I'd better get a move on," she said. "This cake isn't going to decorate itself."

Jeanne's housekeeper rushed into the kitchen. "Miss Brink, Miss Brink! Tommie wants to cancel the party. She is very upset!"

Jeanne followed Gloria back down the hall. Tommie wasn't in her room, where Thelma had spent the night on the fold-away cot, but in Jeanne's room, sitting on the bed sobbing into a pillow.

Next to her was the magazine. The one with Peggy's picture on the cover.

Jeanne's heart fell. She'd been so careful; she'd stowed the magazine in the drawer of her dressing table, where she thought Tommie would never bother to look. But the dressing table was littered with cosmetics, hair ornaments, and perfume, and suddenly Jeanne understood—Tommie had snuck in here to borrow Jeanne's things, to prepare for the party.

Jeanne's heart broke for Tommie. All of this disappointment in one day was too much: to know that her classmates shunned her—then to see her mother's photograph on the magazine.

Only the package from Peggy was still safely hidden in the closet. Jeanne had nearly relented and allowed Tommie to have it, but Thelma had talked her out of it last night.

"It'll be worse, knowing she isn't here," Thelma said. "It will just be a reminder that she left. The sooner she forgets all about her mother, the better."

And now, it was Jeanne's fault that the wound had been reopened. She sat down on the bed next to Tommie, took her head in her lap, and stroked her hair. There were clumsy smudges of rouge on the girl's cheeks, and her hair had come undone. It didn't matter.

Thelma sat down on Tommie's other side. She picked up the magazine and slid it under the bed with a significant look. Jeanne would get rid of the magazine later.

"Why isn't she here for my party?" Tommie sobbed. "Doesn't she care about me anymore?"

"Now that's enough," Thelma said firmly. "Your mother has a job to do and that's just the way it is. You've got lots of nice things here, and your aunt is every bit as nice as any of those other mothers, isn't she?"

Tommie's sobs were growing hoarse with exhaustion, gradually turning to heartbreaking whimpering.

Gloria poked her head in the door. "Miss Jane Weatherby is here."

Thelma's and Jeanne's eyes met. "You get her ready," Thelma said. "I'll go entertain Miss Jane."

WHEN JEANNE LED Tommie—halting, shy—from the room five minutes later, her hair had been repaired, her face washed, her tears wiped away. Jeanne had dabbed a bit of perfume on each of Tommie's pale wrists.

Jane Weatherby was sitting at the table with Thelma, cutting out paper hearts. They were meant for a game the girls were to play later, but Jeanne knew that by giving the little girl a task, Thelma had made her an ally.

"Hello, Jane," Tommie said formally, and Jeanne was struck by her near-imperious tone, so like her own when she'd been a schoolgirl. Jeanne had not been very nice to the other little girls when she was in first grade, but at the moment she was pleased to see Tommie hold herself back a bit. "I'm glad that you could come to my party."

It was as though some switch had been reset. Girls continued to arrive, their mothers openly appraising the apartment, which Jeanne had just had redone top to bottom. Ivory silk dupioni drapes hung from the tall windows, the walls were papered with a bold Colefax & Fowler stylized print, and she'd bought all new furniture from Heywood-Wakefield. Jeanne knew that the apartment made up in style for what her address lacked in cachet, and that these women would spread the word to the mothers who had shunned the party about this curious, perhaps dangerous single woman who was living successfully on her own.

The judgments they made today could chart Tommie's social course for the next few years at least, and Jeanne had prepared well. The tea cart was set with her mother's coffee service, one of the few beautiful things that Emma Brink had owned. Gloria's luncheon—pinwheel finger sandwiches, ham salad, individual gelatin molds—was laid out beautifully on lacquered trays Jeanne found at Florence Knoll. Jeanne was wearing a smart Claire McCardell wrap dress, a nod to the nascent American couture industry, and of course there was her figure—as trim as ever, the envy of these women whose post-childbearing bodies had softened like water-soaked sponges.

But it was Tommie who seized the day and made it her own. Whatever she'd resolved, after her tearful tantrum, she was different now. The clumsy taunts and snubs that had wounded Tommie as recently as yesterday now glanced off her harmlessly. Besides, the other girls seemed oddly cowed. Maybe it was the apartment's chic glamour, so different from the old-money mansions to the north. And maybe it was the enormous collection of dolls and clothes and toys in Tommie's room, gifts from Thelma.

But Jeanne knew that mostly it was Tommie finally hardening herself to her mother's absence, shutting off her heart to further hurt. She held her head high as she led the girls on a tour of the apartment, showing off Jeanne's wardrobe of shoes, her dressing mirror, the racks of clothes and handbags. She showed them the polished Gaggia espresso machine in the kitchen, the ice maker in the new refrigerator. She made up a story of how a baby had fallen down the mail chute and died.

During the party games her voice stood out above the others—bossy, demanding, sly. When one of the girls pouted after losing a game of pin the tail on the donkey, Tommie announced, "You might as well stop or you'll have to sit by yourself in the kitchen," in a voice so like Peggy's that Jeanne did a double take. She opened her gifts with theatrical timing, pulling off the paper slowly, thanking each girl with a sigh that suggested the gift did not quite meet her expectations. Somehow, she'd mastered the art of indifference, and the girls lapped up her scorn like kittens at the milk dish.

She held her composure until the very end. As the last girl's mother was gushing over the party favor that Jeanne had made by a seamstress they sometimes employed at the showroom—little velvet purses embroidered with each guest's initial—Tommie tried to slink from the room.

"Come back here," Thelma said, grabbing her arm and hauling her back. "Please tell Betsy how much you enjoyed having her at your party."

"I didn't, though," Tommie said, staring up at Thelma in feigned innocence. "Betsy smells like boiled eggs."

All three women looked at her in shock. Betsy—who was, it was true, an ungainly little thing, with a red birthmark shaped like a large comma on one side of her face—burst into tears. "I do not, I do not," she wailed, pressing her face to her mother's coat.

But Jeanne recognized the resignation in that mother's eyes; she too had lost sleep over her child's social woes, she too suspected deep down that there was some damage she would never be able to repair.

"I'm so terribly sorry," Jeanne said to the mother, but there was a part of her that felt pure secret joy, that there was now to be a new class outcast, and it would not be Tommie. "Tommie, that was perfectly awful of you. Apologize at once."

"Oh, I'm sorry," Tommie said through heavy-lidded eyes. "I didn't mean to hurt your feelings. Maybe you could borrow some of my perfume if you like." Then, turning to the mother before any of them could react, she said, "Genevieve gave me a bottle of Little Lovely. It's just for girls. It comes in a pink glass bottle."

"How—how nice," the mother said as her daughter wiped her eyes and sniffled.

"We'll have to get the girls together to play," Jeanne said.

"That would be very nice."

Thelma ushered them to the door, and when they were gone, she turned and collapsed against it. "I'm too old for this," she said, and it was there in the blue circles under her eyes, the sagging of her skin, the echoes of the pain and exhaustion Jeanne had glimpsed earlier.

But she seemed happy.

They decided to go out for tea while Gloria cleaned up. Jeanne went to fetch Tommie, but she was fast asleep on the floor of her room, clutching the shabby old stuffed rabbit that Peggy had bought her with her very first paycheck.

Thelma

It seemed fitting that the restaurant at the hotel he chose, half an hour away in Ridgewood, should be drafty and dark. She drove herself in the first car she'd ever owned, a 1950 Nash Rambler, and found him sitting at a table nearly hidden in the back, wedged between the serving door and a tall ficus tree.

"Imagine running into you here," she'd joked when she arrived—and then she'd seen the look in his eyes, and knew that it was worse than she'd feared.

But later, after the dinner had been brought and taken away, nearly untouched—because one still had to go through the motions of ordinary life, still had to speak cordially with the waiter who had no idea of the poison you carried inside you, the seconds ticking away all the things you thought you had time for—some of her good humor returned.

"I'm not afraid, you know," she said over coffee laced with Irish whiskey.

"Please, Thelma. Let's not talk any more about it tonight."

"Look, Jack. I'm not just another one of your patients. You don't have to protect me."

"Did it ever occur to you," he said, "that it's not you I'm protecting? That despite everything you've accused me of—all the mistakes we've both made—I still love you?"

"Don't," she said automatically, for it had been a rule since the first time and it would be a rule the last time she ever saw him, because what he had told her would not change their arrangement. Then she softened a little. "You do know I want the best for you," she said gently. "There's still time, for you. I would hope you would make the most of it."

"Time for what?" he said in a harsh whisper. "Time to replace you? Is that what you want from me? To stare in some stranger's eyes and never stop wishing it was you?"

"Of course not," Thelma said, and then she couldn't help it. She laughed. The diners at the next table looked over and smiled—perhaps they'd noticed the handsome older couple, their fine clothes, his gold watch, her still-lovely face. "Time for you to make an honest woman of your little Ukrainian girl. Or to go back to Patricia. Make her happy, be the husband you should have been."

"You're cruel," Jack finally said. "You've always been."

"Oh, hush now, let's go upstairs," Thelma said. Because in the end there was that—always, there had been that.

MUCH LATER, WHEN the first pink glow of dawn was seeping through the window, they woke. They watched each other, not talking, as they dressed, Jack knotting his tie with the same practiced speed as the first time they'd been together, Thelma zipping a far nicer dress than the one she'd worn then.

He walked her to the door. She would go first; he would wait, though surely the porters and concierge knew exactly what was going on.

"When will I see you again?"

"Oh, Jack." She sighed, smoothing his collar as she'd once done for Henry. "Don't ask me questions like that."

His mouth worked; he searched for something to say. There wasn't anything, of course. Men were so unequipped for moments like this.

"All right. Call me in two weeks. We'll figure something out."

His kiss, dry and cool and papery, seemed to linger. On the drive home Thelma put her fingers to her cheek and let herself imagine it sinking into her skin, branding her poor body with his benediction. She would not see him in two weeks. She would not see him again, because from this point on it would only be worse, and he would only see her deterioration and know he was losing, losing, losing her.

At home she set her bag down in the hall and leaned against the wall, tired already though the day was only hours old. She would make a pot of coffee and sit with the papers and drink a cup, and then, perhaps, she would go to bed. She had no calls or appointments today; Mondays were reserved for the books. Tomorrow, she would feel better. Tonight, she would call Jeanne and lie to her, tell her that the doctor said she'd be good as new soon.

She'd rinsed her cup in the sink and taken off her shoes

when there was a knock at the door. She padded to the door in her stocking feet.

It was a messenger, a young man with a cloth cap. "Telegram for Mrs. Thomas Holliman, ma'am."

Thelma automatically reached for it before realizing that it was not intended for her, having somehow only heard "Mrs. Holliman," then stood staring at the envelope in her hand for so long that the young man grew embarrassed. He cleared his throat and stepped off her porch, and she thanked him and closed the door, then ripped open the envelope. It was wrong of her to open a telegram meant for Peggy; but it was a minor transgression compared with everything her daughter-in-law had done.

She read through the brief message. A sob escaped her as she sank to the floor and read it again:

THE NAVY DEPARTMENT WISHES TO INFORM YOU THAT THE BODY OF YOUR HUSBAND THOMAS HOLLIMAN WILL BE RETURNED TO YOU AS PER YOUR WISHES. ARRIVING BY TRAIN BRUNSKILL PA 0930 THURSDAY OCTOBER 12.

REAR ADMIRAL JACOBS THE CHIEF OF NAVAL PERSONNEL.

Thomas was finally coming home.

Eight

Greige

*Greige, of course, means any fabric which is not fully pro-
cessed; which is neither bleached nor dyed. Bolt upon bolt
of it, waiting in the warehouse, can be an eerie sight: pale
columns of nothing, against the sepia shadows of the dye
vats and pallets. You may feel as though you are looking
at an old photograph, when in fact what you are seeing is
sheer possibility. Will the order come in for palest wiste-
ria or shocking violet? Will it be embroidered, overdyed,
glazed, tucked? Anything, you see, can happen next.*

October 1951

Peggy

Peggy was in Newark, where they had finished refurbishing a section of the misses department in order to feature the new fall Peggy Parker Originals collection. Advertisements had been placed in the paper and invitations mailed to the store's best customers.

Peggy and her team had learned from each show, tweaking and improving along the way, and she was feeling much more confident than she had the first time. The ladies filed in, a plainer and less affluent group than those she'd already addressed, and Peggy mentally adjusted her planned remarks to focus on practicality and durability. She shuffled the rack, choosing a Dacron-cotton ensemble to lead with, and reviewed the changes in the order with the models before retreating for her customary solitude before the show.

The Newark store manager was a portly man who seemed better suited to selling farm equipment than fashion. He looked chastened as he kept to the edge of the room, staying out of everyone's way, glancing at the script that Peggy had developed. She'd offered it merely as a suggestion, but she hoped he wouldn't venture too far from the remarks she'd prepared for him and would allow her to conduct the show.

Peggy only half listened to him as he read verbatim from the sheet, welcoming the ladies and drumming up their fervor with a promise of a take-home gift and the luncheon to follow. She'd adopted a little private routine for luck before going out into the audience: she touched her earlobes, left and then right, feeling the comforting smooth round surface of the rose gold earrings, the only tie to Thomas that she still had. She made a sign of the cross—she still went to Mass every Sunday, at a church on Mulberry where she was one of few non-Italians, sitting alone in a pew near the back and ducking out after Communion—and then, finally, she put her hand in her pocket and touched satin. It was Tommie's hair ribbon, which had been in Peggy's purse the day Thelma had ordered her out of the house because it had fallen out of Tommie's hair on the way to school and Tommie didn't want to wait for her mother to retie it. Now, it was her only physical connection to her daughter, and she took it with her everywhere she went.

"My darling," she whispered, rubbing it for luck. Then she took the stage.

"Ladies of Newark, hello!" she said, clapping. The ladies roared their delight and joined in, and the "Fall Fiesta" was officially begun with thundering applause ringing throughout the second floor.

An hour later Peggy's part was done. Two salesgirls served squares of pink sugar-dusted cake and another served coffee. The models posed and allowed themselves to be admired like prize poodles, and the department manager and her assistant took orders from a long line of enthusiastic customers.

"Miss Parker," a handsome young man called. A reporter, for the *Star-Ledger*, perhaps; she was becoming accustomed to press coverage and had built time into her schedule for an interview and photos.

But today she hoped she could put the young man off. She was tired; she had dinner scheduled that night with the manager of the Newark store and the regional marketing director, and she longed for nothing more than a nap before she had to dress and fix her hair all over again.

"I'm so sorry," she said. "But I've got to dash. Please talk to my assistant—there she is, in that fetching little hat—and we can set up a time to talk, yes?"

The man turned away, disappointed, and Peggy scanned the room looking for her exit. She'd become expert at spotting the gaps in crowds, the lulls in conversations, that allowed her to make her escape.

And then her eyes fell on a woman standing in the corner of the room, watching her, a veiled hat shadowing her eyes. But Peggy would have known her anywhere, from the set of her narrow ankles, her graceful neck and slender waist, the way she clutched her hands to her chest as if holding her heart in place.

Peggy's breath caught in her throat, and for a moment she was frozen, watching her sister moving toward her through the crowd, astonishment giving way to sudden terror. She raced to meet her and seized her sister's hands. "Oh God, is she all right?"

Jeanne squeezed back, her eyes brimming with tears. "Tommie's fine," she said, her voice thick with emotion. "It's Thomas, Peggy. They're finally sending him home."

Jeanne

She had planned to be furious but the fury had withered even before she stepped out of the taxi. It had been easy enough to learn that "Peggy Parker" would be appearing less than an hour away; when she called the Fyfe's switchboard yesterday, the operator had misunderstood her inquiry and told her, regretfully, that no more tickets remained for the event. Jeanne had told Tommie only that she had to go to a meeting that might run late, and Gloria would pick her up at school and give her her dinner.

To Anthony, she had said nothing at all. Lord knew he'd been patient with her; she'd been waiting for the right moment to introduce him to Tommie, but until then, they were limited to once- or twice-a-week rendezvous, cut short so that Jeanne could be home for the sitter, a teenage girl whose parents had given her a strict curfew. Jeanne had given him a version of the same story about Peggy that she had told the nuns—that her sister was institutionalized, that she was ill—so there was no way she could explain the current crisis without exposing her lies.

She'd intended to use the train and taxi rides to fine-tune her fury at Peggy. She wanted to make Peggy understand how badly she had hurt them all by leaving. Thomas's body would be in Brunskill in less than twenty-four hours, and the military escort would be expecting Peggy to be there, but before that happened Jeanne meant to make Peggy understand that Thelma would be the one to make all the decisions about the funeral, no matter who was listed as next of kin.

"You probably don't have time in your schedule anyway," she'd planned to say coldly. It wasn't fair that Peggy should have the honor of burying her husband, when all that Jeanne had been accorded was to sit in the pew behind Charles's family, squeezed between several of his cousins. Her name was not even mentioned in the program. She was not invited to stand in the receiving line. Charles's mother was in no condition to make introductions, so many of the guests never even knew that she was the woman whom Charles had promised to marry.

Even in this last act, she had been forced to accept half measures while Peggy would receive full recognition.

But as the taxicab crawled through the late afternoon traffic along Broad Street, her resolve faltered. She remembered how Peggy had locked herself in her room after learning of Thomas's death nine years earlier, how she hadn't eaten or bathed for days. She'd loved him, once; Jeanne had worried then that her love would consume her, would leave nothing left over. Instead, Peggy had slowly become someone else. As the cab pulled up in front of the grand redbrick and limestone entrance, Jeanne gave up trying to hold on to her cold, hard resentment and steeled herself to witness her sister's heart breaking all over again.

"They're finally sending him home," she said, and Peggy's face had gone white with shock. But she quickly regained her composure, taking Jeanne's hand and leading her through a service door into the network of hallways and storage used by employees. Peggy knew her way and moved so fast that Jeanne could barely keep up, and they didn't speak until they exited the building and crossed the street to the hotel where Peggy was staying.

"We can talk in my room, but I need to make a call first," Peggy said. Jeanne watched in astonishment as her sister placed the call from the telephone in her elegant room and directed whoever answered to cancel all her plans for the evening. So Peggy had her own staff now; Jeanne marveled at her curt self-assurance. Somehow, the two of them had both left the past further behind than either ever dreamed.

Peggy put down the phone. She was sitting in the room's only chair; Jeanne perched on the edge of the bed. "How did they finally get permission to send the body back to America?"

"I really don't know any more than what I've told you," Jeanne said truthfully. "Someone from the navy called the house, but he didn't have a lot of details either. Thelma's hoping that whoever is escorting the body . . ."

"The body," Peggy echoed, stricken. Jeanne wanted to offer her comfort, but the gulf between them seemed too great. How formal they were with each other now. How like strangers.

"I'll come to Brunskill in the morning," Peggy said. "I can

be there by the time the train comes. I'll . . . I can get a room at the Falls Hotel."

"Wait," Jeanne said. "You can't—Thelma's going to be the one to meet the train. You don't have to be there. It will be better if you're not."

"Of course I'll be there," Peggy said, but Jeanne could see that she hadn't thought it through. How would they ever get through this? If word got out, there were likely to be crowds at the train station. In the thick of the war, the arrival of flag-draped coffins had become almost commonplace; but now that the pace had thinned to a trickle of bodies being sent home from temporary burial sites in the Pacific, people were turning out again to honor the dead.

There might be a little crowd of them, with signs and tiny flags. Photographers from the local paper would be there. Maybe the mayor. And there they would be, the dead man's mother and his daughter, his wife's absence a gaping hole.

People would talk. The seeds of the story they'd planted—that Peggy had been sent away after a breakdown; that she'd been maddened by grief—would spread. Tommie was too young to understand now, but how long did they have until she started asking questions? Until she heard uncharitable gossip and demanded answers?

"What about your job?" she said, a little desperately. "The Peggy Parker story?"

"I can't believe you're asking me that," Peggy said. "This is my *husband* we're talking about."

"You can't do this to Tommie," Jeanne burst out. "You can't

just—just suddenly show up and, and make her think you're back in her life! And Thelma, she hasn't been well, you haven't seen her but there's something—there's something—"

There's something wrong with her, she was trying to say, but suddenly she was crying too hard. It was a thought she'd never dared speak out loud, despite Thelma's weight loss, her refusal to eat, the visits she'd canceled. All of which Peggy had missed.

"We'll figure it out," Peggy said, almost desperately. "Let me call the hotel and see if I can get a room for tonight. We can go back to Brunskill right now."

"Your *daughter* is in *Philadelphia*," Jeanne reminded her, "and while I'm sure you've lost track, she's still too young to travel by herself."

"Oh, God, Jeanne, I know that, I know, it's just—" Peggy blinked rapidly, then pulled a handkerchief from her purse and dabbed her eyes. "But she has a nanny, right? Could the nanny bring her and . . ."

"This is for *me* to figure out," Jeanne said, trembling with fear and anger. "I'm here as a courtesy. I—we—thought you should know. But there's no need for you to come."

Peggy blanched. "You can't keep me away, you can't—"

"You were with him for a few *months*," Jeanne said. "He's been dead for years. I'm not going to let you put Thelma through—put *Tommie* through—"

The words wouldn't come, because how could she describe her fears for Tommie, her refusal to let the girl suffer any more heartbreak because of Peggy's selfishness? How could Peggy dare to show up and risk upsetting Thelma now, when she was so weak?

But Peggy hadn't seen either Thelma or Tommie in two years. She couldn't know about the changes in either of them.

"I'm going back alone now, to my apartment," Jeanne said, suddenly exhausted. "I need to be with Tommie; I want to be there before she goes to bed."

Emotions passed over Peggy's face that Jeanne could not identify. "You've become a real little mother, haven't you?" she finally asked quietly. "What do you tell her about me?"

"We don't talk about you. I don't give her your letters."

"I didn't suppose you had. But what does she know about why I left?"

"We told her you've got an important job to do. We try to keep her from seeing your picture in the magazines."

"It wasn't meant to be forever," Peggy said, almost desperately. "Only until I got things sorted out, until I could get a place for us both—"

"Oh, stop it," Jeanne said. "It's *me* you're talking to. Don't lie to me. Tell yourself whatever you need to believe to get through the day. But don't pretend you ever meant to have her with you."

"Things could be different now. I've got money. A lot of it. She can come and live with me."

Here was the moment that Jeanne had dreaded and feared. She had sworn she would never allow Peggy to hurt Tommie again. But she hadn't factored Thomas into her plans. He was a hero now, and if the press sussed out that Peggy Parker was actually his wife, they wouldn't be able to resist the sensational story.

Of course, Jeanne could go to the press too, and tell the truth about her sister, how she'd abandoned their child and walked out on her mother-in-law. That might dampen the papers' enthusiasm for the war-widow angle.

But either way, the stakes were too high, because it was Tommie who'd be caught in the middle.

"Peggy." She tried to soften her voice, swallowing down her bitterness and fear. "Once Thomas has been given a proper funeral, and things settle down again, maybe you can visit Tommie. But right now, she's too vulnerable. She's had to live with the fact that you walked out on her, that she had to move away from the only home she'd ever known—"

"*You're* the one who moved her to the city," Peggy protested angrily. "You won't let me see her, won't give her my letters—"

"We have done what we believed was right for her," Jeanne shot back. "*I* put her needs first every time. She finally has *friends* now, did you know that? Little girls who come over to play. Her own bedroom. Room for all her toys."

She saw Peggy do the calculations, saw her trying to add the months and years to the child she remembered. "She can have all of that in New York," Peggy said uncertainly.

"What makes you think she'd be happy there?" Jeanne demanded. "You can't keep this up, all of this—running around. I see the society pages, you know. I hear the talk. You're out every night of the week."

"That's not true!"

"And what are you going to tell *him*, anyway?" Jeanne and Thelma had pored over photographs of the couple in *Vanity Fair*, posing at a ball the night he proposed. "The news that you were *married* might come as something of a shock, don't you think? Oh, and the press will love it."

She watched the implications dawn on her sister and took little pleasure from her horror.

"Daniel is—that's over," she said uncertainly.

"Oh! Really?" Jeanne pointed to her sister's left hand. "Why aren't you wearing his ring? I understand you accepted it."

"I—I don't wear it for travel," Peggy said. "I don't . . . Jeanne, listen. There are things you don't understand. Please, I need to talk to Thelma. I need to—"

"She doesn't want to talk to you," Jeanne said forcefully. In truth, Thelma had been curiously unconcerned about Peggy; she was wholly focused on Thomas now. Frank was with her; Jeanne had implored him not to leave her alone.

I can't believe it, she'd said, over and over, since she got the news. *I can't believe he's finally coming home.*

Peggy was searching her face. "She's still my child," she said in a small voice. "I . . . still love her."

"Like you loved Thomas?" Jeanne said icily.

"Of course I did," Peggy said, aghast. "You know I loved him. How could you doubt that?"

Jeanne stared at her sister, regretting her words. No: she didn't really believe that Peggy hadn't loved her husband. Or her child. It was just that there was something broken in her sister, some inability to care for others. She had been too much of a child herself, too caught up in her own needs, her impulses and fleeting desires.

But the woman in front of her had changed. She was on the cover of magazines, her name known to women all over the East Coast. She had money and power and did not seem to be afraid of either.

Had Jeanne misunderstood her, all those years when she'd aimlessly haunted their home? Underestimated her? Had all of them?

"I'm sorry," she said, hearing the hollowness in her own voice and hating it. "I have to go. I'll call you when it's all over."

"Please," Peggy whispered, but she made no move to stop Jeanne as she strode to the door. "Please."

Jeanne stepped into the hallway and shut the door behind her, the sound muffled by the thick, expensive carpet, and hurried to the elevator.

What had they done? How had they lost their faith in each other? If only they'd held on—if only they'd been more generous with each other. If only they'd known that grief wasn't forever, that life inevitably would carry them someplace new.

The elevator reached her floor and Jeanne stepped inside, barely nodding to the other well-dressed passengers. She crossed the well-appointed lobby without really noticing it and stepped out into the drive. A brisk wind had come up, spitting rain. Jeanne turned up the collar of her coat as the bellhop tried to flag down a cab for her.

She was heading home, to Thelma and their work, the lives

they'd carved for themselves. To Tommie, who needed her. She would protect what they had made. Thomas would finally receive the honors due him, and would be laid to rest next to his father. In the spring, Jeanne and Thelma would help Tommie plant flowers around his headstone.

But Jeanne understood now that Peggy would not give up. That her sister would come for Tommie and that there was nothing they could do to stop her. Legally, they had no right to the child; and with some clever management of the press, Peggy could easily spin the story in her favor. Six years after the end of the war, America had a powerful hunger for happy endings.

Thelma would accept her daughter-in-law back into the fold if it was the only way to stay in Tommie's life. In the calculus of love, Jeanne knew that she—with no blood connection to Thelma—would always come a distant second to her granddaughter. Perhaps Thelma would move to New York. There was money now, enough for all of them.

Jeanne would be left behind. She would run the mill and honor their father's memory and, she supposed, buy a house of her own someday. She would go back to being only Tommie's aunt; she'd visit on holidays and the occasional summer weekend. Anthony would grow weary of her sadness and leave her, and then she would be a spinster; perhaps eventually she'd become an eccentric.

If Peggy played her hand, all of this would come to pass. And once again there would be no place in the world left to Jeanne.

Peggy

After Jeanne left, Peggy collapsed on the luxuriant bedcovers, clutching herself, making herself so small she thought she might disappear entirely. Thomas, back on American soil. Back home. It was almost more than she could fathom. Every time she thought she might fully absorb the news, an image would come to her—the soldier who'd delivered the telegram when Thomas was killed, exhausted from having to break too many hearts. Jeanne's face crumpling in on itself eighteen months later when Charles's father called with the news of his death in Italy. Being wheeled down the hall in the hospital after she went into labor, with Jeanne holding her hand right up until they took her into the operating room.

Holding her newborn daughter, alone.

If her Thomas had been alive he would never have allowed her to suffer such crushing loneliness. Thomas had been more than other men, better than other men. "I'll send angels to watch over you until I come home, darling," he had said that day at the train station, holding her close, whispering in her ear as his mother hovered too close. And Peggy had believed it. Stupid, naïve, unforgivable—but yes, she had believed it.

The guilt had followed her everywhere. There hadn't been a day since she betrayed him that she'd ever forgotten or not known she was being punished. The pain and shocking mess of

Tommie's birth, the horrible sameness of the days with an infant. The infected, cracked nipples; the awful light-headedness of sleep deprivation, the changes in the body she'd once taken for granted. And Tommie, insatiable, irrational, unforgiving.

Peggy deserved all that and worse.

She thought of poor Rose Scopes, dead by her own hand but only because Peggy had given her the push. Rose had only been a bystander. Peggy had ruined everyone, had hurt so many. Why she hadn't just told Jeanne the truth, Peggy didn't know. But Jeanne would know soon enough.

Peggy roused herself and went to the mirror. She splashed water on her face and blotted it with one of the soft towels. Her reflection stared back, her makeup smudged, her eyes red. What if, instead of going back home tonight, she went to Philadelphia? She would stay up all night; she would wait outside Jeanne's building, and when they emerged in the morning, she would snatch Tommie up and run, straight to an attorney's office, who would . . .

The reflection seemed to sneer at the ludicrousness of the thought. Did she imagine that Tommie, who hadn't seen her since that awful day that she walked away, would be glad to see her? Besides, Tommie would be different too: Could Peggy keep her resolve when she saw her daughter older, taller, wiser? Capable, perhaps, of understanding how completely her mother had failed her?

The truth was that Tommie as a baby had been hard enough. Tommie as a *person*—an individual with opinions and dreams—was unfathomable.

And what was she to tell Daniel? It was a damning admission to reveal to a man whose life was subject to public scrutiny, who was keenly aware of his stature in society. Daniel had chosen her partly because of how well she was received by the press. But the attention she would bring his way if the truth about her was revealed would not be welcome anymore.

Her reflection seemed to distort and blur, but it was only her own tears. Peggy sagged against the bathroom wall, feeling the cold tile against her skin. She remembered a day at the shore, shortly after she and Thomas had started going steady. It had been a group of them that day; they all crowded into a train car and arrived in the shimmering heat of a late September afternoon, and the boys whooped and hollered and carried the girls like Egyptian goddesses to the blankets they'd spread on the beach. Late in the afternoon she'd fallen asleep in the sun, and when she woke, Thomas was lying next to her, propped up on his elbow, staring at her with a funny little smile on his face. Peggy had bolted awake, her hands going to the straps of her swimsuit. "What?" she'd demanded, looking about for the others. "What?"

"Just thinking," he'd said. "Wondering what you'll look like when we're old."

"Oh, what an awful thing to think about! I'll be ugly, and wrinkled, and I'll have yellow teeth and—"

"And you'll still be the most beautiful girl in the world," he'd said softly. "I don't care what happens, Pegs. You're meant for me and me for you."

He'd been wrong, of course. They'd been like children,

carefree and careless, believing in fairy tales. Neither was meant for anything at all. She was Peggy Parker now, and their love might as well have never existed.

Peggy wearily sank down to the edge of the bathtub. Everything that had happened, she had brought on herself . . . but who was to say it would have come out any better if she'd behaved perfectly? It was like one of those old-fashioned stereographs she remembered from childhood. You held it up to your eyes and—like magic—you peered into a whole other world, mustachioed gentlemen chasing blushing women in voluminous skirts. But Peggy had always wondered, even as a child, what had happened next. It was unknowable: when you put the thing down, the image vanished. And yet it lived on in her mind.

If she could go back in time—to that beach, to that sultry afternoon—and do everything differently . . . well. There would be no Tommie. And that alone was enough—enough to give Peggy the resolve to do what must be done.

She stood and fixed her face, adjusted her clothes. Threw her things into her suitcase and called down to the desk for a cab.

"WHAT WAS SO urgent, love, that you had to see me right now?" Daniel spoke lightly, but there was a faint edge of irritation in his voice. Even in light of what she'd come here to do, Peggy marveled that she hadn't noticed it before. Or, rather, if she were truthful with herself, she had noticed and chosen to push it deep down inside her. With a man of Daniel's stature, one had to accept a bit of impatience, an expectation that the world would conform to his wishes. After all, he was accustomed to getting what he wanted.

"Well," she said. Daniel had mixed her a drink without being asked, the gin rickey that somehow had become her signature cocktail. They were in the living room in his sprawling home in Connecticut. Several times before, during a cocktail hour in this room, Peggy had grown bored by the conversation among Daniel's friends and let her mind wander to the dead wife. Had she played the gleaming piano? Had she chosen the paintings that flanked the fireplace, or had a decorator?

Had she and Daniel ever made love here, when their daughter was small, when they'd come home giddy and a little drunk from an evening out, after they sent the sitter home?

The drink Daniel handed her was perfect, a little sliver of lime floating in it. She sipped slowly, buying time. Daniel sat down next to her, his tumbler of bourbon balanced on his knee, and reached for her hand. He knew that she kept the ring in a safe in her townhouse when she traveled, but she could feel his faint disapproval as he turned her hand over before lacing her fingers with his own.

"There are some things I should tell you," Peggy began. "Things I probably should have said before. About me, about my past."

His hand stilled on hers. He shifted, almost imperceptibly, away.

Somehow, he knew what was coming—hadn't they both, almost from the start?

Thelma

"This is going to be a very exciting day for you," Thelma said. She was sitting on the painted wicker chair in Tommie's room, part of a set she'd given her granddaughter for her birthday. There was a matching dressing table complete with a small oval mirror, and a monogrammed sterling brush and comb. Tommie loved to sit in front of the mirror, but rather than play dress-up, she sketched her own reflection in her notebooks.

The chair was uncomfortable, but then again, most everything had begun to hurt. It wasn't just the stomach and back pain anymore. The disease was reaching into her bones, spreading through her body. Thelma had lost eighteen pounds already, pounds that even six months ago she would have been delighted to see disappear. She would continue to lose, she supposed, until she had to be put in some room somewhere, to finish dying . . . she didn't like thinking about that, and it wasn't because she was afraid. It just seemed like a lot of fuss when she already knew the outcome.

A problem for another day.

Because tomorrow, Thomas would finally be returning

home. Today she and Tommie would ride back to Brunskill, where she had given the house a deep cleaning. The room where Tommie had spent the first eight years of her life with her mother had been returned, as best Thelma had been able, to the state it was in when Thomas lived there. His plaid bed-spread had been brought up from the basement. His dresser had been stripped of the flowery shelf paper Peggy had put in it. His portrait, resplendent in his naval uniform, sat in pride of place. When guests came back to the house after the funeral, they would see it as it was, when he had lived at home.

The dining room, which more and more Thelma treated as an office, had been cleared. She'd had to put the ledgers and adding and duplicating machines in her own bedroom, but that was all right. Once the funeral was over, it could all go back as it was.

She'd gone with Frank to choose a casket, a handsome, sim-ple one with brass fittings. Arrangements had been made for the mortuary to meet the train and take care of transporting the remains. Some women from St. Katherine's were prepar-ing the luncheon. The church basement had been offered, but Thelma wanted people here, in her home. She would do what she could in the time she had left to protect Thomas's memory, even if it meant exhausting herself hosting the mourners.

She had one nagging worry: it would be only natural for people to ask after Peggy. Surprisingly, only Mrs. Slater had made the connection—the version of Peggy in the news was different enough from her old appearance that most people didn't realize it was her. But they would have to be prepared to tell the truth now—the version of the truth that Thelma had devised for Mrs. Slater, anyway. She just hoped that people would have the sense not to bring it up in front of Tommie.

If the press figured out the truth, they'd have a field day. But Peggy was a clever girl, a survivor. Thelma was reasonably sure that whatever story Peggy told to explain herself, the press would eat it up, playing it for emotional appeal. She'd have to forgo her current beau, of course, and stay out of the news for an appropriate length of time. But she'd get another chance. Girls like her always found a way.

As long as she didn't come after Tommie.

Thelma had done things that the world might not forgive her for. But she was weak and growing weaker. She no longer had the strength to protect all of them. And so she had to choose.

"Are we going to the museum?"

Thelma forgot that she had promised to take Tommie to see the Costume Institute's exhibition called "The Seeds of Fashion." Thelma knew that Tommie was only interested because the exhibit advertisement was a fashion illustration like the ones she remembered her mother making. Ever since her birthday party, Tommie had been obsessed with her mother, and it broke Thelma's heart to watch her trying to revisit the memories, already going hazy, from before Peggy left.

"No, sweetheart, not the museum, not today. We're going back to Brunskill, to my house—we're going to be having some special visitors."

"Who?" Tommie said suspiciously, putting down the Baby Mine doll that Jeanne had given her for her birthday.

"It's—well, you see, there is going to be a special funeral for your father. He didn't get to have a real one when he died, but now we're going to bury him in the cemetery next to your grandfather." Thelma had prepared this little speech earlier, wanting to avoid mentioning anything about the body, to squash Tommie's curiosity about where it had been all this time and focus on the ceremony. Because how was she supposed to explain to an eight-year-old that Thomas had been hastily buried in a dirt field with only a wooden marker for the last nine years? How would she describe what had been shipped home, what was now sitting at Grenholm Mortuary, waiting to be buried?

Confusion and distress flitted across Tommie's face. "I don't want to go."

"Well, you must. You're his daughter," Thelma said, more shortly than she would have liked. She didn't have the energy for an argument today.

"Is Mama going to be there?" Tommie asked. Her eyes were wide and blue, a navy tinged with brown edges, unlike Thomas's faded cornflower ones.

"No, of course not, darling." Thelma should have anticipated this. "You know your mother is very, very busy in New York City."

"Well, she was married to him. If I have to go, why doesn't she?"

A sharp ache in Thelma's back nearly took her breath away. If only Jeanne was here; handling Tommie was too much for her today.

"Because we told her not to," she snapped between gritted teeth. "And that's that, so let's not hear any more about it."

"You told her she couldn't come?" Tommie asked, dumbfounded. "But I could have seen her there!"

"Thomasina," Thelma said warningly. "That's enough."

"No it isn't! If Mama's not going then I'm not either! She loved him, she told me. She used to cry because he died. I *remember*. It's your fault she won't come. She hates you."

This was news to Thelma. She'd seen Peggy cry over things—a botched haircut, a sad movie, sheer exhaustion when Tommie was small and inconsolable—but never over Thomas.

"You don't hate me," she said flatly, her irritation impossible to ignore. It had been like that lately, her emotions more insistent, her reserves growing thin. "Tommie, you're being ridiculous. Auntie Jeanne has already packed your suitcase and you're coming with me."

"I don't *want* to go. What if Mama comes here while I'm gone?"

"Your mother's not coming here," Thelma snapped. "Not ever."

"Yes she is." Tommie's face set stubbornly. "I wrote her a letter. I asked her to."

"When did you do that?"

"At school."

Thelma guessed—hoped—that Tommie was fibbing. "Tommie, listen to me. I know you—you miss your mother, but she is much too busy to come."

"No," Tommie said, suddenly leaping up, knocking over the doll wardrobe. "She is *not* too busy."

"But what matters right *now*," Thelma continued doggedly, "is that Uncle Frank will be here soon, and I expect you to be ready to go. We need to do something with that hair. And you need to have your lunch."

"I'm not hungry."

"Tommie!" Thelma yelled it, and finally she seemed to have the girl's attention. "Your father *loved* you," she finished, inadequately.

"No he didn't. He never even met me. And besides, I hate him!" Tommie ran from the room, her footsteps echoing through the apartment. Why, why had Thelma insisted on doing this alone?

She got painfully to her feet and followed Tommie. One foot had fallen asleep and it clumped awkwardly on the floor, tingling almost unbearably. Tommie had gone to her hideout in the closet under the stairs, where she liked to go with a book and a flashlight whenever she was cross. Jeanne had allowed her to take some old blankets to sit on, and sometimes Tommie fell asleep in there.

She stood outside the closet door. "You need to come out this instant, missy," she said. "Uncle Frank is going to be here soon."

"I'm not going, I'm not! I hate you! I just want my mom!" Tommie's wails were muffled and pitiful, and yet they did nothing to diminish Thelma's irritation.

She rattled the doorknob, but Tommie had locked it from inside.

"I hate you! I hate you!" was her only response.

The ache in Thelma's spine took her breath away. Something twisted—something new, a further insult to her system, and she collapsed against the wall, gasping for breath. She pushed her hand against her lower back and tried to press the pain away but succeeded only in bringing black spots to her eyes. She breathed in, out, in, out . . . until slowly the spots receded and the pain shrank just enough that she could stand all the way up again.

She staggered to the living room, already regretting the way she'd spoken to Tommie. Now she would have to wait out the child's tantrum. But she was just so tired. She'd lie down for a few moments, they would both calm down . . . and then Frank would come and they would go home.

Home, with the echoes and the ghosts. Where soon enough Thelma would be nothing but a memory too.

"THELMA? THELMA, GOOD God, are you all right?"

Thelma roused herself from a hazy dream of Thomas as a child, dressed in a military uniform far too large for him, unable to walk or move because he kept tripping on the too-long trousers. In the dream she had been calling out to him, but he could not hear her.

Someone was squeezing her shoulder gently. She blinked and saw sunlight streaming into the room. So she'd fallen asleep again in the afternoon . . . but wait, she wasn't at home, she was at Jeanne's, in Jeanne's bed with the white matelassé—

"Oh!" she said, scrambling to sit up. She was at Jeanne's and here was Frank, come to take her and Tommie home. She'd promised to be waiting at the curb so he wouldn't have to find a parking spot, and now she'd gone and fallen asleep. Frank didn't know about her troubles, and he was looking at her with a quizzical expression.

"I'm so sorry, I just . . . I'm sorry, Frank."

"But where's Tommie? Did Jeanne come for her?"

"Jeanne? No, I—" The tantrum from earlier came rushing back to her, and she ducked her chin in embarrassment. How could she explain that an eight-year-old had gotten the best of her? "She's in her room. Probably fast asleep. She was so cross, earlier."

"No, I checked."

"Well, then, she's up to something. She likes to hide, you know." Thelma sighed. "She's having a hard time understanding, about the funeral. The . . . body."

"But Jeanne, the front door was open. When I came up."

It took a moment for Thelma to understand what he was saying—and then she felt sudden fear. It had never occurred to her that Tommie would leave the apartment on her own, that she'd run away. But she'd been so angry. *I hate you*—she'd said it over and over again.

Thelma bolted out of the bed and tore through the apartment, ignoring her pain. She checked the closets, under the beds, in the kitchen cupboards—but Tommie had vanished. Thelma went back to Tommie's room and searched, and sure enough, Mummer was gone . . . Mummer, the doll with the porcelain head and soft body and real human hair that Thelma had given her for her second birthday, handled now until the ivory-colored cotton was grayed and fraying, the hair knotted and pulled from the hard skull. Tommie loved that doll and still slept with her at night.

"She's gone," Thelma gasped. Frank stood uselessly in the doorframe, looking stricken. "We've got to find her."

Everything was going to pieces.

Tommie

Tommie had ridden the train a million times, and she knew where her aunt kept a stack of dollar bills in the hall table to pay the grocery delivery man. Sometimes Aunt Jeanne let her take a few bills from the drawer and hold them all the way to the train station, where she would slide one, hot and moist from her hand, through the curved opening in the glass of the clerk's window.

She took the whole stack of dollars today, just in case, and she felt a little bit sorry about it because it was kind of like stealing. But Grandma had been so mean to her that it seemed like it might only be fair after all. Surely, if Aunt Jeanne knew the way that Grandma had spoken to her, she would never have allowed it.

Tommie was a bit hungry, actually. She walked by the bakery where they sold cookies shaped like little leaves, with chocolate in between. Aunt Jeanne always allowed her to tell the counter girl what they needed, with a "Please, ma'am" and her best thank-you. Today, though, Tommie was going to New York City, where there would be so many wonderful things to eat—her mother would be so surprised and happy to see her that she would say, *Never mind how busy I am today, you are more important, my beautiful daughter, so let's go and get some ice cream.*

Thinking about her mother gave Tommie a nervous sort of feeling, her face getting hot and her tummy going a little bit dizzy. Earlier, when she had found the package in the pretty wrapping paper, she'd known that she should have waited. Only, Grandma and Aunt Jeanne didn't understand about Mama. She knew Mama sent her nice things sometimes, because she'd heard them talking about it. And she knew that they kept Mama's packages to themselves because she had been so bad at school, because Sister James caught her running in the halls again and because she clapped the erasers inside the classroom when it wasn't her turn and got chalk dust everywhere. And because of what she did to Nancy Craig even though it was Nancy's fault because she cut in line and took the last yellow placemat and all that was left were the brown ones.

Tommie knew she was a wild girl, and a sinful one, and her greatest fear, the one she had never even told Aunt Jeanne, was that this was why her mother had left in the first place. That was why, when she got to New York, she was going to behave much, much better than she ever had before. She would go to whatever school they had in New York without complaining, she would eat prunes if they were served for lunch, she would keep her bedroom neat and tidy. And she would stop drawing in the classroom when she was supposed to be listening.

She had arrived at the heavy doors at the station, and she walked inside with the rest of the busy people coming and going. The familiar smells of coffee and tobacco and ladies' perfume and cooking grease and motor oil teased her nose as she threaded her way through the crowd to the row of ticket windows. A lot of trains were coming and going at this time of day, that was why there were so many people. Tommie stood politely in line with the men in their hats and the ladies in their coats, and noticed with satisfaction that as usual none of them looked as nice as Mama or Aunt Jeanne or even Grandma. It was important to look one's best, that was something Tommie had known practically since she remembered being alive, and it didn't take much more effort to look neat than to look all thrown together, and even if a girl didn't have a lot of money there were ways to make the most of what she had. Mostly, these were things Tommie knew from before

Mama left, when the three grown-ups would talk as though she wasn't there, so far above her, their voices like the leaves on trees overhead, but that was only because she used to be small.

Not anymore, though. Tommie was eight years old now, and she was almost as tall as the shiny ring on the lamp in Aunt Jeanne's bedroom, and when her turn came she asked nicely for a ticket to New York City, saying thank you like Aunt Jeanne always told her.

The ticket clerk pointed to track number three and Tommie followed the signs, down two sets of stairs to the tracks underneath the city. You could catch a train here that would go all the way to Chicago, which was much, much farther than New York. The train was waiting there but the doors were closed and people waited with their suitcases and briefcases and handbags and baskets. She studied the map on the wall like Aunt Jeanne sometimes did, but a man bumped into her and didn't say he was sorry, and then *another* man asked her if she was lost and she thought she might cry. Instead she told him "No, sir," and then the doors opened and the conductor stepped out and Tommie hurried around him and into the car, taking the first seat she saw and sitting up very, very straight.

When the lady next to her put her ticket in the little metal clip, Tommie did the same. It wasn't as much fun without Aunt Jeanne there to watch her do it.

She didn't stare at the other passengers, because that wasn't polite. When the train started moving her tummy did a funny little lurch, and then the conductor was coming down the aisle with his hole-poker, clicking it over and over while he said "Tickets, please" in his loud voice. He barely glanced at her when he punched her ticket and Tommie felt very grown up, since he obviously thought she was old enough to be here by herself. A train passed in the other direction, heading into the station as they were pulling out, and you could make yourself dizzy if you tried to see in the windows while it was going past. But then, the train broke into the sunshine and Tommie blinked from the brightness.

Tommie hugged Mummer a little tighter, under her coat, and peeked at the woman next to her. She was even older than Grandma, and her eyes were closed and her hands were folded in her lap, on top of a shiny pocketbook with the edge of a handkerchief peeping out from the latch.

The whistling and rattling and the sound of the engineer's voice were familiar comforts. Tommie listened carefully to each announcement the engineer made, but she didn't hear him say New York City. That was okay, because Tommie knew it was far away, farther than Brunskill, farther probably than she'd ever ridden before. Each time the train stopped she looked at the station signs, searching for familiar words, but the names were long hard jumbles of letters and none of them looked like a place her mother would go.

After a while she got sleepy. Maybe, she thought, it would be all right to just close her eyes. She would keep listening, though, and when she heard the engineer say "New York City," she would thank him politely as she got off the train, and he would think—*My, what nice manners that little girl has.*

Jeanne

Jeanne turned the page in the sample book, the swatches of fabric spilling onto the table. Jerome Goodwyn was a new prospective account, a tall, somewhat portly man with a voice strongly accented with the South, and red hair going to gray.

"Dad died before he could see all of this," Jerome said, puffing around the stem of the pipe he'd just lit, then gesturing with it to indicate the whole of his showroom. It was a smaller space than Charming occupied, a cramped suite only two blocks away. Jeanne had done her research and knew that after their father died, the Goodwyn brothers had moved their dressmaking enterprise north even as the cotton industry had moved south.

"It's quite visionary of you, really, to bring your—em—southern sensibilities to this market," Jeanne said, a delicate acknowledgment that they were swimming against the stream. The same migration that had put her father out of business—more than two-thirds of the silk mills in New Jersey closed in the late 1930s—had closed down many other textile manufacturers, forcing them to the South.

Goodwyn hadn't seemed to mind that Jeanne had come by herself. Ordinarily Uncle Frank would be here, but he was with Thelma today. Jeanne would go up tomorrow for the funeral, but they had all agreed she should not cancel today's meeting.

She had spent much of last week preparing for this pitch, and if she could convince Jerome Goodwyn to place an order for their fall line, Charming would be running at full capacity, generating capital they could use to add another loom and hire more workers.

"You're known for your classic American styles," Jeanne said, launching into her prepared pitch. "And America has embraced modern fabrics like no other nation. Your past-season catalogs offer an idea of how well our textiles might complement your contemporary line. But we think you can go even further. We think you can make inroads into the markets that have so far snubbed domestic fashion."

She took a breath before her next statement because now she was on her own. Generally when meeting with prospective customers, she deferred to Frank. But Frank disagreed with her on this: Frank believed they needed to continue to pursue moderate sportswear manufacturers and leave high fashion to the established vendors. Because Europe shied away from synthetics, his reasoning went, so too would high-end American manufacturers.

"We think you can find a foothold in American couture," she finished.

"American couture," Jerome echoed. "There is no such thing. Omar Kiam, Herbert Sondheim, Ceil Chapman—they're all doing off-the-rack."

"You've just made my point, Mr. Goodwyn," Jeanne said. "That is the future of American fashion. Already we are seeing the beginning of a trend away from the ultra exclusive salon. Even women who can afford to shop anywhere are buying ready-to-wear. Fresh, youthful, active"—she ticked off the adjectives on her fingers—"even *practical*, these define the new American style. And rather than leaving this market for others, we're suggesting that you embrace it."

Jeanne had promised Frank that she would wait until after the funeral to draw up any proposals for the Goodwyn brothers, but there was no harm in laying the groundwork now. Her work was the one thing that could take her mind off the rest of it.

"We didn't offer a single dress in last fall's collection under fifty dollars," Jerome said. "We have no intention of competing with Sears. Our brand has always been synonymous with quality and attention to detail."

"And you've never used a synthetic textile," Jeanne said. "You've equated quality with tradition. I'm suggesting you reconsider. Our fabrics are ideal for your market: a woman who values quality and exclusivity, but also practicality and her own time. Who thinks that four afternoons spent in the fitting room for a single dress are four afternoons she could have spent doing something else."

Jerome studied her with a bemused smile. "You sound like you've been talking to my wife."

Jeanne laughed. This was the point at which some of her clients made a comment along the lines of, "And what does Mr. Brink think of all of this?" or "Are you authorized to offer these terms, or do you need to consult with your boss?"

"I'd be delighted to send your wife our catalog," she countered.

She would not allow herself to think about the gathering taking place twenty-five miles away, in the house where she'd once been marooned like a castaway on an island, a time that already had taken on a dreamlike quality in her mind, a place in her history occupied by someone she used to know.

She had this. *This* was her due, her solace.

"How do you achieve this . . . what would you call this finish?" Jerome said, fingering the pinked edges of a six-inch square of a fleeced wool-nylon blend. He'd landed by chance on Jeanne's favorite color in the line, a grayed aquamarine that evoked stormy seas. "Luster, that's the word that comes to mind."

He'd succeeded in lighting the pipe again after his first attempt failed, and puffed at it carefully, filling the showroom with the sweet smoke.

"You're a mind reader, Mr. Goodwyn," Jeanne said. "We are considering using that very word in the name. Perhaps with an alternate spelling to evoke a continental feeling—*l-u-s-t-r-e* . . ."

"Clever," Jerome chuckled. "I sometimes think you could sell a Virginia lady a brick of cow manure if you gave it a French name."

There was an urgent knock on the door. "Excuse me for a moment," Jerome said, getting up to open it.

Thelma, flushed and out of breath, leaned heavily on Frank's arm in the doorway.

"What are you doing here?" Jeanne gasped. "Is everything all right?"

"No," Thelma wheezed, her hand to her throat. "Tommie's gone. She's run away."

Peggy

No one would recognize her now, Peggy thought ruefully as the cab dropped her in front of Grenholm Mortuary. She was wearing a plain gray skirt and sensible shoes and an unadorned cardigan. Her hair was tied back with a scarf and she was wearing large sunglasses even though the day was cloudy. Her plan was a simple one—she would ask to sit with her husband's casket, until the rest of them arrived. Thelma wouldn't make a scene, not here. And Peggy would make it clear that she wasn't asking for anything other than a chance to make Tommie understand that if things had only turned out differently, both her parents would have loved her so much.

The memory of Thelma's anger, the day she cast Peggy out, was something she would never forget. But there, in the awful chasm hollowed out by Thelma's fury, was room for a tiny seed of hope. Because her mother-in-law had never told Jeanne the truth about what had happened. Peggy didn't know why:

maybe she wanted to protect Thomas's memory; maybe she wanted to keep Tommie from ever finding out.

And in keeping Jeanne ignorant, Thelma had allowed the attachment between Jeanne and Tommie to grow in a way it never could have if Jeanne knew Tommie was Charles's daughter. Last night in Newark, Jeanne had been almost brutal: *Tommie stays with me.*

Peggy had always known that Jeanne loved Tommie. In the first, terrible days following the birth, when Peggy could barely find the energy to get to the bathroom and could not stand to look upon her own infant, she'd marveled at how quickly and naturally Jeanne had taken to her niece. The guilt of those weeks, when she knew in her heart that Jeanne loved Tommie more than she yet could, now seemed like a blessing. Because Jeanne had cared for Tommie when Peggy could not.

Strange, now, to think how important the men had once been to them. How they'd stayed up talking and making plans those summer nights when she'd been eighteen and Jeanne had been nineteen, believing that what they felt was love, a love great enough to sustain them. How stupid they'd been, with war lapping at the shores, neighbor boys soon to be coming home in boxes, mothers' wails echoing in the streets. How arrogant, to believe that they would escape.

Which had been the greater wrong? The things that Charles had done to her that night . . . or the fact that Peggy hadn't fought harder to prevent them? She would never allow such a thing to happen now, but she wasn't a foolish, naïve girl anymore either. It was impossible to make sense of it all, even now that so much time had passed.

Peggy couldn't change the past, but she would devote the rest of her life to trying to make a place once more in her daughter's life—and if someday Jeanne allowed her back, she would consider herself lucky. But she could atone to one person now, even if he was dead.

She walked with some trepidation to the mortuary door. The day had turned gloomy, a slate sky hanging heavily over the town, stirring up eddies of wind like an irritable child, tossing leaves and litter about.

Peggy slipped inside, the dolorous bell chiming softly deep in the recesses of the building. She spotted a polished brass ashtray on a low table of the reception area and suddenly longed for a cigarette. She could almost see Thomas in her mind's eye, over a decade ago when she had first been invited to Thelma's house as his guest. After dinner he'd invited her to walk, and they'd smoked under the tree where his father had once hung a swing for him, on the street where he'd learned to ride a bike. He'd been so handsome, her Thomas, a boy-man glowing with enthusiasm, his love for her a natural extension of his love for his dog and his car and the track medals hanging on his bedroom wall. He—they—had been so innocent, and the thought brought a new wave of grief, a wistful, forgiving kind of regret.

A man came into the foyer. He was dressed in a black suit, his hands folded.

"I'm Peggy Holliman," she said, using the name that Thomas had given her so very long ago.

"Mrs. Holliman. I am very sorry for your loss. Your husband is at peace in the casket that your mother-in-law chose for him."

"I'd like to be alone with him for a while, please," she said, and the hitch in her voice must have been convincing, because he led her down the hall without another word, to what remained of the man she hadn't deserved and could not keep.

Tommie

A lady in a big dress that smelled like onions woke her up. The other lady, the one she'd sat next to, was gone. Nearly everyone was gone. The train had stopped moving, and the lights had come on inside their car.

Tommie sat up and looked out the window. They were on a platform underground. She wondered hopefully if they were in New York City yet.

The lady leaning over her spoke again. "*Dziecko?*"

Tommie didn't know what she was saying, but she seemed to want something. She repeated the same words again, but Tommie couldn't understand. She had a funny way of talking, as though she had a piece of licorice in her mouth, but she smiled too, and didn't seem angry.

"I'm looking for my mother," Tommie explained. Then she suddenly realized that she wasn't holding Mummer any longer. She looked frantically around, on the seats, underneath them, up and down the empty train car—but the doll was gone.

She started to cry. She was hungry and Mummer was gone and she wasn't sure how to find her mother and she was afraid she had made a bad, bad mistake. Maybe Aunt Jeanne was terribly angry with her—maybe she wouldn't even come looking for her. Maybe she would never see Aunt Jeanne again, or Grandma.

"Ah, *chodź ze mną*," the woman exclaimed, and took her firmly by the hand. Tommie didn't resist. The woman kept talking and led her toward the train's exit.

They walked out on the platform and up some stairs, and through halls and corridors and more steps, up and down until Tommie was thoroughly confused. They arrived at another, narrower platform crowded with people, and when a train came hurtling into view, everyone pushed forward, Tommie and the woman along with them.

They got on this new train, the woman pushing her ahead, but all of the seats were taken. Tommie held on to a pole, burying her face in the woman's heavy skirts, comforted by her steadying hand on her shoulder as the train rocked and jolted and picked up speed, only to screech to a stop moments later. People got off, but others got on; Peggy counted one, two . . . seven stops until at last the woman took her hand again and led her off the train.

Now they were up above a busy, crowded street. The woman smiled and prodded Tommie toward the stairs, down to the sidewalk. The men hurrying by wore heavy coats and sturdy boots; the women wore scarves around their heads and carried shopping bags and babies. All of them spoke like this woman, fast and confusing. Delicious smells poured from the buildings, both familiar and strange, and Tommie's stomach growled so loud that the woman laughed. She said something that didn't sound mad at all, and Tommie found herself hoping that the woman might give her something to eat.

After they had walked a block or two, they came to a building with stone steps like Aunt Jeanne's, except not as nice. There was a dog on the landing with a boy who was trying to get him to sit, which made Tommie smile. The dog looked friendly, but she didn't dare ask to pet it.

They walked inside the building and took the stairs up, up, up until Tommie's legs hurt and her breath was ragged, and then the woman took a key from her purse and said something to Tommie. She seemed to be expecting an answer to her question, but Tommie had no idea what she had asked. The woman tutted and opened the door, and they walked into a warm room with a table in the center and old chairs and lamps and pictures cut from magazines for decorations. On the table was a cloth as pretty as anything Aunt Jeanne's company ever made, with big flowers in red and pink and yellow.

The old woman called out, and an old man and two young men came into the room, and looked at her with surprise.

The woman put her hands on Tommie's shoulders and pushed her gently forward and said something, and then everyone was talking at once.

Peggy

Peggy sat for a long time in the room with the gleaming casket. At one point she stood and bent over it, resting her face on its polished, cool surface. Her hair had come free of its scarf and Peggy hadn't bothered to fix it. Someone looked in on her at one point; Peggy didn't bother to acknowledge them.

Moments might have passed, or hours. She kept expecting Thelma to walk in, and she had no plan for that, other than to drink in this time as fully as she could and make sense of it later. The walls were well insulated; no sound came into the viewing chamber. The electric candles in the sconces on the walls flickered endlessly, casting their ersatz shadows on the wallpaper.

Peggy's heart broke for her dear boy, for the joy and daring in him. It was wrong that he'd been left in the soil of another continent for so long, but war had no sympathy for the order of things, war took what it would. But now Peggy understood that what was in the casket was also not Thomas: that the essence of him had left his body and traveled like milkweed silk on the wind, wherever his spirit needed to go. Maybe he'd been with her, through everything she'd endured since then. Maybe he'd been there for the birth of his daughter—and yes, yes, in this quiet and sacred space Peggy finally understood that Tommie *was* his daughter, in the only ways that mattered—in the stories they would tell her and the love they would wrap around her.

Maybe, just maybe, he'd already forgiven her.

EVENTUALLY, WHEN NO one came, she left the mortuary and began walking the narrow stairs and sloping streets, rising above the commercial district into the stepped row houses that had housed a century's worth of millworkers. She had planned to check into the hotel but instead she found herself back on Thelma's street, exhausted, as night fell. She was ready to give up, ready to submit to Thelma's fury, but she was also determined to be at the funeral tomorrow and if there was going to be a scene it might as well happen now, before the mourners gathered.

But no one was home; no lights were on in the house. After standing on the porch for a long time, Peggy finally took the spare key from under the mat and let herself inside.

She walked slowly through the house, turning on lamps, a flood of memories coming back to her, but everything was different. The old sofa had been replaced by a new bouclé couch, and there were other modern touches here and there. A new clock on the kitchen wall. A new electric kettle.

She didn't dare go into Thelma's room, but the room that had been hers was transformed: it was exactly as Peggy had first seen it, when Thomas brought her home so many years ago. The plaid blanket was made up neatly on the bed. On the shelf where she'd kept her perfume and her sketchbooks and pencils were Thomas's trophies. Above them was a pennant for the University of Pennsylvania, where Thomas had once hoped to join the Quakers track team.

Peggy sat down on the bed, her hands resting on the soft, worn wool of the blanket. This bed had once been hers, but now she longed to envelop herself in the faint traces of Thomas that lingered.

She slipped off her shoes and pulled back the covers. It was just for a moment. She'd put it all back as it was before. She closed her eyes, and thought about the boy she'd loved.

A KNOCKING AT the front door woke her. It seemed like only moments had passed, but her mind was groggy and maybe she'd fallen asleep. Peggy bolted from the bed, mortified, tugging the covers into place so they wouldn't know what she'd done.

But as she straightened the pillow it occurred to her that Thelma wouldn't knock, not at her own house. She looked out the window into the night and saw a police car parked at the curb.

Her heart banged in her chest. Were they here for her? Had someone reported her breaking in? A panicked protest was on her lips as she hurried to the door.

She opened the door and at first all she saw was the police officer, his shiny cap and smooth-shaven face and kind eyes.

And then she looked down and saw her daughter.

"Mama!" Tommie cried and threw her arms around Peggy. "I thought you'd be in New York. I was trying to get there."

"This was the only address she could give us," the policeman explained. "She said her grandmother lives here."

Peggy fell to her knees and gathered Tommie into her arms and pressed her face into her hair and held her tight, unable to speak, her tears falling freely. And she wondered in the depths of her heart if Thomas had somehow had a hand in bringing her baby back to her.

Epilogue

August 1952

Jeanne

"You're as nervous as a colt," Anthony said, as Jeanne checked her hair in the mirror for the third time. "How about a drink?"

"I don't think so, darling," she said. "It's silly, anyway. It's just half a dozen people."

"Half a dozen *journalists*, you mean. So you're entitled to be a little bit excited."

The buzzer sounded and Jeanne practically ran to answer it. The press conference wasn't for another hour yet, and Frank was taking care of setting up the showroom for the photographers, but she wanted to be there to greet the reporters. Pauline Rehr was going to be there from the *Times*, and Anne Yardley from *Women's Wear Daily*, and others whose bylines she'd known for years. Charming Mills was announcing its exclusive line for Perrodin today, the first of the European couture houses to feature American-made fabrics in a collection.

She threw open the door and was nearly knocked over by her niece. Peggy followed her daughter into the apartment, resplendent and shy in her pale pink suit and hat, a silvery feather curving down almost to her cheek.

Jeanne laughed. "Peggy! You look like a—a giant begonia!"

Anthony had come down the hall to greet Jeanne's guests. "Hello, Miss Thomasina, how lovely you look today," he said, bowing.

Tommie giggled like she always did. "You *still* talk funny," she said, an ongoing joke between them, and barreled into the apartment. Jeanne had left her room unchanged since Tommie went to live with Peggy at Thelma's house after Thelma's death last fall, two months after Thomas's funeral.

For now, Peggy had stepped into Thelma's shoes and, with the help of an accountant they had hired, was learning to manage the books. Peggy Parker lived on, in the person of a fiery failed actress from California who had no design experience at all but who was brilliant at public appearances. But Peggy Holliman was content to live quietly on the money Thelma left her, working part-time and taking care of Tommie, learning the business that would someday be her daughter's legacy.

"How are you, really, dear?" Peggy said, taking Jeanne's

hands as Anthony went off to sit on the floor of Tommie's room and listen to her chatter.

"Good." Jeanne drew a nervous breath. "I think. Anthony brought up marriage again."

Peggy burst into laughter. "Most girls would be thrilled!"

"You turned down *your* last proposal," Jeanne pointed out.

"Mmm. More like had it respectfully withdrawn. Can a girl get a drink, please?"

As they walked into the living room, Tommie's shrieks of laughter echoing through the apartment, Jeanne let Peggy go ahead of her, so she could study her sister for a moment. Peggy was as lovely as ever, but there was a confidence about her that had never been there before. She talked about Tommie more than any other subject these days, and she'd actually called Jeanne in a panic last week to ask her how to get marshmallows out of the hair of one of Tommie's friends.

Jeanne had no illusions that Peggy would ever be the sort of mother Thelma had wanted for her grandchild. But before she died, Thelma had given them both her blessing. "I thought I knew what was right for all of us," she'd said, shortly before she slipped into a coma two days before her death. "I made so many mistakes."

Peggy and Jeanne had both protested in the hushed voices they'd taken to using in her bedroom. Out in the living room, the day nurse was doing homework with Tommie.

"No," Thelma had said. "Don't. It's all right. I just want to . . ." She paused for a moment as a wave of pain passed over her face. "I just want you girls to promise me that you won't doubt yourselves. Just take what you deserve from life."

It was the last time she'd been entirely coherent, and Jeanne knew that Peggy cherished the moment as much as she did, though they never spoke of it again.

Peggy had mixed them each a gin and soda. She handed Jeanne her drink and raised her own for a toast.

"To Charming?" she suggested with a smile.

"To us," Jeanne replied, and they touched their glasses, the clink of crystal one of the loveliest sounds in the world, after the laughter of a child and the whisper of a lover and the hum of the treadle as the needle works its magic in the cloth.

About the author

About the book

Insights,
Interviews
& More . . .

Meet Sofia Grant

Vanessa Lopez

SOFIA GRANT has the heart of a homemaker, the curiosity of a cat, and the keen eye of a scout. She works from an urban aerie in Oakland, California. ∽

Story Behind the Book

I REMEMBER the first time my mother told me to watch my sister while she ran into the store, leaving us in the backseat of the station wagon with our scornfully indifferent older brother. It is my first memory of taking up the mantle of "women's work," and I was more than ready, at seven, for the job.

Mom emerged from the fabric store with a card of buttons, and it's these I remember even more than the dress they were intended for. The buttons were butterscotch yellow, smaller than dimes, smooth and slightly domed—and embedded in the plastic was the suggestion of a shimmering star, like a precious sapphire. You wanted to both admire and *eat* those buttons, they were that gorgeous.

They were to go down the back of the bodice of the dress, and I remember my mother's hands—firm, impatient—on my shoulders as she lifted the pinned and basted garment over my head to check their placement. Her mouth was full of pins, so she tugged at me insistently to make me stand up straight. I would wear that dress until the cotton thinned and faded, the rickrack edging so hopelessly curled no iron could ever flatten it again, but that day, it was new and still smelled of sizing sizzled under the soleplate.

My mother was not one to share her inner life, and so sewing became a ▶

3

Story Behind the Book (*continued*)

kind of language between us. I intuited
that proof of her love for us could be
found in the hours she spent hunched
over her Singer. She made a shirt for my
father early in their marriage, which—
over fifty years later, after their divorce
and her long illness and death and his
remarriage—he still owns. She made a
throw pillow (brown bouclé, appliquéd
with an eagle) for my brother that graced
his tiny basement bedroom, defiantly at
odds with its shelves full of Star Trek
books, his Dungeons and Dragons
figurines. For my sister and me there
were matching navy cotton ottoman
sundresses with wide sailor collars; we
wore them to a summer festival and the
sun burned our shoulders.

I remember the things I sewed too,
and in the remembering is the narrative
of our relationship. Sewing was our
language, and woven through the strict
lessons (how many seams did I rip out
until she was satisfied?) was the heady
knowledge that Mom was conferring on
me the tools of femininity. I was, if not
yet a woman, at least an acolyte on the
path to becoming one. Sewing, with
apologies to my daughter and her peers,
seemed firmly the realm of women and
girls, and I was as eager to master it as I
was to shave my legs or curl my hair into
a Farrah Fawcett flip.

As the years ticked by, I sewed for
economy. This will be incomprehensible
to a generation reared on Forever 21 and
H&M, but in the 1970s and early 80s it
was still cheaper to sew a garment than

to buy ready-made. I was broke, so I made my prom and high school graduation dresses; I made Bermuda shorts and sundresses during my preppy college days. The Izod alligator gave way to the Ralph Lauren pony, and I had a dorm-room cottage industry of embroidering faux logos onto polo shirts and sweaters. No one could tell the difference between my version and the real thing.

I graduated and got a job—a *real* job, far better than anything my mother could have hoped for. I met a man; I sewed black-tie gowns, bridesmaid gowns, my wedding gown. I sewed maternity clothes and baby clothes and doll clothes, curtains and slipcovers, baby quilts and school raffle quilts. The children grew, they left for school, their father and I divorced, and I was too sad to make much of anything for a while. I gave away my fabric stash, my patterns, my half-finished projects: let someone else take up the needle, for I needed to gird myself for my own second act.

But just as you'll never get a blood stain out of cotton once you wash it in hot water, I never was able to quash forever the urge to pick up the spool and the thimble and a patch of cloth and go to work. Handwork calms; it's better, sometimes, than speaking to a therapist. At forty-nine I was back to the basics, an overcast stitch and tiny knots bitten off with my teeth, finding solace in English paper piecing hundreds of tiny hexagons into . . . well, nothing. ▶

Story Behind the Book (*continued*)

They're still in a box somewhere, misplaced in my latest move, waiting to be made into a pillow or a throw.

It's the journey, you know.

These days it's writing that's got me in its grip. I scrawl and type and move the words around with every bit as much fervor as I once did working furiously to finish a dress in time for a dance. I wish my mother had had a chance to see my book in print; I wish I could hand her a finished copy with the same quiet satisfaction and lack of ceremony as she once handed me a patched pair of jeans. We're scrappers, makers, dreamers, she and I, and I can only hope that she would delight as much in my made-up story as I did in that long-ago yellow dress. ∽

Q&A with Sofia Grant

Q: **The Dress in the Window** *opens at the end of WWII, when Americans celebrated the return of peace to the world. But your characters hardly count themselves lucky or prosperous.*

A: I think the popular contemporary notion of the end of the war—immortalized in that Times Square photo of the soldier kissing a pretty girl—glosses over the horrific losses from which the world would take a long time to recover. It was a very different era, of course, when a sturdy emotional constitution, an ability to "buck up," was encouraged and pain was considered something to hide away. We know that many soldiers who returned from that war suffered their traumatic memories in silence, and that many women who lost sons and husbands and lovers lacked outlets for their grief.

This is fascinating fodder for the type of story that reveals its characters' inner lives in a slow and tantalizing fashion, which is what I set out to do here. I sometimes think that readers would be startled by me and my friends, who can pour our hearts out over a single cocktail, but can't sustain a sense of dramatic tension long enough to properly recount a good piece of gossip. Fiction, of course, is another matter entirely—thank heavens! ▶

Q&A with Sofia Grant *(continued)*

Q: *What made you choose the fashion industry as a backdrop?*

A: The years following the war were marked by a sea change in style whose scale is difficult to comprehend now. When Christian Dior debuted his "New Look" in 1949, the uproar it caused represented a major social shift. The lean, spare, serious styles of the forties—dictated by rationing and scarcity as well as the androgynous uniforms adopted by women pressed into service in the jobs soldiers left behind—gave way in an instant to an outrageous celebration of femininity. Women who'd proudly rolled up their sleeves, like Rosie the Riveter, now seized hungrily on bouffant skirts and sweetheart necklines and demure, soft shoulders.

It was an illusion, of course, that would be shattered a generation later by the Feminine Mystique and a new era of feminist thinking, as well as even more shocking developments in the fashion world. But what interests me are the ways women coped with having to subvert the independence and freedom to which they'd been so recently—and briefly—introduced. Fashion gave them an outlet to express themselves during and after the war years.

Q: *Do you consider yourself fashionable?*

A: I wrote much of this novel while wearing a man's fleece-lined flannel shirt and a pair of yoga pants with a large stain on the thigh that resulted from a late-night dash to Chinatown for Sichuan noodles. Fashion, it is safe to say, eludes me.

But I do appreciate well-chosen clothing on other people. My mother was the sort of woman who took pride in looking sharp. She would never have worn a garment that had not first been tailored precisely for her figure—or, for that matter, one that did not compliment her. I can't imagine measuring up to her example.

Q: The sisters' relationship is volatile but also obviously deep and powerful. Do you have a sister of your own?

A: Indeed I do, and I treasure her more than I can say. I hope that she will detect in this story an apology for the times I have been hurtful and mean, and an appreciation for all the grace she has brought to my life.

Q: Many of the men in this story are dead—and they don't seem to be missed either.

A: I sometimes think it takes an extraordinary man to rise up above society's expectations of his gender, and that may have been especially true in the middle of last century. It's all too easy to be a cad when boorish behavior is not only tolerated but encouraged. But moments of kindness, gallantry, and even heroism shine through all ▶

Q&A with Sofia Grant *(continued)*

those shades of gray. I don't think that Leo and Frank and Henry and Thomas were bad men . . . but men were irrelevant in many ways to the place and time in which my characters found themselves. (Until, of course, the magnificent Anthony Salvatici appeared!)

It was also important to me to give Thelma sexual agency, as a mature woman with some hard miles behind her. It didn't seem true to her character to mourn the loss of her unremarkable husband. I think we tend to think of our foremothers laboring stolidly but chastely through middle age—but I suspect that we do them a disservice. And, of course, there's the fact that I'm Thelma's age, and I'd like to think I've got a few saucy moments left!

Bibliography

Cantwell, Mary. *Manhattan, When I Was Young*. Boston: Houghton Mifflin, 1995. Print.

Colman, Penny. *Rosie the Riveter: Women Working on the Home Front in World War II*. New York: Crown, 1995. Print.

Feininger, Andreas, and John Von Hartz. *New York in the Forties*. New York: Dover Publications, 1978. Print.

Hirsch, Gretchen, Karen Pearson, and Sun Young Park. *Gertie Sews Vintage Casual: A Modern Guide to Sportswear Styles of the 1940s and 1950s*. n.p.: n.p., n.d. Print.

Laboissonniere, Wade. *Blueprints of Fashion: Home Sewing Patterns of the 1940s*. Atglen, PA: Schiffer Pub., 1997. Print.

Lisicky, Michael J. *Wanamaker's: Meet Me at the Eagle*. Charleston, SC: History, 2010. Print.

Litoff, Judy Barrett., and David C. Smith. *Since You Went Away: World War II Letters from American Women on the Home Front*. New York: Oxford UP, 1991. Print.

Marcus, Hanna Perlstein. *Sidonia's Thread: The Secrets of a Mother and Daughter Sewing a New Life in America*. Charleston, SC: CreateSpace, 2012. Print. ▶

Bibliography *(continued)*

Olian, JoAnne. *Everyday Fashions of the Fifties: As Pictured in Sears Catalogs.* Mineola, NY: Dover Publications, 2002. Print.

Olian, JoAnne. *Everyday Fashions of the Forties as Pictured in Sears Catalogs.* New York: Dover Publications, 1992. Print.

Palmer, Alexandra. *Couture & Commerce: The Transatlantic Fashion Trade in the 1950s.* Vancouver: UBC, 2001. Print.

Przybyszewski, Linda. *The Lost Art of Dress: The Women Who Once Made America Stylish.* New York City: Basic, 2014. Print.

Reid, Constance. *Slacks and Calluses: Our Summer in a Bomber Factory.* Washington: Smithsonian Institution, 1999. Print.

Walford, Jonathan. *1950s American Fashion.* Oxford: Shire Publications, 2012. Print.

Whitaker, Jan. *Service and Style: How the American Department Store Fashioned the Middle Class.* New York: St. Martin's, 2006. Print.

Wilcox, Claire. *The Golden Age of Couture: Paris and London, 1947–57.* London: V & A, 2007. Print.

Yellin, Emily. *Our Mothers' War: American Women at Home and at the Front During World War II.* New York: Free, 2004. Print. ❧